A Lady's Guide to Selling Out

Center Point
Large Print

Books are
produced in the
United States
using U.S.-based
materials

Books are printed
using a revolutionary
new process called
THINKtech™ that
lowers energy usage
by 70% and increases
overall quality

Books are
durable and
flexible
because of
Smyth-sewing

Paper is
sourced using
environmentally
responsible
foresting methods
and the
paper is acid-free

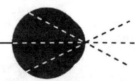

**This Large Print Book carries the
Seal of Approval of N.A.V.H.**

A Lady's Guide to Selling Out

Sally Franson

CENTER POINT LARGE PRINT
THORNDIKE, MAINE

This Center Point Large Print edition
is published in the year 2019 by arrangement with
Dial Press, an imprint of Random House,
a division of Penguin Random House LLC.

A Lady's Guide to Selling Out is a work of fiction.
Names, characters, places and incidents are the products
of the author's imagination or are used fictitiously.
Any resemblance to actual events, locales, or persons,
living or dead, is entirely coincidental

The text of this Large Print edition is unabridged.
In other aspects, this book may vary
from the original edition.
Printed in the United States of America
on permanent paper.
Set in 16-point Times New Roman type.

ISBN: 978-1-64358-047-0

Library of Congress Cataloging-in-Publication Data

Names: Franson, Sally, author.
Title: A lady's guide to selling out / Sally Franson.
Description: Center Point Large Print edition. | Thorndike, Maine :
    Center Point Large Print, 2019.
Identifiers: LCCN 2018047425 | ISBN 9781643580470
    (hardcover : alk. paper)
Subjects: LCSH: Self-actualization (Psychology) in women--Fiction. |
    Self-realization in women—Fiction. | Large type books.
Classification: LCC PS3606.R42258 L33 2019 | DDC 813/.6—dc23
LC record available at https://lccn.loc.gov/2018047425

TO MY NANCYS
FOR BELIEVING IN ME

A Lady's Guide to Selling Out

1
BRANDS, BRANDS, BRANDS!

I guess you could say this whole thing started the day we tacked Ellen Hanks's face to our vision board and began thinking seriously about how we could best take this incredible human being and turn her into a brand. Ellen Hanks was *the* face of Minneapolis's *Real Housewives* franchise, and she had, just a few days before, approached People's Republic Advertising about integrating her brand identities. PR was *the* best boutique agency in town, and Ellen needed our help. She'd launched a number of her own personally branded products—low-cal vodka, protein bites, and shapewear called Shape UP—but she felt these brands lacked inter-, intra-, and meta-coherence. They didn't reflect, she said, her core values. She'd put us on retainer for what we were calling "cohesive brand management," to not only support the growth of her consumer base but to add value to the life of each and every Ellen Hanks girl. Which is why we—Annie, Jack, Lindsey, and I, the crackerest-jack team PR had ever put together—found ourselves on that dreary March day puzzling over Ellen's giant face and its implications.

In fact, it was the Ides of March—I've always had a soft spot for days when famous guys got murdered—and I was wearing palazzo pants in the hopes of appearing more European. Despite the freezing temperatures, I was also wearing open-toed shoes in the hopes of dressing for the weather you wanted, not the weather, in Minnesota, you'd ever get. My best friend Susan once said my optimism bordered on derangement, and I told her they'd probably said the same thing about Gandhi. She'd said she doubted it, and I'd said greatness always seems deranged at first, which was something I thought about while writing in my diary sometimes, and a paraphrase of a quote I'd read on Pinterest.

Together the four of us looked like an advertisement for the kind of glamorous urban life you could have if you went into advertising: three stylish and beautiful women, and a fetching gay. Well, it pains me to say that Annie wasn't empirically beautiful, but when you put her with Lindsey and me you tended to, in your mind's eye, gently round her up.

"I am loving—" Jack said. He paused, placing one putting-the-man-in-manicured hand atop his checkered shirt, beneath his bow tie. "*Loving* what I'm seeing here." He was our team's senior art director; it was his job, in other words, to create the "visual ethos" for each branch (print, digital, film) of a brand's campaign.

"Uh-huh," Annie said, nodding. "Absolutely. Uh-huh." Annie was a copywriter, a fresh-faced twenty-three. Annie wore a lot of cardigans and was very diligent. She worked hard, much harder than the rest of us. She was talented enough to know she did not have a ton of talent; fear of unworthiness gave her a near-alarming level of commitment. But by then I'd read enough books about female leadership to know that true torchbearers ruled not by fear but inspiration, so I took Annie under my wing, complimenting her cardigans and praising her work and giving advice I don't think she asked for but, I believed, might need someday. Annie returned this kindness with devotion, which only compounded my natural beneficence. She also didn't mind, during long meetings, serving as an appreciative audience member for the rest of us as we waged our usual campaigns.

"Here's what we do," Jack said. "Full-page glossy, put it in *O* and *Us Weekly*, we airbrush the face, add a fan to the hair, then her name at the bottom with the logo." He blocked out the words in the air with his thumbs and index fingers. "ELLEN HANKS—"

"Ellen Hanks," I said. "And then the tag. 'Housewives take no prisoners,' or something."

"Casey, enough with the tags. We don't need a tag," Jack said. He was irritable that morning. His shih tzu, Johnny, needed eye surgery.

"I think we might need a tag," Lindsey said, cringing. Lindsey cringed when she said anything controversial. She'd gotten an art degree at RISD, painting tiny dolls on china saucers. A year or two after graduating, when it was clear she could not live by the bread of her Etsy store alone, she turned her saucer eyes toward advertising.

Recently Lindsey'd gotten into what she called the Healing Arts. She drank weird glops out of mason jars and was always suggesting that I hold crystals and smell things. "Here," she'd say when I complained of fatigue, and push a tiny brown bottle my way. "It's for energy."

"So's this," I'd say, and glug down an entire Americano.

"We don't need a tag," Jack said impatiently. "All we're doing is creating brand recognition."

I put my hands on my hips. "Yeah, but people won't understand what the ad is *for*."

Jack put his hands on his hips, too. "So we'll put the names of her product lines at the bottom."

While we bickered, Annie looked back and forth between us like a cat trying to keep track of a laser pointer, bless her. When she watched, the part of me that felt I needed an audience to exist was, in that moment, satisfied. Jack and I went on like that for a while, more for sport than anything. Boredom crept into our edges like blackness on those old-timey photographs. It was

12

important for our mental health to keep it on the periphery.

"We can't just use her face, Jack," I said. "Her face alone doesn't mean anything."

"What are you talking about?!" Jack said. "Her face is her entire brand identity!"

Finally Lindsey interjected. "You guys," she said, cringing. "Seriously, let's chill for a second."

"Fine. Take it to the windows!" I flounced in that direction.

People's Republic took up the entire top floor of a downtown building, and the first thing people usually noticed were the floor-to-ceiling windows, complete with window seats and decorative pillows. "Take it to the windows," in PR speak, meant to take a break from whatever earthly problem or disagreement you were wrestling with. There were little shelves of organic snacks by the windows, and at the end of the day we often kicked back there with a glass of wine from the well-stocked Sub-Zero. The refrigerator and pillows and snacks—not to mention the couches and dartboards and graphic prints on the wall (my favorite one said I LIKE YOU), plus the sound of people bouncing tennis balls, deep in thought, on the concrete floor, and the whimsical doodles on the whiteboards—were all of a piece that added up to this whole idea that we should feel at home while we were at work.

Or really that there was no difference between home and work—that work was fun! This is what we loved to brag about to our friends the most, friends who were stuck in less exciting jobs, slogging through Excel spreadsheets or legal briefs or outdated software at a nonprofit that had seemed noble at twenty-two but at twenty-eight seemed poor and sad. We got to go to work wearing artfully ripped jeans and scribble on Post-its and stick pictures of reality TV stars to movable felt walls! And we got paid for it! In fact, we got paid quite a lot!

Lindsey, Jack, and I made jokes about being sellouts when we went out drinking after work, which happened frequently: the joking and the drinking. I guess we wanted to prevent someone else from saying it first, something we all feared. For me, that someone was my best friend Susan. We'd both been English majors in college, where we met, and even now, almost six years after graduation, I could feel her accusations boring into my skull. *This?* she'd say with her relentless blue eyes. *This? We stayed up till three every night talking Marxist-feminist theory, and you're writing campaigns for slimming underpants?*

Susan was the kind of friend where all she had to do was say "underpants" a certain way and I would double over laughing. I loved Susan more than anyone else in this world. Before I met her, I'd spent my whole life feeling a few clicks on the dial away from everyone I knew. Not that you could tell necessarily—I was popular and all that growing up, lots of friends, guys buzzing around like big horseflies—but there was this static in the air when I was around other people. Sometimes I'd even cancel plans, feigning illness, in order to stay home and read novels and fiddle with the antenna in my brain, trying to get a clear signal. Sometimes I'd go days, weeks, without it, the dull hiss unceasing. The static only seemed to stop, or my brain could only tune in to the world properly, when I was taking walks or reading novels. In other words, when I was alone.

Oh well, I'd thought then, sucks for me I only get clarity by myself, everyone else seems to be getting on fine. Weirdo. Probably best to pretend that static doesn't exist. That was right around the time I started partying, and exercising all the time.

But when I met Susan I swear I could hear a low hum from somewhere deep below her rib cage that precisely matched the one in mine. I was eighteen years old, and it was the first time I understood what it meant to be kept company. From the inside out, I mean, not just a warm body thing. I feel sad when I think about that sometimes, that it took so long, that my whole life I'd been lonely and didn't even know it. But there's joy in that too, a kidlike joy, like when you run home crazy thirsty after playing outside all afternoon and glug down a glass of water. You think, Jesus Christ, why'd I let myself get so thirsty in the first place? And also: what a relief.

"I bet Ellen's a bitch," Jack said. He was lying on his back on a window seat, knees knocking, his hands resting on his stomach like a Buddha. "On the show she's such a bitch."

"What are you talking about?" I said. "She's not a bitch. She just doesn't suffer fools!"

"I don't think they're fools. They're lost, you know?" Lindsey said. She sat cross-legged on a bright blue ottoman, opening a fresh bottle of kombucha. "Like, in the culture." She took a sip. "Wait, she's the one from New Jersey?"

Annie's face brightened because she knew the answer. "Uh-huh. She came here because her ex-husband got a job as CEO at—"

"Blah blah blah," I said impatiently. "And they got divorced, there was a prenup so she didn't get any money, but thanks to her hard work and beauty and brains she managed to claw her way back up from nothing." I didn't know how anyone could *not* know the story of Ellen Hanks. Besides the minor celebrities who stuck around after going to rehab at this glitzy place outside of town, there weren't *that* many ambitious people in this city. I should know. In my work at PR I'd tried to curry favor with all of them—and foist myself on more than a few.

Ellen, however, was an exception, maybe

because she was often flying to New York or L.A. or wherever it is people jet off to when they'd rather live somewhere else. I never saw her around town, which bummed me out, because after watching two seasons of her show I'd developed what I guess you'd call a girl crush on her, that weird feeling of wanting to touch another woman's hair and press her cheek to your cheek and tell her all your secrets while maybe kissing her a little, just maybe, or maybe even more than that, maybe even smushing your face in her breasts, but then again, maybe not, I dunno, it was hard to say.

"You know, you guys kind of remind me of each other," Jack said. He was scrolling through Facebook, absentmindedly "liking" this post and that.

"Hello," I said, "you just called her a bitch!"

"You're a bitch too," he said. I gasped, though I was not in the least offended. He craned his neck to look at me. "Lovable bitch," he explained.

"Couldn't you guys see Casey on TV?" Lindsey said. The kombucha was reviving her. She sat up a little straighter on the ottoman.

"Oh my God," Annie said. "Totally."

"You guys, stop it," I said, but they all knew I meant *continue please.*

"Seriously!" Lindsey said. Lindsey loved saying nice things to people. It was one of her best qualities, but also weirdly the most

17

irritating. I think she thought it would make us love her better—she'd had a difficult childhood, bad stepdad and whatnot, and seemed to think her full-time job was to try to make the rest of us happy. Sure, I liked all the little presents and handwritten cards, the affirmations on the hour, every hour, but sometimes they were exhausting. Sometimes I wanted to pull her aside and tell her: it's okay, don't you see we love you a whole lot already? But you couldn't say that sort of thing to Lindsey. She crumpled easily.

"Seriously," she said again. "You're both super funny, super sexy, super, like—"

"Oh, I don't know about all *that,*" I began.

"Bitchy," Jack interjected.

"I was going to say driven," said Lindsey. She took another delicate sip of kombucha.

We didn't come up with much else to tell Ellen before she arrived that afternoon. It didn't matter, though. We were in new territory—a person, not a company, asking us for branding advice—and the most important thing was to make Ellen feel comfortable. For *her* to get to know *us,* and for *us* to get to know *her.* How could we create a brand campaign for a person if we didn't even know the person? Or anyway, that's the sort of thing we told ourselves while we snacked and gossiped and tumbled around the Internet checking Facebook/Twitter/Instagram, avoiding work and taking what I liked to call the modern cigarette break. I didn't make that up, I stole it from somewhere, but I didn't tell people that because it was nice to feel like you were the person with all the good ideas.

Celeste Winter, my boss, and the founder of People's Republic, tended to like my ideas. I was considered, not unbitchily, to be one of her favorites. Which was, I thought, also not unbitchily, fine by me, seeing as this favoritism was the direct result of my hard work, not to mention raw talent. Celeste was one of those bosses who was notoriously difficult to please, and who took pleasure in this fact. She'd been a hot young public relations girl in New York in the early nineties before cocaine got the better of her. She'd come here for rehab, then stuck around here to relaunch her career.

The fact that Celeste was hard to please only made me want the job more. I chalked this up to my childhood. People my age were very interested in their childhoods. Our parents shouldered a lot of blame. We worked through our childhoods and against our parents using therapy, self-help books, and light-to-medium Buddhism from apps and meditation tapes. From my own journey of self-discovery I came to understand that even though my mother, Louise, wasn't an alcoholic, her mother was, and this stuff trickles down in families like water in old buildings. For example: when my grandmother wasn't drinking, she'd get so obsessed with cleaning that she made my mother tiptoe on the edges of carpeted rooms so as not to mess up the vacuum lines. My mother wasn't that bad, but every Saturday morning she'd still haul me out of bed for chores and make me clean for hours until the house was up to her specifications. Which is how I learned that a large chasm exists between a child's skill and a mother's specifications—a chasm that, so far, had yet to improve with aging.

I'd applied for this job right out of college. When Celeste sat back in her chair during my interview, arms crossed, her face primed for disappointment before I'd so much as opened my mouth, I wasn't surprised; I felt right at home. *Mama!* It's like that experiment I read about in Psych 101. When baby chimps, removed from their mothers at birth, are given bare wire hangers in the laboratory with bottles attached, they automatically turn the wire hangers into mothers. It's pretty cute, actually—they snuggle the hangers at night, play little games with them, et cetera. But the funny thing is, even when scientists *remove* the bottles from the wire hangers and attached them to other, more comfy, cloth-covered hangers, the baby chimps always prefer the wire hangers. In fact, they prefer them so much that they basically starve to death.

Anyway, instead of talking about my qualifications in the interview, which I'd assumed would impress Celeste about as much as a baby chimp could wow a hanger, I'd done a little emotional jujitsu. Celeste was closed to me; I wanted her to open. But how? In jujitsu, you use the energy of your opponent against them. If Celeste were a stone, I would be . . . the dynamite that blasts apart the stone in a rather haphazardly controlled detonation.

So I decided on the element of surprise. Instead of listing my extracurriculars or five-year goals, I'd embarked on a stream-of-consciousness think piece about the previous night's episode of *Survivor*. I told her that, if I were on the show, I'd start by wearing my tribe bandanna as a bikini top so everyone would underestimate me. "Then," I said, leaning forward, "just as they start making nice, letting their guards down, because they think big whoop, who cares, I'll be voted off anyway, right? BAM! I'll get immunity in a physical challenge thanks to my high-intensity interval training and exploit all their weaknesses in my alliance-building."

When I was done with my exultations, Celeste had uncrossed her arms and was tapping the pads of her fingers together. "Fascinating," she'd said in the voice I now know means that she can smell money. "Tell me. How would you describe yourself?"

"A real bulldozer!" I'd said.

Celeste hired me on the spot. She said that we were going to hone that skill, capitalize on it. And we did. Which is how I became the youngest creative director at PR. *Authenticity* and *innovation* were fast becoming buzzwords, and apparently I had both in spades. While my colleagues went off to silent retreats, hired life coaches, and joined soulful gyms in order to quote-unquote tap the strength within, I could no more untap myself than Zeus could prevent Athena from springing out of his head. That's what ideas felt like when they came to me: it was involuntary, occasionally painful, and a lot of times it was all I could do to get to a pen and paper fast enough to scribble it down before another one was shooting through my synapses like cannon fire, ready to spring out of my head again.

It didn't take long for this quality to shine through at PR. We had a client, early on in my tenure, who sold backyard equipment and trampolines. Trampolines had been getting a bad rap for years in parenting magazines, and the company wanted a campaign geared toward the discerning, safety-first mother. Something cheeky, they said, but classy. The ideas being thrown around were literal to the point of being excruciating. *Take the leap. Jump high*—all bland inspirational mumbo jumbo. Then I said,

"What about something like, 'Ladies, meet your tramp'?" And all eyes turned in my direction.

I took over that account soon enough, and others. I was complimented on my "freshness." I became a praise-seeking missile. It wasn't hard to hit the targets, because it turned out advertising was full of people trapped in some awful purgatory between expression and repression, and while a good many of them did their best to unravel whatever was trapping them so they could, you know, come up with their own ideas or be themselves or whatever, others seemed perfectly happy to live this weird half life, half-ass their work, and bide their time. Though of course, that being said, other people are always more complicated than we make them out to be.

I heard the elevator ding and looked up from my computer, where I'd been toggling between websites dedicated to eating naturally, decorating minimally, and spring fashions I desperately needed, and social media. I'd posted a photo on Instagram of my and Lindsey's shoes—we were wearing the same brand, but different styles— and added a ton of hashtags, but so far only three people had liked it. Three people! It was rude, the lack of attention. But these apps were designed to addict you. Like any addict, I loathed my dependence just as desperately as I craved a hit. I kept refreshing every few minutes, toggling between despair that no one liked me and the hope that soon they would so the post might, algorithmically, ascend atop the heavenly news feed. Sure, this emotional yo-yoing was kind of tiring, but what else does one do at three-thirty on a Tuesday?

Celeste and Ellen stepped out of the elevator, both shortish brunettes in towering heels. The difference between them was that Ellen looked like she belonged on reality TV. Her hair was blown out—I think she might have had a weave—and even at a distance I could see the layers of painstakingly applied makeup on her lips and eyes. Everything she wore was tight: tight jeans. Tight silk blouse, tight leather jacket, casings for her tightly wound interior. Tightly wound in a fun way, though, like one of those pistols in cartoons that only shoots bouquets of flowers from the muzzle. She was so skinny her head looked like it was the wrong size. So did her purse, which was leather and the size of a tent.

Celeste, on the other hand, dyed her hair so brown it was almost black. She only wore black, too, billowing tunics and tailored pants. Her hair was air-dried and tucked behind her ears, and she wore no makeup. I guess when you're successful enough you can stop caring so much what you look like—that is, unless you became successful *because* of what you look like, as Ellen had. The thing to know about Celeste is that she wore a gold rectangular pendant every day that was secretly a switchblade. She'd cut anyone who messed with her; I should know. I'd seen it, metaphorically of course, all the time.

Jack, Annie, Lindsey, and I were all at our desks, which was actually just a long, shiny white table that held our computers. PR didn't believe in hierarchy, or privacy, or personal space. The only person who had an office-office was Celeste, and even that had glass walls. I liked the open layout, it made me feel like I was a part of something, like movies set in newsrooms, where everyone's sitting on top of desks, one foot on the ground, all pleated khakis and rolled-up sleeves, trying to figure out how to take down the big guy. The difference between those movies and my office was that we had much nicer furniture, no one would be caught dead in pleated khakis, and we offered up the best parts of ourselves as choice meat for the big guys.

Celeste signaled to us without looking—just an arm in the air and a snap—and we knew to gather our things and meet them in the conference room. Which wasn't a room at all, just a cordoned-off area with raw wooden beams, like the frame of a house under construction. It was furnished with sofas, very square armchairs, and a reclaimed-barn-wood coffee table. When I got there, having speed-walked the way you did in elementary school right after a teacher yelled at you to stop running, I saw Ellen tapping away on her phone like her life depended on it.

"Ellen!" I said. "Casey Pendergast. Creative director, *Real Housewives* devotee, and huge fan of the Shape UP." I lifted up my shirt a little, to show her I was wearing some. "Huge fan of you in general. And just so you know, if Monica had come to *my* house and accused *me* of trying to come between her and Jacqueline, I totally would've started a fight too."

Ellen looked up. "Jesus Christ, finally!" she said in her Jersey accent. "Someone sees it from my point of view!"

Turned out Ellen was just like me: she could strike up a conversation with a stranger as if she'd known them forever. While Jack, Lindsey, and Annie filtered in, and Celeste returned with a Venti-something from the Starbucks on the building's first floor, Ellen and I talked a lot of shit about Monica and how unfair it was that the producers got to cut and splice whatever they wanted in the editing room. "I swear to you," Ellen said, "I swear on my mother's grave, it was Monica who pushed me first. Do you believe me? It wasn't my fault! You don't push a girl from Jersey, anyone could tell you that. What'd she want, a peace treaty?"

I could feel Celeste's eyes on me as Ellen and I chattered on, could feel that she was pleased with my performance. If I won Ellen over, Celeste might even compliment me after the meeting. A compliment from Celeste was like Genghis Khan telling one of his conqueror-minions that he hadn't done *that* terrible of a job lighting that village on fire. It meant a lot, both because a compliment was hard to come by and because he had the power to kill you.

"All right, let's get going," Celeste said when Lindsey had finally returned after she had forgotten her crystals and had to run back to her desk. I could see her fingering them in the pocket of her blazer, finding a solace in them that made no sense to me. You can't squeeze love from a stone! I wanted to tell her. But Lindsey, as I've said, was a sensitive being. Once, when I joked that her purse sounded like maracas when she walked because of all those supplements she carried, she excused herself to the bathroom and didn't come back for twenty minutes. When she did she was red-eyed and quiet for the rest of the day. I felt so bad that I texted her that night to apologize. *i was being stupid,* I wrote. *overcaffeinated and punchy.* Lindsey, being Lindsey, not only forgave me immediately, but had a vial of something called Rescue Remedy waiting for me the next morning. "For your anxiety," she said.

"Everyone, Ellen. Ellen, everyone. Casey you've already met, it seems, but this," she said, going in order around the table, "is Jack, Annie,

Lindsey. Senior art director, copywriter, art director. Oh, and this is Simone."

Simone, Celeste's assistant, whom I loathed, appeared behind the Eames chair Celeste had brought in to avoid the indignity of a couch. Simone was tall like me, but two sizes smaller, because she ate raisins and Diet Coke for lunch. "Pleasure," Simone said. Her voice had the sweetness of a rotten peach. Simone's family was rich, which made her careless, insouciant. She didn't care about paychecks, and it showed. For whatever reason this made Celeste like her, which in turn made me want to destroy her. Plus Simone had a terrible habit of walking into the kitchen right as I was trying to eat junk food secretly.

Celeste tucked a piece of hair back behind her ear. "I want to keep this short and sweet. Ellen has somewhere to be, I have somewhere to be, and nothing ever gets done after a half hour in meetings." She waved a hand toward us. "Tell her what you're thinking. I know it's only been a couple days, but you've been working hard." She looked at Ellen. "I work all my girls hard. They don't like working hard—they can leave."

Jack opened his mouth to speak, but I caught his eye: *Leave this to me.* "Ellen," I said, "we are all dying for this campaign. Dying. DY-ING. I don't even know how many hours we've spent so far, hundreds maybe, imagining where we might take this. So far we're really committed—I mean, *literally obsessed*—with using just your face as the image. Your face in Times Square, your face along Mulholland. Billboard size. Your face on the back of *Us Weekly*. Ellen Hanks, Ellen Hanks—everywhere you go, there you are. People can't escape you, you're gazing down at them, looking up at them, you're all around them, you're everything they see. You're everywhere, they can't escape you, but they can't get enough of you either."

"Huh," Ellen said. "I'm listening." She leaned forward and recrossed her legs.

"So what draws them in is the face. Your face. Your face becomes even more of a household name—well, household something, faces don't have names I guess—anyway it becomes even more famous than it already is. The more familiar it becomes, the more they like it, they warm up to it, they forget that you broke Monica's nose—"

"Barely broke it," Ellen muttered.

"—and got indicted for tax evasion. And then," I said, pausing for a breath. I was making this all up as I went along, following my instincts, which is generally how I did my best work. "Then what we'll do is consolidate and streamline all your brand logos—the vodka, the nutrition stuff, the shapewear, whatever else—"

"*Hello,* don't forget my skin care!"

"Right. Your skin care—so they're all complementary. Jack here"—I motioned to him—"has a better eye than anyone I've ever met, and he is determined, DE-TER-MINED, to give you something better than these girly silhouettes and cursive writing that these other Housewives are using. The brand logos will go in the corners of the page, or billboard, sort of like a playing card. The fine print at the bottom shows all the retailers where the brands are sold. We just feel that you're *so* beautiful," I said, leaning forward and looking her in the eye, "and *so* popular, that anything else will just get in the way."

Ellen smiled involuntarily, the way a person smiles when someone tells them something about them they already know to be true.

"But we have to come up with a tag," I said, "something that lets the consumer know that it's not just your brands we're selling, it's *you* we're selling. Because, hello, people want to *be* like you, they want to be your *friend,* and it's our job to make them feel that's possible. So whatever it is we come up with has to really, like, represent who you are. What it is that's so unique about you that people should not only be buying, but emulating. We already know," I said, "that you're an amazing businesswoman, a white-hot MILF, a reality star, a badass Jersey girl—and that might be enough for some people. But what those other people want?" I leaned back and settled against the couch, opening my arms in welcome. "Is you.

The real you. The Authentic Ellen Hanks. The you *The Real Housewives* doesn't let us see. And we believe that if we can get our customers to see that, you will have a very lucrative—not just fan base, but *brand* base."

It surprised me sometimes, how moving I could be. Sometimes I even gave myself goosebumps. I felt in that moment that I had been charged with very important work—not just for Ellen, but for *society*. By helping Ellen reflect her core values to the world, we were, by proxy, helping all women do the same. They would see her face everywhere, and it would empower them. Women are taking over the world! they would think. Yes, it was very valuable what we were doing. Female empowerment was a cause I cared about deeply.

"So tell us," Lindsey said. She stopped fingering her crystals and reached across the table to grab Ellen's acrylic-nailed hands. "Who are you, really?"

Her words hung in the air for a second. Annie was busily taking what I assumed were minutes on the awkward keyboard of her iPad. Jack fiddled with his bow tie and sniffed, miffed, I was sure, at how little he'd been allowed to speak. Jack thought that just because he'd been bullied in high school he had the right to bulldoze over us girls in meetings like every other guy I knew. Over the past couple years I'd corrected that assumption.

Finally Ellen turned to Celeste and said, "Holy shit, I'm, like, crying right now." She reached into her purse and pulled out a Kleenex. She dabbed her eyes. "I'm fucking crying right now and I don't even know why. I love it. You guys are amazing. You're fucking geniuses. Let's do it." She turned to Celeste. "I thought you were full of shit when you said you invested in your clients, but now I know you do." She blew her nose. "You really do."

Celeste looked over at me and nodded imperceptibly, code for *well done*. My heart soared. I felt, as I always did in such moments, as if I'd been offered a rare jewel, which was, I guess, true, since nothing is more rare than a withholding person's admiration. Once in high school I'd approached my mother after my friend told me her parents gave her twenty bucks for every A she got. It had got me thinking, or rather stewing. "Why don't I get rewarded for good grades?" I'd complained that evening. "I got an A last quarter in every class except drawing."

And Louise, without even looking up from rubbing Curél into her hands, said, "Because good grades are what we expect from you."

I sank farther into the couch and daydreamed about a future where Celeste introduced me to clients as her protégée and took me out for weekly lunch dates. "Just the two of us," she'd say when she invited me. Meanwhile, Annie was tap-tapping away on her iPad as Ellen began telling her life story with the aim and accuracy of a sawed-off shotgun. This was Annie's job as a copywriter: to pull the vague, half-formed ideas out of clients and knit them into a cohesive story, a story that could then be distilled all the way down to a tag. I heard bits and pieces of her childhood ("Parents hated each other. Of course they stayed together, they had no money, what else were they gonna do?"), her youth ("I don't remember a lot of it, to be honest. Lots of cigarettes, though, a lot of chicken fingers"), and her marriage ("Scum of the earth. If it weren't for that restraining order I would've set his house on fire").

She must have talked for some time, I was daydreaming and only half listening. The next thing I knew, Celeste was tapping her watch and saying something about getting Ellen to her next thing. We all stood up, then, did that weird dance of trying to figure out if it had been a handshake or cheek kisses or hug kind of meeting. I personally went for a hug and kiss, because it wasn't every day that I had the chance to meet Ellen Hanks. Her body felt like a hanging skeleton against mine, but I could feel the energy zinging through her like a live wire.

"You," she said to me as we embraced, "are a fucking star. A star. Hey, Celeste," she said to my boss, who had stepped outside the scrum so as not to bother herself with animal rituals of comings and goings. "You know this one's a star, don't you?"

"Oh, I know," Celeste said. "That's why I hired her."

After Ellen and Celeste headed for the elevators, Jack, Lindsey, Annie, and I all congratulated ourselves, and each other. "Such great note-taking, Annie," I said, giving her a hug, which made me feel very doting and maternal seeing as the top of little Annie's head only reached my chin. I took Lindsey's hands and squeezed them as earnestly as I could without ruffling my sense of irony. "You were so giving to her, I could totally feel you shining out all that positive energy."

"I was really trying!" Lindsey said, as sincere as a person could be.

"And Jack," I said, putting a hand on his checkered back, "I know I didn't let you talk, but you know that was just for the sake of the company, right? Because I mean"—I smiled not unbeseechingly—"you know I love you. I *cherish* you."

"Whatever," Jack said, in that no-man's-land between kidding and not. "Love you too."

Which was true, so much as you can love people whom you don't know well, or whom you only know in one setting. It was only four-something in the afternoon, and Susan and I weren't meeting

34

until six, but I figured I'd surprise her by showing up at her work, a photography studio out in the burbs, where she assisted a guy who specialized in senior pictures and family portraits—cheesy, Sears-style stuff. She claimed she hated it, but I'd always thought it was sort of perfect for her, as a way of paying the bills while she worked on her novel. It got her interacting with people, she got to play with kids, and it was so anachronistic, just like Susan. Who knew there was still an industry for senior pictures when teenagers were snapping a hundred selfies a day?

"I'll see you guys tomorrow, yeah?" I said, rummaging around my workstation for the lipstick I'd stuck somewhere. When I found it, I swung my purse over my shoulder and blew them a kiss. "You're the best."

"You're the best," Lindsey said, blowing me a kiss back. She was sitting at her desk, probably about to open Photoshop. That and Illustrator were what, as junior art director, Lindsey used to execute Jack's so-called visions, but a lot of nights she stayed late to use the software for her own creative projects. Recently she'd taken to refurbishing old dollhouses and taking photographs of the rooms, before and after she wrecked them with razor blades and matchstick fires. I think if Lindsey had been living her best life she would have lived in a remodeled barn in the countryside and engaged in gentle activities all day, but Lindsey had $140k in student loans from RISD that were not going to pay themselves.

"No, you're the best!" I said.

"We're all the best," Annie said from behind her computer. She was going to stay late too, most likely to try and come up with some tagline ideas. Sometimes I felt sad for Annie because she worked so hard but so often had very little to show for it, but I couldn't get wrapped up in other people's sadness. It derailed me. It's why I had to stop watching the news. All the refugees, fighting, shootings—how can people stand it. Watching it, I mean, let alone living it. I'm not saying tuning out's the best way to cope, but listen, some of us have got to keep our heads above water for the sake of sound government, slimming underpants, and bustling commerce.

"We're the best," Jack said, motioning to himself, Lindsey, and Annie. "And you're *ridic*."

"So true," I said airily, and headed for the elevators.

2

PERSONAL BRANDS

I'd wanted to be a star for as long as I could remember. All babies emerge from the womb screaming for attention, but most people seem to grow out of this impulse. I never did. As a lonely only child, my favorite way of amusing myself was to pretend I had many friends—imaginary friends who let me entertain them. My Middle Western childhood was a blur of make-believe and community theater and homemade movies shot on a camcorder so heavy my mother had to buy a tripod before it busted her shoulder. When adults asked me what I wanted to be when I grew up, I would scratch my head and explain that while I couldn't say for sure, I was considering comedian or talk show host.

"You know, you could be both," my Aunt Jean told me once. I was six years old, and we were playing in my room as I composed a new song on my thumb harp. Aunt Jean lived in Los Angeles, where she produced experimental films. She had short silver hair and a sharp sense of humor and wore trousers with a sharp crease and big shoulder pads and T-shirts with the sleeves rolled up halfway. I trusted her because she bought me neon sweatshirts and didn't laugh at bad jokes and rolled her eyes at half the things my father said.

That visit, I snuck out of my room to eavesdrop one night. Louise was telling Aunt Jean—her sister—she was hoping to write a book on parenting, and Aunt Jean was saying all these nice things about me. "I think she might be the first artist in the family," she said. To which Louise replied, "She also gets very high scores in math."

When Aunt Jean told me I could be both comedian *and* talk show host, I remember looking at her gap-mouthed. Everything shocks you as a kid. Over a lunch of grilled cheese and tomato soup, Aunt Jean told my mother to introduce me to Lucille Ball, Gilda Radner, and Lily Tomlin. "You know what," she said, "I'll even send you some tapes. I've got reams of *SNL*."

"She's too young for that," Louise said. This was before I knew that when adults who have known each other a long time talk about one thing, they are actually talking about a hundred other things, some of which are too molten for the bounds of civilized conversation. "She won't understand the humor. It's vulgar."

"It's not vulgar," Aunt Jean said. "It's political."

"It's gauche."

"Oh for God's sakes, Leezy, listen to yourself."

Louise took a small sip of soup. Then she put

her spoon down on the place mat and dabbed delicately at her mouth with her napkin. When my mother finally broke the silence, it was so big and strange you could have fit a beached whale inside. She tried to make her voice sound sweet but the sweetness had cracks all over it. "Children need routine, especially a child as sensitive as Casey. You learn this quickly as a parent."

Aunt Jean was not a parent. She lived with a woman my mother insisted on calling her roommate until I was in my twenties. In her eyes I saw all sorts of things I didn't have words for at that age: something about their own mother, the drinking, how even when the drinking was really bad everyone had to pretend it wasn't happening. These thoughts were making Aunt Jean sad, but also mad. It didn't make any sense to either of them, how such a gap could exist between them, when they'd come from the exact same place.

I couldn't take the pressure of this gap. So I spilled the rest of my tomato soup in my lap. "Owwww!" I wailed. "It's boiling!"

Aunt Jean and my mother sprang into action, temporarily united by my error—grabbing paper towels, ordering me to change my pants so we could run the soiled ones under cool water, scolding me for not being more careful. I still got in a little bit of trouble, but I didn't mind. I had done what was necessary.

• • •

Back in the day, Louise had been a first-rate PhD candidate in clinical psychology. She was at the top of her class when she found out she was pregnant and had originally put her dissertation on hold only to get me up and running. Yet for various reasons, including my father, Rake, and the intensity of his work travel, she'd never returned to it. Louise checked off the era's requirements for good mothering—dinners from scratch, packed lunches, school chaperoning— as easily as she'd breezed through her orals, but something was off about the delivery. I couldn't find her, even when she was right in front of me. A thick wall of glass. By my tweens I'd run headfirst into the wall often enough that I grew wary of her, though at the same time I could not stop ramming my head into the glass, trying to make her see me.

Of course, I didn't know what anxiety meant back then. I didn't know that the glass wall might not be a wall at all, just the insularity of a quicksilver mind that, bored and hungry, had begun to cannibalize itself. I also didn't know that the hard stuff that happens to someone when they are little never really goes away. I was the center of the universe, or so I thought, and believed that my mother's off-ness was my fault. After I did something dumb like knock a glass of grape juice over with my jazz hands, I'd kneel beside

40

my mother as she mopped it up, offering help she always refused, all the while hearing the thoughts in her brain, clear as speech. *It wasn't supposed to be like this.* When I heard this, I tried to transmit straight from my brain into her brain using my antenna, *I'm sorry, I'll do better, I'll be the daughter you wanted instead of me.* But the thing is, it seemed a flaw in her original experiment, my falling so far from the tree. I never could do better, the conditions weren't right. For a long time I tried to change the conditions so she could finally be happy, but I didn't know how. Eventually I got angry instead.

Given all that, my ambivalent relationship with my mother, I mean, it meant a lot when Ellen told Celeste I was a star. *Mama!* But it had also given me a funny little tremor in my brain, one I'd first felt around my twenty-eighth birthday, a shimmering feeling of existing in two places at once: the life I'd imagined for myself, and the life I was currently living. Before turning twenty-eight I had been able to maintain, as many people did, that however many hours I worked at my day job, however successful I was becoming at PR, advertising wasn't *really* what I was doing with my life; it was just what I was doing *right now.* Then one day I opened *Us Weekly* and realized half the celebrities in it were my age or younger. I began waking up in the middle of the night with sweaty half-baked thoughts: when will

I start living the life I've always wanted, like my refrigerator magnet tells me?

My car was a little silver import that had seemed California-hazy with glamour and luxury at point of sale, but now seemed more and more like the car a teen starlet drives until she gets a DUI and her parents take it away. It moved with zippy ease through the snarly downtown traffic and toward the portrait studio where Susan worked. Right as I turned on Top 40 radio, my phone rang. I looked at the screen. It was my mother. Speak of the devil. Reluctantly I answered, because I still couldn't bring myself to ignore her. "Hi, Mom."

"Hello, Casey," my mother said. Unlike other loved ones who adopted nicknames for me over time—Case, Case-Face, Case-a-rama—Louise only called me by my given name. Funny enough, it was not even a name she wanted. My father had chosen it. I think it still horrified Louise, WASPiest of WASPs, that her daughter was called something so quotidian, because she said "Casey" gingerly, like it might spoil in her mouth. "How are you?"

"Fine." I pulled onto the highway. It did not occur to me to go into further detail. Louise did not have what you might call active listening skills. She preferred conversing in one of two ways: giving advice, or monologuing the concerns of her own life. Whatever I said was usually followed up with a "that's nice" before she cleared her throat and deposited her entire existence upon me.

"That's nice," she said.

"What's up?" I passed a billboard advertising something called a fruit-blasting chiller. The next billboard offered a four-thousand-dollar reward for the return of a young African American boy who'd gone missing.

"Just calling to say hello. Did you receive the book I sent you?" This was Louise-code for *Why didn't you call to thank me for the book I sent you?*

"Uhhh . . . yes! I did! Thank you." A package from Amazon was sitting on my mail table, unopened. This was another of Louise's favorite forms of communication, sending books she thought I needed. The last one was called *The Spirit of Intimacy*. The one before that was a collection of poems chosen by the host of her favorite public radio show, and before that a book on parenting adult children. "Your children are not your children," it began.

"Very thoughtful of you," I added.

"What do you think of it so far?"

"It seems"—I wondered how much of a refund I'd get if I returned it unopened to Amazon—"really useful, I think." There were things in my wish list I was coveting, including the latest from a Nigerian novelist I loved, also these Kegel balls that were supposed to make you tight like a virgin.

"We read it in book group," she said. My mother did not have any friends, really, but she did have activity partners. "I thought of you because—"

Right about here I tuned out, because I no longer listened to my mother. It seemed important to listen to her when I was a kid because no one else did except Aunt Jean. Sometimes if my mother talked for a long time some of the sadness around her mouth and eyes would go away, even if she wasn't talking about the source of the sadness, but about dumb things like the neighbors' garden and our washing machine. But I stopped once I went to college and heard other girls talking to their mothers in the dorm and realized that some mothers actually listened to their daughters. I had not forgiven Louise for not being these other mothers yet.

"Huh," I said as I drove and Louise continued speaking. "Huh. Interesting." I was thinking about how I needed to get groceries delivered; I was out of leafy greens.

"Anyway, I should go," I said finally as I pulled into the portrait studio's parking lot. "I'm meeting Susan for dinner."

"Oh," my mother said. She sounded confused. "Okay. Say hi to her for me."

Susan had a soft spot for my mother, one

44

of the few flaws of her character. Whenever I complained about Louise, Susan would say I was being too hard on her. Susan would say it wasn't her fault; it wasn't even that special. Mothers have been messing up their daughters since the beginning of time. Hello, just look at my grandmother. I'd say, well, hell, that's why I'd never have daughters and Susan would say oh, classic Casey, always taking the easy way out.

The studio was sandwiched in a strip mall between a Panera and an independent bookstore named Wendys's, unrelated to the fast-food chain—it just happened to be started by three women named Wendy. Susan was crouched down trying to stuff a very fat toddler into a very red snowsuit. The studio had been rearranged to resemble a festive winter scene, complete with a snowy, coniferous backdrop and a couple of toboggans perched in front of an artificial tree. Susan's boss and the owner of the studio, Dudley—a bald little toadstool of a man— was talking to the toddler's father, one of those corporate guys who stands with his legs far apart and talks so loud his face and thick neck are always red. The guy was wearing a white turtleneck and a Norwegian sweater. His wife, one of those yoga-gaunt women, also in a white turtleneck and a Norwegian sweater, was standing above Susan, giving her instructions about the zipper. "Try not to pinch him," she said. "He doesn't like being pinched."

Then why not dress your fat baby yourself? I wondered. At that moment Susan looked toward the door. I waved and mouthed, "Don't mind me!" and pointed toward the cramped lobby and the plastic chairs that looked like they'd been stolen from an elementary school classroom. In a stage whisper: "I got off early."

She gave me a thumbs-up before turning her attention back to the toddler, whose mood had changed like weather on his face and the forecast said squalling. The wife's supervision was irrelevant. Susan was better with children than anyone else I'd met; I think she felt less anxiety being around them than she did around grown-ups. While the family completed an elaborate sequence of Christmas card shots, which seemed preposterous, seeing as it was March, I checked my Instagram, my Facebook, my Twitter; I scrolled through my RSS feeds and pretended to read *The New York Times*. Time disappears a little when you're on your phone. Space, too. Or maybe it wasn't time disappearing, it was me.

I rattled back to real life only when I heard something that seemed worth hearing: the wife telling Tad (her husband) that she didn't like the way his sweater pulled. Tad barked, "Jesus Christ, Lisa, can I get off this goddamn sled?" Susan was reassuring them that everything looked great, they were beautiful, such a beautiful family, it would be a lovely Christmas card, no they were smart to do it early, you know how busy the holidays get. Dudley, committed but talentless, snap-snapped the photos dutifully. How he stayed in business must have been through word of mouth and sheer affection, because he was the least businessy man on earth.

Time passed, how much, who knows. I was filling out quizzes about what kind of person I was and looking at panda GIFs. Before I knew it Susan had plopped down in the plastic chair next to mine, smelling as she always did of cigarettes and hair and the French perfume she wore, her only concession to luxury. Meanwhile, the family was being pushed gently out the door by Dudley. "Tallyho!" Dudley was saying. Dudley always said odd things like that.

I slipped my phone back in my purse and slapped my thighs. "Shall we?"

"God, yes. You okay here, Dudley?"

"A-okey-dokey-chokey!" Dudley said.

"You're not going to stay too late, are you?"

Dudley chortled. "Me? Why, this fella's got his card full at the dancing pavilion this evening!" His Adam's apple bobbled under his teal turtleneck and sweater.

"Can you at least go get a panini? You love those Panera paninis."

"I'll grab something in a bit here, don't you worry."

"Really? Will you?" Susan looked at him, hard. She crossed her arms.

Finally Dudley put his hands up. "All right, all right," he conceded. "I'll get a panini."

"You take care of him like he's your doddering relative," I said as we walked across the parking lot. I beep-beeped the doors unlocked.

"He is my doddering relative," Susan said, opening the passenger side. "He's got a cot in the back and a hundred cans of tuna fish stacked by the sink and catastrophic health insurance."

"You don't even have health insurance," I reminded her.

"I'm afraid he's going to break a hip."

"It's not your job to take care of him," I said. "He's your *boss*. He's supposed to take care of *you*. By paying you more than $11.50 an hour and overtime when you stay late helping screaming babies with bows scotch-taped to their heads."

"That was one time. And he can't afford to."

"Then why not stay his friend and look for a better job?"

"I like my job."

"But the money!"

Susan frowned. When we were together, in diner booths and darkened movie theaters, Susan and I played a fun game of make-believe where things like salaries, taxes, and student loans didn't exist. She looked out the window. "I don't care about money."

I should have stopped right there, but I couldn't help myself. Sometimes our make-believe drove me nuts. "Everyone cares about money!"

"I care about him."

"You can care about both!"

"Casey, enough."

I let out a whuffing sound and put the car in reverse.

Susan and I were both flyover-country girls selected randomly to room together at our fancy East Coast liberal arts college, where students often confused Iowa with Idaho. I'd chosen the school because everyone in the brochure was preppy and good-looking. The previous summer I'd read a novel about a girl from St. Louis who attends a famous prep school on scholarship, and while it was meant to be a satire of the upper class, I'd read it more like an instruction manual. Nothing's more Midwestern than plotting escape from one's origins, and I planned on a full reinvention of myself upon arrival.

I didn't talk to Susan until move-in day, though not for want of trying. Susan heard phone messages not as an invitation to call back but as something to wait out like a mosquito in your bedroom: irritating, sure, but it'll die eventually. The prospect of college dorm life held no promise for her; she would endure our tiny sixth-floor double, she solemnly informed me after our parents left, as Solzhenitsyn endured the gulags: for the sake of novelistic material.

"Okayyyyy," I'd said uncertainly. "So the mini-fridge should go—"

"*Please* don't ask me about stuff like that."

She'd been wearing a big John Lennon T-shirt and clompy boots and looked not so much like a girl as a wild creature. She dug a crumpled pack of cigarettes out of the back pocket of her black jeans and offered me one. I shook my head, affronted by her dismissal and gall. Shrugging, she went over to a window and pushed it open, stuck her head out, struck her lighter.

"You're not allowed to smoke in here," I said. My hands were on my hips. I sounded like my mother.

Susan said nothing, just exhaled and looked out the window, her complexion rosy against the gray sky.

"Fine," I said, motioning to the refrigerator and the space beneath my lofted bed. "I'm just going to put it here then."

"Go ahead," she said without turning around.

"*Fine,*" I said. I felt defensive. She seemed to be asking me to account for myself, why I was a person who thought it important to discuss mini-fridges, and I realized I did not know.

At the tone in my voice, Susan turned around.

She looked at me, and I held her gaze, even though I was nervous. I felt her eyes go inside me, settle right upon my heart. After a moment, she motioned to the space beside her.

I shook my head. "I don't smoke."

"Do you breathe?"

I'd learned to be a person from other people and TV, but Susan wasn't like other people or TV. Where I came from, girls talked about clothes and boys and each other. I didn't know what else people talked about, so I defaulted to the banal pitter-patter of college freshmen everywhere: where were you from, what did you want to study. When I asked her the latter, she took a deep drag of her cigarette then exhaled. "I want to be a writer," she said. Then she corrected herself. "I *will* be a writer."

I had never heard anyone my age speak with conviction before. Conviction wasn't cool then, irony was. "How do you know?" I said.

She shook her head. "I've always known."

"I like to read," I said. "I'll read your books. I read all the time."

Susan turned to me, and I saw her take in my mall clothes and Valley girl lilt and highlighted hair a little differently than the first time around. She smiled. One of her front teeth was crooked, which mysteriously made me want to hug her. "What do you read?" she said.

It turned into an all-night conversation, one

51

aided by a bottle of peach schnapps Susan'd smuggled from home and burritos we got at the campus convenience store. Susan and I had loved a lot of the same books growing up: *A Wrinkle in Time*, *Bridge to Terabithia*, the Narnia series, Judy Blume, Lois Lowry. We'd devoured them, cried over them, stuffed our backpacks to overflowing on trips to the library, got chastised by our mothers for staying up too late and ruining our eyes with flashlights. Our tastes had veered come adolescence, with me diving headfirst into The Baby-sitters Club and Sweet Valley High, and Susan embracing Tolkien and other fantasy, but we both loved Agatha Christie, and our reasons for reading were the same.

See, I'd never told anyone about the antenna in my brain before, how I felt like an alien because of the static I heard around other people. How the sound of the static changed depending on their mood; how I could hear, amidst the static, their thoughts and feelings, even when they tried hard to hide them. But for some reason that night, I told Susan. Susan said, "I know what you mean." I told her that when I read books the air around me sounded clear and sweet, and she nodded, like, *yes exactly*. I told her that deep down I thought books might be better than people because people were always pretending, but right as I said it a little voice in my head added *but not anymore*.

I felt shy around her, but a different shyness than I felt around boys, more tangly. I'd never met anyone so alive before. We went everywhere together that first year, Susan and I, arms linked like paper chains, so inseparable everyone thought we were either lesbians or had grown up together. "No," one of us would explain in a singsongy voice. "We just got lucky."

That night we went to our "weekday place," which was different from our "weekend place," because on the weekdays we didn't want to tire ourselves out by trying to appear more civilized than we really were. Our weekday place was a pho restaurant in Susan's neighborhood, which was my neighborhood, too, except the part where Susan lived wasn't as filled with, well, white people—people who looked like her and me. My half had gentrified, hers hadn't yet. The restaurant had fluorescent lights and tan booths that wheezed and sank whenever you moved. Most of the time it was empty. But the bowls of soup were like barrels, just ten bucks, and we loved the mango bubble tea. Susan and I hadn't lived together in a few years—different income brackets and whatnot—but we still ate like roommates, like hyenas around a wildebeest carcass. In the midst of our chewing and slurping we made our way through a mile-a-minute conversation on everything that had happened since we saw each other. Because so much had happened! Even though it'd only been three days.

I told her about meeting Ellen and how well the pitch had gone; she told me about the trans girl who had come in for her senior pictures and stood proudly below a wooden gable in a prom dress she'd made herself. "I helped her with the boobs and everything," Susan said. "She can't get the hormones and stuff till she's eighteen, so she has these silicone gel things. The nipples you buy additionally I guess, but they're self-adhesive. I just kept thinking about how when we were in high school, no one had even heard of, like, gender identities or gender fluidity or whatever." Susan rolled her eyes. "So if this is where we're headed"—she lifted up her bubble tea—"cheers, America, maybe you're not completely screwed."

"Yeah, true." I'd taken a sip of my own bubble tea, and I felt the tapioca squish uncomfortably around my mouth. "But remember last week, when you went out to shoot that soccer team and all they talked about was Internet porn and the girls they were banging?"

"Yeah." Susan paused and dropped her chin so that her hair created that familiar wavy curtain. She was quiet for a moment. "I forgot about that."

"Yeah."

"Yeah."

"People are stupid," I said, "but not all people."

Then I shoved a bunch of noodles in my mouth, chewed, and pushed the sludge out through the crevices of my front teeth. "Jush look a' me!"

Susan laughed. I was good at making Susan laugh. Physical comedy was her weakness.

Eventually she said, "So Ellen. You really liked her."

"You would too." When she raised her eyebrows I added, "She wasn't fake at all. At ALL. She was—I mean, sure, she's a reality star. She's kind of self-obsessed and her proportions are—well, she looks like a bobblehead—but she was totally on the level." I finished chewing my noodles, swallowed. "Just because she does reality TV doesn't mean she's a garbage person, you know."

"I never said it did," said Susan.

It was her tone, God, that tone, the slight uptick on the *did* that reminded me we were in contested territory. "Advertising is a tumor," she'd said when I'd come home, elated, after Celeste had hired me at my interview. It was the summer after college; we'd moved to Minneapolis together right after graduation to do the whole urban twentysomething thing. Susan was dead set on remaining unemployed for as long as possible, living on a small inheritance from her grandmother while writing full time, whereas I was hoping to make a nice bourgeois living while remaining bohemian on the inside. "A bulging, cancerous mass on the human condition. You haven't even gone to any auditions yet. Why are you giving up already?"

I'd promised Susan that after we moved to the city, I was going to sign up for an acting class, try out improv, audition for a small theater, do something related to what she insisted on calling my "artistic life." I had done little with my "artistic life" in college because, I told her, I was busy *living*. But the real reason I avoided most of that stuff was because I didn't know how, and I was too scared to try. I'd been bred only to meet or exceed expectations others came up with.

Not to mention the fact that being seen was humiliating. You learn that, as a girl, over time. "Casey Pendergast, she's so annoying," I'd overheard a girl saying in the middle school bathroom while I peed and changed one of my first tampons. "She's so *loud* . . . about *every-thing*." I know it was a long time ago, but I've never forgotten that moment: the humiliation that leaked pungently from the deepest crevasses of my body. Girls are mean. Wild animals, really, stuck in tight zoo-y confines. What I'd learned in school—way more important than the subjects— was that it was okay to stand out, but only if you stood out in the right way, with looks and body and stuff. Not too much though, and the less you talked, the better. Even then a lot of girls would probably hate you.

Susan wasn't like that. She's the one who taught me the words *misogyny* and *patriarchy*. Not even my teachers had used words like that.

Susan and I had fought the day of my hire at PR. I needed creature comforts, my champagne tastes had me up against the wall. Two-hundred-dollar shearling boots couldn't buy themselves, and I'd rather burn in hell than ask Louise for money. Susan had stood her ground. The argument turned arty and high-concept, but in the end what we were really saying to each other was *I'm afraid we're not as similar as I thought we were, and that scares me.*

We eventually called a cease-fire that had endured now for almost six years. As I'd moved up the ranks at PR, trading my time for money and, I guess, my own ambitions for someone else's, I could tell Susan still disapproved. But Susan disapproved of everything, most of all herself. The world was not as it should be. *We* were not what we should be. What that meant on the daily was that Susan worked at a job she didn't really care about and spent most of her time and energy working on a novel I feared she'd never finish. She'd get on a roll, stop herself, berate the path she'd chosen, start over, celebrate the breakthrough she'd made, then the whole thing would start all over again. There were piles of stories and poems in her apartment that were finished, or seemed finished to me, but Susan refused to do anything with them. "They're not done yet," she'd say when I needled her to send them out. "I can feel when things are done, and these aren't."

You can't change people, even your best friend. Most of the time you can't even offer suggestions, they'll just bounce off the surface like asteroids glancing off the moon.

"Let's not talk about work," I said, putting down my chopsticks. "Did you finish the book?" I'd lent her the first novel in a four-part series by an Italian woman about an intense female friendship spanning fifty years. Usually Susan was the one giving me recommendations, but I'd seen this one blurbed in *Entertainment Weekly* and gobbled it up while Susan worked her way through some depressed Norwegian guy's journal.

"I devoured it. I didn't even want to wait for you to finish the second, so I went to Wendys's and bought it myself."

"What part are you at?"

"They just got to Capri."

"That's where I am too! Do you think she's going to have an affair with that student?"

"Yeah, unless her husband kills her first."

And we were off to Italy, where we spent the rest of dinner, on an island neither of us had visited but could envision so clearly I could even taste the ocean salt on my lips.

When I grabbed the check and insisted on paying, as I usually did, Susan winced. "I feel like your ward, or something."

"You're not my ward," I told her. "You're my broke-ass friend."

Her face twisted up, like her features no longer worked together properly, which happened when she got ashamed.

"Listen, when you get your book deal you can buy me like, a hundred dinners. I'll keep tally in my journal and we'll make sure it's even in forty years. Deal?"

She sighed. I could tell she didn't like it, but she knew me. There was no getting around it when I was hell-bent on something. "Deal."

Susan was going to walk home, her apartment was only a few blocks away. It was easier to do those blocks in the cold months, when winter garments made our bodies impossible to distinguish. Come summer, that same walk guaranteed the kind of catcalls that could make your hair stand on end. "Girl, I want to RIP that ass up!" one guy had shouted at me the previous June from the back of an SUV. I had shouted something equally obscene back at him, along the lines of fuck you, then he and his friends'd laughed, then I'd roared they'd better not be laughing at me, and then they'd laughed again, and then I'd cried when I got home.

"Text me when you're back in your apartment," I said. "'Kay?"

She nodded. We put on our bulky coats—it was still freezing. Outside Susan twisted up her long hair then stuck her beanie on top and pulled it down low over her head.

I said, "I yove yoo," and gave her a hug.

"I muff moo," she said into my hair.

Somewhere in the distance a horn honked. A siren began its sad twirling. As I got into my car I could see Susan crossing the intersection. A guy in front of the corner store was watching her, arms crossed over his chest. He was going to say something to her, I just knew it. I clenched my keys in one fist and felt for the pepper spray at the bottom of my purse. I'd only used it once, when I'd been out till closing time and the cab I'd ordered to take me home was late. A guy had approached, said some things. I didn't spray him till he touched me. I'll never forget the sound of his screams as he doubled over and staggered. How for a moment, just a moment, I'd believed I was the bad guy as he kept screaming *What the fuck, what the fuck, what is wrong with you?*"

Across the street I could tell that Susan saw this guy too: a change in her gait said so. She crossed to the other side of the street to avoid him, my beautiful friend, shoulders shrugged forward and hatted skull bowed deferentially. *I'm sorry,* I'd said to the guy while he cupped his hands over

60

his eyes in prayer, in agony. Boy, oh boy, did the world break my heart some days.

My apartment was on the top floor of one of those charming old mansions they'd converted into condos once developers figured out people would pay a whole lot more for old buildings than new buildings, so long as the old buildings were basically like new but kept the crown moldings and high ceilings. I'd kept my illusions of bohemia about as long as I'd kept my promise to take acting classes. Now I was as bohemian as a Restoration Hardware catalog. I vacuumed for fun—thank you, Louise—and thought a lot about bowls and fussed when I noticed a spot on a chair I'd purchased after it'd come recommended on a blog that believed apartments could be designed as therapy. I came from enough money that I took it for granted that objects should be more than functional, they should be beautiful. Though I'd been broke in college and right after, this was different from being poor. Poor was an abstraction to me, but unfortunately so was privilege. What I mean is: I knew I had privilege, but I couldn't *feel* privilege, the way a fish can't feel water.

I did try, though. I watched documentaries. About once a year I'd volunteer for something, and every couple months haphazardly contribute money to a Kickstarter campaign.

I settled into my evening routine, which, since I'd lived alone for a few years, had been perfected through many nights of solitude and reading self-improvement websites. I made a cup of hot water and lemon, which was supposed to detoxify me, poured a very civilized amount of M&M'S into a teacup, which was supposed to satisfy my sugar cravings, hung up my palazzo pants and silk blouse into a color-coded closet, which was supposed to cure my anxiety, put on a chemise and matching shorts, which were supposed to make me feel cozy, yet sexy, and sank into the gray mid-century sofa I'd spent a small fortune on and secretly wished was more comfortable. I opened my laptop, which was still there from the previous night, unlocked my phone, and spent a good half hour just "liking" things and responding to messages. Sure, I'd have brunch after spin class with Emily. Yes, Uncle, the article you sent is very interesting. Everyone was talking to each other all day, every day. Sometimes even I, who Susan once described as "a human geyser," got a little exhausted by it.

But you had to keep up. I sure as hell wasn't going to be one of those hipster douchebags who bragged about their flip phones and claimed they'd quit Facebook three years ago. Casey Pendergast did not get left behind, anywhere, anyhow. I accepted that part of being a person nowadays was that you had to maintain your personal brand. The personal brand I was going for was someone who was beautiful, fun, smart, funny (but not so much as to inspire the crueler kinds of envy), cared a lot about style (I posted a lot of home and wardrobe pictures) *and* a lot about substance (I posted thoughtful articles and commentary on education and light social-justice issues)—all in all, basically someone you couldn't help but like. I wanted people to scroll through my Instagram and think That is Casey Pendergast! It was exhausting, but it was necessary.

Despite my long hours at PR and my own self-consciousness, a few weeks before my twenty-eighth birthday had served as a catalyst to reignite my childhood ambitions, which had, as Susan had predicted, been extinguished entirely after a few months of working at PR. After going on a whim to an open casting call for *The Bachelor*, held in a Marriott ballroom filled with self-esteem issues and women ten years younger than me, I'd decided I needed to put myself in fewer situations where the end result was me crying in Whole Foods and stealing fistfuls of chocolate raisins from the bulk aisle while googling *personal trainer*. The entertainment industry required a more tactical approach for a woman my age. I had a network; it was time to use it. Thanks to a commercial director I'd met through PR, I'd gotten hooked up with a local production company that specialized in commercial voice actors. My big break had come when I'd been invited for a callback for an organic dairy farm's new campaign. After it, at my request, the production company forwarded me the audio from the audition.

Eagerly I clicked the email attachment. I heard rustling as I took off my coat in the sound studio, idle chitchat. My voice sounded high: the sound guy was cute, an involuntary reflex. The commercial director, Scott, had come in, asked if I needed anything—water, coffee, an apple to help with dry mouth.

"No, thank you," I heard myself say tremulously.

"Then let's get started." He explained the concept behind the commercial: a new cow had come to the farm. The new cow was a vegetarian—only grass. The other cows didn't like her because she was quirky and different. "You're the new cow," he said. "Can I hear you moo?"

"Moo!" I said.

"Great. You're a natural. Now imagine you're younger, a little more insecure."

"Moo—oo?" I said.

"Beautiful. Now you've got a stomachache because the other cows put pig slop in your food."

"Moooooooooo," I said sadly.

It was not the audition I'd ever imagined for myself, back in the days where I played prima donna for my stuffed animals, but then again Kathie Lee Gifford had probably never dreamed of getting drunk on the *Today* show for a living, which proved that everyone had to be flexible.

"Great, Casey, gorgeous," the director said. "Now the cow's a little more alluring, a little more sexy, she's gotten some attention from a bull and she's feeling—"

"Moo-oo-oo-oo-oo. Moooooooooo!"

"Amazing, I love it." He clapped his hands twice. "Thank you, beautiful! We'll call you!"

Buzzing with adrenaline—the email said I'd hear back by the end of the week—and the sugar from the M&M'S—the latter had unleashed the monster in me who could only say two words: "MORE SUGAR!"—I opened the dating app on my phone, the one designed to make intercourse easy and efficient. I checked to see if there had been any new matches, or messages, in the past two hours. Indeed there had, including a brief missive from a square-jawedly handsome fellow named Chad. Chad, based on his photographs, enjoyed gym mirrors, boats, and bars that put a red glare in his eyes. I did not reply to most messages I was sent, but Chad's question intrigued me. *do you work at build-a-bear?*

I wrote back right away. *haha, no. why?*

Chad did not reply right away, so I scrolled through the other messages. Lots of *hi, hello, what's up Casey? how r u doing on this beautiful day?* Boring, boring, stupid, boring. No one who relies on stock phrases can be good in bed. Chad replied soon enough, as I knew he would, because I know the intricate wiring of a horny male dick.

i want to stuff u

Okay, Chad, I thought. Easy does it.

I could have left it there, but because I could not help myself, because every girl, no matter how contrary, becomes her mother, I wrote *but then shouldn't you ask if i'm a build-a-bear BEAR? i.e. you can't stuff build-a-bear EMPLOYEES?*

Chad did not reply to this, which was fine. Experience had taught me there were plenty of other Chads in the sea. This particular app represented and had helped codify the general philosophy of my generation. People are like playing cards in a game of Go Fish. You try to collect the ones you like; and the ones you don't like, you try to get rid of as swiftly as possible. Sure, there were better ways of treating people, but how were we to know what they were? Our parents had plunked us in front of their personal computers as soon as the retail price became reasonable, and there we had learned to flirt in a chat box and always think that beyond what was in front of us, there was probably something better.

Sure enough, another Chad appeared a minute or two later. Actually, this guy was named Sam, but it didn't matter. Sam, according to himself, was a lawyer who was *hopin to get more into music. DJing and stuff.* He sent me a song I should listen to, which in this app counted as romance. I listened to maybe half of it.

:) i like it, I wrote.

i like you

you don't know that

;) oh really

We went on like this for a while. It was fun the way games are fun when you're half paying attention, an easy way to pass the time. I wasn't sure what winning meant in this game, but I believed it involved not caring very much. About the other person, I mean. In my experience, men were either trying to gobble you up or running away to avoid the vulnerability of hunger. But, I mean, so was I.

what r u wearing?

I looked down at my pajamas. My makeup was scrubbed off. On the computer screen was the summer-weight down comforter I'd been considering purchasing.

nothing

tease

you call this teasing?

I sent a photo I'd taken for another guy. All this and more, from the privacy of my own home. A whole bed to myself, nothing upsetting or smelly. We worked each other to climax, or so we said, through a sequence of increasingly explicit messages. He asked me what my fantasies were, and I repeated something I'd heard in a European film, something about doing a bunch of strangers on a high-speed train. Much better than my original answer, which was not to cry after coming.

When we were finished, and texted good night with vague promises of "next time," I fell asleep hugging my decorative bolster pillow, like if I hugged it hard enough, it might one day pull a Velveteen Rabbit and hug me back. There was more to life, I was sure of it, but when I listened to the stillness for my clear signal these days all I heard was static. The static was too loud, so I turned on the television, and fell asleep to canned laughter.

3

The Blue Ocean

About a month later, when I came into work—
actually it was exactly a month, Tax Day—
there was an email waiting from Celeste. I was to
"stop by" her office at ten, the official start to our
working hours, "for a quick chat."

My watch, a fancy thing given to me by a
former boyfriend—one of those finance guys
whose generosity, consciously or not, always
operates on a balance sheet—informed me it
was 10:33. This was usually when I arrived, as
I did not believe in working hours so much as
I believed in work. My philosophy was: smart
people work faster, and therefore shouldn't have
to be there as long. Plus, I'd slept badly the night
before, caught up in a recurring and disturbing
dream that had me backed into a corner of the
Build-A-Bear warehouse. I didn't remember
much, but, boy—tufts and fluffs everywhere.

Still, I felt terrible. I did not like letting Celeste
down. I prided myself on being her faithful steed;
you could say a good chunk of what psychologists
called my "self" depended on this steediness.
The thought of losing this identity for a reason

as dumb as showing up late one morning—okay, many mornings. Most mornings. All mornings. Usually Celeste herself didn't appear till noon. And yet—

"Shit," I said to my computer screen.

"What is it, hon?" Lindsey said. The slim bangles on her wrist jangled as she reached her hand out to give mine a squeeze. Lindsey had the softest hands of anyone I knew, also the smallest. It was like holding hands with raw chicken breast. She was at her station right beside mine, working in Photoshop on the final mock-ups of Ellen's face for the new ad campaign, which was set to go live the following week. The tag we'd finally decided on was simple: *ALL REAL.*

We were pleased, but Ellen had freaked out when we'd first shown her the print. Apparently there were many lines that needed to be removed. As a result Lindsey had spent the past four days doing God-knows-what brushing and filtering and screening to make sure Ellen's face was up to Ellen's standards. I myself couldn't notice a difference, but I think something happens to a woman's brain when she hits puberty, then again when she hits forty: she can no longer see herself objectively, only as a monstrosity. The prettiest forty-year-olds get this way the most, maybe because they're so attached to the rewards for physical perfection, whereas everyone else had to get used to their monstrousness at an early age, find coping mechanisms for it: a sense of humor, say, or a unique take on current events, maybe an online shopping addiction.

"Uggghhhh I am such an *idiot*," I said, dropping my purse on the floor and rummaging around my desk for—what?—something to take the anxiety away. I found the Rescue Remedy Lindsey'd given me and squeezed a whole eyedropperful onto my tongue, though the directions said to "gently place" one or two drops in a glass of water. Goddamn hippies; I didn't have time for gentle placement! "I was supposed to meet with Celeste, like, a half hour ago, but I took my work email off my phone so I could, like, achieve balance or whatever but now"—I opened a vial of lip balm and compulsively smeared petroleum over my mouth—"I just look like a shithead. I don't know if I should go see her now or hide under the desk until she comes looking for me."

"Just go now. It's not a big deal."

I shoved the balm back into my cluttered makeup bag and looked up. "Seriously," Lindsey said. She gave me a reassuring smile. "It'll be fine. Celeste loves you. That's not going to change."

That was the thing about Lindsey. Right when you might not want to take her seriously, dismiss her and her Healing Arts, she'd tunnel right into the center of your brain, where all those secret and often sad thoughts lived, and she'd speak right to them.

She pulled what looked to be roll-on perfume out from behind her iMac. "Put this on your wrists," she said. "It's for grounding."

My pulse whizzed from caffeine and anticipation. "I don't need grounding," I said. "I was born grounding!" I took it from her and put it on anyway.

Smelling like a feminist bookstore, I knocked on Celeste's glass door. She was sitting at her desk with her laptop open, and she motioned for me to come in. She was wearing black, as per usual, which stood out against the accoutrements in her office, which were completely white, including the book jackets on her Lucite shelves. It was like being inside a Rorschach test. Hard to get an accurate reading from inside the inkblot, or was it. *Mama!*

"So sorry I'm—" I began, but she cut me off, motioned for me to sit down in a chair whose sleek lines and hard finish had the comfort of a church pew.

"You majored in English, didn't you?"

I blinked twice and crossed my legs, so as to protect my dignity. Spring had sprung, which meant I'd taken to wearing short dresses that couldn't decide whether they wanted to fully cover my ass. This one was wide, though, to offset its minimal length. It had become trendy to wear cloth boxes. "Yes. Why?"

"What do you know about Ben Dickinson?"

"Ben Dickinson?"

There were things I'd been hoping Celeste would ask (Hey, kid, you've got talent, do you want to be a star?), things I'd been dreading she'd ask (What's wrong with you? Do you want to get fired?), and then some banal stuff in between, but in no universe had I imagined a left-field question like this.

"Ummm—" I smacked my newly petroleumed lips. "He's a writer. Lives in town, I think. Wrote a novel that came out last fall, which I haven't read, but I'm pretty sure my friend Susan has. I know it got good reviews, and I saw on Facebook there's some event with him at a theater downtown—"

I was running out of steam. Celeste was looking at her computer screen, frowning, clicking on links I could not see. Her shoulder-length bob was more unkempt than usual, and despite her red light facials or whatever, she looked tired. Haggardness was something of a badge of honor around People's Republic, a sign you were sacrificing yourself to a higher power. There was a Venti Starbucks on her desk, a bottle of water imported from France, and one of those energy drinks that comes in a vial because a larger dose would give you a heart attack. "Susan," she said absently. "Your friend. Also a writer, yes?"

"Yes! She's incredibly talented. Hasn't published anything yet, but she will, I know she will." I was impressed Celeste remembered Susan. Though I talked about Susan all the time, I wasn't used to Celeste bringing up anyone's personal life. Celeste, so far as I could tell, did not have a personal life, and her tacit expectation was that neither would we.

"Would you say you're good with writers?"

"Uhh—" I rubbed my lips again. "I guess? I mean—sure. Writers are just like everybody else. They love to talk about themselves, or their writing, and if you pay a little bit of attention they'll love you forever. But oh my *God* are they sensitive. Sometimes that makes them sweet, but not always. Once I was at this party with Susan, and this little group was going on and on about this writer they'd known in grad school who was famous now but at parties he'd never bring booze, just drink everyone else's, and they were, like, *eviscerating* him for this. And it was years ago! I was like, you guys, this is a *party,* let's stop talking and dance already! But they wouldn't! I could never get a single one of them to dance, not ever. Not even when I twerked and my boobs fell out of my shirt."

Celeste didn't respond, just kept clicking.

"So, anyway," I finally said. "What's all this about?"

A long pause. I shifted in my seat and thought about how maybe I could have left out the part about my boobs falling out of my shirt. My chest grew hot, the way it did when I got too excited and spoke without modulating my foolisher tendencies. When Celeste looked up, her dark eyes reflected the cool lamplight like black magic. I had the uncomfortable sense of entering a high-stakes negotiation, one in which she alone knew the terms.

"Have you heard of a business strategy called Blue Ocean?" she said.

"Uhhhh . . . no?"

This felt like the wrong answer, but what else was there?

"Have you heard of Cirque du Soleil?"

"Yes," I said. "I mean, hello, Vegas is *literally* my favorite city in the world."

This was true. Vegas looked to me how a bit of crinkled tinfoil looked to a drug addict: so much promise beneath so much shininess! Every time I went I felt like I'd been baptized by the holy waters of the Bellagio, born anew by the excess of free drink tickets, VIP passes, and other perks handed to me by club promoters who decided my appearance passed muster for discounted rates.

Celeste shut her computer. She rested her elbows on top of it, interlaced her fingers below her chin, like a teacher at three o'clock who finds herself very, very tired of teaching idiots all day. "It's the 1980s," she said. "The markets are recovering from Carter's disastrous handling of the recession. People are making money on Wall Street, they've got cash like never before, and they want to spend it. They're taking vacations, they're going to Disney, they're trying out upscale restaurants, but they're not"—she corrected herself—"they've *stopped*—going to the circus." She pointed at me with both her index fingers. "Why?"

Another trick question. I considered it, or rather, tried to look as though I was considering it while flies buzzed idly around my brain. "Well," I said. I thought of the time I went on a field trip to a traveling big top and I'd cried in front of my whole class when I saw the elephants in chains. "Circuses are disgusting."

"No, circuses *were* disgusting," Celeste said. She ticked the names off on her fingers. "Ringling Bros., Barnum & Bailey, Big Apple—all hemorrhaging money. Industry's dead in the water. The founders of Cirque du Soleil knew this, so do you know what they did?"

"Started training preteens in Chinese acrobatics?"

Celeste leaned forward, and a strand of dark hair fell out from behind her ear. She put her palms up. The switchblade necklace dangled and clattered against the Lucite desk. "They discovered whole new waters."

Then she leaned back, tucked in the unruly strand, and reached for her Starbucks. She took a long swallow, satisfied, it seemed, with her ability to drop bombs onto hapless targets.

"So Blue Ocean is a new—" I paused. "Um—industry?"

"No." She drew out the vowel, like I did with Annie when I was patiently explaining something but secretly wanted to thwack her upside the head. "It's an uncontested market space within a saturated industry."

"Ohhhhhh, I see," I said, though I did not.

"In contested markets, the water is red from companies fighting for market share and devouring each other. Cirque du Soleil was blue because no other circus could compete with it. Nothing like it had ever come before."

I shifted again in this dumb block of a chair, then again, trying to get comfortable. "I know there's an analogy coming with this and PR, but I'm not following you yet."

Celeste took another sip of coffee. She took pleasure in this—knowing something I didn't, making me wait till she was ready to give it to me. Me, I didn't like holding anything back from people. It made me feel all stuffed-up inside.

"How many advertising agencies are in this town, Casey?"

"Six good ones, maybe. Double that in total."

"Would you consider that a red or a blue ocean?"

Well, now she was being patronizing. "Red," I said. There was a little tone, I have to admit. I added, "Obviously."

"How many people like Ellen live in this town?"

"What do you mean, people like Ellen?"

"People trying to create and capitalize on notoriety through product creation and endorsement."

"Well, hmmm." I cocked my head and looked up toward the ceiling. A large mirror hung on the wall. Its wavy glass made it impossible to see yourself clearly. "Minneapolis is technically a second-tier city, so not nearly as many as in New York or L.A. But I can think of at least twenty off the top of my head—"

Local cooking show people, reality show veterans, bloggers, YouTube and Instagram influencers—they were everywhere, pressing cards into my hand, appearing at some event or another at bars or so-called lifestyle boutiques, posting self-promotional status updates and highly stylized photographs designed to make the rest of us feel fat, poor, boring, and envious. That sounds a bit resentful, but I suppose that's because I *was* resentful: they were naked with their attention-seeking in a way that I wasn't, but sometimes wished I could be.

But how, how? First there was the matter of dignity. Also that antenna that let me know how other people were doing and thinking and feeling. You can't in good faith start an Instagram account dedicated to your daily fitness regimen if you have this antenna, you just can't; you'd die a thousand deaths before you got your first jump-lunge off the ground. Self-awareness was a liability among personal branders, not to mention other-awareness. You had to, as the saying went, *do you*. Which so far as I could tell meant act with impunity.

"And is that a red or blue ocean?"

"Okay, okay," I leaned back in the chair as best I could, given its stiffness, and put my hands up. "Uncle! Red."

Celeste looked at me like I'd just spoken Portuguese. "Uncle?"

I cocked my head, surprised. "It's what you say when—"

Before I could continue, she was talking again, opening a slim drawer in her desk and pulling out one of those dense food bars. "I have no problem with staying in a red ocean," she was saying. "People's Republic was founded in a red ocean, and we've done very well for ourselves. I've done very well for myself," she said, mostly to herself. "But our capabilities are outgrowing the current business model." She unwrapped the food bar, which had the size and consistency of

79

a cockapoo turd. She took a bite. Chewing, she said, "And that's where you come in."

"Me?" I felt my eyebrows go up to my hairline.

My astonishment was not a drill. When you grow up in the Midwest, especially if you attend public schools, you're conditioned toward the average. Sure, homogeneity is the source of our racism, but it also makes it easy for us to get *along*. Differences, including intelligence or talent, are shamed and amended, so that we might be compressed to a tolerable middle. Everyone is comfortable because no one is exceptional. Most of my high school class graduated straight to the community college down the road.

Celeste swatted away my incredulity. She did not suffer modesty any more than she suffered fools. "Yes, of course you. Don't be ridiculous."

Nothing made my heart swell more than someone powerful telling me I was special. On a large scale, I think this is how fascism works. On a small scale, I listened with slavish devotion as Celeste went into a lengthy explanation of how successful entertainers make most of their money. Turned out it wasn't through the work itself— music or movies or shows—it was through sponsorships and endorsements. Big, meaty deals that allowed big, meaty corporations to align themselves with the reputation of whatever lucky schmuck they chose to be their "face." People less real-famous and more Internet-famous were doing the ratchet version of this all the time: writing "sponsored" posts for companies who sent them free swag, earning a percentage of profits if a reader bought something after clicking the embedded referral link. "But there's a glut of these people," Celeste said, yanking off a piece of nutritional taffy so hard I thought her teeth would break. "The traditional mixing of personal and corporate branding is tired. We go into that market like we're doing with Ellen, we'll be fine, we'll hold our own. But I don't want to just hold our own."

She set down the near-empty wrapper and opened her computer back up, started typing. I knew what Celeste wanted. She craved power the way a college virgin craved sex: all back half of the brain, all alligator impulse. In some way or another she must have gotten screwed over, big time, early on in her life, or maybe just the opposite. Otherwise I could not account for the unabashed aggression that kept her scrambling to the top of every mountain, every hill, hell, every gravel pile.

When she turned the computer around, I saw a white screen and a word I'd never seen before typed in Helvetica.

"Nanü," she finally said.

"Nanü?" I said.

"PR's new branch," she said. "Brokering corporate opportunities for the last untapped creative influencers. Designed to create fresh content for companies that need to hit the reset button, and long-term financial solutions for influencers who have none."

I flipped back through the conversation we'd just had, trying to put the pieces together. Celeste wore that irritated expression she got when she remembered she has a faster brain than the average model. She said: "Why do you think I asked about your friend? I'm talking about writers."

I burst out laughing.

"Are you crazy? Writers aren't influencers! Influencers are like, seventeen-year-olds with a YouTube channel!"

Celeste smiled a crocodile smile. "Yet. Writers aren't influencers yet. 'Yet' is the name of the blue ocean game."

I was still laughing. Cognitive dissonance does that to a gal: less humor and more the body gasping *Does not compute!*

"Sorry, sorry, but I just can't see this happening. Writers are like—I mean, Susan has to lie down after she goes *grocery shopping*. These people walk around with no skin on. I really can't imagine them wanting to plug further into social media—"

"Do you know what makes excellent skin?"

Celeste said. "The best skin?" She paused. "Money."

Before I could protest further, she further launched into her pitch. Companies that had fallen out of favor with the general public, or perhaps had never been in favor—oil companies, utilities, recalled meat companies, Dippin' Dots—could no longer afford or attract real celebrities as spokespeople; no legit star would sign with them. And these lower-cost aspirational celebrities, like Ellen, as well as fledgling social media influencers, were too concerned about dignifying their budding brand to work with these unfavorable companies. But well-known authors, who already had plenty of cachet, were the penny stocks of the fame market. Not only did they have a credible brand name—at least among "intellectual-spendy upper-middle-classers," as Celeste called them—they also had what these companies really needed and wanted: creative capital whose best functions were language-based. With Nanü serving as broker, these companies could hire authors to be the face (or voice, for the less attractive ones) of their company, or simply hire the authors to help reshape and rebrand their identity through text-based social media platforms.

When she was finished, I scratched my effortless-looking bedhead hair, which had taken thirty-five minutes and two different hot irons to arrange, and thought: when Susan hears about this, she is going to lose her shit.

But what I said was: "I can see how this would be useful for the companies you're describing. But the writers? I dunno. I still can't see them getting on board. Not just because of like, social maladjustment. The ones I know hate, and I mean like, *despise,* you know, consumer capitalism—"

Now it was Celeste's turn to laugh.

"I know, I know," I said. "It's cliché."

Celeste was still laughing. I had gotten her good.

I said, "But seriously, Susan doesn't even buy shampoo, she mixes water with baking soda. She says the beauty industry is a con."

"Oh God, that is rich," Celeste finally said, wiping the corner of her eye with her ring finger. "Straight out of central casting."

I could feel myself getting a little defensive. "Well, you don't have to put it like that. It's a serious difference in values. I really can't see *real* writers lining up to, whatever, tweet for Exxon—"

Celeste heard the edge to my voice. It steeled her own. "You'll be surprised what people are willing to do once you put the right dollar amount on the table."

I wrinkled my nose. "I don't think it's that simple."

"It's always that simple," Celeste said. She sat

up straighter, her spine a rod. "I've been doing this for twenty years, and I promise you. It's always that simple." She reached over the top of her laptop screen and clicked the forward arrow. Up popped these pie charts on the screen that compared authors' current average earnings (from advances, royalties, foreign rights, speaking engagements, and whatnot) with the projected earnings from Nanü, with consideration given to levels of sponsorship and levels of something called "creative engagement." The difference in numbers, even at the lowest tier of engagement, was like the difference between a cake pop and an entire cake.

"Holy shit," I said.

Then I said, "That is a lot of money."

Celeste said, "And when these writers have this kind of money, when they're not struggling with teaching jobs or menial office labor—think of all they'll be able to do. They can finally"—she paused meaningfully—"get back to writing. Whatever they do with Nanü isn't going to take up nearly as much time and energy as what they do now to make ends meet. And further-more, it's ridiculous, frankly almost criminal, how little capital publishers have to work with this day and age. Poor things. Working so hard and having so little to show for it, financially or otherwise—"

"Huh," I said. "You have a point."

"As Darwin said, adaptation is the key to survival."

"Did Darwin say that?"

Celeste continued. "The partnerships which Nanü alone can broker, thanks to the network I've built for two decades from the ground up, are crucial to the financial and behavioral health of these writers, like your friend, who"— she laughed again, it was somewhere between malicious and benevolent—"let's be honest, aren't exactly known for either."

She went on to explain that she'd gotten the idea for this enterprise the night after we'd first met with Ellen, while listening to a public radio program about belief and spirituality. "Ordinarily I can't stand that sort of thing," she said, rolling her eyes. "But the author they had on was very compelling. Julian North, have you heard of him?"

"Julian North?" I said.

I had more to say, but before I could Celeste continued. "He was talking about the fact that it had taken him ten years to write his new novel because most of his life was taken up with family, teaching, freelancing, editing, cooking, dentist appointments, what have you. And what I realized as he was talking was that someone like Julian might have a mid–six figure salary at the companies we work with and yet here he was, teaching kids to write poetry at some public university for $60k a year and editing cover letters on the side. What a shame, I thought. Here we have talent with huge potential and zero outlet for it. The man is brilliant—"

"Oh my God, isn't he?" I interrupted. "He's amazing. He *literally* changed my life."

I wasn't bullshitting, either. Julian North was something of a hero of mine; he'd given a talk at my college sophomore year. Though I'd never heard of him prior to the visit, Susan had insisted I come with her to his reading. "Ugh, why?" I remember saying, splayed pantsless on my twin extra-long. It was fall, which meant we'd already cranked up the radiator. "I'm busy."

"With this?" Susan pointed to the DVD case on my bed. On the front was an image of a curly-haired woman looking wistfully at the New York City skyline. "Case, you know you can't watch too many episodes in a row, or you'll get sad. The book is good, trust me. It's just the kind of thing you'd like."

"Readings are boring. I can read the book myself."

"What's the last book you read?"

I stared up at the ceiling. "Ummm . . . Machiavelli."

"Actually read, not the SparkNotes."

"That's not fair!"

Susan was more tolerant of my vices those days, indulgent even. And I was less self-absorbed, more willing to appease. It was the honeymoon phase of our friendship, and subsequently, it did not take much more coaxing for me to haul myself out of bed, repants myself, and head with her to the auditorium.

It'd been a packed room, not just with students and faculty but college-town citizens who prided themselves on living in a place with such fine opportunities. Susan said hello to the four people at our school that she liked, I said hello to whomever I could get my hands on, and we sat in the front right corner along with other students from Susan's creative writing workshop: girls and boys who wore large glasses and looked at you with recrimination if you used outmoded cultural references. I got along well with them, or about as well as a bull gets along with china.

The lights dimmed and the provost came onstage, followed by Julian North. Tall and silver-haired, his gesturing hands thick and capable, he gave an hour-long speech on why writing was the key to self-knowledge, reading a revolutionary act, and compassion the radicalism of our age. It was the usual inspirational college stuff, I guess, but at the time it moved me the way a waterfall crashes through the placid river beneath it. I remembered something I'd always known and too often forgot: that reading meant more than escape. I remembered walking in the woods near my house with my science book after we'd learned taxonomy in school; I remembered pointing to the trees while saying out loud, "You are a birch, you are a maple." I remembered resting my hands on their trunks and how they felt like cheeks; I remembered knowing them and in turn, being known.

That's what Julian was saying up there. How words saved you from yourself. How when we called things by their right names we became bound to them, we were freed from the great alone. "We must write our hearts," he'd said at the end of his address. When the house lights rose, I pounded my hands in applause and turned toward Susan with tears in my eyes. She nodded; there were tears in her eyes, too.

We got in the long line to get our books signed. When it was my turn, I couldn't stop babbling about how much I loved his speech and how I loved to read and how just then he made me feel so human and boy, come to think of it, maybe I should become an English major, too, just like my best friend Susan.

He smiled graciously. "Thank you," he said. "I'm glad you came." But it was the way he said it. Or was it the eye contact? I believed, then, that an understanding passed between us. He saw my entirety, and accepted the lot. I was not used to feeling this acceptance with anyone besides Susan, certainly not with a man. *To Casey: Write on! Julian,* read the inscription in my book. The words seemed both encouragement and imperative. I was certain he had chosen them just for me.

The very next day I'd marched into the registrar's office and declared my English major. I didn't want to be a writer myself; the act of composition had never interested me. But I did want to be around writers, start reading again, use the parts of my brain that could do more than flirt and banter and skid through classes by the skin of my teeth. No, I wanted to sink in my teeth. I wanted, more than anything, meaning.

Meanwhile Celeste was saying more about what went on in Julian's radio interview, the marketability of even his casual ideas, how it all seemed meant to be. "It's meant to be," I echoed reflexively. What was meant to be? It was hard to be a person and a mirror simultaneously. "Totally meant to be."

"I'd love for you to talk to Julian at some point—" Celeste said.

"Oh wow, really?" I said. The thought made me feel funny inside. I shoved the funniness into the drawer where I kept all my repressed objects.

"—providing all goes well. But for now I need you to work on bringing Ben Dickinson on board as our proof of concept. I spoke to him and he's expressed tentative interest in running the Instagram and Facebook accounts of Waterman

Quartz fountain pens. They have a new line, WQ, they're hoping to market to younger men. Take him to lunch today and work your magic, will you?" She reached into the drawer where she kept her food bars and pulled something else out. "Which reminds me. I had this ordered for you."

She handed me an American Express business gold card. It had the word *Nanü* and my full name, Casey Cornelia Pendergast, stamped on it in silver. This beautiful gold card had the same color and promise of Vegas and Times Square and the Wild West and the very best dreams of the United States of America. When I took it in my hand and felt the weight of a nearly unlimited line of credit, I couldn't help it, I sighed, "Oh my God!" in orgasmic release.

"I trust you, Casey," Celeste said. She stood up and came around the desk, put her hand on my shoulder like a minister giving a small child a mix of chastisement and blessing. "And I'm looking forward to seeing what you're capable of."

"Oh *gosh*—" I said. I put a hand over my heart. It sounds silly to say I wanted to cry in that moment—Celeste was my boss, asking me to work more, granting me a credit card to be used solely for business expenses—but I bet Moses felt just as strange and sentimental when he was promising a burning bush that, sure, he'd help an entire population of slaves flee Egypt. Sometimes you get asked to do weird things for weird reasons, and you don't entirely understand the nature of the assignment, and maybe it feels a little off, but maybe it also feels a little, you know, *on*. A little special, I mean. A far cry from dull. And so at the end of the day you just have to go with it. Because what's the alternative to taking these chances? Staying the same old person doing the same old thing, the only difference being what television series you stream at night?

"This is a big opportunity for you." Celeste's thumb dug into my shoulder blade. "I believe you're very well-suited for a leadership position at Nanü."

"Yes!" My voice had a whinnying quality.

"A position you'll have the opportunity to create as you go, with maximal growth opportunities."

"Wonderful!" More platitudes ran out my mouth as more complicated thoughts struggled to form in my frontal lobe. Susan was going to be appalled. There was a chance that I, too, was already appalled, but this was hard to pin down. When I was around Celeste's magnetism, my moral compass malfunctioned. True north turned upside down; the dial bobbed and weaved.

Still, I could not stop clutching that credit card in my hand. Credit was promise. Promise of money, yes, but also promise of a future in which I could have anything I wanted and nothing could hurt. Not even the one-line rejection from the director of the organic dairy commercial saying, thanks but no thanks in response to my callback audition. Money, as Celeste said, made for excellent skin. You could love money, and everyone knows loving is way easier than being loved back.

Celeste's hand was cold, even through my blazer. "Simone made a reservation for you and Ben at Horse & Stable for twelve-thirty. She should be sending an e-dossier too, with relevant asset info and the terms of creative brokering."

"Asset?" She nodded. "Asset—author, right."

Celeste removed her palm from my shoulder, a signal that I should stand. Which I did. "And Casey?" she said as I headed for the door, smoothing the butt of my dress.

I turned around. "Yeah?"

"For now Nanü is, for all intensive purposes, a need-to-know sort of project."

"All intents and purposes," I said without thinking.

Just the slightest nod toward irritation appeared in her upper right lip.

"But of course!" I said. "Yeah. Of course, yeah."

"I'll be bringing people on, a few at a time, assuming all goes well. But without a proof of concept I don't see the need for any big announcement."

"Sure, sure."

"Just keep it on the down-low for a while."

"Okay." I shifted uncomfortably. "What should I say when people ask what I'm doing?"

"Tell them I've got you on a personal project or something." Celeste lifted her bony shoulders. "They shouldn't be asking anyway. They've got questions, they can come to me."

"Okay." I shifted again. Subterfuge was the sort of thing that wreaked havoc in the office. Too many women. Secrets drove us crazy, especially if they made it harder to figure out the pecking order. I think Celeste knew this, and so she used secrets cannily, tokens of power to be fought over and distributed. I was terrible at keeping them. Though I loved the power they afforded, I also hated their divisiveness. Even by being in Celeste's office this long, I knew I was in for it when I got back to my desk. People would ask what I'd been doing in there, and it would take all the strength I had to keep my mouth shut. "No problem. *Hakuna matata.* Everyone's going to know eventually, I guess, so no biggie."

When she didn't answer right away, I said, "Right?"

She walked back to her desk and sat down without looking at me. Maybe she hadn't heard me. "Remember to tell Ben he's not selling out.

He's buying in. This is what progress looks like."

"Right," I said, palming the credit card with affection the way Lindsey handled her crystals. I opened the glass door. Simone was sitting there, her desk angled so she appeared to Celeste's visitors as a gatekeeper. She typed furiously at her keyboard, as if the matters at hand were of national significance instead of something like scheduling. With her silky blouses and slender neck and countless hours spent in hot yoga classes, she was the kind of girl who took pride in never buying her own drinks at night. "Guys buy them for me," she'd say with a toss of her dark head. Though she was only five years younger than me, technology moved so fast she belonged to an entirely different generation. From the minute I met her, about a year earlier, I understood she had her heart set on stealing my job. "Are you married?" she'd purred, two seconds after we shook hands. When I shook my head, she said, "But you're going to have kids, right?"

As I walked past her, she said, "Check your email," in a voice that could frost the spring grass. The nerve! Her jealousy sunk fangs into my ass.

"I know," I said. My voice was equally cold. "She already told me you sent it, thanks."

I sounded like a thirteen-year-old, and I did not

95

care. What I wanted to communicate to Simone but could not, directly, was: I AM VERY IMPORTANT! SHE THINKS I AM VERY IMPORTANT! WAY MORE IMPORTANT THAN YOU!

"Fine," she said, giving me the old up-and-down, classic mean-girl stuff. "She also wants a status update after lunch."

"I *know*," I said again, though I didn't.

"Fine. Enjoy your lunch then," she said, and looked back at her computer.

"You enjoy your—" but there was nothing I wanted her to enjoy. Sometimes I think life would be a whole lot easier if we women could just admit when we didn't like each other. Say it once, real loud, then give each other a wide berth instead of pretending to be friendly. "—coffee."

"I will!" she said. A stevia voice: sweet with an acrid aftertaste. As I stalked away I thought: in future generations, may mothers teach their daughters to be straight with each other.

4

BOYS, BOYS, BOYS!

I did not have what psychologists would call a "great" relationship with men. Naturally, I blamed this on men, namely my father. Rake Pendergast was the kind of guy who did a lot of good for a lot of people and a lot of harm to a few. Because I was one of the few, I hated him with the ferocity of many—which maybe wasn't fair, but what child is fair to her parents? A beloved motivational speaker, subregionally famous, Rake spent a majority of my childhood on the road, exhorting employees to rise to the challenges of the workplace and daring middle schoolers to resist drugs and alcohol. He was so convincing and—okay fine, inspiring—that about every third time we were out in public, someone would stop to thank him for either saving or changing their lives.

The way these strangers looked at him, their faces full of fear and hope and gratitude, embarrassed me with its false familiarity. My father never seemed to mind. "Come here," he would say, opening and wrapping his big arms around them. Rake was built like a football player—he played wide receiver in college—

and moved like one still. That he could crush these strangers with his embrace was precisely what they loved about him: people like to make themselves smaller to fit in something larger. Around Rake there was only one point of view, and this relieved people. They relaxed into his embrace the way a body softens to accept a blood draw or a shot going in.

Not me, though. Rake, for all the good he did, was also a depressive philanderer. It surprised me, even when I was young—too young, really—how seldom adults acknowledged these flaws in his character. Especially, for all her intelligence, my own mother. One of my first memories is when Louise and I dropped by his office, a modest two-room operation inside a shabby commercial building, unannounced. It was midday; I wasn't in school yet, was maybe four. I remember my mother turning up the volume on the radio—a James Taylor song—in our brown Oldsmobile as she pulled into the parking lot. She reapplied lip balm and mascara using the rearview mirror and smoothed out my little cardigan, re-pinned my barrette. "You be good," she said to me, which was something she said often.

When we entered the front office, after climbing two flights of stairs, I knew something was wrong because the air felt funny. Rake didn't see us at first. He was sitting on the edge of his secretary Jeanine's desk, leaning forward and laughing softly. "You and I are a lot alike," he was saying. "I've always thought so." Jeanine's face was high with color as she fingered the chunky glass beads around her neck.

Jeanine saw us before my father did. I saw her drawn-on eyebrows raise, her lipsticked mouth curl into a cracked *Oh*. Her teal suit jacket with gold buttons was too big for her. At the sight of her expression my father turned around.

"Hi honey," my mother said. I saw surprise move like the shadow of a manta ray across my father's face before he rearranged it liquidly into a pleasant expression. "Well, look who it is," he said, and moved with ease off the desk to give Louise a kiss on the cheek. He picked me up, and I felt the change between my two parents as clearly as I could feel temperature. I never liked it when my father held me. There was something sour in his body.

"Hi Louise!" Jeanine said too brightly. My mother smiled stiffly with her hands in half fists. My father kissed me on the temple. I moved my head away. "She's a daddy's girl," he told Jeanine, and bounced me a little.

On the car ride home, Louise told me that we should feel sorry for Jeanine because she was a single mother who hadn't gone to college. "It isn't easy for those women," she said. What had happened, she was saying, hadn't actually happened. No, my mother never again brought up what Rake had said or the way he sat on Jeanine's desk or why he used that slick-wet voice I didn't recognize. She never brought up the drinking, either, nor the temper nor the late-night phone calls for which he'd disappear for hours into the garage. This turning of a blind eye from a woman who otherwise missed nothing continued to disorient me for years after, had perhaps disoriented my whole life. Love was a mental disorder, denial more than a river in Egypt. It turned out that if you closed your eyes you could believe anything, absolutely anything, about someone, even if all evidence pointed to the contrary.

Yes, yes. Louise was an empiricist, and she still got duped. I was an emoter, and I couldn't help but rage on her behalf. Nary a moment would pass after my father came home from a business trip before—with the help of adolescent hormones—I would set upon him with complaints and accusations. They were the same ones Louise had but would never dare articulate as she stood there, with her damp rag, silently wiping the countertop. Why hadn't he been there for my violin recital? Why did his coat smell like cigarettes? He was home three hours later than he said he'd be; where had he been?

Ah, but my father built his life and livelihood on the sands of unimpeachability. Look at how hard he worked, he'd shout, how much he did for us, how spoiled I'd become in my mother's hands. "Stop it, both of you, stop it!" Louise would say. She had not the strength to fight him, and when he felt like it, Rake rewarded her weakness with affection. The worst fight we ever had, he got purple in the face and balled up his fists, and though he didn't hurt me, he could have. That's the day I realized my father would do anything to protect himself. Male lions kill cubs all the time, you know. Monkeys too.

Horse & Stable was one of those elevated American restaurants popping up everywhere those days, where traditional was trendy and simple meant expensive. Nestled in the warehouse district among skyrocketing rents and lofted condominiums, the building had once been used to mill blue-collar grain. Now the white-collar types who frequented it were triathletic men who talked loudly about microbrews, and women so smooth they looked like dolls from a mold. I'd been there before with people from PR, but never with Susan. Susan wouldn't be caught dead in a place like this.

Simone had reserved a table for two, but I took it upon myself to move the reservation to the bar. I didn't want a block of reclaimed barn wood coming between Ben and me. There was an art to these types of conversations, a craftsmanship to the con. If I had learned anything from Rake, it was the art of persuasion. Even when he was in a checkout line, Rake would look at the sales clerk like he or she was the prime minister. In response, or in thrall, to his charisma, they'd fall all over themselves with gratitude. Sometimes we got discounts, sometimes free stuff. Celeste thought desire boiled down to money, but I, I thought it came down to value. People wanted to feel like they mattered, and the thing is, they rarely did. If you led them to this feeling, as Rake knew, they'd give you pretty much anything: trust, loyalty, coupons, and, as I'd learned through advertising, slavish brand allegiance.

Not to toot my own horn, but I was preternaturally good at making people feel good. At work, yes, Ellen was a case in point. But also in life. Women were trickier, but men, I could get them to do pretty much whatever I wanted. It's hard to explain but I guess it boils down to this: I sensed what they were missing, and I gave it to them. Or was it that I emptied myself out, so they could fill me? Whatever the case, it did not hurt that I was a hellcat in bed.

Point is, I was unconcerned by the prospect of getting Ben Dickinson on board for Celeste. Why wouldn't he, I practiced saying in my head, want to enter into an exciting new relationship with fountain pens? A relationship, per the e-dossier I'd grabbed from the printer before leaving the office, that could guarantee him enough money to last easily through the end of next year? My legs were bare and freshly shaved, spring's latent sexual energy bursting from between them like a broke chrysalis. I smoothed my hair and tucked part of my bob behind my ear and thought: God help you, Mr. Dickinson, for the devil sure can't.

I took out the printed pages from my purse and spread them out on the rustic wood of the bar. It was a few minutes before twelve-thirty, but I took the liberty of ordering my usual cocktail of beverages from a bearded, suspender-wearing man who looked like he belonged in a Jules Verne trilogy: hot water with lemon, coffee, Diet Coke, club soda, hot tea, and kombucha. I had read in a magazine that drinking liquids all day curbed your appetite and also detoxified your system. On my dating app profile, *detoxification* was one of the six things I couldn't live without.

"Anything else?" Jules Verne asked, one bushy eyebrow raised.

"Why, yes," I said, just to annoy him. "I would also like some cocktail peanuts."

His face turned a shade of smug, something that was happening more frequently in upscale restaurants. Bartenders start using eyedroppers to make their own bitters, suddenly they're God's gift to the restaurant industry. "We don't serve cocktail peanuts."

"Well then," I said. "I will have your finest

bowl of warm olives. And please—no bread on the side."

Jules Verne left, undoubtedly annoyed that he was being forced to wait on a customer. I turned back to the dossier. Ben's biography was straightforward enough: three years older than me, grew up here, parents divorced, went East for college, moved to New York, dabbled in publishing, had a story published here and there, and then had made a splash in the literary world the previous fall—and a gentle wave outside of it—with his debut novel, *Next Please*, a comic romp through the trials and tribulations of an unemployment agency during the recession. He'd moved back here recently to help care for his mother, who'd sadly been diagnosed with early-onset Alzheimer's, but his publisher had him traveling a lot to shill the book. An investment like a book tour, I'd learned from hanging out with Susan and her friends, was rare in publishing, and I made a mental note to ask Susan, as soon as I got the nerve to tell her about this new venture, whether this investment could be chalked up to Ben's talent or mere winsomeness. Likely it was both, since I saw that he'd made appearances on a couple late-night talk shows, which writers never got to do unless they were extremely charming and/or good-looking.

I learned, too, from the dossier that Waterman

Quartz, the pen company in question, had been a respected firm back in the 1950s, but its reputation had slid steadily in the past couple of decades with the rise of emails and three-dollar packs of made-in-China pens. The line, WQ, that they wanted Ben to "support" on social media, was supposed to appeal to the kind of man who bought old-fashioned shaving kits and wore old-fashioned work boots and talked about "slowing down" and cooking "slow food." A man like my bartender, Jules Verne, who seemed nostalgic for an era a hundred years before his birth. It seemed a profitable enough marketplace to me. Why, even on the walk to Horse & Stable I had passed a men's store selling tin mugs and Swiss Army knives and something called raw denim.

Jules came back with my beverages and olives, and I became so engrossed with sipping, munching, and musing that I did not notice a man slipping into the cushioned bar stool next to mine and motioning to the bartender for a cup of coffee. When he tapped me on the shoulder I looked up and blurted out unthinkingly, "Shit! You're him!"

"I am him," he agreed. "If by that you mean I am me."

Ben Dickinson looked nothing like he did in his author photo. His aspect in the photo in question was churlish intellectual: spectacles, prominent chin, humorless, scowling features. The guy in front of me wasn't wearing spectacles and his hair was longer, a sandy mane. He looked younger, more good-natured; his face was inquisitive, handsomely unusual. He wore a velvet blazer, of all things, and of all things raw denim, both of which fit him well enough to reveal the lean physique of an athlete. The attraction I felt was so immediate that I instinctively crossed my legs.

Business, I told myself. Business business business business business.

I opened my mouth to talk, but for once I couldn't find anything to say. So I sat there, mute, until he reached out his hand.

"Ben Dickinson," he said. "Jesus, I hope I am who you're waiting for. The hostess said your name was—"

His hand was warm and dry. Touching him revived something in me, or ignited it. "Casey Pendergast," I said. "Creative director at People's Republic, interlocutor for Nanü, Celeste Winter's right-hand woman. Pleasure to meet you."

"Pleasure's all mine," Ben said. His smile took up a fair amount of his face. There were faint lines on his face, around his mouth and eyes, the impishness of a well-used boyhood. It was one of those smiles you couldn't help but smile back at: a mirroring, connecting impulse. Electricity zinged down my spine and straight into my pelvis. I thought: to see a grown man smile like a boy is one of the lesser-sung pleasures of this life.

I recrossed my legs, adjusting the hem of my dress. "How are you?"

Ben slid out of his stool. He stood and angled his body toward mine, so close I could catch the scent of man shampoo: crisp and piney. He nodded toward my clatter of beverages. "What are we drinking?"

"Don't you mean," I said, having recovered myself, "what *aren't* we drinking?"

He looked at me. No, he looked into me. My body throbbed.

"I'm going to like you," he said, and then leaned over the bar with two fingers up and ordered a couple of whiskeys.

My God. So annoying, and yet so exquisite, to be in the position I usually put other people in. Ben was one of those people you couldn't say no to, and believe me, I tried. "You're terrible!" I said, some two hours later, slinging back an oyster in a half shell and washing it down with a flute of champagne. The lunch crowd had petered out by then, and it was just the two of us at the bar, the restaurant nearly empty.

"You're terrible," he said, chucking down his own oyster. "Profligate spender of company money."

"Who said this was on the company?"

"You did, half a drink in."

"No, I said it was on the company if you behaved yourself."

"My sense is you'd rather I didn't."

We were like that right away, he and I, falling into a repartee that signaled, as it always does, that we immediately wanted to bed each other. Talk like that, it's as good as sex, sometimes better; an attraction both rare and beyond reason. Unreasonable, even. Causes decent people to throw whole lives away and indecent ones to do worse. I mean, I'd met Ben solely to pitch and close the deal, and yet for hours all I could do was banter and catch his eye while in the meantime my body burned.

It was not just that Ben was handsome, intelligent, funny. I'd been with plenty of guys who possessed such qualities, though admittedly rarely all three. There was something else. We were, from the get-go, like tennis partners, *well matched*. What exactly matched between us was harder to say, but I felt this matching as soon as he sat down beside me, and I know he felt it too. Which was why I could not pull myself away from the pleasure I took merely in sitting beside him, seeing his eyes light up and crinkle when he laughed, his posture lively and erect.

Jules Verne glided up to us. "How's everything tasting?" he said to Ben. Since Ben's arrival, he'd begun to address questions to him exclusively.

"Great!" I said. I used a lot of tone. I wanted this tone to say: hey bucko, look at me, I am not this man's enfeebled hausfrau; I'm the bad bitch who's about to pay for everything.

"Anything else I can bring you two?" he said to Ben.

"We'll take the check," I said to him.

Ben looked at me with mock horror. "So soon?"

"Some of us have to work, you know."

Jules Verne looked back and forth between us. "So . . ." he said to Ben. "The check?"

Ben waved Jules off. "Thanks. We don't need the check just yet."

"We'll take the check," I said imperiously. "Thank you."

"I'll give you a couple minutes," Jules said. As soon as he was out of earshot, I let out a whuff of displeasure.

"Do you see how he does that?" I said. "Only talks to you?"

"Guy's an idiot. Anyway, I work too, you know."

"Sure you do."

"I also play video games and keep up on Reddit."

"Ah, that's comforting," I said. "Captain of industry, right here."

Ben leaned back in his stool and crossed his arms, cocking his head to the side as if working out a puzzle in his brain. He put his feet on the rungs of my stool with a sense of ownership I found both irritating and extremely sexy. "You're a bit of a workhorse, aren't you."

"Psssh. Me? Who just allowed you to turn a business lunch into a three-martini party? Yes, that's right," I said, leaning forward. "I *allowed* you. Because I'm *generous*."

"I bet it's surprising to some, since you come off initially like a wild child. But look," he said, spreading his arms out wide. "We're getting to know each other. Establish rapport. You can't rush that."

"We don't need to get to know each other. This is a business meeting, not a date to see if we're likely to breed and buy real estate. What I need for you to do is sign a few papers and be on your merry way."

He smiled. That smile. I smiled back because: biology.

"You want to buy real estate with me?"

"Oh, please."

"I'm flattered."

"You shouldn't be. I said that's *not* what this is. I already own real estate, thank you, and I only brought that up to explain—"

"A condo of one's own, is it? You strike me as the condo type."

I was getting flustered. He was more in control of this than I was, which I didn't like. As Oscar

110

Wilde said, everything was about sex except sex. Sex was about—

"Into girl power, and all that feminist jazz," Ben continued.

Jules Verne appeared again, and I snatched the black folder out of his hand and stuck the gold credit card inside. "Thank you *so* much," I said. "Everything was *delicious*."

"And for the record, I'm not a workhorse," I informed Ben after Jules went off to swipe the card. "I'm a fun horse."

Ben laughed, genuinely.

"Can we talk shop for, like, a second?" I said, checking my watch. "We've been here for—God, I don't even know how long. Walk me back to my office. Obviously we're getting nothing done here."

Jules reappeared with the receipt and a pen, and as I scribbled my name on the exorbitant tab, Ben stood and placed my blazer, which I'd shrugged off hotly at one point, upon my shoulders. He left his hands there for a second, and I felt something I had felt only a few times in my life: a man's protective instinct, different from possessiveness. There was, beneath his cleverness, solid good-heartedness. He had returned home, despite the prestige and attention he was getting elsewhere, to care for his mother. In that moment I found myself strangely honored by his attentions: that he would see through and still accept me.

. . .

The walk back to the office was brisk and efficient. I told him what Waterman Quartz was asking him to do, and he seemed more amused than anything. He asked what the workload would be, and I guessed that it would be one, maybe two hours a day, especially if he scheduled posts ahead of time. The trick with social media was to *appear* like you were always working, I explained, not to always *be* working, so if he had a busy week he could front-load a bunch of photographs, status updates, and whatnot, line them up, and have a social media deck fire them off for him. He considered this for a moment, and then agreed faster than I had expected that he would.

The money, he explained, was so he could hire an in-home aide for his mother, whose decline was more rapid than anyone had expected. He was loath to put her in a nursing facility, but she became confused when left by herself for too long, and her husband, Ben's stepfather, worked all day. From Ben's tone of voice I understood that he did not like his stepfather. The money from his book was good, he said, better than most, and there were promises from his agent and editor that another contract was in the works for his second, but none of it was substantial or steady enough to support both him and his mother. "It's a clusterfuck, really," he said.

"Sometimes I wish I'd gone into accounting."

I screwed up my face. "Do you really, though?"

He laughed, and reached his arm up to brush the budding springtime leaves of one of the trees that lined the sidewalk. "No. Sometimes I wish I wished. Mostly I'm okay with the fact that I'll never be rich. But my mom—"

"I understand," I said. And I did, or I thought I did, or I tried my very best to.

"Say," I said after a minute. "I've been meaning to tell you. My best friend's a writer."

"Yeah? Who?"

I told him about Susan. "She hasn't published anything yet. She's a genius, honestly, a virtuosic talent, but she just gets so—I dunno, heady, I guess, about putting herself out there."

"Happens frequently with writers, as you might imagine."

"It's like she's terrified to make a single move because she sees too many possible outcomes or consequences to that move, like on a chessboard. She simultaneously lives only in the past and, like, twenty years ahead of the rest of us."

Ben glanced over at me. "You're very observant."

I shrugged, blushed. "I try."

We walked in silence for a minute. A man busking on the sidewalk began a pan flute rendition of "My Heart Will Go On."

"I've been thinking about her a lot today

because I'm sort of dreading hearing what she has to say about Nanü—I mean, about you working with us. She's going to compare it to the Fall of Rome. She literally compares everything to the Fall of Rome. Caligula—is that the emperor's name? The guy that started out okay then devolved into a greedy tyrant?"

Ben laughed. "Why?"

"I'm just saying, Susan hates advertising. Plus she has sort of a—an exaggerated view of the artist's role in society."

"I get that. Most artists in their twenties do."

"And older. Hel-*lo,* James Baldwin."

"Hello, English major." Ben side-eyed me appreciatively. "Who knows, maybe Nanü is the Fall of Rome. But honestly, the older I get, the less able I am to see the world in absolutes. For me, working for Waterman Quartz isn't representative of anything except the fact that I need money to help my mom out."

"Susan wouldn't buy that. She'd say something about the—oh, what would she say—the systemic degradation of language into quote-unquote salable content in which you're now complicit."

"To which I'd say, artists've always made shit for the sole purpose of making money. You think those old masters painted a bunch of old women with dogs in their laps because they were called on by the Muse?"

I made a mental note to remember that line.

As we kept walking, we passed by a toothless woman panhandling, her cardboard sign saying something about homelessness and sickness and anything at all would help. I never knew what to do when I saw such people. Louise had taught me never to give money because, she'd say with a wrinkled nose, you never knew what they would do with it. But that reason never felt good enough for me to justify walking past these folks, straight-faced, gaze ahead, pretending, for my own sake, that I lived in a world where they did not exist. A few years before I'd taken to keeping granola bars in my purse to give away, but one time a burly flanneled guy, clearly mentally ill, had pushed the offering away in a frothed-up fury. "I don't want your filthy food!" he'd slurred. "Gimme your filthy money!" After that I had kicked the habit.

Ben stopped, dug into his back pocket, and pulled five dollars out of his wallet. "Thank you," the toothless woman murmured. "Beautiful couple. God bless."

It seemed silly to explain to her that we were not a couple, seeing as we'd likely never see her again. Plus the sound of the words pleased me, like an unresolved chord resolving in my head.

"We're not a couple," Ben said to her, dissonantly clanging me back into the present.

"*Definitely* not," I said for good measure.

"Beautiful couple," she said again. Her eyes

had a film over them, the way eyes get when they look out onto a world only they can see. "A lot of hair."

We laughed about that as we continued. It was true: we each had a good head of hair. Though normally I hated the "we" that so many couples used, I understood that afternoon, or re-understood, why people did it. *We*'ve got a lot of hair. It was a tool of sorts with which you could knock down the hard jail bars of the *I*. Outside those bars, you could stand up a little straighter. *We*'re in this together.

We passed a popular Mexican place, a fast-food chain that had taken over the industry with pound-and-a-half burritos and promises of healthfulness, naturalness, organics. Just the year before, famous authors' words had started appearing on the company's take-out bags. Bon mots, poems, quotes you could easily digest. This seemed to give further credence to Ben's point: writers and corporations had a normal, even symbiotic relationship.

But I remembered what Susan had said when we'd stopped at the restaurant last fall for burritos to-go on our way to the movies, right around the time this ad campaign started. On her paper soda cup had been a little story from one of the great white men of our current century. A little story, in fact, that I liked a great deal. Something about kindness and change. But as soon as Susan saw it, her face darkened and closed. "What the hell are they doing?" she'd said.

I'd been digging into my bag for a handful of tortilla chips and hadn't seen her furious expression. With my mouth full I'd said, "What're who doing?"

"Bullshit neoliberal propaganda," she'd said. She had raised her voice to address the entire restaurant. "You guys know that this meat is constantly getting recalled for E.coli and none of the food is actually good for you, right? That they're just trying to make money?" She held up her cup and pointed to the story. "This guy? They *paid* him to manipulate you into forgetting all that with this gauzy bullshit feelgoodery. But you see any voices of color on these cups? You think any of the people behind the counter will see a wage increase if this entitled dude's story causes sales to spike? Stay woke, people. Life's too short to buy into this fuckery." And with that she'd thrown her cup, along with her uneaten burrito, straight into the trash.

My first thought as she stalked out of the restaurant was: oh, *come* on.

My second: even if she gets hangry at the movies, she is *not* allowed any of my burrito.

Burning with embarrassment—although, what did I care, the people staring were people I'd never see again—I'd followed her outside, where she'd been trying unsuccessfully to light her cigarette. As she turned the lighter over and over with a grating click, cigarette dangling from her mouth, she said, "I cannot be*lieve* that motherfucker signed on to shill burritos. Give me a *fucking* break."

"Actually he didn't say anything about the burritos—" I'd started, but stopped when I saw Susan glaring at me. Our patience for each other had been eroding steadily for years by then, but slowly enough that we could look straight ahead instead of down, distracting ourselves, pretending the common ground beneath our feet wasn't disappearing. Once in a while, though, events demanded we clock the loss. This clocking had such a cataclysmic effect that the first time it happened I had to take to my bed for two days to watch British television. This was maybe a year after I began working for PR, after I'd invited Susan to be my date at one of the award ceremonies advertisers are constantly throwing for themselves. I'd picked her up wearing a rented Dolce & Gabbana dress and my first pair of designer shoes; Susan had slid into the car wearing Timberlands and a torn rayon dress. "I didn't have time to shower," she'd said, shrugging.

That night Susan had proceeded to get riotously drunk and talk heated nonsense while sitting with her legs splayed wide in her chair. I knew Susan drank too much when she was nervous, but there was something else to her drunkenness that night. Susan had a destructive streak: her capacity to ruin was just as powerful as her capacity to create. What she was saying to me that night through her actions was *I don't respect any of this*. And there was nothing I could do about her acting out, which is precisely why she did it.

Our fight came to a head in the bathroom. Lots of tense words and arms crossed followed by crying. Eventually we forgave each other, but you don't forget these moments: they form patterns in the mind. They leave a bone bruise.

Walking with Ben, feeling the movement of his fingers just inches away from mine, I shook these memories from my head. Susan was intractable; I was not. That's what made me so good at my job. I was no philosopher, no moral imperialist; I didn't even know what *neoliberalism* meant. As much as I'd admired Susan's principles over the years, they could be, on a day-to-day basis, extremely off-putting. Lecturing an entire fast-food restaurant on the dangers of propaganda? People don't respond well to moralizing, I could have told her, but Susan wouldn't have listened. She couldn't read people the same way I could. She was interested in them, but only in the abstract. After zero real inquiry or curiosity about them, she came up with stories about them in her head. If you thought about it, that was no more charitable than encouraging these same people to buy burritos.

Oh, that was good. I had to remember that line, in case I needed to zing it at her later. All writers are propagandists, I would tell her. All of you are trying to convince us of what to think or do. It's just in advertising we're not as sneaky about it as you.

When we got to the entrance of the People's Republic building, I started toward the door, expecting Ben would follow me inside to sign the paperwork, but he stopped me. He was meeting a friend, he said, and had to run. I felt a jealous ache. I didn't know if I was jealous of the friend—was it just a friend?—or jealous that the world he moved through was so much bigger than mine, full of midafternoon coffees and time uncolonized by the marching armies of commerce. Perhaps he looked down on me for my position. A true intellectual he was, I thought, and here I was not even knowing what neoliberalism meant. Probably, I thought, he was attracted to women who were more like him: serious, ambitious, capital-*a* Artists who had not given up on their true aspirations and did not spend what little free time they had on frivolous home decoration and trending exercise regimens. He did not say this, but I believed I could see it in his eyes. Never mind that he was wearing sunglasses and that, when I looked at him, I saw only my tiny reflection tinted in amber.

With my earlier confidence sputtering out like air from a leaky balloon, I pulled out the dossier from my bag and handed him his contract, telling him in a voice far less lively than the one I'd used at the restaurant that I'd appreciate if he wouldn't mind signing it before he took off. Sad, I think, how quickly anxiety severs connection. How often we got in our own way.

Ben very courteously said, of course, he'd forgotten all about the contract, he'd sign it right away. He used the wall of the building as a hard surface to scribble his name on the final page.

"Someone should teach you to read the fine print," I said, watching him.

"I trust you," he said.

It was the second time someone had said that to me in one day. It startled me, coming from him, whom I'd already begun to say goodbye to, to dismiss as a onetime flirtation. I said lightly, "Careful, that's gotten a whole bunch of boys like you into a whole bunch of trouble."

"There are no boys just like me," he said, capping his pen with his teeth.

"Is that so." When I took the papers back from him our fingers brushed.

"Sure was nice to meet you, Casey Pendergast."

"Sure was nice to meet you, Ben Dickinson."

"See you again, I'm sure," he said. He stood there, considering me, and then he leaned forward and brushed his lips to my cheek. Hot breath. The soft skin of my earlobe. The fullness of his mouth. The way it pressed up against my ear's crevasse, tickling the invisible hairs inside.

All at once I was having trouble staying upright. I put a hand on the wall of the building and watched him saunter down the busy avenue, hands in his pockets: an unmistakable figure, so different-looking from the scores of barrel-chested businessmen hurrying about in their pale blue button-downs. I exhaled, looked down at the contract. Next to his name he'd written a note in tiny cramped block letters: *I'll call you*. Then he'd drawn an arrow and written *Cross this out*. I put my other hand over my heart, and then I did.

5

ANGELS AND DEMONS

Walking to my car after work I texted Susan to see what she was up to. My drunken afternoon giddiness had faded to a headachy malaise, and I was dying to go somewhere quiet with her and eat salads and talk about our feelings. Or rather, talk about my feelings. Talk about my feelings about Ben. I had a lot of feelings that I needed to feel! Process. Share. Feel, process, share. Rinse with wine and repeat.

Susan texted back and said she was on her way to a reading. *Wanna come?*

Where is it? I texted back.

Present Moment

I groaned. Present Moment was one of those bookstores that had a resident cat and catered toward men and women who wore socks with Birkenstocks, used the word *lover* instead of *partner,* and believed the path to liberation was through astrological readings. But so much had happened that day—a new work project, a new man—that I was dying to fill her in on, I was willing to subject myself to this hairy semblance of a bookstore, whose self-described "radical progressivism" seemed mostly to mean they radically only cleaned the bathroom once a year.

I knew, of course, that what I had to say to her would go over poorly. I could imagine it already: she'd press her intense, Susan-specific rhetoric upon me about the ruled and ruling classes, Celeste's so-called internalized misogyny, the doomed nature of so-called heteronormative relationships, white men and their so-called acolytes standing on a three-legged stool of racism, sexism, and capitalism, et cetera, until I capitulated not from agreement but exhaustion. But Susan was my family, and that's what family is for: you exhaust them, they exhaust you, but underneath all that lies a watchful and ferocious loyalty.

I texted back. *Ok fine. Who's reading?*

My friend Gina and some other ppl. You'll like her. She's a slam poet ;)

Omg stoppppppppppp

All these years later, Susan wouldn't let me live down the three months my junior year when I'd convinced myself *I* was a slam poet. As part of the English major we were required to take a creative writing class: I'd chosen poetry, because it seemed easiest. The professor, who insisted the class call him J, commuted in from New York City and spoke with a lot of pregnant pauses. A few years before he'd had a part in *Def Poetry Jam*, which he mentioned several times on the first day of class while wearing a T-shirt that said EAT THE RICH. That same day he'd made us write and perform our first poem. Mine, inspired by his T-shirt, was about rich people not picking up dog poop. J seemed to like it. He snapped his fingers, which I later learned was called a "poet's snap." He said, "Man, I *dig* it."

Pretty soon I was saying I dug stuff, and had harnessed the power of my own poet's snap. College was an impressionable time for me, what can I say. Or was I always this prone to suggestion? In any case, I bought a pair of Chuck Taylors and developed what I believed to be a socialist aspect. I wrote poems about my father and the effect of media on body image. I believed they were very good. Then I saw the video one of my classmates had uploaded to the college intraweb of our end-of-semester jam.

It was, how can I put this. Horrifying. Like watching a toddler dance recital, minus the chubby-kneed charm. "What the hell *is* this," I'd said to Susan once I showed it to her. I was furious, I guess because what had happened in my head did not seem to be reflected accurately by reality. "Amateur hour?"

"Um," Susan had said delicately. "Yes?"

I'd sent a furious instant message to the videographer, demanding he take the video down, and thrown out my newsboy cap. Six years later I considered myself a "recovering slam poet" more than a "former slam poet," though if it weren't for slam poetry I might never have gotten my job. A year later, I'd had my senior exit interview with a college career counselor, and when asked about my favorite classes I'd mentioned J's. The counselor had smiled at me the way you smile at that lady in Thursday night Zumba who practices moves in the mirror after class. "Hard to make a living from poetry," she'd said from across her cluttered administrator's desk, while behind her a wall of books, all variations of *What Color Is Your Parachute?*, loomed menacingly down at me. "But if you enjoy it, it's certainly something you can do on the side." Then she'd asked if I'd ever considered advertising. I had not. Then I did. Perhaps it is not an overstatement that this woman, with her Talbots blazer, had changed the course of my life.

Plus, Susan wrote, *free food!*

Sometimes it made me sad that Susan had to think about things like free food. I was making six figures, I owned my condo, I could afford to eat whatever and whenever I felt like. But I knew there were things about my life that made Susan sad, too. We both refrained from saying these things out loud because sometimes the sadness we feel when we look at the lives of our friends just shouldn't be articulated.

Anyway, I told Susan I was on my way, and before I could think better of it, typed *Btw what do you know about Ben Dickinson?* With my heart in my throat I pressed Send, for once grateful that texting by its very nature forced language to become extremely casual and not, say, lovestruck and obsessive.

Her response came immediately. *Not much. Liked his book, know people in town who know him. Why?*

Wheeeeee! I thought. *Tell you in person,* I wrote, and chucked my phone in my bag before opening the car door.

What Susan had neglected to mention was that the reading was a celebration of something called the Duende, which in my initial understanding, thanks to the sandwich board positioned outside the bookstore, was a magical goblin who breathed words out of his mouth in an olde English cursive: Meet your duende tonight!

The crowd inside, maybe twenty people, was about what you'd expect: hippies and vegans and freegans and folks who looked like they had yet to return from their last acid trip. An island of misfit toys who were perfectly happy living outside the traditional confines of society, while still remaining reasonably middle-class. I spotted the bookstore's owners, two older women, Pat and Patty, who lived together and worked together but weren't, as Susan had once explained, *together*-together. Both were wearing

Wiccan pentacles tied around their necks with leather cord and sack dresses of earnest hemp fabric. With the help of a few volunteers, they were clearing space in the back of the store, unfolding metal folding chairs, and assembling a makeshift stage. The store's black long-haired cat, Whiskers, swished, augural, around their feet. Gregorian chants thrummed through the speakers.

I spotted Susan talking to someone who I assumed was her friend Gina. Susan was wearing a long black vest, slim black pants, block heels that made her even taller than she already was. It had taken her a while to shed the band T-shirts and ripped, ill-fitting jeans of her adolescence, but when she finally settled on a monochrome wardrobe it was for her, I think, a great relief. Her outer trappings finally reflected her inner life: imperious blacks and whites. In contrast, Gina wore a pale blue T-shirt and thick black glasses, had a pageboy haircut and assumed the retiring posture of a true introvert: shoulders slumped, chest concave, prepared at any moment to crumple to the ground in social surrender.

I interrupted their conversation with the tact of a gale force hurricane.

"Hi!" I said to both of them. And to Susan: "I need to talk to you and I'm STARVING."

Susan and Gina exchanged a glance. I linked my arm through Susan's. "Nice to meet you," I said to Gina in the same fakey tone of voice I used with Simone. Then I dragged Susan by the arm toward the food table.

"Be right back," Susan called over her shoulder.

"Casey," she said as we walked. "Rude."

"I just really wanted to talk to you. *Alone.*" Around us the bookshelves contained volumes as obscure as they were dusty. "Also, why didn't you tell me this was a *magical* reading? You know I don't like magic."

"Duende isn't magic. It's an energy."

"Oh. Well then. *Pardonnez-moi* and *namaste—*"

Susan frowned. "You wanted to come. Stop making fun."

"I'm not!" I said. "Okay, fine, I am."

At the food table a Hawaiian-shirted, cargo-shorted bald guy cut in front of us and started slopping food on his plate with big metal spoons. He had the spread-out-wide air of entitlement that a lot of old white guys have, even if they've never amounted to anything. The food on offer fit the night's theme: half devilish (devil's food cake, deviled eggs) and half angelic (angel food cake, angel hair pasta). Even the coffee in an old-fashioned silver percolator came out of a large can that was branded DEVIANT DEVIL COFFEE with a picture of old Satan with his pitchfork and horns.

While we waited I told Susan that I had some good news and some bad news and which did she want first.

"Well, I only have bad," Susan said, and laughed a little. "A clusterfuck of story rejections. Yippee."

"Oh, muffin." I reached over and squeezed her arm. "But you *tried*. That's huge. I mean, even a year ago you wouldn't have sent out anything."

"Yeah, because there's no point." She laughed again. It was the cynical laugh she used when trying to cover up anguish. The metallic sound made me wince.

I squeezed her arm again. "Yes there is. All artists get rejected. It's part of the process. Look at—I dunno—the Impressionists." Susan rolled her eyes, but I continued. "They weren't always hanging in waiting rooms, you know. The establishment *hated* them. It takes a while for people to catch on if you're trying something new. You have to be patient."

"Easy for you to say. You're not the one getting filleted by strangers on the daily."

"Because I can't. I don't have it in me. You do."

"It's so stupid," she said. She cast her eyes sideways, down toward the floor. "Even if they accepted something, it's not like anyone reads these magazines. They read their Facebook feed and like, clickbait listsicles about celebrity weight loss. I'm spending months on these stupid short stories for what? Fifty bucks and ten people in a grad program?"

"No, because you're a writer. It's what you have to do. It's what you're *meant* to do."

"Ugh. Only rich white people say that sort of shit."

"Hate to break it to you, but we are rich white people."

"*You* are."

Here we go, I thought. I held my tongue, though there was a lot I wanted to say back to her. About how you can't abdicate privilege, for one thing, any more than you can refashion your own reputation. About how childish she seemed, after my long *actual-work* day, with her insistence on seeing people and culture as toxic absolutes.

Finally Susan asked, "Anyway, what's your bad news?"

Well, the timing wasn't great, but the conversational ball was already rolling downhill, and at the end of the day what can you do about gravity? I told her the bad news wasn't, per se, *bad,* only that Celeste had put me on a new project in which corporations would provide patronage to talented authors in exchange for a small piece of the authors' creative capital. I used this exact language because I wanted to practice my pitch with a straight and undilemmaed face. "I mean, I don't think it's bad," I said again for good measure. "I think it's a great opportunity for writers to make a little more money, you know? Pay off the mortgage, pay off the car. Send the kids to private school. The only reason I said it was bad was because, I mean, I knew *you'd* think it was bad." I picked up a paper plate, handed it to Susan, picked up another for myself. I feared the sloppiness of this buffet, but it was time to summon my courage for the sake of interpersonal harmony. "But you don't think it's *that* bad, do you?"

Susan didn't respond right away, which didn't surprise me. It took her a long time to match the right words to feelings. In college, before I understood this, I would constantly harass her in the quiet. Now I kept talking because gravity is unforgiving. "I just wanted to tell you because you know I don't keep secrets from you. Celeste said I'm not supposed to talk about it, but I mean, how can I not talk to you about it, specially since you're a writer too?"

Susan still wasn't saying anything, so I tapped her on the shoulder. "Hello? Hello, hello?" I twisted up my voice so I sounded like an old-timey radio announcer, which normally she loved. "We're standing by for a report from the field from one Miss Susan—"

"Casey, stop," Susan interrupted. She picked up a deviled egg. Susan and I had both dabbled in eating disorders back in the day—in our socioeconomic bracket, what girl hadn't—but had mostly set them aside once we'd discovered all the million things that were more fun. Deviled eggs, for one thing; sex, for another. "Don't song-and-dance me like I'm one of your clients. Why do you even care what I think?"

"Fine, no song and dance." I looked warily at the table and all the food it held. If history had proven anything, it was that no good could come from buffets. "I just don't want you to be mad at me."

"Why would I be mad?" Susan scooped a spoonful of deviled ham with a plastic spork.

"The usual reasons. You hate advertising. And now advertising is, like, creeping into your industry."

She turned toward me, spork in hand. The ground-up ham looked like cat food. "You know what the definition of insanity is?"

"Umm—" I thought for a second, then snapped my fingers. "Easy. Sophomore year. Wearing miniskirts when it was like negative twenty degrees."

"Doing the same thing over and over and expecting different results."

"Okay, sure," I said. "But do you know what the *other* definition of insanity is?"

"Oh my God, stop with the joke line already."

"Okay, okay." I was put off by her exasperation. I took on a piece of angel food cake. "I just thought you'd at least want to talk about it more. You know, like we used to. You say stuff about assembly-line creativity, I talk about creative capital, you say plutocracy, I say Pluto the dog—?"

"No, thanks."

"Why?" I sounded whiny. A long time before I'd realized I needed Susan to be my sounding board, the opposing force off of which my best thoughts ricocheted. She didn't let me evade difficult questions with clever jokes or allow me to change the subject; she pushed me. Harder than I wanted sometimes but, I also thought, exactly as hard as I needed. I thought that if she and I could have a serious conversation, I could make peace with my own position. I couldn't get there without her, so I baited her: "It's not so simple, you know. Ben Dickinson's going to use the money to get his mother—"

"Ben Dickinson's in on this?" She looked at me with genuine astonishment.

"I had lunch with him today. That's why I asked you about him. Which leads me to the good news—"

"Fucking Celeste," Susan said under her breath. Ah—bait taken. I grabbed a few limp crudités and followed her toward the folding chairs. Susan hated Celeste. Always had, though you'd think she'd at least in theory appreciate that I had a powerful female boss. But to Susan, Celeste wasn't actually interested in shifting the sands of power in any way beyond aesthetic. Celeste had power and used it, as Susan had put it a bajillion times, to quote-unquote reinforce distorted messages about women, and was clearly more interested in amassing her own fortunes than changing the status quo. "She manipulates you," she'd told me once after I'd had a bad day at work—some pitch gone sour. We'd been drinking wine all evening, and in vino were being very veritas. "She wants you to be just like her. You're not, but you are gullible. If you keep trying to impress her you're either going to drive yourself crazy by pretending or"—I remember the pain at the corners of Susan's wine-stained mouth—"spend so much time pretending that eventually you *do* become just like her."

I'd laughed it off then. "Oh, please. I'm not like Celeste at all!"

But Susan hadn't laughed with me. "I'm serious. I do not trust that woman. I don't know what she has on you that keeps you working there."

She makes me feel special! I'd wanted to cry. Susan didn't get it. She assumed that, like her, people walked around with a clear sense of who they were. But some of us girls wait dutifully to be told. Celeste was someone who told me who I was and, unlike with most people—my parents especially—I didn't hate the answer. But it's hard to speak plainly like this, even with your best friend, even with yourself. So I'd drunk more wine instead.

Before I could get any further with needling Susan into a response, Gina came and sat down next to Susan. "Hey, you guys," she said, in a voice so muted and affectless I had to bend over to hear her.

"Gina, this is my friend Casey. Casey, Gina. Sorry we left you like that," Susan said to her. To me: "Gina's an incredible poet." To her: "I can't wait to hear you read tonight."

Just as I was registering that Susan hadn't used the word *best* before *friend,* hadn't said anything about *my* incredibleness at, say, creative directing or dance fitness, either Pat or Patty took the stage to welcome everybody and introduce the night's first reader. I settled in and prepared myself for two hours of earnest droning. I forked a piece of cake into my mouth, listened ironically to a rail-thin man talk about train hopping, and waited for a good snarky one-liner to pop into my head so that I could lean over and whisper it to Susan.

But when one came to me *(Why do sad writer boys love pretending to be hobos?)* and I looked over, I saw that Gina and Susan were murmuring with each other. Gina! I hated her. I would smite her with my thunderbolt of Susan-specific expertise. *Bet you don't know her favorite Counting Crows album,* I would thunder as soon as Susan was out of earshot. *Yeah, that's right, Gina, if that's even your* real *name. Bet you didn't*

136

know she secretly likes Counting Crows either. Oh, but who was I kidding. I didn't have the heart to smite Gina. I only felt the pang of left-outedness that dated back to kindergarten, even before that, an ache that did not lessen with time but rather that time added to with layers. Watching them, I understood awfully for the first time that Susan had a whole life that had nothing to do with me. No wonder she didn't care about what I was doing at work. I was too outdated for her milieu, which was currently filled with bespectacled poets like Gina and Marxist punks and grad students who spent the mornings on their dissertations and afternoons on their novels. Intellectuals and artists, self-described and self-important. Probably they looked at me the way I, too, had looked at friends who invited their high school and college friends to parties. They were fine most of the time, nice enough, but often it was clear that they had served as useful way-sides on the road to someone actually becoming themselves and did not belong at later exits.

These thoughts were socks tumbling around the dryer of my brain, hot and constant. Sure was easy to feel inadequate in this world. But I didn't just feel inadequate. I felt many things at once. There were probably German words for these sensations, complex nouns like *competition-friendship* and *IneedyoutoremindmewhoIamness* and *occultbookstorespecificsorrowatlosingyour-*

bestfriend, but these sorts of ambiguously poetic constructions didn't exist in English, so I was stuck with my sadness. So I emotionally ate cake.

The reading was fine. Good, even, if I allowed myself to see it purely for what it was, to let it stay, as the old saying went, "in its lane." But charity, according to a recent online quiz, was not one of my top three virtues, so my mind continued to drift and ruminate. I'd put my phone on vibrate, and when I heard it buzz in my purse I leaned over and dug for it with a sense of relief. Finally, something besides the present moment to occupy my attentions.

It was an email, I discovered, turning my body discreetly away from Susan, from my contact at the production company that had gotten me the audition for the organic dairy commercial. The tone was apologetic. The company was "streamlining" its talent in order to "incubate" their business, and while they were grateful for the opportunity to work together, albeit briefly, they would be moving forward without me. In other words, they were firing me, even though I'd never worked for them in the first place.

Stupidly and involuntarily, tears sprang into my eyes, like in gym class when you caught a basketball too hard in the chest. I didn't want to cry—there was no reason to cry, I was losing something I'd never had in the first place, I'd dipped a mere toe in the waters of another kind of life while my real life remained intact—but look, the body knows what the mind doesn't want to admit. In such moments I was reminded that there was this whole bloody, desirous animal beneath this well-groomed exterior of mine. One always feeling and wanting things too hard. She stayed there, relentless, this animal. No matter how hard I pushed her, muted her, numbed her silly, she never went away.

I sniffed and blinked the tears back. I would not feel anything unless I had to and no one could make me. I put my phone back in my bag and returned, arms crossed, to the scene in front of me. It was Gina's turn. From Gina I learned that duende was not a magical word-breathing goblin at all, but a force with which human beings could create. It came up like a reverse lightning bolt from the earth; one had to wrestle with it the way Jacob wrestled his angel. It was a power, not a work, Gina quietly slammed. Action, not thought. Blood, not brains. At once I longed for that force to come up through *me,* fill *my* blood, power *my* work, offer *my* life the meaning I'd always longed for and could not quite find. But oh, maybe Susan was right, that sort of longing—what am I meant to do, blah blah—was reserved for spoiled rich people. So I made like an angel-wrestler and shoved it right out of my head.

• • •

I went over to Susan's apartment after the reading. She needed a ride home, and she'd just finished reading a book that she wanted to give me, a book of poems. Accepting the offer seemed like a way to repair, or at least start repairing, the crack between us that seemed every day to be widening. Hell, maybe I would actually *read* it, and we would stay up late talking about it the way we did years ago.

Susan's studio apartment was in no more disarray than usual. She'd always been messy, but in the years since we'd lived together her living habits had taken on a feral quality. Her unmade bed, really just a mattress on the floor, was piled with books and papers, and a dirty plate and fork sat atop her bedside table. She used a folding table in her kitchen, owned two scuffed-up armchairs, and had nothing but rice, beans, and canned tomato sauce on the exposed pantry shelves. The only thing of quality she owned was her writing desk, which had been given to her by her grandmother and sat in the middle of the room. It, too, was covered with books and papers. We took a seat in the armchairs and faced each other, our legs tucked beneath us, the way women do when they talk in yogurt commercials.

"You want a drink?" Susan asked me, and pointed to a bottle of rye on the floor by her desk.

I shook my head. "I started at noon, thanks to my new friend Ben."

"Oh *yeah*." Susan leaned over and picked up the bottle from the floor. "I meant to ask what happened with him."

While Susan poured herself two fingers, I recounted the afternoon Ben and I'd had together, careful to leave out just how much I'd liked him. That needed to stay between me and me for a little while. Susan's and my sacred ritual of talking about boys was a decade old at that point, however, and the ease with which we both settled into it comforted me. I'd tripped on a worrying wire at the bookstore, feeling the space between us, but maybe it was nothing, that wire. A false alarm. A trick of the imagination addled by drinking for three hours straight. "Point is," I concluded, "he's totally amazing and I think I'm in love!"

Susan smiled, because she knew I was kidding. We weren't cynical, but we were cool—there was a difference. Love was for single women who bought bridal magazines, pinned on Pinterest, and made careful lists of the qualities they were looking for in a boyfriend. Probably they had parents whose marriages were held together by something more substantial than real estate and denial. Probably they did not think much about just how useful myths of romantic love are for existing power structures and birthrates.

Ah, but beneath this jadedness of ours, as is usually the case: a whole compost heap of hope and hurt. I longed for love, what human doesn't, but I feared love was a lie—or, at best, temporary. Susan had this compost pile at the bottom of her, too, though she dealt with it differently than I did. Susan was too sensitive for casual affairs, attached fast and hard, was devastated for a long time after they ended. As a result, she abstained for long periods of time. At times I felt she thought this tendency toward observation in lieu of participation made her superior, that she looked down her aquiline nose on my messy, frequent, and all-too-human exchanges.

But that last part could have been just a projection. What can be said for certain about Susan was that she did not crave the attention of men the way I did. She did not seek it out with, for example, the intensity of someone who's fallen down a hole and is waiting either to be rescued or for the hole to be filled with rainwater she can float in.

"Speaking of love, before I forget—" Susan said, and abruptly jumped up from her seat. She trotted toward the walk-in closet, which she'd converted into a giant bookshelf. Besides the bathroom, it was the only separate part of her studio. "—the book."

"Speaking of books," I said, standing up myself

and wandering over to Susan's desk. "How's the novel going?"

"Good. Fine. Terrible. You know how it is."

"You figure out how to raise the stakes yet?" Susan's novel was a bildungsroman about a group of friends who originally met at summer camp. Her worst fear was that it was boring.

"No. It's still all backstory, no story."

"Something big needs to happen." I moved some papers around. "Maybe to Sheila." Sheila was Susan's main character, a struggling writer. Sheila was not at all, Susan would insist on telling people, based on herself.

"I know, but I don't know what it is yet."

"Can I read it? You haven't let me read it in forever."

"Not yet!" Though a wall separated us, I could hear her tone. It meant *Don't fuck with me on this*.

I picked up a sheaf of papers and started leafing through. "What about the story you just sent out? Can I read that at least?"

"Maybe later!"

That same tone of voice. Instead of forcing me back from the edge whence the tone came, something pressed me forward. There was a secret part of me that liked edges. I picked up another pile of papers. A sequence of poems based on a photograph by Diane Arbus. I picked up another pile of papers. The short story in

143

question. The thing about pushing on edges is that if something breaks—if *you* break—at least you know what happened. You're not waiting.

I stuffed the papers in my bag. Pure impulse, lizard brain, the same brain that swiped through hookup apps as I walked down the street and ate entire bags of tortilla chips at eleven p.m. and cheated on boyfriends and lied to Lindsey and went drunk shopping. The front part of my brain, meanwhile, was formulating my justifications if and when Susan figured out what I'd done, noticed the pages were missing, caught me red-handed. I would say, *I wanted to give them to Ben, Ben knows people, he said he'd call me, he'll put this in the right hands.*

What I would not tell her was that I, too, had been rejected that day. That if my dreams were just superficial delusions I could at least live vicariously through hers. I would not tell her that I envied people like her and Ben because they had never felt they had to grow up and let go of their childish things, the things they loved and were passionate about. I would not tell her that sometimes I wanted to punish her for this, for having such a clear vision for her life. I would not tell her that I needed to do something drastic so that she would not go away.

Because if I passed the story on to Ben, and this jump-started something for her, there would be no chance that we would stop being friends. *See the logic?* I would say. Yes, I was preparing to say and not say everything that was in my head, but in the end there was no reason. I was back in my armchair, arranging myself to look as though I'd been resting idly, by the time Susan emerged from the closet.

"Here it is," she said triumphantly with the book in her hand. It was a slim volume written by an American woman in the seventies. Susan told me she'd lived in Greece for a few years and had come back from the Hellenic wilderness with a light in her eyes and this fistful of poems. Reading it, Susan said, would change my life.

"I can't wait," I said, which was not true. I did want it to be true, though.

When I got home, before I went to bed, instead of swiping on my hookup app or buying shoes, I opened this volume of verse. The first poem in there was about a girl dressed in white. Her hands were gnawed off, her nails gone. She lived in a beautiful garden, but she was covered in blood. She'd done it to herself, the poem said, so she wouldn't have to feel the other things.

The poem didn't say what these things were. It didn't have to. A girl comes into the world knowing these things. I myself knew them well.

6

GAME OF BROOKLYN

Rake died of an aneurysm my junior year of college. Came out of nowhere. When my mother called and told me the news, it was a late-February afternoon, and a grimy fog had begun to settle over the matted-down grass in the commons and dirty piles of snow. I walked across campus in a daze and looked up at the bare trees. Through her own tears Louise kept murmuring "Mama's here, Mama's here," but I could not feel her, and never had.

When she finally asked, quaveringly, if I was all right, I said that I was. Though I knew in some terribly clarifying way that I was not all right, and would not be all right for some time. It's common as dirt, parents dying before us, and yet when it happens we can't help but think bewilderedly: why has no one prepared me for this? The answer, of course, is that we would not have listened.

After I got off the phone I wandered into the student union, where luckily I found Susan. She was sitting in a big leather chair, her face buried in a library copy of Sartre's *Being and Nothing-*

ness. I stood in front of her until she looked up. Then I put my hand on her armrest for balance.

"My dad died," I said, swaying back and forth a little.

Her eyes widened with shock. I opened my mouth again but I couldn't find the words to explain what I already knew in my body to be true: that my life as I knew it was ending.

"I have to go home," I finally said. "For the funeral."

Susan put her book in her bag. "I'm coming with you."

I shook my head, faced the floor, bobbed and weaved.

She stood up and reached out to catch me. "Yes, I am." Yet by the time she took me by the arm, my mind had already wandered off. The thing about losing your mind is that it rarely announces its departure. It doesn't cut your ear off or leave you raving in the streets or stick your head in the oven. All it does is slip away when your back is turned.

At the funeral Susan served as my proxy with the bereaved while I hid behind oversized sunglasses and silently contradicted every beatifying story they told. *He helped save your marriage? Well, he ruined his own. He got you into AA? He drank in secret every night!* Louise, on the other hand, swanned around the church, relieved, I think, by the beatification process,

148

its forgiveness of any obligation she might once have felt to reconcile her husband's duplicitous nature. A death in the family knocks everybody into highly subjective and private realities, and, at least for a while, the realities my mother and I lived in would find no overlap.

There's no way to explain the following year except to say that grief ripped through my body like a hurricane rips through trees. I slept with more people that year than I had in my whole life. I made a hundred new friends and abandoned them with impunity. I lost weight, gained it back. Six months later I gave away half of what I owned. I rarely thought consciously about Rake, which was, I suppose, the whole point. I wish I could say that eventually I emerged from that time triumphant, but in truth I emerged like the survivor of any natural disaster: intact but permanently shaken. No, I did not learn anything from my father's death except how fragile I am, how fragile any "I" is, and to be honest I've been trying to calm down how much I know this ever since.

Though there is something else I learned. One day Susan took me to the park down by the river near campus carrying tinny portable speakers and a pack of cigarettes and a cheap bottle of wine. It was summer, but I could barely feel the warmth on my skin. We drank the wine and smoked the cigarettes and listened to a new record by a group of riot grrrls who by now were women and still believed the world had hell to pay. I was going through the motions of being a person but was, I thought, made of nothing inside.

"Do you remember Reepicheep?" Susan asked suddenly. She was lying back on her elbows on our tattered blanket, facing the river.

"The mouse from Narnia?" She nodded. I was sitting up, and curled my knees into my chest. "Yeah. What about him?"

"Remember what happens to him at the end?"

"He goes sailing off on his own, I think. From the *Dawn Treader* to the edge of the world? I can't remember why."

"Because he had to," Susan said. A cargo ship lurched through the muddy waters, belching smoke in the air. Somewhere birds had to be chirping, but I couldn't hear them yet.

"I know you're out at the edge of the world right now," she continued, still looking out at the river. She was using a twig to dig into the dirt beneath the long grass. "And I might not always be able to go there with you. But whenever I can I'll try to drop down into your boat." With this she turned to look at me. "Paddle with you for a while."

I couldn't look at her. It was so embarrassing, being a person. Being loved and seen without any disguising contraptions. Eventually I managed to say, "You will?"

"Of course I will," she said. And she squeezed my arm.

So I guess I learned that, too.

Life, turns out, is chock full of learning opportunities. We learn from life like a nail learns from the hammer that keeps clocking it on the head. If I had the choice, frankly, I might choose to learn a little *less,* even if it allegedly makes me a better person, because listen, it hurts to get whomped on all the time.

Luckily some learning doesn't hurt as bad as, for example, death, not to mention the imminent loss of your best friend to a retiring nemesis named Gina. Like the learning I did for Celeste! After signing Ben on with Nanü, I threw myself into Celeste's new enterprise with renewed gusto. In addition to performing my regular duties as creative director at PR by day, I devoured books by MBA types at night and impressed Celeste in the mornings by casually dropping terms like *anti-structuralist strategic thinking* while we waited for the Keurig machine to finish its wheezing drip. "I am just, like, *all about* innovating value right now!" I said to her the day after I finished reading a book called *Playing to Win.* "Would love to ideate with you when you get a chance."

It took a couple weeks for her to finally pull me into her office, but when she did, her email said that she had exciting news. When I arrived in her doorway, Celeste was pacing around in her tall-tall heels, her black cocoon cardigan billowing around her like a cape, her face narrowed and intent and gazing at something invisible in front of her. She looked surprised to see me, even though she herself had beckoned.

Perched at the edge of her desk, and tapping one foot insistently on the cement, Celeste explained that she had just heard back from Waterman Quartz. Ben's official start date as their social media guy was, Olé!, Cinco de Mayo, still a week away, but he had done as I suggested and was scheduling out tweets and posts and photos on a social media dashboard. The CEO himself had been so impressed that he'd immediately called Celeste. As soon as she had gotten off the phone with them, she emailed me.

I don't know exactly what that CEO guy told her, but it was substantial enough that Celeste was acting pretty intense. Which was saying something, because Celeste wasn't exactly a casual person. Over the years I'd tried to imagine Celeste as the party girl she claimed she once was, but the only way I could parse it was that when she was in her twenties, she hadn't yet figured out a way to aim that intensity, and the energy had spun out everywhere. But she'd trained herself out of that. She'd become the skilled practitioner her intensity required. Seeing

152

her direct it with such overwhelming focus toward her goals was one of the things I admired most about her.

Anyway, she mentioned something about venture capitalists now being interested in Nanü's concept. I didn't know anything about venture capitalists except what I'd learned from an hour-long drama on premium cable, but I had enough context and imagination to guess that there might be some money on the table now, maybe even big money, and that since I was already a part of Nanü, some of this big money might end up trickling down to me. I remembered what Celeste said when we'd first started talking about this stuff: that people were willing to do surprising things once they were offered the right dollar amount. I did not think of myself as greedy, and yet I could not stop images of well-designed homes and tropical locations from flitting like a slideshow through my head.

Celeste was vague on the details of these potential investors, what an investment by VCs would actually mean on the daily, but she did tell me that she would be needing me over the next several months to help establish what she called Nanü's "portfolio." Having a proof of concept, a.k.a. POC, a.k.a. Ben, was one thing. But what Celeste really wanted, and what I assumed the VCs were asking for, was a total of ten partnerships brokered between authors and corporations. This would establish enough precedent that Nanü appeared to be truly a blue ocean, and not just some one-off success with a local company's social media accounts and an up-and-coming writer like Ben Dickinson.

Ben. I hadn't heard from him since our lunch, though I'd thought of him often. More than often. I'd thought about him all the time. In the shower, walking down the street, before I went to bed, when I woke up. How embarrassing, since we'd only spent a few hours together. Though it would have been possible to get his number from Celeste and text him myself, I was too proud for that sort of business.

Luckily Celeste didn't notice how I started when she mentioned Ben's name. She was intent, rather, on explaining to me that she had gotten in touch with the important people she knew, who in turn had gotten in touch with the important people *they* knew, who had dug up a number of names and contact information of authors who might be interested for whatever reason in Nanü's version of "creative engagement." The first name she mentioned was Wolf Prana.

"Wolf Prana?" I said, and wrinkled my nose.

To be honest, I didn't know much about him, only that Susan hated his guts. He was thirty-seven, a California-born Stanford dropout who had hopped on the Twitter train early and prolifically, and, for reasons I couldn't quite understand, had become incredibly Internet-famous. He was a poet to begin with, but his Internet fame, per Celeste, had allowed him to go on to do all sorts of different things. He founded a magazine, made a documentary short about himself, had a gallery show with his photography. In short, a capital-*i* Influencer and New York man-about-town. What Celeste didn't mention, however, was that he also had a terrible reputation among women. Grabby hands, explicit DMs, or so Susan said.

"I want you to fly to New York to get him," Celeste said matter-of-factly. There was an Italian athletic wear company, big in the nineties and now a relic. Wolf was well known for wearing tracksuits everywhere as part of his personal brand. Celeste had discovered this by scrolling through his Instagram feed and had, very cleverly, I thought, put two and two together. Wolf could not only wear this company's apparel, Celeste explained, he could write, direct, and star in an Internet-only commercial for the company, one that could be embedded in all the social media platforms in which Wolf was already enmeshed. His level of "creative engagement" would have to be subtle, though. Prana's "alt" fans were a touchy bunch and wouldn't take kindly to their fearless, seemingly antiestablishment leader churning out sponsored posts for an untrendy company. But Celeste was confident that we could find a way for the company to sponsor him without looking like the company was sponsoring him.

When she used the word *we,* she motioned to the two of us, her and I. It made me happy. *Mama!*

"Here's how I want to play this at the office," she said, still perched on the edge of her desk. She looked like something out of *Advertising Age,* one of their frequent glossy spreads about a no-nonsense CEO succeeding in a tight marketplace. "I don't want word getting out to any other agency about what we're doing, so I still want to keep things relatively on the down-low. Those of you working on it—just you, plus Jack, Annie, and Lindsey, for now—I'm going to have you sign NDAs. No point in getting people excited over something that's not real yet."

"By 'something' you mean the venture capitalists?"

"I mean changing the whole face of advertising." Celeste stood, crossed her arms. Her fingers rested elegantly on her toned triceps. "I mean changing the world. Because of what we do, because of our *singular vision,* artists will never go hungry again."

I mean, yes and no. I mean, no. I mean, that was certainly untrue. But around Celeste, much like with Susan, there was no such thing as untruth. It was impressive, how much Celeste herself believed what she said, how true she could make it seem. And as I've said, I was very impressionable.

"Sure," I said. I crossed my arms, too. Sometimes I found myself studying Celeste very carefully, like I used to study music videos in middle school, try to memorize the steps so I could try them out later, alone in my room. "I mean, duh! So exciting."

Celeste flicked one wrist in a gesture of casual dismissal. "And if anyone outside of your core team asks what we're doing, tell them they can come talk to me directly." She knew as well as I did that no one would. Celeste was not what you'd call an approachable boss. You did not go directly to her unless you were bleeding.

"Okay." I smoothed my pencil skirt. "Wait. Did you say *my* core team?"

She smiled. "Say hello to a ten percent raise and your new title. Senior Creative Director for People's Republic, and Nanü's Head Asset Manager."

Somewhere in my head I heard a game show bell go off, watched as confetti fluttered through my brain. In reality, I put my hands together like a cymbal-clanging monkey and clapped. Ten percent! Ten percent! Who knew how much happiness I could buy with ten percent? Perhaps I could now even hire an assistant, outsource the boring parts of life so I could get back to important stuff, self-improvement, what lifestyle bloggers called "self-care." We could not heal the world without first healing ourselves, they said. And healing ourselves took a whole lot of time and a lot of money, not to mention lavender oil.

"Thank you!" I said over and over, like a tearful beauty pageant winner. Though PR prided itself in theory on minimal hierarchy, we all jockeyed for better titles. Between my exhortations of gratitude I thought smugly: looks like *someone's* never going to have to clean the coffeemaker again.

When I got back to my desk, I saw that Lindsey, Annie, and Jack had been waiting for me. Ellen, we'd discovered earlier that day, had penned a memoir. The book was set to launch in the summer, but she'd just gotten into a huge argument with the art department at the publishing house, whose potential covers for the book were, according to Ellen, *extremely* off-brand. She was asking us to work with the art and copy departments to get the cover and jacket flap more "on message." The four of us had been scratching our heads all day, having never worked with a publishing house before, and certainly having never written a book jacket. We'd been drafting and redrafting a reply, but we didn't know what to say. Heck, we didn't even know that kind of interference with a publishing house was allowed.

"*So* sorry, you guys," I said a little too apologetically, which could be read either as *I'm as sorry as I've ever been* or *I'm not sorry at all.*

"It's okay," Lindsey said. Those wounded eyes of hers! I'd met a lot of people in my life, most with about the average mix of goodness and badness, but Lindsey, she was a good person right down to the bottom. Not a drop of what the believers would call original sin.

"Where were you?" Jack said in a miffed voice.

"Ohhh," I said. "Celeste and I are working on something. She'll tell you about it. I have to go to New York in a few days, though, so if this Ellen stuff doesn't get wrapped up before I go, you guys'll have to take care of it without me."

"You're going to New *York?*" said Jack. Office politics, they were tricky. Most of the time we told ourselves we were all in it together, but of course that wasn't true. If someone got pulled off of one project to work on another, we got jealous. If someone got to travel and we didn't, we got jealous. If someone got a promotion and we didn't, we got jealous. It was the same as kindergarten, except as adults we were expected to know how to deal with these feelings. But the thing is, no one had ever taught us how to deal, so we had to bottle it all up: pretend to be happy and talk shit about each other and then feel bad about talking shit and get worried about our own futures. Then on the drive home we'd cry, or just honk the horn and yell at other drivers with the windows rolled up.

The healthiest of us, the best we could do was "unpack" this stuff in therapy.

"Uh-huh. She'll fill you in, I'm sure, eventually."

"Why can't you just tell us?" Jack said.

"Because she wants to."

"That makes no sense," he muttered under his breath. He was such a snarkfish sometimes. But, look, so was I.

"Is anything wrong?" Annie wiped muffins crumbs off her lap, having not heeded one of my first and most urgent pieces of advice: that carbs were the enemy within.

"Not at all! It's all good, really good. I'm not trying to be cagey, there's just a lot going on right now." It was important that whoever Celeste deemed the Chosen One did not act *too* chosen. As the saying goes: Jealousy, yay! Mutiny, nay.

The trip to New York was brief—just an overnight. I flew out in the afternoon, and that night Wolf was slated to host a party for some hipster magazine I'd never heard of. After my admittedly pushy request, Simone had booked me a room at the Ace. It would have been more convenient to stay in Brooklyn, but I believed the Ace and I were better suited.

The timing was crunched, though. By the time I'd checked in to the hotel, I barely had time to take a forty-five-minute shower under and between a hundred rain spigots, sweep the entirety of the complimentary toiletries into my suitcase, order a kale salad from room service, drink wine from the mini-fridge, dance jubilantly to my favorite female pop icons, put on my face, remove my face (the eyeliner was no good), put on a new face, try on all the outfits I'd brought, hate them, hate my body, spiral into a sad time, despair while eating a bag of corn chips, and get entirely redressed over a thick layer of Spanx.

I was just about ready to head out the door, with the suit of armor that good taste and expensive personal care products provide, when my phone chirped. I was glad it did, because I paused in my tornadic preparations enough to spot Susan's poems on the desk. I'd brought them along in case Wolf and I had a chance to chat about them. He knew so many people, an endorsement of her work from him could mean a lot, or maybe he could even get them into a publisher's hands. I shoved the poems into my bag and reached for my phone. The text was from a number I'd never seen before.

Want to get a drink before your thing?

I wrote back right away. Did Wolf have my phone number?

Wolf, is that you?

Pause. Three dots let me know the person was typing.

Nope.

Who is this???

Have you been waiting for this moment your whole life?

Another pause, three dots.

Or at least two weeks?

Another pause.

Celeste gave me your number.

I grinned. Oh, I grinned. I wrote back right away.

Texting, not calling? I expected more from you.

Might as well burn with Rome.

Wait, you're in New York?

Workshop and reading thing. Do you want to get a drink or not?

I didn't understand how I could smash up against so many people every single day and not feel a thing, and then this one person, all he had to do was send a few words and I was gone. A goner. Knowing he was in the same city, who knew where, but close enough it sent a rush of pleasure down my centerline. I wanted him. And it was not a light hunger.

It was hard to know what to do with that hunger, since we'd only just met. The force of my desires could be a lot, even for me. Luckily, texting turns all feeling into banality. If Paul Revere had forgone his midnight ride in favor of

SMS, all the warning the colonists would have had is a shrugging *british r comin :0*

As a compromise, we agreed to meet for a quick drink at the bar across the street from where the party was, an establishment that distilled its own liquors and concocted craft cocktails. It had a rustic aesthetic, but it was the sort of rusticism dreamed up by urbanites who fantasized about the "simple life," going "back to the land," maybe had tried slaughtering their own meat once, a humbling experience they continued to bring up for years after. The long wooden tables were unfinished, the strings of Edison bulbs hanging from the high ceiling white and soft, the clientele sophisticated and good-looking. Unfair, how the median level of attractiveness in New York was so much higher than everywhere else. My outfit, which had seemed so à la mode when I'd packed—wide, high-waisted black pants, a sheerish and sleeveless white blouse over a lacy bralette, and black cutout booties with brass grommets up the sides—all of a sudden seemed too . . . well, how can I put it. Brooklyn women wore black T-shirts and scuffed shoes and unwashed hair and somehow looked impossibly chic. I, in contrast, felt like a Carrie impersonator from Omaha on the *Sex and the City* bus tour.

Ben was at the bar already, talking with the woman behind the counter, who looked to be about twenty-one. She had the whole waifish heroin chic thing going for her that caused my hackles to rise. I didn't want to do what I knew I was about to do, but I didn't know how to stop myself. "Beeeeennnn!" I cried out a little too loudly, and I made an elaborate show of hugging him and touching his arm, so as to communicate to the bartender: the boy is mine.

This wasn't necessary, of course. She had already disappeared to get someone else's drink, and for a second I thought about how much energy I'd wasted over the past few years trying to keep and hold a man's attention. No wonder women got breast lifts and plastic surgery and Botox—women I *knew,* not just Hollywood types—before *and* after they hit thirty. A woman's window to power is very small and always shrinking. Some women, knowing this, shrink right along with it.

Ben fit perfectly into this Brooklyn milieu. He had started growing a beard, which suited him, and had on a plain white button-down and jeans. I felt ridiculous because he was looking at me quizzically, having apparently asked me a question I hadn't heard. A barback was setting two drinks in front of us and Manu Chao was playing loudly over the speakers and Ben's face was so open and expectant that I took a big breath, shoved my chronic female malaise aside, and heaved my best foot forward. "What'd you say?" I said, and helped myself to a drink.

"I said it's good to see you!" he said a little louder. This sort of bar prided itself on din. Being heard was less important than being seen.

"Oh!" I said, probably too loudly. "Yes! And you too! I had such a great time last time!" I kept jabbering in this vein because that's just what happens when I get excited, also what happens when I've spent a long time thinking about someone without actually talking to them in person. Most of the time this tendency toward rhapsodic fantasy ended in disaster: I'd wind up disappointed that the remarkable man I'd concocted out of bits of remembered detail and dreams had little or nothing to do with the dull pedant in front of me.

But with Ben it was different. Just sitting next to him for a second had my whole body vibrating. A physical charge, a tectonic disruption, no less measurable than electricity. As soon as I sat down next to him, words began to form way down below my solar plexus and, slowly, began traveling up through my back brain and into my frontal lobe: *I could totally fall in love with this guy.*

But that was ridiculous. I didn't know Ben. There was no such thing as love, anyhow; love was a delusion shared by two lonely people. I told myself that I must be suffering from delusion and thus must, severely, keep a tight rein on my actions. Anything I was feeling or wished to do was just a trick of the old hormones.

And we did work together, after all. It was unprofessional, I said to myself, bad for business, what would Celeste say? So before I could think better of it, I ended my monologue about how great it was to see him again and what I'd been up to in the interim with what I thought was a sassy and independent, "Oh, and just to be clear, I am *not* going to fuck you."

I'm not sure what was more embarrassing. Knocking over the highball glass in front of me and watching it roll to the floor and shatter, feeling strangers' eyes burning the back of my skull accusingly (I was *that* girl), or the look on Ben's face in reaction to my pronouncement: half surprise, half total amusement. It was a very dumb thing to say, because the thought of fucking him was A-okay fine; I just didn't want to love him. "Oh for crying out loud!" I said, jumping off my stool and crawling on the floor, trying to pick up the broken glass. "My bad. If you're wet, sorry about that—"

As I kneeled with one palm filled with glass fragments, I realized I'd put myself right at eye level with Ben's crotch.

"Oh dear," I said, and scrambled to my feet. Ben was really laughing at this point, slapping his palm on his leg. I apologized to the barback, who'd returned with a broom and a mop, and sat back down, desperate for a drink, but I'd just spilled my drink, and had nothing to take the edge off the stabbing humiliation. As if on cue, Ben passed me his, and I took a couple big gulps. This turned out to be a big mistake. It burned, it burned! Locally distilled whiskey, it burned! I coughed and gasped.

"Anyway," I said, once I'd handed him back the glass. I crossed my legs and interlaced my hands primly over my knees, determined to proceed as if without incident. I cleared my throat. "Where were we."

Ben started to say something, but just then I heard my phone chirp. I put a hand up primly. "Hold that thought." Simone had texted, that sneaky devil. *Where the fuck are u??? Wolf says he's been lookin and you're nowhere to be found????????*

Coming!!!!!!!!!! I texted back. *Sorry!!!!!!!!!!* Then I added a grimacing emoji.

To Ben I said, "Well, well, well, as revelatory as this has been, I have to go." Then I added, with some back-brain impulsivity: "Unless you want to come."

"Already?" Ben looked disappointed, or was I just imagining it. He shook his head. "I would, but I can't stand that guy."

"Well," I said, standing up uncertainly. "Maybe we could meet up later? I'm only in town till

tomorrow, but I thought we could maybe"—
Ben smiled then, a cat-eating-the-canary sort
of look—"as friends," I added, "colleagues"—
why in God's name were these words coming
out of my mouth?—"go to a museum, or something—"

My phone chirped again. It was probably
Simone. "Shit, I really have to go," I said. "I'm
going now, byeeee—"

I leaned in to give him a hug. Before I could,
he kissed me. On the mouth. Nothing big or
anything, no slip of the tongue, but there was the
shock and pleasure of feeling his lips on mine.

"Catch you later, Pendergast," he said. We were
on a last-name basis now.

"Oh for crying out loud," I said again. Then
I smiled real big. Huge, really. You can try and
try to deny love, but, like pain, it insists on
acknowledgment eventually. Often it insists
on even more, insists that one restructure one's
entire way of being, but luckily this process
is slow and incremental so we don't balk and
skitter off. Point is, I wasn't thinking about love
when I was kissing Ben. I wasn't thinking at all,
only being. Of course, you could also say that
being without thinking with someone, I mean
genuinely, is the definition of love itself.

Listen, the party was unbearable, and there's a lot
I'm willing to bear for the sake of a party. But

parties are never fun when everyone's afraid to be themselves. That's the first thing I noticed as soon as I got to this converted warehouse/gallery space. A person could not ask for better circumstances—dim lights, not-bad DJ, luscious alcohol, wide dance floor—and yet all the darkly dressed and disaffected youths just stood around in tight huddles, death-gripping their plastic cups, looking about furtively like small forest animals sniffing for predators.

It sounds strange, but I felt instinctively tender toward these people. Writers, I'd figured out over the years, were solitary creatures. To join a crowd, to participate, would mean to stop observing, and I think this was pathologically impossible for them. Which is sad, if you think about it, because as much as joining and participating can lead to awful things—Nazism, for example—it also leads to wonderful things. Like karaoke, and barbecues, and intergenerational dancing at wedding receptions. Poor writers! No one, at this party, was willing or able to join anything beyond their own ruminations, and therefore it was a real dud.

In lieu of fun, a couple of bespectacled gentlemen were selling magazines behind a table for twenty bucks a pop. They were dressed like dandies, or the Wright brothers. People milled around, idly flipping through the issue. I picked one up. There was an emaciated woman on the cover, dressed in white. *The Minimalism Issue*, the cover line said. It was the era of rich people throwing out all their things. I set it down. I knew deep down that I was a maximalist at heart.

It didn't take me long to find Wolf; I just had to spot the clump of fanboys and -girls that followed him everywhere he went like peewee soccer players. I disliked him at first sight. Wolf even walked with smugness. From the looks of him—average height, mushy build, shifty eyes and bad posture—he'd been something of an outcast growing up. And, like many former outcasts, had seized upon his newfound popularity with a tyrannical zeal.

"Glad to finally meet you," he said, smiling with his mouth only after I'd introduced myself and broken up his coterie. He led me by the elbow to a corner of the room so we could speak privately. All his mannerisms felt so stagy I had to resist the urge to guffaw. It was impossible to take this guy seriously, maybe in direct proportion to how seriously he took himself. He gestured for me to take a seat at a wrought-iron high top table. "How are you?"

"I'm good!" I said in a voice an octave higher than the one I normally use. And then, made efficient by the desire to have sex with someone who was not the person in front of me, I proceeded to launch into a mile-a-minute pitch about why he should start being sponsored by and producing content for the Italian athletic wear company. While I talked Wolf kept smiling. It was a smarmy smile; I knew it well: I'd been getting it ever since I was sixteen. He was not really listening to what I was saying, just humoring me because he found me sexually attractive enough to do so.

"I need a cigarette," he said, right when I was getting to the part about the importance of subtle endorsement strategies. "Come outside with me."

I know I didn't have to go outside, but look, I was trying to get the whole thing over with. The party was in full swing, and when I'd come through the front doors I'd seen plenty of people outside smoking. But Wolf didn't go to the front, he led me out back, past the bathrooms and out to the alley, which smelled of garbage. Once outside he lit a cigarette, sighed, and exhaled a plume of smoke. He offered one to me, but I refused.

"That's better," he said. "Too loud in there."

I nodded. I began again. "Anyway, as I was saying—"

"You like dick?" he said out of the blue.

"What?" I thought I'd misheard him. "Sorry—I think I—"

"You heard me," he said. He was leaning against the brick wall, one foot up, like a wannabe James Dean. I didn't know whether to laugh or run. Fear and absurdity get mixed up a surprising amount of the time. When a bad thing starts to happen, the wise guy in me looks around and pipes up, thumbing toward the situation. *Can you believe this shit?* Wolf took another self-conscious drag.

I started to laugh, an involuntary nervous-system response, no different from a possum's flopping over and playing dead. "That's—" I said, between giggles. "That's—what are you talking about?"

Wherever the laughter was from, Wolf didn't like it at all. Or maybe he liked it a lot. In any case he stubbed his cigarette out against the brick and sidled toward me and started slobbering on my face. He might have described it as kissing, but I can assure you this was not the case.

"You do, don't you," he said into my ear between his slobbers. His breath was hot and rank. "I can tell." He felt around, grabbed the space between my legs roughly. "You love it."

"Ummmm," I said.

I was flipping lightning-fast through possible responses in an impossible situation, unable to figure out how not to hurt his feelings or cause him to act any more aggressively than he already was. He was grunting a little, insistent, like a dog trying to get peanut butter from the inside of a chew toy. And I was kissing him back, I *guess,* or I wasn't not kissing him back, I'd say the fault proportion between him and me was around 90/10, same as a head-on collision. When Wolf finally paused, leaning back to get a better look at me, I instinctively touched my face, just to make sure it was there. This was not how I was expecting the evening to go.

"Should we go back to my place?" he said. His curly hair, styled like a fifties greaser, was falling across his sweaty forehead. He was one of those guys whose face wasn't bad-looking from far away, but up close his yellowing teeth and pockmarked complexion stood out. The flaws seemed to worsen when he opened his mouth.

I had to be delicate about this. In order to talk to a guy like Wolf you had to remain permanently deferential, tacitly assure them at all times they were in the dominant position. "I mean," I said, "I would love to, but—" I scraped around the edges of my brain, looking for a reason. Illness: no, too obvious. Death in the family: same. Feeling fundamentally unsafe: he wouldn't care. All the smarts in my brain disappeared into a poof of smoke. Until—"Wait!" I said, pushing him gleefully back. "We can't! You're hosting! This is your party!"

After that, Wolf made me wait around for hours, the very end of the party, till he would talk to me again. Maybe he was sore that his advances had been rebuffed, maybe it was just another power trip. He was going to sign with us, of course he was going to sign. He just wanted to fuck with me. Show me who's boss. Sometimes men seemed so dumb and naked and obvious in their actions it baffled me that we lived in a world where they ruled it. Then I remembered the advantage they had—they could hit women really hard. Rape us too.

I occupied myself for the remainder of the evening by thumbing through my phone, scrolling through family and vacation pictures taken by people I barely knew, filled with rage at this dumbass Internet poet wasting my time. Finally at three a.m., Wolf sidled up. "I'm wrecked," he said. "Mind if we put off work stuff till tomorrow? We can get coffee or something."

I smiled sweetly. "Sure. That sounds great." If he was going to make me ingratiate myself with him, oh, he'd see. I'd ingratiate him into the ground. He was going to make me miss going to a museum with Ben so that I could stare with hatred at him through the steam of an Americano? Fine, just fine. I was going to get what I wanted from him, and no matter what he did, he was not going to get what he wanted from me. I don't just mean sex—I mean my respect.

"Cool." He stood there, weaving a little. He was drunk, probably also high. "Thanks for coming."

"Absolutely," I said, in as soothing a voice as I imagined a mother used with her screaming, idiot baby. "Thank you for having me."

7

CAPITAL PICKLE

The next morning, Simone emailed me at some ungodly hour, letting me know there'd been a change to my itinerary. Surprise! Mary London, resident queen of the American short story, was expecting me for tea at the women's college where she taught, just north of the city.

It took a few readings of the email for me to understand. Celeste actually *knew* Mary; they'd gone to college together back in the day. Huh. Celeste knew Mary *London?* Mary was Susan's favorite writer, my second favorite, right behind Julian North. Susan discovered London in a college fiction workshop and had in turn gotten me into her by laughing so hard at her collected stories that I'd eventually made her start reading them aloud. London's cutting humor was as finely orchestrated as any comedian's stand-up act, but unlike most comedians, she also wasn't afraid to crack your heart into smithereens.

Apparently Celeste and Mary were the same age, but I'd always pictured Mary London to be ancient, maybe because I believed only old people could be wise. It occurred to me, not for the first time, that there were elements of

Celeste's life I'd only get glimpses of through the chain mail that wrapped around most of her affairs. Most people are unknowable to us and, what's more, they prefer it that way. Anyway, I was going to take a train upstate, which Simone had already booked. It left in a few hours.

This all seemed very exciting, like I was on a big mission for a top-secret government agency. I felt like I was playing make-believe in my childhood bedroom all over again, this time with piles of money at my disposal. *Affirmative,* I wrote back to Simone. *Copy that.* Then, from the comfort of my California King, I called and called and called Wolf until he drowsily picked up with a " 'sup."

I commanded that he meet me straightaway at the café downstairs. "I don't have a lot of time today," I said haughtily. "I have another meeting this afternoon." Listen to me! How busy and important I sounded! I was a professional businesswoman with an iron fist! I rummaged around my memory for bits of dialogue from no-nonsense prime-time workplace dramas. Then I added, "And *don't* be late."

Wolf showed up at the Ace not an hour later, a surprising show of punctuality, given his Brooklyn address, and more proof that the best way for me to get a leg up in the world was to watch more TV. I'd saved us two stools by the windows that faced out onto Twenty-ninth. I found comfort in the hustle and bustle of the Ace, of the trustfund babies, creative professionals, and wealthy tourists that filled the Parisian-style, light-filled coffee bar. Being around fancy people and fancy things had always put me at ease. It's not even that I was born with that big of a silver spoon in my mouth—it was more that I'd always felt I'd *deserved* a big silver spoon in my mouth. For a brief period in fifth grade I'd even convinced myself that I'd been switched at birth and was the secret daughter of Princess Anastasia Romanov.

Point is, the question I was always trying to answer in my daily affairs was: how can I make this banal shit more glamorous? Today I'd already answered that question by dressing like a French woman—high heels, ripped jeans, red-and-white striped shirt, fitted trench coat—and ordering, instead of my usual Americano, an espresso in a tiny cup that arrived with a mini-*macaron* on its tiny saucer. Eating and drinking out of tiny things made me feel, as the French would say, *très* chic.

Wolf, on the other hand, looked terrible, probably because he'd just gotten out of bed. Seeing him there, far from his natural habitat, I was struck by the precariousness of the roles we assign ourselves, how tenuous this idea of *identity* really is; how much of ourselves relies on context. Here in the Flatiron District, in the bright glare of morning, Wolf's ultra-niche demagoguery had no place. He appeared meek and chastened by the peacockish displays of wealth and health and good grooming around him. He was not the king of the Internet poetry scene; here there was no such thing as an Internet poetry scene. Here, he was not *allowed* to assume the alpha position, the bullying self, he got to be in other places. Because here, barely a few miles from Brooklyn, they gave zero fucks about him.

Yes, there was something about Wolf's hangdog look, the unease with which he shuffled to the bar to get a coffee, that rustled and awakened what I must shamefacedly call my own inner bully. I saw him fumble with his change at the counter, and I felt that electric rush that accompanies the sudden awareness that the power in a situation is totally up for grabs. Ions crackled the air around me; a twisted kind of pleasure narrowed my eyes. You fuck with me? I said silently to his back. I fuck with you. You disrespect me? I disrespect you. After the female praying mantis mates, incidentally, she devours the male head to toe.

"I need you to do something for me," I said, once he'd sat back down. "Before I forget."

I was daring him to try, just try to say no, try to gain the upper hand, but I knew as well as he that he wouldn't dare. I had something on him now. I knew something about him—that he could not make me unknow. This didn't mean anything among his sycophants in Brooklyn, but I was pretty sure I could parlay it into something here. Power's too damn circumstantial. Wolf's shoulders were slumped; he curled into himself as he took a sip of his coffee. "Sure, yeah, what's up?"

"Take a look at these, will you?" I took Susan's poems out of my purse and pushed them across the bar. "They need a home, and I need you to find it for them."

"Uhhh . . . okay. Yeah."

"I mean right now."

He looked at me. "You want me to read them right now?"

"Uh, *yeah,* I want you to read them right now," I said, "and I want you to tell me where to publish them."

"Who's Susan Anderson?" He was slumped still, leafing through the pages.

"My best friend." I was going to use this man-child, as he used people. If I had any compunction about lowering myself to his level, I sure couldn't feel it at the time. Helping Susan and beating him at his own game, the old two-birds-one-stone maneuver, ah, it made me feel like a ruthless Russian czarina. Life was very grand sometimes.

I let him read for a while. Then I crossed my arms and said, "So?"

"These are great."

"I know," I said, though I felt a flush of pride at Susan's talent. "So what's the plan?"

I personally watched him email three editors with a query. That seemed satisfactory to me.

"Can I keep these?" he said after he'd sent the last one. "Just in case I run into a few people."

"Of course," I said in what I believed was a benevolent tone of voice. I felt very queenly just then, very competent. "You bcc'd me on those emails, right? And you'll forward me their replies?"

"Yeah, definitely," he said. "I hope something works out."

"Well—good." I scratched my head. Wolf was being so obliging and diminutive, and coupled with his poor-orphan aspect—I don't know how bullies punch down for so long, it was already giving me a backache. Perhaps Wolf wasn't threatening after all. Perhaps he was just *insecure*. All the impotence he must have felt in places like the Ace got stored up, sublimated, and transmuted into aggression, because deep down he didn't love himself, thought he never could, was too wounded to try.

To soften him up into signing with us on the spot, I asked him about his childhood. I listened for God knows how long about his issues with his mother, how as a teenager he'd gotten into drugs and it'd taken him a long time to pull out of that scene, how angry he was that other poets were prone to dismiss his work because it wasn't canonical enough. That was the term he used: *canonical.* He felt alienated from the poetry community, but it wasn't his fault that his career had taken off and he'd gotten these amazing opportunities. He worked really hard, and at the end of the day he didn't care what they'd think about this sponsorship bullshit because, you know what, YOLO.

He went on and on like this, sometimes it was hard to be patient, but I was because I knew at the end he'd sign the paperwork. Which he did. Which he probably would have done all along, but both of us were used to a certain pas de deux when facing off with the opposite sex.

When we said goodbye outside the hotel—I was hailing a taxi to take to the train station, cutting it dangerously close to my departure—we shook hands like we were real colleagues who'd just brokered a successful deal, not two strangers who'd smashed faces not twelve hours before at a random event space in Brooklyn. It was drizzling a little, the sky was a melancholy gray, which contributed to my involuntary twinge of empathy for the sad, mixed-up man before me. After all, it was my job—wasn't it?—to take care of men who were soft and vulnerable and needed help with their personal evolution.

"Don't forget about those poems, yeah?" I called to him as I slid into the cab. He waved and nodded as I shut the door. I remember thinking as we pulled away from the curb: that poor thing.

One thing I've always loved about work is that it doesn't let you dwell. Weird sexual thing with a guy you work with? No matter! Hopelessly falling for a guy you've only hung out with twice? Forget about it! I didn't have control over a lot of things in life, but I did have control over my workplace performance. No, life doesn't come with an instruction manual, but Celeste did, she was giving me instructions all the time.

Simone had emailed me a number of PDFs—commencement speeches, opinion pieces, reviews of her most recent book—to look over on the train on my way to meet Mary London, which, in the wake of my successful encounter with Wolf, I proceeded to do with a sense of extreme competence. With all the hullabaloo I hadn't slept particularly well so I picked a sparsely populated car in order to uninterruptedly listen to soothing meditation music and focus, focus, focus. I had an app on my phone that dinged when I was supposed to work and dinged twice when it was time for a break, and I followed it as reverently as a nun to her canonical hours.

I read as much by and about Mary as I could, as well as the plan for "creative engagement" that Celeste had cooked up just for her. It was a company that People's Republic already represented, a plus-sized clothing chain called Encore. Encore was currently undergoing massive rebranding in an attempt to get rid of their suburban-mom affiliation and get on board with the fashionable full-figured women who—smartly, I thought—had banded together on the Internet to demand better sartorial choices. Yet Encore couldn't lose their suburban moms entirely, for they were the company's bread and butter. It was a fine line to walk, which is where we came in.

Encore's chief marketing officer happened to be a big fan of Mary London, and Celeste had managed to convince her that the solution for the rebranding dilemma was to employ a writer she already adored. Mary had a sterling reputation as an author and happened to be full-figured herself. She was beloved among the kind of book-clubby woman who would share Mary's arch think piece about sexism on Facebook the same day she joined Jenny Craig. Even the suburban-mom customers who didn't fit that bill, who had never heard of Mary London, could still appreciate whatever witty copy London would undoubtedly come up with. The biggest selling point of this offer to Mary London, so far as I could tell, was that it meant she could quit her teaching job, which allegedly she hated.

I was so engrossed with my work that I lost track of my surroundings. It was easy for me to lose track of myself; sometimes I even forgot I was a person. I'd get so into whatever I was doing, or let's be honest, *whom*ever I was doing, that what you might call my self sort of lost its boundaries. A malfunctioning of my cell walls' selective permeability, I guess, to the point that the whole universe seeped in. At such moments I felt less like a human being and more like a loose jumble of thoughts and sensations held together by the equivalent of a too-stretched rubber balloon.

So you can imagine my surprise when I eventually realized not only that the train had stopped moving beneath me, but that we had arrived at my stop. "Hold that door!" I hollered, disoriented but determined to continue on with the sense of unwavering industry that was emblematic of our countrymen. I scooped up my bag and my trench coat and swooped out the doors just as they were closing.

The college where Mary taught was located in a small and picturesque town right on the Hudson, two hours from NYC. Both college and town had a weird friendliness about them that reminded me of a *Twilight Zone* episode about women who slept in age-defying Tupperware at night. People smiled and waved on the street, and the drivers always stopped for pedestrians. These overt displays of neighborliness creeped me out, despite having been raised in the Midwest. I preferred cities like Berlin and Philadelphia and New York, where the people were rude, the smells ripe, the garbage uncollected and spilling out onto the street. Because at least then you knew where they *kept* it.

But here in this quaint hamlet, where the median income had to be well into the six figures, the garbage was divided into an elaborate system of recycling, composting, biodegradable trash and the shamefully unbiodegradable, et cetera. They wanted visitors to know that even their garbage was better than everyone else's, and this impressed me, truly. I was always impressed by the minor improvements it was possible for a person and a society to make in order to live their best lives. Right then and there I vowed to devote myself to creating more civilized garbage, not the reeking stuff I took out the back door of my condo building and threw into a green dumpster with pizza stains on the side. You could buy very nice garbage cans for the home now. A couple hundred dollars, not too bad, and enough to make you feel like a less shameful person.

Mary was holding office hours that afternoon, and I was planning to go straight to her. On my walk over, I called Susan. "You'll never guess where I am," I said in lieu of greeting.

"Where?" It sounded like she was with other people. This made me self-conscious, like I was interrupting something I wasn't invited to in the first place. I plunged ahead anyway.

"On my way to Mary London's office." I was on a winding sidewalk. On either side spread the green, expensively maintained lawn and tall oak trees of the college mall. Behind that, the ivy-covered brick and stately facades of old buildings. The names of people who had hoped to live on forever were etched into the marble at the top of these buildings, and while these people were still dead, I concluded there were plenty of worse ways to take a stab at immortality. Like starting blogs or wars, or building a casino chain.

The walk itself was filled with lively young women, trans women, women of all shapes and sizes and colors, all walking and talking with books in their arms or nodding along to music no one else could hear, courtesy of the white buds in their ears. There was an air of entitlement and self-assuredness about them that I found beautiful. But it was beautiful in the way autumn is beautiful: because winter was coming. Winter, in this case, being the world they faced as soon as they stepped off the grounds of this institution, a world that had not been especially designed for their care and maintenance as this place was, and in many cases had been designed just the opposite.

Susan said, after a pause, "Why are you on your way to Mary London's office?"

"Because believe it or not, Celeste knows her! They went to college together, isn't that nuts? I'm literally going to walk into her office in like three minutes."

"That is nuts."

"Should I get something signed? Can I tell her about you? I mean, obviously I'll tell her about you, but what should I say?"

"Don't tell her about me."

"Of course I'm going to tell her about you! You're her biggest fan!" Being around all this youthful confidence was reviving me from the unsteadiness I had felt on the train. I picked up a stick from the ground and started waving it around like a little kid. I felt vigorous, buoyant. "What if I called you while I was with her so you could talk to her yourself? I mean, it's a once-in-a-lifetime opportunity, might as well use it!" I paused, reconsidered, all the while still hacking at the air with my stick-sword. College campuses brought out the spoiled child in me. "Or at least, like, the first-time-in-your-lifetime opportunity."

"That's okay. Thanks, though."

I frowned. "Why?"

"Because it's awkward."

"Pssssh. It's only awkward if you make it awkward!"

"No, *you're* making it awkward by trying to make me do something I don't want to do."

"Jesus Christ." I paused. "Are you *mad* at me for being here?"

There were still ambient noises in the background. Susan said, "No."

"If you're mad, just say so."

"I'm not."

"Then"—I looked around at the Elysian lawn— "why does this feel strange?"

"It doesn't feel strange."

"Where even *are* you right now?" I blurted. She felt so far away. I wanted to find her.

"I'm at a coffee shop."

"You're writing?"

"I have the day off, yeah."

There was a time, not long ago, when I knew Susan's schedule to the hour. Now here I was, halfway across the country, and I didn't know a thing about what she was up to. I didn't even really know who she was, or who she was becoming, or trying to become. Just because we knew someone yesterday is no guarantee we'll know them tomorrow. People drift away for all sorts of reasons; it's the commoner scenario. What broke my heart was that I thought Susan was the exception. She was my sister, I had told myself, as many others among us have told themselves when it became clear they needed more family than their family. She was, not to put too mushy or melodramatic a point on it, the first and only person in my life who'd loved me unconditionally.

But not anymore, apparently. What I hated even more than the distance in her voice was the fact that she was pretending it was not there. Susan and I, we'd always been straight with each other. We didn't fight like girls, we used to say. We fought like boys, pulled no punches. If only things could stay the same, remain as we prefer to remember them, pure idyll.

"I've been reading that poetry book you gave me before I go to sleep at night," I said. A last-ditch effort to establish contact.

"Yeah?"

"I love it." My voice got thick, I didn't know why, or I did, but I didn't want to.

"I'm glad."

I said, "It makes me cry."

"Awww."

That was the worst—the distance of that *awww*. Like how an acquaintance on the street would respond if I'd said I was thinking of buying a puppy. The opposite of what I wanted to hear. *I knew it would,* I wanted to hear her say. That's why I gave it to you. Your soul is starving, I know that, and I know you know it too. With others you can pretend, but you can't with me, and I wanted you to read those poems so they could do for you what they did for me. We will never not be dying but there are ways to keep alive. We don't always understand each other, but I will always be alive with you.

But that was not what she said.

"Anyway," I said, "I'd better go. Just wanted to call and tell you about Mary."

Susan sounded like she was on another planet. "Have fun."

"I will!" I said. My eyes were getting all stupidly wet. "I'll tell you all about it!"

After we hung up I broke my stick in half and threw the pieces on the college grounds. I did not want to play with it anymore, and I no longer liked all these happy people.

Mary was meeting with a student when I arrived at her office. I took my place dutifully at one of the chair-desks in the hall. Her door was partly open, and I could overhear the conversation taking place. A young woman with a chippy voice was prattling on about the witches in *Macbeth*. Asking if they were real or not real, that sort of thing. The question was meant to function not as a question, but as an avenue toward getting Mary to tell her what to write about in her paper. A tactic I knew quite well, having deployed it many times myself.

"The point is not whether the witches are or are not real," Mary drawled in reply. "The point is a matter of delusion. As a writer I'm very interested in delusion. Likely most of us live in deceit one way or another. Live by it, too."

The student seemed very impressed by this.

"So the possibility you're posing of the witches' realness is both superficial and irrelevant. What's important is that Macbeth believes they are real. He believes he has a prophecy to fulfill, and as you can see, he fulfills it with impunity."

The young woman puzzled over this for a moment. From the hall I could almost hear her IQ straining against its boundaries. "So the witches are like, symbols?"

"We're not meant to wonder about the witches," Mary said. She was being patient, more patient than I could have been with this color-coded-binder sort of girl who was looking for her straight-A answer. "We're meant to stand back in wonder at the power of belief. Even you"— she laughed—"are convinced that you have very important things to do in the world. As I was, as all young people are." She laughed again throatily. "Some of us will go on believing this. The rest will believe right up to the point the world crudely proves otherwise."

The hair on my arms stood up. I can't say why, only that it felt like she had given an answer to another question entirely. A moment or two later, the girl (blond, cable-knit sweater) appeared in the doorway, and Mary London appeared behind her. Mary wore a long black dress, and her brown hair, marked with strands of silver, was parted down the middle and hung unstyled past her shoulders. She looked like she had seen a lot in her life, reseen stuff too.

"The one and only Casey Pendergast, I presume," she said with a faint smile. She motioned me into her office. "Come in. I've heard a lot about you."

Mary's office was eclectic, to say the least. One wall was covered with tapestries, a Japanese tea set sat on a side table, books overflowed from the floor-to-ceiling shelving and onto the large windowsill and floor. I hung up my coat on a rickety scrolling coat-tree, and she gestured for me to take a seat on one of the two matching armchairs situated on either side of the tea set. "Would you like some tea?" she asked me in her odd, drawling voice. Yes, sure, I said. "Love some."

We were quiet as she prepared the tea, a ritual that she seemed to move through as effortlessly as breathing or walking. She struck me as the kind of person who preferred silence, who digested words like they were a heavy meal. I tried not to pepper her with questions and conversation, though, boy, was it difficult to sit in the quiet. I was not used to being quiet with another person. Quiet meant sadness. Didn't it? It was my job to entertain her. Wasn't it?

I'm not sure what Mary London was thinking about in the quiet, but I doubt she was thinking about how quiet it was and wondering if the quietness was all right and worrying that it wasn't. Something told me that Mary did not think about stuff like that, she just did what she wanted, and I immediately liked that about her.

"So, you went to college with Celeste?" I said as the electric kettle came to a boil, when I couldn't stand it any longer, bursting into speech like a Casey-in-the-box.

Mary poured some kind of loose leaf tea into an infuser and dropped it into her teapot. She didn't answer at first, and I assumed she hadn't heard me. Then she said, pouring the water into the teapot, "Do you know what we called her back then? *Fleabag.*"

I laughed, then I clapped a hand over my mouth. Thou shalt not defame thy boss! "Why?!"

"She'd go down to the city on the weekends. Wouldn't return for days at a time. Told us she was staying at fleabag hotels with older men like it was her badge of honor, proof that she was leaving the rest of us behind." Mary laughed, not unkindly, as she recollected. "She made her own life difficult. Girls are merciless. Care for a scone and fresh cream?"

She reached under the table and pulled out a paper plate covered with tinfoil. "Would I!" I said. I pulled back the tinfoil and grabbed a hunk of buttery biscuit, dipped the corner of it into a Dixie cup filled with clotted cream. It was a treat I might not have indulged in on my own, but it felt right to eat pastry with Mary. She was not vain; I could sense it. Her lack of vanity must have rubbed off on me, because I pushed the whole scone into my mouth with one steady movement, like a suitcase at an airport's security checkpoint. "Wow," I mumbled, still with my mouth full. I realized that, besides the espresso and *macaron* I'd had at the Ace, I'd eaten nothing all day. "This is really good."

"Have another then!" she said. She was so genuinely kind. "Have some tea!"

We ate, we drank, we talked and talked. Mary was exceedingly reasonable about Nanü and, I thought, rather flip about how her role might affect her status as high literary icon, maybe because she'd resigned herself to doing pretty much anything to get out of her tenure. She was tired of the academy. "Don't let them fool you," she said. "Though they'll go on and on about my awards and show me off like a prized donkey when the donors come around, the academy is just as tired of me."

Though the college had afforded her financial stability—"I've made peace with the fact that I'm a woman of rather enormous appetites"— she'd started teaching later in life, and the income wasn't enough to allow her to save for retirement. Nanü was a fast and easy way out of what she kept calling her "capital pickle."

"It's either that, or die tomorrow," she said. "As of now I can't afford old age."

"Don't say that!" I said. I did not think the macabre was funny. Far from it.

"Growing old is expensive, at least in this country. No safety net, and it's getting worse."

"What about the money from your books?"

Mary laughed and laughed. "You little lamb," she finally said. "There's still so much of the girl in you."

I stiffened. "Well, I don't know about that. I'm twenty-eight, almost twenty-nine, after all."

Mary's eyes glinted. "I see."

"The books, though? What about the prizes? Didn't you win a MacArthur at one—?"

"What there was"—Mary made a gesture like smoke disappearing into the atmosphere—"is all gone now. You could say I specialized in divestments."

Mary spoke cryptically like this from time to time: she enjoyed, like many teachers, making *le grand statement*. Though I felt obligated to bang out the fine print of her "creative engagement" contract—she'd create the tag for Encore's national rebranding campaign, rewrite the website, write the product descriptions for their new capsule collection, dress in their clothes (gratis, natch) for her new author photo—she seemed uninterested in these particulars. She'd already decided to make her bed; it was time to lie in it,

195

no matter what that meant. For some reason this made me feel strange. I guess it's not fun to sell an idea to someone who's resigned themselves to it before you even arrived.

"May I ask you," she said as she was signing the paperwork, "how you ended up here?"

"You mean *here* here? Well, I flew in yesterday afternoon and this morning I took the Metro-North after, well, that's a whole other—"

"No, no," she said, capping her pen and handing the manila file folder back to me. "Working with Celeste, I mean."

"Well, I was an English major—always had a way with words, I guess. Actually that reminds me, I almost forgot." I rummaged into my bag, which was resting at my feet, and pulled out Susan's crumpled short story. "This might be a little, you know, unpro*fesh,* but my best friend Susan is also a writer. Insanely talented. Afraid to put herself out there but she's got the"—I snapped my fingers—"you know. The *thing.* The thing that makes you really *feel* something. She'd die if she knew I was doing this but"—I pushed the crumpled pages toward her—"would you read her story? I think it's good. I mean, I don't know much, but—"

Mary smiled. Her eyes were bottomless. "You're a good friend."

"Well, depends on who you ask, and on which day."

"I'm happy to read your friend's story."

I clapped, involuntarily, and clasped my hands to my chest. "You will?!"

She blinked a couple times. Her pupils were large, nearly swallowing up the ambers of her irises. "At my age, I'm rarely moved," she said after a moment. "But I remain moved by loyalty. You still haven't answered my question."

"Question? Oh, right. I guess Celeste just liked me right away. I mean, I liked her too," I added quickly. "She's been good to me, we've been working together for a long time. And the chance to help out amazing writers like you? Celeste says I've got a real knack for it."

Mary's eyes were bright and watery now, like the sea. "Careful what people in power tell you about yourself," she said. "Most often what lies behind it is greed."

On the train ride back to the city I thought about what Mary said. The expense of old age, loyalty, greed. It reminded me of something that a professor had said about Chekhov. Chekhov had worked by day as a country doctor, and said the writer's job was not to cure—there was no cure—but rather accurately identify the symptoms of the human condition. Later, when I'd finished reading *Uncle Vanya*, I remembered sitting, stunned, at my library carrel, reeling from Sonya's last speech about work and death and work being the only thing to do until death. Not because it was sad, necessarily, or because I was sad. Because it was *true*. Meeting with Mary London had provoked a similar, albeit milder, combination of unsettledness and solace. It was clear the woman didn't miss a thing. And it was increasingly possible that since the salad days of *Uncle Vanya*, maybe I had.

I stared out the window at the row houses and cinder block buildings framing the train tracks as we rumbled and lurched back to Manhattan. It was early evening, and the twilight gave a romantic purpled hue to even the most run-down of developments. I had no concrete thoughts, no plans, no judgments; I just pressed my nose to the glass and watched the world go by with the wistfulness of a creature far from home.

I took out my phone and texted Ben. Why? I'd lost my mind and temporarily gotten a better one, one less self-conscious yet more self-aware.

Hey, turns out I'm still in New York. Any chance you're around? Staying at the Ace.

When he didn't text back right away, I put my phone on Do Not Disturb and sat on it. I vowed not to look at it again. I looked back out the window and I tried to find my inner peace. I heard someone yelling at their kid and I thought: I *will* have inner peace. It was getting harder to find my inner peace because we were almost back at Grand Central, and the other passengers were already jostling and crowding to be the first ones out the door. Right around the time a big bald guy pushed me out of the way on the stairs and then said "Ex*cuse* you," my inner peace peaced out completely.

I walked back to the Ace, instead of cabbing, in the hopes of finding it again. I broke my vow on that walk and checked to see if Ben had texted. He hadn't. Oh, what was the point of these human relationships. Putting yourself out there, being vulnerable, opening your heart, was all so humiliating and would in one way or another end in tragedy. Perhaps it was time to give up on humans and become one of those ladies who carries a dog in her purse, feeds it specialty foods from the organic market, and clones it so there's a replacement waiting when the first one's dying.

And then, what do you know, who do I see sitting on a leather wingback chair the moment I walk into the hotel lobby?

Ben stood up when he saw me. We hugged, and he smelled just as I remembered, like himself.

"Hi," he said into my hair.

Of course we were going to sleep together. We'd both known it from the minute he sat down at Horse & Stable a few weeks prior. I'd gone back and forth in my head so many times about how to play it with him. I was going to make him work for it, I was going to appear aloof, I was going to make him guess and beg until I was good and ready.

Or I didn't have to do any of that. After one drink at the bar I asked him, plain and simple, "Do you want to go upstairs?"

Once we were upstairs I took off all my clothes and said, "Oh hell, here goes nothing."

He took one finger and traced it up the center of my sternum, over my clavicle, down my arm. "Here goes everything."

8

LOVE IN THE TIME OF MONTAGE

Whoever has starry-eyed notions of falling in love doesn't know love; they only know television. Physically, falling in love is a rather awful ailment. Stomachaches, loss of appetite, sleeplessness, not to mention the debilitating anxiety—not that much different from a particularly rough bout of food poisoning. And yet, that spring, I was happier than I'd ever been.

Or no, that's not right. I don't much cotton to happiness; at least, not in the way it's talked about these days, with the tracking apps and how-to books and self-proclaimed gurus with packed stadiums. What I felt with Ben, in those first days, I don't have words for it. And I don't want to look for them, because they'll sound boring and trite when they come out of my mouth, when in fact those days were the most beautiful to me, perhaps the most beautiful of my life. Oh, my heart! My heart. I feel them still.

And still, while love is the best experience a person can have, it's the worst to try and talk about. Not only because every listener has not only heard it a thousand times before, but because she secretly believes that no love can compare with what she herself has had already.

But since we're here, the best I can do is explain that it felt like Ben and I took hands that night and leapt headfirst into the ocean, and since then had been swimming farther and farther beneath the surface in the hopes of touching bottom. I had never known a person all the way before, not even Susan, wouldn't even say I had really known myself—or that my self was fully formed enough to know. But we were learning together, he and I. We revealed, and the other revealed us. The first time I cried in front of him wasn't because I was hurt or mad, it was because he was looking at me so kindly when I was talking, about what I can't even remember, that I didn't know what to do with myself. "What's the matter?" he said, and gathered me in his arms. I used the opportunity to dry my eyes and blow my nose on his T-shirt. "Nothing!" I honked muffledly into his shoulder. "I'm just . . . not used to feeling so . . . not-alone!"

And it was the same for him too, I think. There was a melancholy to Ben that not everyone could sense beneath his joviality, but I sensed it, and he could tell I sensed it, though we never talked about it directly. It relaxed him, maybe, my knowing it was there and not minding. Brought his walls down faster, walls he camouflaged with politeness and humor but were, beneath the ivy, thick as brick. The sadness was partly circumstantial, having something to do with his mother's illness, but the other part, I'm pretty sure he was born with. Most writers are born sad, live sad, die sad, which is not to say sadness is their only capacity. Indeed, Ben's novel, which I read on the plane ride home from New York, was hilarious and very joyful. But one cannot know joy without knowing its opposite, cannot be funny without too being sad, and this, I have to say, was Ben's great gift: a full and lively spectrum. Yet unlike Susan, he did not tend toward the extremes of this spectrum; he was grounded by a practical nature and good instincts, which made him less ruminative, and easy to be around.

A couple weeks after I got back from New York Ben met Susan for the first time. There was a gallery opening uptown that I knew Susan would go to, so I made a point of inviting Ben to go with me. The art at the gallery was mediocre, but honestly, that's true most of the time. The accompanying book called it "mixed media." The bo-, bro-, and fauxhemian crowd was full of the usual suspects, a mix of creatives and professionals and a new subgenre called creative professionals. There were women in loafers and odd hats, queers talking about queerness, men who generally looked uncomfortable. I asked

Ben to get us glasses of wine while I went and tracked down Susan, whom I eventually found peering at a large photograph of a hairy man's arm holding a flower.

"Hi!" I said three octaves higher than my usual speaking voice, the universal female code for *Let's play nice.* I went in for a hug. "How are you?!"

"Hello pooky!" Susan said, hugging me back. She was with Gina again, who began inching away as soon as I appeared, or perhaps with her introvert camouflage she just blended in with the wall. "Fancy seeing you here!"

"I wanted to see you! And the art, of course. Kinda. I brought Ben. You want to meet him?"

"Obviously." Susan was smiling, her cheeks flushed. "How are you? I miss you!" She was in a jovial mood, or the red wine was making her so. Either way I was happy for the warmth. Before I could answer Ben's arm snaked around my right side, wineglass in hand.

"Speak of the devil," I said, taking the plastic wineglass and turning around to smile at him in thanks. "Ben, Susan, Susan, Ben."

I looked on anxiously while they exchanged hellos, like the parent of a kindergartner who really hopes their kid won't fuck up and humiliate them by proxy. I found myself trying to engineer the entire social situation so as to dictate a successful outcome for my loved ones. Before either of them could finish a sentence, I would interject something like, "That's *just* the sort of thing Ben would say," or, "Did you know Susan is *also* left-handed?"

When it was clear they didn't need me anymore—turned out they had lots to say to each other; they were both reading the same book, some Spanish novel in translation by a guy I'd never even heard of—I hung back and listened for a few moments, proud and happy. I left them alone and wandered the gallery for a while, looked at papier-mâché sculptures of meat. When I came back, they didn't seem to notice me at all. As the minutes ticked by, I began to sulk. *Pardonnez-moi, remember me?* I wanted to interrupt. *The very special and important person who brought you together in the first place? This incredible gal right here with a heart of gold, Friday-night attitude, and tight booty?*

Frustratingly, it appeared they did not remember, immersed as they were in a comparison between the literature that came out in Franco's Spain with that of Pinochet's Chile. Meanwhile, I got progressively drunker by comparing the wine that I'd stolen from Ben in my left hand—if he was too busy talking about dictatorships to drink it, I grumbled, *someone* might as well—with that in my right.

When Susan finally excused herself to use the

restroom, Ben turned to me with a grin on his face. "She's fun," he said. "Really smart. I can see why you like her."

"Mmmhmmm." I stacked the wineglasses and crossed my arms over my chest.

"You two are sweet together." He looked at me. "You okay? You look tired."

"I'm not tired." Men should know by now that saying a woman looks tired is like sticking a fat bear paw in a hornet's nest.

"You want to get something to eat?"

"No, thanks. I'm pretty tired."

"What?" Ben laughed. "You just said you weren't!"

"That's not what I meant." I shifted my weight. After a beat: "Did you just forget I was standing there or something? Or did you not want to talk to me anymore? Or what."

"What are you talking about?" He looked baffled.

"I understand you guys are gonna want to talk books and stuff." I sniffed and shrugged my shoulders. "I just thought it was rude."

Ben cocked a brow. "Me getting to know your friend you brought me here to meet?"

"You know, if you'd rather hang out with her and Gina tonight, that's fine."

He threw up his hands. "Casey! Where is this coming from?"

Decades of competing for the attention of men,

I could have said. Instead I said, "Ummm, from you guys *ignoring* me?!"

"I don't even know what to say to that, it's so far from true."

Say you won't leave! I wanted to drop to my knees and beg him. Instead, I put my hands on my hips and roared, "Say you're *sorry!*"

Yes, it took a while to clean that one up, not until I'd stomped around some more and eaten four tacos and sobered up and tearfully admitted at one in the morning after much bluster and evasion that I'd been jealous and insecure and suffered chronically from impostor syndrome around him and Susan, not to mention the chronic issues simmering wordlessly between Susan and me. "I'm sorry," I sniffled, wiping my eyes. "For taking my garbage out on you."

I could only assume now that Ben would run screaming in the other direction. But in fact the opposite was true. "Come here, you goofball," he said tenderly at my kitchen table and pulled me in for a hug, the peppery detritus from the tacos getting cold on our plates. "It's okay." He kissed the top of my head. "You're okay. I adore you."

Lord. If only it were easier to be adored, to receive the affection we've always longed for, to heap it back on the person generous enough to put it on offer. But it's a lot harder to take in good stuff than bad. We keep goodness suspiciously at arm's length, waiting for the other shoe to drop, since at one point or another all of us were loved imperfectly.

Or at least, that's what I found myself thinking about on various airplanes in the peripatetic days following that interaction. In late May I traveled to Vermont to poach another potential asset, the highbrow, *New Yorkery* nature writer Tracy Mallard. One of Tracy's essays about loons had made its way onto that short list that high school teachers use for teaching composition, so she was something of a household name, at least among people who paid a modicum of attention during English class. Nature's Harvest, another established client of People's Republic, best known for their granola bars, was hoping to use Mallard to get their brand, as Celeste put it, "back to nature." The sugary granola bars, once a nationwide staple in children's lunchboxes, were now the sort of thing on parental "banned food" lists, or what you'd only reluctantly pick up at a gas station.

Nature's Harvest was too calcified to do anything about the nutritional content of the granola bars, but their marketing department was all right with spending a lot of cash decalcifying their reputation. After several conference calls, we'd coaxed them into making new compostable wrappers with animals on them, in honor of the 0.05% of profits that would now go to the World Wildlife Foundation. Inside the wrapper, we'd put a little bon mot from Tracy. When, on the first call, someone in the Nature's Harvest marketing department suggested it would save time and money if they, instead of contracting with Mallard, paid for the rights to use her previously published work, Celeste handled the dissent with the deftness of a career diplomat.

"Everyone's quoting someone these days," she said smoothly. "Even the parking garage beneath our building has a Gandhi quote on the wall. It's not enough to use Tracy's outdated content. We want Tracy to develop original content for us, and solely us. Something no one else has. Casey and I are also going to ask her to sign away any rights for anything outside her books so that in the end the only place people will be able to read Tracy is through a brand to which they know she is deeply committed: Nature's Harvest."

We *are?* I thought, alarmed. The marketing team murmured in approval. "I wouldn't have thought of that," one of them said.

"No, you wouldn't," Celeste said in a soothing voice. "And that's why you hired us."

Scheduling a visit with Tracy ended up being tricky. It was well known that she was a little crazy, that she talked to animals. She also had very specific times she was willing to talk to me. I pulled into the gravel driveway in my rental at 4:45 p.m. Per the instructions I received from Tracy's assistant, Harriet, I waited in my car until exactly 4:50, then headed for her old farm-house. At 4:53 I knocked on the front door, then crouched down and put my eyes up to the mail slot. Naturally, with all this tiptoed pageantry, I expected a madwoman to open the door.

"May I help you?" A pair of eyes, blue-gray, appeared on the other side of the mail slot. The voice was tremulous and soft and sounded the way sunlight felt on bare arms after winter.

"Hello there!" I said in a voice that I hoped sounded like my yoga teacher's. "Peaceful greetings to you! My name is Casey Pendergast, and I'm here to spend a very special afternoon with you! I also brought you cheese!" I dropped back from the mail slot in order to hold up the gourmet basket I'd bought in town.

"Did Harriet say you could come?" the voice said.

"Yes, she did!" I said. "Harriet even said she had left us fresh iced tea!"

After a moment there was a rustle, then the sound of the door unlocking. I scrambled to my feet. Before me stood a small woman, at most five two, hair arranged in an unkempt, graying bun on the top of her head. She wore soft cotton pants and matching tunic, along with socks and Birkenstocks. But her face was like nothing I'd ever seen. Though the day was overcast, her wrinkled visage was golden, radiant. Some bulb was lit up in the back of her head.

"Come in," she said in her sunlit voice, fluttering like a bird with her small, thin hands. "Come in."

Her house looked the way you might imagine a hippie's house in Vermont to look—prayer flags and woven rugs and Mexican blankets folded over the back of the couch. It was very quiet and sparsely furnished and smelled like essential oils, save for the corner where three big, old, lumberly dogs were snoring on mattress-sized dog beds.

"Jacob, Moses, and Rumi," Tracy said, pointing to them.

"Can I pet them?" I asked. She nodded. I went over and let them nuzzle and lick my hands.

"They're rescues," Tracy said over my shoulder. "They found Jacob on the side of the road, hit by a car. Moses and Rumi came from the same litter, a box of puppies dropped off at the shelter in the middle of the night. They're my guardian angels. Yes, you are," she said to them in a singsong voice. "Yes, you are."

I loved dogs. I could have petted them all day, had their breath not smelled like mustard gas. I stood up and wiped the saliva on my pants, dry-cleaning bills be damned. "They're adorable. Do they like cheese? I brought cheese."

Tracy clapped her hands. "They love cheese!"

Her enthusiasm was genuine. Everything about her was genuine; she was like quicksilver,

moving from emotion to emotion with a naked-
ness I wasn't used to seeing on adult faces. It
disarmed me. Alarmed me, even. I was so unused
to that degree of sincerity that I found myself,
strangely, wanting to protect myself from it. Or
maybe I wanted to protect her from the likes of
me.

Eventually I learned, while swallowing my
cheese and moral anxiety, that the reason Tracy
was willing to work with Nature's Harvest was
that she wanted to buy the animal shelter where
she'd gotten her dogs. It was a kill shelter, she
explained, not because they wanted it to be but
for lack of revenue. Apparently Harriet had
already met with a lawyer who was going to
help them get their nonprofit status and establish
an endowment in Tracy's name that would
hopefully continue ad infinitum. "So no animals
in Bennington will ever be killed again," Tracy
said, her palms clasped together resolutely.

Her eyes were so bright and hopeful that it
didn't seem worth bringing up, say, abuse, car
accidents, hunting accidents, et cetera. When she
spoke of her dogs and other species she'd fostered
it was clear these creatures were her friends and
family, that she felt more akin to them than to
people. To accommodate this sensibility I tried to
make myself as canine as possible: snuggling into
the couch, chewing enthusiastically. I reassured
her that yes, I was positive no animals would be

harmed by her signing a contract with Nanü, that in fact because of us, Nature's Harvest would be cooperating with the World Wildlife Foundation to save even more animals than she, Tracy, could save on her own. At the sound of this, Tracy lit up. "Oh, good!" she exclaimed. "Oh, glory! I knew your heart was in the right place! I knew it from the moment you walked in the door!"

Well, let me tell you. It felt . . . not great . . . hearing her say this and then putting a document on the chipped mosaic coffee table that basically said Nature's Harvest, and Nanü by proxy, would own the distribution rights to all Tracy's writing, minus what was published in book form by her New York publishers. And yet this is exactly what I did.

Be it the cheese, or my gut in serious conflict in my brain, I came down with a case of indigestion. "I'm so happy you're happy," I said, as my stomach burbled and lurched.

"*I* am so happy," she said, and clasped her hands to her chest girlishly. "Just when it seems possible to give up on the world, a young person like you comes along."

"Oh, stop," I said, as my gut continued to grumble. Didn't Tracy deserve to be saving animals without signing all of her intellectual property away? Then again, there are always trade-offs to be made, that's what living in a democracy is all about: the best possible solution for the greatest number of people. Or animals, in this case. Tracy's shelter was a perfect example of idealism and pragmatism lining up with one another. It was a cause she cared a lot about, and she couldn't do what she wanted without Nature's Harvest's money. And really, what was worse for Tracy, having to spend a few hours writing inspirational messages for granola bar wrappers or weighing countless litters of dead puppies on her conscience?

"Tell me about you now," Tracy said as I was putting the signed contract in my bag.

"Oh, but I should let you go!" I said. I was going into my obsequious mode, an equal and opposite response to seedy behavior. "You must be exhausted!"

"Do you enjoy your work?" Tracy said, as if she hadn't heard me.

"I do! I love it!"

She nodded. "But perhaps it's not the right work for you."

I shifted uncomfortably on the couch. I'd ended up with a Mexican blanket wrapped around my legs. "I don't think that's true. After all, I get to help writers like you achieve your dreams and reflect your core values to the American people!"

"But you have your own dreams."

"No, I *don't*." The words shot out of my mouth before I knew what I was saying. Nothing makes you correct someone faster than when they've just said something about you that's dead-on correct. "I mean, this is my dream."

She smiled and continued to pet Jacob, who had sidled up and rested his flat head on the couch cushion. I felt like she was trying to communicate with me at a decibel I couldn't hear, too high for a regular person's frequency. "Anyway," I said, putting down my empty cheese plate and half-empty glass of iced tea. "Thank you again for everything. I'm available by phone or email if you have any questions, and I'll tell Harriet that too."

At the front door, she leaned over and hugged me goodbye. She was so slight and fragile. I wanted to take care of her. She must have felt the same way, because as I skipped down the porch steps and down the driveway she called out, "Be careful in Vegas!"

I turned around in surprise. "I'm not going to Vegas."

She was waving, then she stopped. "You're not?"

"I don't think so."

"Oh, silly me. I'm always doing that. Mis-hearing things." She laughed, unperturbed. "Travel safe now, Casey. The world is such an unruly place."

"I dunno, I feel icky about it," I said to Ben later that night. I was filling him in on the most recent developments of my moral dilemma over FaceTime. There was a lot you could do with another person over long distance, thanks to technology. I was lying on my side on the hotel bed in my underwear, looking at my phone, which I'd propped up on the pillow next to mine. Ben's face filled the screen, save for the corner where I could see myself. Often, instead of looking at him, I'd find myself worrying about the hotel room's lighting and criticizing my own features.

Ben grimaced. "Yeah, that's tough. Most writers are pretty clueless. I can't think of a single one of my writer friends who could even tell you what the price of milk is."

I stiffened a little, though I was still draped in a self-consciously artful repose. "Do *you* think we're taking advantage of her?"

"I don't know." Ben scratched his head. His unruly hair was sticking up everywhere. Seeing him rumpled like that turned me on terrifically. "Maybe if she's that fragile?"

"It felt like I was bringing a lamb to slaughter."

"But if she's *willing* to slaughter herself so the pit bulls can be redeemed—"

"Ugghhhh, God, that's terrible!" I flopped on my back. I was tired of having a moral dilemma. It was the first one I'd ever contracted, and I could see why people avoided them. They didn't make you *happy*. They weren't *fun*.

"We should keep talking about it. It's interesting."

I turned over on my side again and propped my head up with a bent pillow. "Is there something wrong with you? Some genetic defect you have that makes you a good listener but is also going to give you, like, liver disease?"

"Why do you say that?"

"Because I've never met a dude who's not just waiting for his turn to talk about himself?"

Ben didn't laugh like I thought he was going to. In fact, he looked a little dismayed. But this was one of my favorite subjects, so I kept going. "Even the guy sitting next to me on the plane, *oh my God,* wouldn't stop going on about his trail races and how many miles he earns from work travel. It's like, you idiot, don't you see I'm reading *Us Weekly* and I *do not care?*"

Ben frowned. "Maybe he just wanted someone to talk to."

"We all want someone to talk to," I interrupted. "Men just think they have the right to that whenever they want."

He made a whuffing sound. He cast his eyes down toward his lap.

"I mean, not you," I added. I concluded, "But most of you. Anyway, we can talk about something else. How was your day? How's your mom doing?"

Ben talked about his mother rarely. Though he

217

was open about most things—his work, friend-ships, even past relationships—something in his eyes flinched every time I brought her up. I don't think he believed that I could understand. When we're hurting, when the thing hurting us is very much in the present tense, it's hard to believe that anyone else can understand, even, or maybe, *especially* when they've been through the exact same thing.

Ben didn't answer right away. Finally he said, casting his eyes back up at me, "I'm not like that, you know."

"Like the guy on the plane? I know!" I said. "That's what I just said! But a lot *are*. Trust me." I took the opportunity to tell him what had happened with Wolf in Brooklyn. It was the first time I'd said anything about that night out loud, and it was harder than I'd reckoned. Ben kept shaking his head as I talked, until he finally said, his voice grittier than usual, "I *knew* that guy was an asshole."

"I know you knew. Everyone does."

"I wish I'd gone with you to the party. I could have done something—"

I waved my hand. "Oh please. It's fine now. I'm fine. I'm just telling you 'cause, I dunno—"

Ben looked grave. "'Cause there're reasons you see the world the way you do."

I nodded. "And there're reasons you see the world the way *you* do."

"I want to understand them."

He looked so earnest that I couldn't help but smile. "I want to understand yours, too."

My next assignment took me straight from Vermont to Reno, Nevada. It was my task to bag Johnny Hard, one of those guys who'd made a name for himself writing about sex, drugs, and rock 'n' roll in the seventies and held a unique place in the hearts of sexed, drugged, and failed male rock stars and burnout writers everywhere. Poor down-on-his-luck Johnny was living in a Motel 6 across from a coin-operated laundromat. It took a fair amount of coaxing to get him to undo the chain on the door. He'd lost a number of teeth since his days of wine and roses and spoke with an aggravating and paranoid lisp.

"Leasch me alone!" he cried when I first started pounding on his door. White Castle was coming out with its own version of McDonaldland—Castleville—and Celeste had convinced them that Johnny should both be a model for one of their new characters, Castlesnitch, and write the commercial treatment. "They want a strung-out addict to write their script?" I'd asked, mystified. Celeste's reply was terse. "Appealing to their demographic."

"Johnny," I said, knocking on the door. "Come on." I rummaged through my purse, where I had a number of Fruit Roll-Ups, and slid one through the crack at the bottom of the door. In the dossier, Simone had included an interview in which he, high as a rocket, had described Fruit Roll-Ups as "my motherfucking favorite food, man." I had this down to an art by now—do research on the assets' preferences in advance and bribe them accordingly.

He grunted in receipt. "CIA sench you?"

"I'm with Nanü. We talked on the phone, remember? Like an hour ago?"

I could hear him chewing. "That a CIA schubsidiary?"

"No, it's an advertising agency. We've found a blue ocean in the branding market. Now specializing in matching uncapitalized-upon cultural assets with struggling corporate interests?"

I heard him smack and swallow. "Bullshitsh." Then I heard a clunk. It was approximately the sound of a body dropping to the floor.

"Johnny?" I rapped on the door. "Ummm. Johnny?" No response. "That's it. I'm going to get management to open the door."

"Don't talk to management!" he cried, suddenly throwing open the door. "They're after me!"

By the time it was over it made for a good story, which I relayed to Ben and Susan one hot early summer evening at a beer garden, as fireflies blinked above us and the sky took its sweet time changing from sunset to dusk. I'd arranged the weeknight get-together when I got back from Reno in an attempt to get back in Susan's good graces, seeing as having fun together is the quickest way to reestablish fading intimacy. "The hotel room seriously looked like something straight out of *Celebrity Rehab*," I said, leaning forward, my elbows resting on the picnic table. Ben was next to me, Susan across. "Pre-intervention, I mean. Like, there was all this tinfoil? Not to mention the pill bottles and pipes and liquor. The guy looked like he weighed ninety pounds soaking wet, so I took him to IHOP and bought him Rooty Tooty Fresh 'N Fruity pancakes. His request, obviously."

"Did he sign the contract?" Susan took a sip of her oatmeal stout. She was the only woman I knew who dared to drink dark beer. "He must have eventually, right?"

"I got him to sign, yeah, but I don't know if he'll remember. I tried to talk to him about Castleville but all he wanted to talk about was what to do with the money. Apparently there's some casita in Mexico and a dog he wants to buy? But it's out of my hands now." I made a show of dusting my palms. "I told Celeste about it. She's going to hire someone in Reno to look after him while he's working, which I thought was nice."

"That is nice," Ben said. He turned to Susan

221

while sticking his thumb toward me. "You should have seen this one giving me the hard sell. None of these writers stand a chance against her."

He meant it in a complimentary way, but given my moral dilemma, I winced. Luckily, Susan let the opportunity to take a dig at Nanü pass her right by. "You think that's good, you should have seen her as a slam poet," she said to Ben.

"That's enough," I warned her.

Ben raised his eyebrows mischievously. "Casey was a slam poet?"

"Nooooo," I groaned.

"Briefly in college, before the Dark Lords pulled her into advertising. Talk about commanding a room. I *still* remember this rhyme she had about this guy Sam she dated who gave her—"

"Okay, okay!" I said, waving my arms. "SOS! Mercy! Give me CPR before I die of humiliation!" On the plus side, we had moved on to my favorite subject: *moi*, myself, and I. I turned to Ben. "Susan was the real standout in our class. I was just fooling around."

"You were a slam poet too?" Ben said to Susan.

"She was the *writer,*" I informed him, pointing at Susan.

"And *she* was the clown," Susan told Ben, pointing to me. "I kept telling her to do something about it—did you know that when she was a kid she wanted to be on television?—but she was always too shy."

Ben looked at me with incredulity. "Casey? Shy?"

"Not in the ways you'd expect. But when it comes to—"

"Well, well, well, I think that's just enough pop psychology for one evening, thankyewveddymuch" I said, checking my watch. It was almost eleven, and the brewery was soon to close. My face felt pink and warm. I wasn't sure if it was from the beer or from hanging out with two highly perceptive people.

"Huh," Ben mused. "Should we sign her up for an acting class or something?"

"Good luck trying," Susan said, standing up. "You can lead a horse to water, but you can't make the horse do the one thing she deep down wants to do already."

"It's true," I said, and went around the table to give her a hug. Perhaps it was a consequence of the late sunset, or the beer, or the lightness in the midsummer air, but there was no rancor hidden in our exchange, only easy familiarity. "On a completely unrelated note, you finish your novel yet?"

"You two," Ben said, shaking his head. "Like an old married couple."

I put my arm around Susan's shoulder and kissed her cheek. "Yup. She's my wife, and you're my . . ."

"Farm boy," Susan supplied.

"Yeah, farm boy," I said. "Baling hay and sleeping in the barn."

As Susan pedaled away on her bicycle, Ben tipsily put his arms around me and kissed both my cheeks, then my eyes, then my lips. "You're not going to keep me in the barn forever, are you?"

I laughed. "Of course not. It was just a joke." Yet while I kissed him, I couldn't keep my mind from drifting toward work, traveling elsewhere, to all the places I had traveled and would soon travel, away from him and alone. The secret that I didn't tell anyone, not even myself, was that I liked traveling, I liked the ungroundedness. No roots, you can't get torn up.

Just a few nights later I found myself in a gazebo in the Sausalito hills with Izzy Calliente, the doyenne of magical realism and soon-to-be label-maker for a new salsa company. The salsa company had offered to not only reward Calliente handsomely for penning spicy Spanish exclamations for the back of their jars, but to commission a sculpture in the Latin American country from whence she came in honor of those who "disappeared" during one of the military coups.

"Idiots!" Izzy had initially cried when I told her about the offer. To be fair, the drawing of the sculpture in question had been of a joyful-looking man throwing his sombrero up into the sky. "We don't even wear sombreros in my country!"

It took a very long conversation with Izzy, one that lasted over two meals and well into the night, to convince her to buy into Nanü. She was the hardest sell yet, by far. Having grown up in a country where the government controlled pretty much everything, it was initially unfathomable to her that she would do anything to compromise what she called "my creative freedom. The one place where I am truly free."

Given my own circumspection about what I was selling, I remained mostly quiet while Izzy talked, planning what I would tell Celeste if and when Izzy said no to the offer. Interestingly enough, however, the more Izzy talked herself in circles, the more she warmed up to the idea. When she finally said yes, it seemed that she herself had flipped a switch in her brain, told herself the right story. I found this happened often, not just with writers. We humans, we can convince ourselves of anything. "Now my daughter can finally pay off those *ridiculous* student loans," she said as she capped the pen after signing the deal.

At the office that summer, a pervasive aura of jealousy was circulating as I fluttered in and out of Celeste's office, leaned my elbows on Simone's desk while she prissily made my travel itineraries (boy, did she love lording her scheduling power over me), and frequently left in the middle of the day for a long lunch and/ or afternoon delight with Ben, a reward, I told myself, for a travel schedule so tight you couldn't even stick a vibrator in it. "What's the rush?" I remember asking Simone as she was booking one flight after another. Simone had answered by parroting a line I was sure Celeste herself had said. "Stay in a blue ocean too long, Casey"—she sniffed—"and someone starts to bleed."

Meanwhile, in my absence, Annie was transitioning to a role Celeste called the Asset Liaison, shepherding our authors through the creative production process inside the corporations. Jack and Lindsey were working closely with Encore and Mary London on the visual side of the store's rebranding. The special treatment the four of us received wasn't going over well with our colleagues. Once, in the kitchen, I heard a couple girls from Accounts talking shit about us and murmuring about rumors of layoffs. "I heard Celeste's planning on selling to some huge agency," a blond Tiffany-braceleted girl named Britney said to the brunette version of herself. They each took a Diet Coke out of the stainless steel Sub-Zero.

"What. The fuck."

"She's gonna take them with her somewhere else."

"They're not even good. Jack's a diva, Annie and Lindsey are lackeys, and Casey must be eating Celeste out every night because otherwise there's no way—"

That was about when I cleared my throat so they'd turn around. "Hi!" I said, and nothing else, so they'd spend the rest of the afternoon wondering and worrying if I'd overheard them.

"You *guys,* I just heard Britney talking shit about us in the kitchen," I said to Jack and Lindsey once I got back to my station. Annie was on one of her many trips to the bathroom. Annie'd taken to hiding in the stalls and playing Candy Crush on her phone when she needed a break from her new position.

Lindsey looked up from her large monitor, eyes wide and hurt. "What'd she say?"

"It doesn't matter," I said. "Did you know there were rumors that Celeste was selling the company?"

"Is that the blond one? Whatever, fuck her," Jack said, flinging a dismissive arm in the air. "Wait, she talked shit about *me?*"

"It doesn't *matter,*" I said again. "But the sale, is that true? That can't be true."

Lindsey shrugged her shoulders and winced. *Beats me,* her body was saying. Please don't hurt me for not knowing.

"*No,* it's not true," Jack said. "You think Celeste would sell this place to some giant corporation? It'd be like selling your own baby into slavery."

"Jack!" Lindsey and I both said, abashed. "You can't say shit like that!" I added.

He sniffed. "I'm gay. I don't have to be PC."

Luckily, I wasn't in the office that much and could mostly avoid these petty dramas. I found myself strolling through a tiny terminal in Cedar Rapids two days later and felt very pleased with myself. Not only had I escaped the acrimony, but no one at that particular moment knew where the hell I was. Given how quote-unquote connected the world was, it felt like a form of liberation, this catapulting through the world like a tetherball yanked from its chain. I was in Iowa to meet Betty Calvinson, the dour grande dame behind such inspirational Christian novels as *Heal Me, Jesus* and *My Love, My Father*, who agreed to write a short story for *Reader's Digest* that "prominently featured" a new, over-the-counter pill for female incontinence. I ate Pepperidge Farm cookies with Betty on her gabled porch and listened to her drone on about her own incontinence, and how she felt it was important that as "a very prestigious writer" she draw attention to the subject. Whatever story you need to tell yourself, I thought, as she held forth on the idea that it was God's will that had brought Nanü to her, so that she might spread further the truth of the Gospels.

With Betty and Izzy and Ben, Mary, Wolf, Tracy, and Johnny, not to mention YA phenomenon Geoffery Turge (writing a campaign for Camel's new cigarettes, Camel Teen), I'd managed to get my asset number up to eight by early August, only two assets away from securing the success of Nanü for the venture capitalists. I was surprised by how easy it'd been to get these writers on board, but I guess Celeste'd been right: people would do pretty much anything once the right dollar amount was on the table. I would have a two-week travel respite in August, but my last stop before it was Milwaukee, of all places, home of Mort Stillman, the aging cartoonist and Holocaust survivor.

I say of all places because Louise had moved there a few years before to be closer to Aunt Jean, who had moved there from L.A. for the cheap rent in the aughts. Unfortunately, Aunt Jean was out of town. Unfortunately, too, my mother was in town. We agreed to meet for lunch at a restaurant on the north shore of the city, not far from the art museum, and in Louise's neighborhood—a part of the city that was very grand and old-moneyish, filled with people just like her.

I hadn't seen Louise since Christmas and, when I saw her, I was struck by how lined her face was getting, how her body was shrinking, getting thinner, though there was also a new softness to her belly. "Hello Casey," she said stiffly into my shoulder as we hugged. Or rather, I hugged, and she patted me on the back. How is this stranger my mother, I thought, and the thought filled me with loneliness.

"What are you getting?" I said once we'd been seated. The menus were huge, and I took comfort in the buffer they provided. I dreaded having to fill the time. Perhaps we could talk about food allergies.

Louise's hands were folded on her unopened menu. "I always get the spinach salad." To an outsider, she probably looked perfectly harmless: an erect, sixtysomething brunette in pearls and a cardigan set. Uptight, sure, but harmless. Most parents seem harmless to the children who are not their children.

But to me, every gesture, every word she said was obliterating. "I'll get that too," I said, imagining myself taking up the giant menu and attacking the table with it, each thwack a reprieve from the millions of words we'd left unsaid.

"So what brings you to town?" she said once the salads had arrived. I looked down and resolutely began shoveling greens into my mouth. I had died a thousand deaths over my mother's lack of interest in my life. I would not die of it again.

"Work," I said, talking purposely with my mouth full. "I got a new assignment."

"That's nice," she said, and took a bite, closing her lips tightly around her fork. As she chewed I braced myself for the inevitable onslaught of

Louise ruminations. But when she swallowed all she said was, "What kind of assignment?"

I blinked. Louise did not ask follow-up questions. "I dunno, you really want to hear about it?"

She nodded and took a sip of mineral water. I took the rare offering of her attention and told her about Nanü, leaving out the parts about my moral dilemma so that I might appear more pleasant and successful. I told her I was traveling a lot, but I didn't mind it, and I got a kick out of getting people excited about something they otherwise would never do. Louise listened while slowly eating exactly one half of her salad. She listened! I felt encouraged, and kept talking more and more. When she finished eating, she put her fork down and placed her napkin on top of the plate. After a second I realized her eyes were brimming with tears.

"Are you crying?" I said, surprised. I'd been talking about Tracy Mallard's animal shelter. "Don't be sad—it'll be no-kill in no time, once the money comes in."

She brushed a single tear away from her cheek. "It's not that."

"What is it?"

She didn't answer, but the tears kept coming. Irritation prickled my skin. *"What?"*

"It's only"—she delicately dabbed her eyes with her napkin—"you sound so much like your father."

My fists instinctively curled in my lap. "No I don't."

"It's just the kind of thing he would have loved to do."

"No it's *not*," I said hotly.

"Honey," she said sadly, and reached across the table for my hand. "It's okay to be sad still. I'm sad too."

"Oh my God, I'm not sad!" I bumped the table so the silverware clanked and the water sloshed in the glasses.

"We all grieve differently—"

"Oh for fuck's sake."

"I gave birth to you," she said, shaking her head. "I know you, probably better than you know yourself."

"No, you don't!" I threw my napkin down and stood up.

"Casey—" Louise started to say, but I was already gathering my things. I fumbled for money and dropped a twenty on the floor. I dropped my scarf and tripped on it. "Leave me alone," I snapped as she reached out to help. And with that I stalked out of the restaurant. Though on some level I knew that I longed for her to comfort me, I did not consider turning back.

Mort Stillman lived in an old industrial part of Milwaukee trying its best to make a comeback, though it's hard to make a comeback when even saying the word *Milwaukee* makes people cringe. Mort had a live/work space with giant factory windows and vaulted ceilings, the kind of place that would go for millions in Tribeca but in Milwaukee was, in Mort's words, "dirt cheap." He greeted me at the door with a cane, wearing a button-down shirt with a small stain on the front. He must have been well into his eighties, and his hands shook from Parkinson's. "Come in already," he said. "Don't just stand in the doorway."

But there was nowhere to sit in Mort's studio that wasn't covered with books. "You want a drink or something?" Mort said. "You want a cup of coffee?" He was leaning against his drafting table with his cane-free arm. The table was covered with drawings, and more drawings were hung on a clothesline by the window. Drawings of dogs, mostly, but dogs acting like people. In one picture of two dogs sitting in a diner booth, there was a speech bubble with one saying to the other, *What we did will be remembered.*

"Love one," I said. A few minutes later, he reappeared with an old ceramic carafe and a box of saltines. We moved the piles of books from the Adirondack chairs by the window, and I ate almost an entire sleeve of crackers. So relieved, I think, to be out of that restaurant and my mother's shadow.

While I chewed, Mort watched and smiled,

urged me to eat more, rested both his hands on top of his cane. I felt very safe with him, right off the bat. Whatever testosterone aggression he might have had as a younger man had already burned through him, or else he never had it. Some men, a few, the ones I like best, just don't.

My spiel to Mort, out of all the spiels for Nanü that Celeste had coached me on, was the one I felt shittiest about. I had flat-out refused the first time Celeste told me what the deal was, but as always, she'd smoothed and soothed me with her rhetoric. "Let's let Mort decide what is conscionable," she said, and added, "and give him the dignity of not deciding for him."

One of the subsidiaries of Burns Industries, owned by billionaire Burns brothers Fred and Donald—a huge conglomerate with all sorts of holdings in everything from petroleum and chemicals to paper production and ranching—had reached out to Celeste not long after one of those nonprofit news organizations had exposed the Burns brothers' shadowy ties and secret money-funneling to a number of extreme political organizations. Some of them so extreme, in fact, as to be flat-out racist. A tape had been released of a meeting between the Burns brothers and one of these groups in which the *n*-word had been used, and the *k*-word too.

The best way, as all bigots know, to seem unbigoted is to make a buddy: *I don't hate*

[BLANK] people, just look at my [BLANK] friend! Burns Industries was hoping to do just this with a new PR campaign featuring rapper Kanye West and Mort Stillman, one of the country's most beloved Holocaust survivors. They didn't want any art from Mort—they didn't care about his cartooning—but were hoping for a photo spread, Annie Leibovitz–style, of the man in his studio, along with a few quotes about how Burns Paper was the best paper and the only paper he uses, or something. In return Burns would not only pay Mort handsomely, but put up a whole bunch of money to renovate Milwaukee's Jewish museum and establish two new wings: one with art by Milwaukee's Holocaust survivors, and one devoted entirely to Mort's life and work.

Mort listened with various degrees of attention—at some points it seemed to drift off to somewhere far outside the window—as I talked. He refilled my coffee without my asking and brought out jam for me to spread on the saltines. I don't think his eyesight was very good, because there were specks on the jelly spoon from its last outing. I also don't think his health was very good, because he was sort of listing to the side.

"Do you want some ice cream?" he said when I was done with the pitch.

"Ummm . . . sure," I said. He shuffled off and came back with two Häagen-Dazs bars.

"There are worse things than not having any

235

money," he said after I'd unwrapped his bar for him.

I unwrapped my own bar, took a bite, chewed. "It's true," I said with my mouth full. There was a bit of chocolate on the side of his mouth. I wanted to rub it off, but I didn't want to embarrass him.

"Americans, I tell you," he said. "You're not used to suffering."

I bristled. "We suffer plenty." *For example,* I wanted to say, *I'll have you know, I just walked out of a very difficult luncheon with my mother.*

"I never said you didn't. I said you're not used to it."

I looked down, and all my ice cream was gone. How did that happen? I wasn't even hungry. I'd read an essay he'd written, one that Simone had included in his dossier, about his wartime experiences. Before the Germans had captured his family, they'd lived in a hole in the ground for two years in the forests outside Warsaw. When the soldiers had dragged him out, his legs were so atrophied they collapsed out from under him. I wanted to ask him how a person survives something like this, how a person can possibly go on being a person, but I didn't know how. He was eating his ice-cream bar quietly. It seems like the more people have lived through, the less likely they are to talk about it. So much of what happens to us, I guess, isn't cut out for chit-chat.

"Sometimes I look around," he said when he had finished his ice cream. "And I don't recognize this country."

"What do you mean?"

"All the lonely people," he said. Then he smiled. In his scratched-up, still-accented voice he sang, "where do they all come from?"

I paused and looked out the window. A flock of black birds swooped across the overcast sky.

"All the lonely people," I sang, turning back to him. "Where do they all belong?"

The song hung there for a second.

"Maybe they belong in Milwaukee," I said finally.

Mort laughed. "You're a good kid."

"I don't know about that." There were papers from a racist multinational business conglomerate in my bag, after all.

"I'll tell you what," he said. "I'll let 'em take these photographs—"

"You don't have to," I interrupted hastily. Now that he was agreeing to it, I wanted to backtrack immediately. I didn't want anything in front of him that was not beautiful.

"—if instead of giving me a wing in the museum they put together a classroom and a little teaching studio. My work doesn't need a mausoleum," he said. "But if we could get some teachers in there. Help the kids draw, make pictures. Saved my life a hundred times over, making pictures." He shook his head. "You never know, maybe it'll save theirs too."

"Is it worth it, though?" I said. "Are you sure?"

"Ah, they can't hurt me," Mort said. "I'm an old man, I'm tired, and I've seen things they couldn't even dream up. I'm not afraid of them. And by doing this I force them to do one good thing with their power." He held up his index finger. "One good thing." He turned his index finger toward himself. "And that's my victory, and their defeat."

9

WHEN THE GOING GETS TOUGH

On my way back from Milwaukee, when I was still ten thousand feet up in the air, the ground beneath a patchwork quilt of farmland, I asked myself what in God's name I was doing getting Mort Stillman to shill for the bloody *Burns* brothers for, what, a ten percent raise and the flush of Celeste's attention? Was I really, as Louise had insinuated, the spitting image of Rake Pendergast? I didn't think so, I hoped not, but since Celeste first brought up Blue Ocean, it felt like I'd put my forehead on a baseball bat and run around in circles; the whole summer I'd been staggering around the country like a punch-drunk kid. The rightside-up world was still out there, I was pretty sure, but it was hard to get back there after so much centripetal motion.

Which I guess is what Susan had always tried to get at: I was too eager to belong to something larger than myself, regardless of the larger thing's broader and more insidious implications. But as she also tried to get at earlier that summer: you can lead a horse to water, but you can't make a horse establish her own morality and make her life choices commensurate with them.

If only I had time, I concluded by the end of the flight, if I just had *more time,* if I weren't *so busy all the time,* my center point would return, the way out of my moral dilemma would become crystal clear.

The next day, a Saturday, was the annual company picnic. I decided it would be the perfect time for me to break the news to Celeste that I needed some time off. A brief sabbatical, as white-collar people say, or a two-week vacation for research and reflection. A respite from the trials of the world, so that I might, as the CrossFit gym across the street from my condo advertised, *pursue my legend.*

I slipped on a floral sundress and gladiator sandals and picked up Ben on my way to the riverside park where the picnic was always held. As a client, Ben'd been invited separately by Celeste, but we decided there was no time like the present to make our relationship known. As we arrived, hand in hand, I noticed three giant inflatable enclosures—a castle, slide, and what looked to be a strange sumo wrestling pit— behind the elegantly catered barbecue. The event planners had put white tablecloths on the picnic tables, and my colleagues were drinking champagne from real stemware. The tacky inflatables must have been a concession to the growing cadre of mommies in the office, whose lobbying for various rights for their offspring had swelled lately.

Around the adults, little kids were running around in white polo shirts and dresses. It was a contest among a certain subset of ambitious parents, seeing whose kids could remain pristine the longest.

"Give me a sec, will you?" I said to Ben, and squeezed his hand. He was wearing a short-sleeved madras shirt and cutoffs. He looked so cute I wished I could cut away the rest of life and focus my efforts solely on pouncing on him. "I'm dreading it, but I think I'd rather get it out of the way first."

"Good luck," he said, and squeezed my hand back. He'd thought my taking time off was a good idea, not necessarily for any abstract notions of good and bad, but because he could tell how awful I felt about my present situation. "Who knows, maybe that's all you need," he'd said, kissing my forehead, "a couple weeks to clear your head."

"I doubt it." I'd solemnly put my hand on his leg. "I read my horoscope. I think this is the start of my Saturn Return."

I began weaving through small clumps of small-talkers trying to get to Celeste, who was holding court with a group of older, well-heeled, prosperity-bellied men. They were in business attire, though the temperature was well into the eighties. Celeste was wearing a white linen sheath with a white gauzy scarf around her neck and with these men looked—not happy, but almost happy. Immediately I became alarmed. Celeste did not wear white, or look happy. I thought: something must be terribly wrong.

"Casey!" Celeste called out in a lighthearted voice, and waved me over. She introduced the men as Chet, Rex, Jeff, and Don, who in personality and aspect seemed all but indistinguishable. "They're from Omnipublic."

"Thanks for having us at your picnic," Chet/ Rex/Jeff/Don said, shaking my hand and chortling for no reason. "Boy, sure is a nice day out here, isn't it? Warmer than they expected."

"You're . . . welcome?" I said, trying to wrest my hand away from his hammy grip. Omnipublic was one of the biggest ad agencies in the country. Something was rotten in the state of inflatable bouncy castles. I remembered the rumors of sales and layoffs I'd overheard Britney recounting in the kitchen, and my whole body tensed despite the sweltering humidity. Would Celeste sell PR just like that? Take the profits from PR and run?

The answer, of course, was yes. Certainly she would.

Celeste told the men to grab a plate of food before the hot wings got cold. I meant to wait at least five seconds after they were out of earshot before saying something, employ a teensy bit of tact, but the words burst out of my mouth: "Are you selling the *company* to these guys?!"

"For God's sakes, Casey, keep your voice down," Celeste said. She took me by the elbow and led me away from the picnicking throng. There are very few scenarios in which being separated from the herd ends up in the separatee's favor, but it's hard to remember that in the presence of a charismatic leader.

"Keep my voice down?!" I cried. "How, when for all I know we're going to lose our jobs?!"

Celeste stopped. "You're not. But the answer to your question is yes."

A wave of relief crashed through my body, but it didn't last long. "You are selling?" My voice cracked. "But why?! You built this place from the ground up!"

And you built me from the ground up! I added silently.

"And it's time for it to keep building without me," Celeste said matter-of-factly. She explained that for several years it had become increasingly difficult to find enough big-fish clients to keep PR independent. There were only about five real advertising agencies left in the country anyway, huge conglomerates owned by holding companies that gobbled up and merged firms just like ours. Just that morning she'd finished intense negotiations with Omnipublic so that PR could at least keep its own board of directors and essentially, she said, operate as a firm-within-a-firm. "No layoffs necessary," she said, anticipating my inevitable next question. "Nothing will change for the employees—the transition is really in name only."

I exhaled. "So I still have a job."

Celeste looked at me like *Don't be a dummy.* "You have more than a job," she said. "For you, the sale is good news." She explained that as the sale was being negotiated, she'd also set up Nanü as an independent agency, one not part of the sale to Omnipublic. With the venture capitalists' investment, Nanü would soon be on the fast track to an IPO. "Which means equity for you and your team," she said, putting a confidential hand on my back. "Especially you, given your leadership position."

"Equity?" I didn't know precisely what equity meant, but I could hazard a guess based on the television I'd watched. "What kind of equity?"

"Fifteen percent."

"Fifteen percent of—" I couldn't help myself. Curiosity killed the Casey.

"Last I talked with the VCs," she said, "they were valuing the company at ten million. Which frankly," she added, "I think is on the low side."

I remember reading a famous study once about kids in a laboratory who were given two choices: eat a single marshmallow right away, or wait ten minutes and get two marshmallows. I knew as soon as I read it that I was a single marshmallow kind of gal. It is hard to think about the future when there is so much sugar in your mouth.

Fifteen percent of ten million was 1.5 million, and it would probably grow and keep growing. I had gone over to talk to Celeste about taking time off, but it was hard, vis-à-vis these numbers, to remember exactly *why* I wanted time off, given the spoils that were headed my way. What was I going to do with that time anyway? Nothing concrete, probably. Nothing *productive*. Probably I'd just waste it on going to the gym and watching TV. By requesting the time off at a tipping point like this, I would likely put this fifteen percent in jeopardy. Yes, fine, it had only been twenty-four hours since Mort had told me there were worse things than not having any money. But it was hard to remember that when you lived in a world where *literally everything* was about money; even the self-help gurus and psychologists exhorting otherwise were charging big bucks for their advice.

As Celeste went on about stock options and seed money, and dollar signs danced in front of my eyes, I decided that, hell, I might as well keep working and amassing my fortune with Celeste for a while, stay *productive,* and keep my moral dilemma—my pursuit of real happiness, or freedom, or purpose or meaning or whatever it was that I really wanted—as sort of a side gig. After all, over the past couple months I'd seen the best minds this country had to offer come to the same conclusion. These writers possessed knowledge, wisdom, and empathy, but none of it gave them power. Money gave them power. And we all needed some power, or we'd be eaten alive by assholes like Rex and Chet.

Not to mention that fifteen percent was a generous number, far more generous than I guessed that Celeste needed to be. I felt a warm rush of esprit de corps at her offer. It was a gesture, evidence I *did* matter to her beyond mere employeeship. I was family to her; I belonged. I looked forward to the day in the near future when she would sit me down on a giant pile of venture capital money and say, wow, Casey, I hadn't noticed until this moment that you're like the daughter I never had. I love you, and I'm so proud of everything you've done, and I'll never give up on you, and what's more I'm excited to see you evolve as an individual and not just an extension of my own massive ego.

"Well!" I said to Celeste, once I'd lifted my jaw up from the grass. "That is great news."

"News that you'll keep to yourself for the time being, of course," she said, patting me on the back in a gesture of finality. "So when the time is right, I can announce it myself."

"Of course," I echoed gravely.

After wandering around tables of gourmet salads and summer cocktails, I finally found Ben inside the bouncy castle along with Annie and Lindsey. He'd met them several times before at summer happy hours. They were all drinking beers and idly taking turns bouncing up and down in their stocking feet. "Silly rabbits, bouncy castles are for kids!" I said, pulling back the mesh curtain over the entrance, yanking my sandals off, and adding them to the pile of footwear outside the castle before hopping up. The inside walls were blocked off in blue and red and yellow, which made me feel like I'd stepped inside a child's paint set. I hopped gingerly on one foot, then the other, then hopped a little more vigorously. "This feels surprisingly good," I said.

"There's something cathartic about it, isn't there?" Lindsey said, taking a big leap into the air.

"Totally!" Annie said, imitating Lindsey's jump, but then she toppled over, spilling the small remainder of beer in her bottle all over the trampoline. "Owwwww" she said, rolling onto her back and pulling her knees into her chest. "My ankle—"

"Poor baby!" Lindsey said, hopping over. "What do you need?"

While Lindsey tended to Annie's ankle with

Reiki treatments, Ben hopped over and offered me his beer. "How'd it go?" Ben said. I pointedly shook my head at the bottle. "Right, right, the gluten."

"Not exactly how I expected—" I began.

"I'm so proud of you," Lindsey said, turning around, apparently finished with her ministrations.

Ben explained, "I filled these guys in already."

Annie climbed hesitantly back to her feet. Lindsey hopped over to give me a hug. "A sabbatical!" She kissed my cheek. "I can't believe it! You're finally learning work-life balance! All it took was you falling in love!"

I started when she used the word *love*. Though I'd certainly been thinking about the word, neither Ben nor I had said it aloud to each other. Ben, luckily, appeared not to have heard, having begun earnestly giving Annie ankle rehabilitation based on exercises he'd learned playing soccer in high school. I pulled back from Lindsey's embrace. "Ah, well, about that sabbatical. Something major just—"

"Did someone say *major?*" Simone appeared behind the mesh curtain, her dark hair keratined and glossy and topped with a Coachella-esque flower crown. How she was able to remain so unsweaty at an outdoor picnic was an aggravating mystery. "Mind if I join you?" Before anyone could answer, she was climbing up. Her jean shorts were so short I thought she might catch cervical cancer.

"No, not at all," I said in a voice that I hoped conveyed a secret message: *Scram!*

Clambering to her feet, Simone delicately pulled her shorts out of her butt and sidled up to Ben with one hand on her hip. "Can I have a sip of that? I'm parched."

Ben smiled and shrugged. "Sure, I guess." He handed her his beer. I shot him a look. "We met by the coleslaw," he said by way of explanation.

Simone laughed, touched his arm under his short sleeve. "You are too funny!"

"Isn't he?" I said with gritted teeth.

"Before, when we were talking, I meant to tell you," Simone said, tossing her hair, turning her back to me, "about this study I read about the health benefits of turmeric in Alzheimer's patients. But you had me laughing so hard it completely slipped my mind!"

I'm going to kill her, I thought, as I watched Ben soak up her flirtations and flattery. I'm going to finish this battle once and for all and vanquish her right here.

That's when I remembered that I *could* actually vanquish her, seeing as there were two inflatable sumo wrestling outfits right next to this bouncy castle. "Hey Simone," I said, interrupting her drivel. "I have an idea!"

She didn't answer, having purposely ignored

me to talk more about turmeric and, I gathered, almonds and blueberries.

"Hey Simone!" I said again.

"What?" she said, not turning around.

"Want to go sumo wrestle with me? Those suits look like they're a ton of fun."

She turned this time, wrinkled her nose prissily. "Thanks, but no thanks," she said.

Ben laughed. "You two? Sumo wrestling? Hard to imagine."

I smiled triumphantly at her. "The writer needs our help imagining."

Simone gave me a dagger look. "I said I don't want to."

"Sure you do," I said. "You just don't know it yet."

"I said *no,*" Simone said. "People have been sweating in those suits all day."

"People have been sweating in here all day too," I said, thwacking her a little too hard on the arm. "Come on. It'll be fun!"

"Do it!" Annie said, testing out her ankle, likely eager to move the locus of humiliation else-where.

"You don't have to," Ben said concedingly. "But if you *wanted* to—"

"I know, I'll take a video!" Lindsey said, taking out her phone.

Simone looked at me with the fury of someone who knows they're about to lose but still has the energy to put up a good fight. "Okay, fine, why not," she said, in a tone of voice that meant *I hate you, Casey P.*

Some forty minutes later, fresh off a best-of-three victory over Simone, my body slick with sweat, my makeup smeared, and hair dampened, I toppled onto the grass, breathing heavily. "Good game," I panted, raising my other hand in farewell to Simone, who was limping toward the beverage tent. She raised her arm and gave me the middle finger as she departed.

"Boy," I said to Ben, who was lying on his side next to me. "That was fun, wasn't it?"

"You were a little rough on her, weren't you?" he said lightly, and nudged me.

"I wouldn't have been," I said, equally lightly, "if you hadn't so enjoyed her trying to get all up on you in the bouncy castle."

Ben paused. When he answered his voice was cold. "What's that supposed to mean?"

"It doesn't matter." I reached for my phone and pulled up Facebook. Wolf Prana had posted a status update that morning that had trended to the top of my news feed. He'd friended me right after we'd met, and I'd accepted because I accepted everyone's friend request, even if they were my enemy.

"Yeah, actually, it does matter," Ben said. He sat up in the grass. "Even if she had been coming on to me, which, by the way, she wasn't, it's not like I would have done anything—"

"But you looooovved talking to her about, whatever, turmeric and Alzheimer's," I interrupted. "Even though you *never* talk about what's going on with your mom with *me*."

"Her grandpa has Alzheimer's! It came up incidentally! There were blueberries in the fruit salad, someone said something about brain food—"

"Wait. Hold on." I put a hand up. "One second." Something in Wolf's post had caught my eye.

Thought about telling you I have a book of words & pics coming out w Phaidon

Next fall then realized I didn't give a shit

There is everyone in the lessening of your wounds

It was that last line, the line about the wounds. That was a line from a poem I had read before. A poem I loved. It was empirically impossible that Wolf could ever write anything I loved. It took some time for what was happening to finish happening and settle in the front part of my brain but when it did—

I was so stupid.

So, so stupid.

"I have to go," I said suddenly, and leapt to my feet.

"Where are you going?" Ben said, shielding

252

his eyes from the sun and looking up at me accusingly.

I re-buckled my sandals. "I'll tell you later. Long story."

"You can't just run away every time we have a difficult conversation, you know."

"I'm not!" I said, in a bitchier voice than I meant to use. I softened. "It's not that. I'll be back as soon as—listen I have to leave right now."

"Oh, come *on*—" Ben started, but I took off across the park, shouting, "I'll be right back!" and digging my keys out of my purse as I ran. I drove like a maniac and didn't stop until I got to the building I was headed for, and because the intercom was busted, I had to wait for a resident to come out to enter. When someone finally did, I ran through the lobby and up the stairs two at a time until, barely twenty minutes after I'd seen the posting, I was banging on Susan's door. This was something I had to explain in person.

Susan and I hadn't seen each other since the night at the brewery, where I thought, more or less, we seemed to be back on good terms. When she opened the door, it was clear she was surprised, though not displeased. I barged into her studio without preamble. Susan's apartment looked even more neglected than usual, which made me feel even sicker about what I'd done.

Dishes were piled in the sink, clothes and papers were strewn all over the floor, and there were chipped saucers filled with cigarette butts.

She must have seen me looking around, because she said, "I've been writing a lot. Sorry for the mess."

"Ha ha, ummm, no need to apologize to me," I said, and added, "Seriously." I needed badly to find a way to move beyond chitchat and into a discussion of some, well, very serious problems that were very much all my fault. If the going got tough, the tough could at least be honest with her best friend about what had happened, due to the road to hell being paved with good intentions, and hope that her best friend could forgive her.

But the thing about friendship, I'd learned over the past few months, was that it was fragile. Millions of gossamer threads connecting one heart to another—it looks like a thick rope at a distance, but up close it's like a spiderweb. All it takes is one clumsy swipe to knock the whole thing down. I wanted so badly for my best friend to be my best friend again. I feared that with the news I was about to deliver, the possibility was about to unravel.

"Can I do your dishes?" I said suddenly. Before she could answer, I went over and started washing.

"Oh boy," Susan said, taking a tea towel and

beginning to dry. "If you're cleaning already, it must be bad. What is it? Did something happen with Ben?"

"No . . ." I trailed off and let the water wash over my hands. "Something else."

"Work?"

"Yeah, work." I stopped washing, closed my eyes, took a breath. "And you."

"*Me?*" Susan laughed, I thought, rather alarmedly. "What does your work have to do with me?"

With my eyes still closed, I started talking. I said the words very fast. "I just saw Wolf post a status update on Facebook using a line from one of your poems. It was a poem, oh God, that I *stole* from your apartment back in the spring, that night of the duende reading, because I had this half-baked idea that I was going to use the writers I was meeting through work to help, you know, launch your career in the literary arts. So I gave a few poems to him when I was in New York so he could send them around to his people or whatever, and he *did,* I swear, I saw the emails with my own eyes, but clearly he's also used them for his own benefit. I don't know how much, though, I've only seen that one line, but I promise you that as soon as I leave here I'm going to call him and demand that he take the post down, and also redact whatever else he's used in his book project, even if I have to call the publisher myself and make a formal accusation of plagiarism."

My fists were clenched under the water by then. "I know that stealing your poems and giving them to Wolf without saying anything to you was a really fucked up thing to do. I completely own that. But I hope you also understand that everything I did really was to try and help you. I guess I just . . . wanted you to stop *hiding,* and help you share your gifts with the world, you know? And I'm sorry. I'm so so sorry, that even by trying to help you I really, really hurt you instead."

There was a long pause. The water was scalding my hands. I kept them there.

"Is that all?" Susan said. "Is that everything?"

"Yes," I said, collapsing inwardly. "That's everything." Except for the fact that I passed her short story to Mary London.

When I opened my eyes, Susan was no longer standing beside me. She was standing by the front door, and it was open. "Who are you?" she said in a trembling voice. She was looking at the floor. "And what did you do with my friend?"

I knew that voice. There was no point arguing with that voice.

"You should go."

Listen, if I were her, I would've done the same thing. Susan felt life as deeply as a fish's gills feel water. So porous, so yielding, until a hook got hold and killed her. I left without saying another word. Such a good human deserved better than my foolish machinations.

But I also wanted nothing more than to stomp on and tear the flesh of her enemies. I'd discovered to be true what I always feared deep down: that my Real Self was pretty rotten, no better than my father or my mother or any other grown-up who only cared for themselves. But maybe I could use this to destroy Wolf and everything he stood for. Fight rottenness with rottenness. Out on the street—I couldn't even wait until I got home—I FaceTimed Wolf. I wanted to see his face, the shifty bastard, while I threw down all the evidence of his misdeeds.

To my surprise—I think there was a part of me that figured I'd just have to rage over voicemail—my phone alerted me that we were connecting. "Whaddup, Casey?" Wolf spoke like he had a bunch of taffy in his mouth. His eyes were stoner-red, his face uncomfortably close to the screen.

"You know what's up." I was furiously walking down the street instead of hopping straight into my car, attempting to blow off the extra steam.

"Is this about the chlamydia?" he said. "I was going to call you but then I figured, you seemed like the kind of chick who got checked any-way."

"Jesus Christ, you idiot, we didn't have sex!" I was yelling now. "This is about the fact that you took the poems my best friend Susan wrote, my best friend WHO NOW HATES ME, and STOLE THEM for your stupid book!"

"Whooooo!" I heard a male voice call after me as I thundered down the street. "That bitch cray!"

"I SAW that Facebook post and YOU BETTER take it down and take out whatever else you plagiarized or I'm going to drag your name through shit all over the Internet. I KNOW people now. IMPORTANT people. WAY more important than you. Ever heard of Mary London? Izzy Calliente? I'm going to call them as soon as we get off the phone. You are DEAD MEAT."

"Yo." Wolf was holding a patronizing, but, I thought, slightly freaked out hand up to the camera. "What're you talking about, homie?"

"Don't homie me. Everyone in the lessening of your wounds? That's not your line, Wolf! You stole that!"

He scratched his head. "Chill, bruh—"

"Enough with the cultural appropriation, *bruh*," I interrupted. "And I have proof. Susan has all her poems on her computer. Microsoft Word date stamps. All it takes is a screenshot of the last edit and you'll be found out so fast your stupid Twitter followers won't even have TIME to shame you, you'll already be so obsolete, you talent-less—"

It was maybe right around this time that I realized there was a presence behind me. I glanced back. Some guy wearing a private security uniform was stumbling behind me. When he saw me looking at him, he said, "Shouldn't be wearing a dress like that in this neighborhood."

"Oh for fuck's sake." I broke into a jog and turned back to Wolf, who appeared to be, whether through drugs or innate male confidence, completely unfazed by our conversation. "Seriously, take it down right now, excise whatever else, or believe me—"

"What—you'll tell some old ladies about it?" Wolf was shaking his head, a funny little smile on his face, the smile of someone who has never once felt threatened, not really, whose reality has never once been impugned. "Casey, girl, you off your meds?"

"IT'S ONLY TEN MILLIGRAMS OF LEXAPRO!" I bellowed. I turned around to see if I'd lost the security guard, but he was jogging behind me. I crossed the street and doubled back in order to return to my car.

"I'm gonna go," Wolf was saying. "Hope you're okay, girl. You know what? Just to be sure I'll call Celeste first thing in the morning and ask her to check up on you."

Well, shit. Wolf couldn't say anything to Celeste. She didn't know about my private dealings with Susan's papers, and would have my head if she did. Conflict of interest, using her connections to make personal gains, it didn't sound good, it didn't sound like the actions of someone with fifteen percent equity. "You better not, you little—"

"Byeeeeeee."

"YOU CAN'T GO!"

Ah, but he'd already disconnected. I broke into a dead sprint. I heard the creepy security guard say, "Where are you going?" as I ran to my car. As I started the engine, the guy came up and put his hand on the passenger-side window, motioning at me to roll it down. I relocked the doors instead. Through the glass I heard him slur, "What's the matter, baby?"

What was the matter? I thought. You're following me to my car and you're asking me what's the *matter?* Well, if he was going to put it that way, I was going to answer that way. With a fury I hadn't felt in a long time, I burst out, slamming the steering wheel with my hands, with what was not even close to the entire answer but was the best I could do at the time, "All of you! I hate all of you! I HATE MEN!"

10

CONTAINMENT: IMPOSSIBLE

It was in this rather odd frame of mind that I wobbled back to the PR company picnic. Late afternoon had transitioned into evening. The blue moon was rising, and the shadows were long on the grass. Thumping summer beats thrummed out of a large speaker system as my colleagues danced and talked and laughed a little too loudly. Every day in advertising was an exercise in convincing ourselves we were having a good— no, *amazing*—time.

Off on one side, Ben was engrossed in what looked like a serious conversation with Celeste, while on the lawn, Jack, Lindsey, and Annie were whacking balls around a haphazardly constructed croquet court. I decided, for the meantime, to let Ben be. I needed to cool off before talking to him again, given everything that'd happened since.

"It's like talking to a child," Jack was saying to Lindsey as Annie bent her knees, took a deep breath, and hit her ball a good five yards away from the nearest hoop.

Annie shrugged. "Oh well," she said to no one in particular. "Your turn!"

"What's like talking to a child?" I said, picking

up a croquet mallet lying in the grass. Maybe it would be good to take out all this fear and shame and aggression on a harmless croquet ball, seeing as Simone was now nowhere to be found.

"You're back!" Lindsey said to me. She hit her ball marginally more accurately than Annie. "Gosh, this is harder than it looks. We missed you."

"On another little mission for Celeste, I bet," said Jack. He looked down and adjusted his stance. He was wearing slim shorts and suspenders, along with his usual bow tie. With a low crack, he hit the ball with his mallet. It went straight through the hoop.

"Nice try, and *great* guesswork," I whipped back. "Not that it's any of your business, *Jack,* but I had a bit of personal stuff to attend to."

"Uh-huh, right," Jack said, tapping his palm with his mallet. "*Very* important business, I'm sure."

I ignored him. I said, "Mind if I take a turn?" Annie and Lindsey nodded. I nudged the ball with my foot toward what seemed like a reasonable starting position. "Anyway, who's the child?"

Lindsey said, "Jack's been having a little trouble with Mary London and Izzy Calliente."

I closed my eyes and pretended the ball was Wolf's head. I took a swing and barely made contact. It rolled maybe an inch forward in the grass.

I threw my mallet on the ground. "God*damn* it."

"It's okay. You can try again," Lindsey said encouragingly. She continued, "Jack's not used to working with artists."

"You're an artist, Lindsey," I said, picking the mallet back up. "Maybe I will try again, if that's okay."

"Sure it's okay," said Lindsey. "We're not keeping score. And even if we were—"

"I meant real artists," Jack said. He looked at Lindsey. "Sorry."

"Um, hello," I said, lining up my mallet with the ball. "Lindsey has a BFA from RISD—do you know what a big deal that is?" I was ratcheting up the intensity in my voice for no reason other than it gave me momentary respite from how shitty I felt about everything else. I took another swing. The ball chopped up in the air and landed fairly close to the hoop. I felt, suddenly, quite pleased with myself. Swinging the mallet jauntily over my shoulder, I said, "Or are you just in a bad mood because Johnny's sick again?"

Johnny, Jack's shih tzu, had gotten a concussion on Wednesday from walking straight into a wall. Apparently his eye surgery had not gone well.

"No," Jack said. "I'm just tired of having to put up with lazy prima donnas who can't do *one* thing without having a hissy fit, falling apart, or feeling"—he dropped his mallet to better dramatize his air quotes—'oppressed'—"

"Sounds like someone else I know," I said, nudging Lindsey, who shook her head as if to say *leave me out of this*. But it was fun to make fun of Jack, comforting even, a welcome distraction from the atomic bomb Wolf'd just dropped on my life and my best friendship. I saw Annie's ball roll the opposite way from the hoop.

She threw her hands up. "For crying out loud."

"Sorry, what?" Jack said. "I can't hear you from all the way up Celeste's asshole."

"You guys," Lindsey said. "No fighting. It's a holiday."

"There's millions of dollars inside that asshole, buddy," I said sweetly. "So sorry you weren't invited."

He looked at me sharply. "What do you mean, millions of dollars?"

"Nothing," I said quickly. Apparently it was impossible for me not to stick my foot in my mouth wherever I went. "Figure of speech."

"There you are," Ben said, approaching our game out of nowhere with what seemed to be forced cheer.

"Sorry—just got back. Took longer than I thought," I said. I snaked an arm around his waist and kissed him on the cheek. He accepted, but did not reciprocate, this affection. "Should we get going?"

He shrugged. His face looked sunburnt. "If you want."

I frowned. "Okay. Oh, but Lindsey," I said, snapping my fingers, "before I forget." She was making one last attempt to get her ball through the hoop. "I got one of those twenty-percent-off coupons for 'our place' in the mail, if you know what I mean. You want to go tomorrow? Maybe go to brunch first?"

"Sure!" Lindsey said, beaming. Lindsey loved being invited places. Unfortunately her turning around to accept my invitation meant that she missed her croquet ball completely. "Oh no," she said. Her voice rose a little. "I missed again. What is wrong with me?"

"It's okay, Lindsey," Annie said tenderly.

"I suck at this game." Lindsey's voice quavered.

"Your place?" Ben said.

I smiled up at him. "It's a secret, ha ha. You can only know if you come with us."

He pulled away a little. "I'm busy tomorrow."

"Oh," I said, hurt by the speed of his refusal. "Well. Some other time then."

On the walk back to the car, Ben and I fell into an awkward silence. The mosquitoes had come out by then; one kept buzzing insistently in my ear. I was turning over what I wanted to say to him—what I'd done to Susan, what Wolf'd done to Susan, what I'd done to Ben himself earlier with my jealous accusations—but the realization that it'd be impossible to get all this out in one

265

piece, or without falling to pieces, compelled me to stay quiet. A couple passed us on the sidewalk, holding hands, the woman with a baby swaddled across her chest. How did these other people do it? I wondered. These normal, well-adjusted people? How did they remain close to each other, close enough to stay in love, to have babies, without all the disrepair?

Ben broke the silence abruptly by telling me that when he was talking to Celeste, she'd been filling him in on the sale of PR to Omnipublic. As Nanü's proof of concept, he'd been offered a 0.5 percent stake in the firm. "Pretty exciting, I guess," he said, though not excitedly. "That kind of money could set a person up for a long time."

"Uh-huh, sure," I said miserably. Might as well keep throwing the shit on the table. "Listen, I want to say sorry about earlier. I wasn't trying to run away. I just saw that Wolf had posted something on Facebook that seriously fucked me and Susan—"

We reached my car and began the drive across town. I told him what I'd done with Susan's poems and how it'd just gone down at her apartment. He listened quietly, shaking his head occasionally, and once let out a very long sigh. The quieter he was, the more I felt it my duty to explain, even defend myself, though I knew deep down that my position was indefensible. My voice pitched up to a whine. "I didn't *mean* for anything bad to happen! It was a stupid thing to do, but I was *trying* to make things better for her!"

We passed the turnoff to Ben's street. Most of the time we slept at my place. "Actually," Ben coughed slightly. "Do you mind dropping me off at my apartment?"

I felt my cheeks grow hot. "I just assumed we'd spend the night at—"

"I'm just tired," he said tiredly.

I circled around the block and pulled up to his building. I put my hands on the steering wheel and looked at him. "I said I was sorry—please don't hold it against me, my being stupid this afternoon—"

"I'm not holding anything against you." He reached out a hand, put it on my bare arm, let it linger there. "I just need a night. I'll text you tomorrow, all right?"

My eyes, those betrayers, filled with tears.

"Casey." He squeezed my arm. "I'm not leaving. It's just a night. Get some sleep. We haven't been sleeping enough anyway."

A few tears traced lines across my cheeks. I brought the back of my hand up to wipe them away. "I know. I know. It's not a big deal. I don't know why I'm so—"

"I'm not trying to hurt you," he said sadly.

"I know." My shoulders shook. Oh, why must the body always have its say. "I'm not trying to hurt you, either. It's just hard, when—I just assume that—" But I couldn't say it. What was there to say? He wanted me to trust him, and I could not. Not because I didn't want to, but because I didn't know how. No one starts playing Mozart when all they've been handed is sheet music and an out-of-tune piano with three keys missing.

I let my hair fall over my face. "Anyway, I understand. You should get some sleep, too."

"I'll see you tomorrow." He squeezed my arm again. "Okay? Everything's going to seem better tomorrow. You have equity, things can't be that bad—"

"Oh, who cares about that." I sniffed and wiped the snot from my nose.

Ben leaned over and kissed my cheek softly. "It's okay. And even though you never believe me, you're okay, too."

The next morning, I picked Lindsey up, and after a long brunch during which we discussed astrology, yogic breathing, and the kitchari cleanse Lindsey was starting on Monday, we made for the suburbs like white people in the sixties fleeing integration.

What Lindsey and I loved best about The Container Store was how they had containers for things we previously didn't even know needed containing. Life was very difficult. There was no way around it. But it got *easier* when shirts had boxes and spices had shelving and you never had any problem finding your can opener. Like the old wives' saying goes: Success begins from the inside drawer, courtesy of The Container Store!

This particular Container Store was located in a ritzy outdoor mall development. Inside, I grabbed a cart from an impeccably stacked row while Lindsey opted for a mesh basket. "So," she said as we made our way down aisle one, which was comprised entirely of colored hangers, "do you want to tell me why we're really here right now?"

Lindsey, bless her, was the kindest person I knew, was even kind when the rest of us were being assholes. I think because she'd been hurt a lot herself, she could intuit the hurt that lay buried underneath our assholery. Hell, maybe she could relate more to us in those vulnerable moments than she could when we were doing just fine. Some people at People's Republic were driven crazy by her vocal endorsement of crystals, "clean" foods, and Transcendental Meditation, but I heard all that talk with a lot of understanding. Underneath it was pain she was trying very hard to get over. Like all injured people with enough money to support the habit, she could be a bit of a navel-gazer, but the great thing about Lindsey was that she was very supportive of my navel-gazing, too.

The words came out of nowhere and I think surprised both of us. "I think I need to leave PR."

A pause. "Okaaaaay," Lindsey said slowly, twisting the slim silver bracelet on her wrist. Lindsey'd had a lot of therapy, and she knew better than to react strongly to outlandish statements. "Why do you say that? Yesterday it was a sabbatical, now you want to quit?"

I burst out, "Well a sabbatical's just not gonna cut the mustard! For one thing, yesterday I also lost my best-best friend, which I'll fill you in on in a minute. For another thing, I just asked a *Holocaust* survivor to pose for advertisements for a racist company. For another-other thing, I told myself that twenty-eight was the year I was going to start pursuing my dreams instead of just working in advertising, and the year's half over and I've barely done anything. And for another-other-*other* thing, I'm watching myself ruin the first good relationship I've ever had by, you know, sumo wrestling my enemies and accusing Ben of all sorts of terrible things. Everything feels upside down and something tells me that the source of it has to do not just with like, astrological forces, but with what we're doing here, with Nanü and PR. It's not right somehow. I can feel it. Can't you?"

I told Lindsey about what'd happened with Ben the night before, with Susan and Wolf, about Mort and Tracy Mallard, about my brief and embarrassing foray into voice acting and how awful it'd been to see my mother in Milwaukee. Meanwhile, we circled around aisle one to an endcap of air fresheners, and then back around to the plastic storage aisle, where tubs of varying sizes and depths were balanced alongside matching lids. The Container Store cared so much about its customers that if you forgot to buy a lid and they forgot to remind you at the checkout, they'd give you a whole new bin and lid for free, *plus* a refund.

"Not to mention," I said, "that the rumors are true—Celeste is selling PR to Omnipublic. She told me yesterday. Which is going to be fine, in the end," I said quickly, seeing Lindsey's Bambi-brown eyes fill up with worry. "You and I are going with her to Nanü along with Jack and Annie, so far as I know. Celeste loves you."

"So far as you know?" Lindsey stopped in her tracks. "You mean you don't know for sure?"

"I mean of course you are! I think. No one's losing their jobs, that much I do know. Celeste was adamant about that. But don't you think— there's something fishy about this whole business?"

I saw her jaw set, unset. It would be hard to talk to Lindsey if she continued acting this way. Once she got frightened, there was no reasoning with her; she crouched and retreated into the animal version of herself.

"Don't worry," I said in a rush. "Don't worry, don't worry. You're going to be fine, I promise."

Part of me wanted to get back to what I was saying before, try to explain this strange, shimmering feeling I woke up with that morning as a result of the upside-downness of my life. An uncanniness, as the existentialists would say. Like if I held my hand in the air long enough it would start to dissolve into the atmosphere, molecule bleeding into molecule. But even between good friends—even with Lindsey—there were certain things you didn't say. Part of what made me, me, I suppose, or made me feel at least a little solidity, was that a part of me remained unshareable.

"What are these for?" Lindsey was looking at a stack of oddly shaped bins.

"Those are to store your shoe trees in, when they're not in the shoes," I said.

I was interrupted by a woman next to us, round and red as a tomato. "My birthday's in September and I told Todd I'm wishing for a closet," she said loudly into her phone. An outdated Top 40 hit warbled over the loudspeakers.

A closet, a closet. I grabbed some sachets off the endcap and threw them in my cart. Was I wishing for a closet? Was that all that was wrong? Was that the source of my unhappiness? I supposed it could be. Oprah's home improvement guy always says that clutter wasn't just physical stuff in our closets; it was anything that got in the way of *your best life*. But perhaps by dealing with the physical stuff *first,* your best life would *follow.* This was also the principle advocated in trickle-down economics.

Lindsey wandered toward an aisle display that held what looked like giant plastic toadstools. "You know, it always surprised me you worked in advertising," she said. She sat down on one of the toadstools and bounced a little. "I told you, I always thought you'd be perfect on TV." Then she bounced too high and lost her balance and fell onto the floor.

"Lindsey! God! Are you okay?" I said, rushing to help her.

"Can I help you with something?" an unfamiliar voice said behind me.

I turned around and saw a man wearing a Container Store apron, headset, and walkie-talkie. "Yes!" I said.

The man's nametag said ANTHONY. He looked at me expectantly, as if waiting for me to articulate what I wanted help with. But I didn't know how, I was waiting for *him* to tell *me* what I wanted, so that I might follow his instructions accordingly. In the silence, I thought of what the woman had said back in aisle two. "Come to think of it, Anthony," I said, rubbing my hands together, "I think I'm wishing for a closet!"

"A closet!" he said, mirroring my hand gesture. "Well then, come with me to our custom Elfa

Design Center." I followed him toward the back of the store. On the way we passed a cardboard stand with about a zillion copies of a book called *Conscious Capitalism.*

Back at the Elfa Design Center, with the help of a large laminated binder, Anthony educated me on the finer points of hidden home design. A place for everything, taken to the extreme. Shelves to hold a single sweater. Wooden racks to help shoes "breathe." The most embarrassing materials of human existence—toilet paper, receipts, photos of people you no longer spoke to—could all be tucked away in a color-coded frieze.

I flashed to an image of my closet as it was—unmatched hangers, unsystematized blouses, spaghetti straps tangled up—and how it could be, and I thought: freedom is just another word for living clutter-free.

"Yes, yes, yes!" I said jubilantly. "I'll take all of it!"

After signing up for a custom financing plan for my custom closet, which Anthony and I designed down to the last in-drawer bra separator, I found Lindsey staring at a wall of kitchen cabinet organizers: light wood, dark wood, white plastic, and clear plastic, all with varying heights. The point was to maximize cabinet space so you could fit as much stuff as possible in them. The Container Store was, among other things, a store that allowed you to acquire more stuff while pretending you had less. Lindsey had dragged her plastic toadstool over to this aisle and was sitting there, staring.

"Wait till you see what I got," I said, crouching next to her. "What'd you find?"

"I don't like it," she said, shaking her head vigorously.

"Don't like what?"

"Do you ever feel like," she said, sort of flapping her hands. "There's no room to be a person anywhere?"

I didn't totally know what she was talking about, but this happened sometimes with Lindsey. What she was talking about seemed to be located in some long-ago moment that kept bleeding into the present when the circumstances unlocked it. Lindsey had told me once that after her mother and stepfather would leave to go out drinking, she would spend the night organizing all the drawers and closets so that everything would be perfect by the time they got home. Sometimes, on stressful days at work, I'd catch her arranging and rearranging the items on her desk to get them at exact right angles to each other.

"Do you want to stay here?" I said, as gently as I could. I don't think these blurred lines between memory and real life were easy for her. "Or should we go get some food?"

She looked toward me with a small, fearful

expression on her face. "Let's get some food."

I helped her stand and carried the toadstool back to its display area. Sometimes I loved my friends the way I imagined a mother loved her children; I wanted to take care of them in the same elemental way. I was feeling peaceful as we headed toward the checkout, arm in arm. I had my new closet and my most tender friend, and we had decided to eat quesadillas together. Life had handed me lemons, and I'd dragged myself to the kitchen to make some lemonade. What could possibly go wrong?

Well, I'll tell you what went wrong.

I can think of so many people I know, who, at least according to social media, have trouble-free lives with trouble-free jobs and trouble-free relationships they present with a real sense of satisfaction. Not me. My curiosity has something to do with the trouble I get into, sure. And, okay, a hot temper. But I have to think that troika of wild-haired Fates looked down at me the day I was born and, with a cackle, sent down a whopping dose of bad luck.

As Lindsey was swiping her credit card at the checkout, I saw Ben out of the corner of my eye. He was wearing the same cutoff shorts as the day before, with a green bandanna in his back pocket. "Oh!" I said, and started to jog toward him.

Then I saw that he was not alone.

In fact, he was with a woman. She was short, curvy, brunette, olive-complexioned. She wore a halter top and shorts and looked fabulous in both. She and Ben were standing in the plastic tub aisle, close together. She had one hand on her hip. They were pointing at different tubs. And they were laughing.

A tesseract kind of happened in my brain when I saw them together. Four dimensions of simultaneous understanding. I cubed the cube of all the men I'd ever known and drew a speed-of-light conclusion. "I'll be right back," I said to Lindsey. "I'll meet you outside."

She looked at me with confusion. "Where are you going?"

"I'll be right back!" I called again as I walked away.

Stealthy as a trained international assassin, I went to the back of the store, behind the Elfa Design Center, so that I might circle around the perimeter and catch Ben red-handed in the plastic tub aisle. What I'd learned from my parents was that denial, as well as plausible deniability, could keep a woman stuck in some bad situations. If I were to confront Ben directly in the moment, he might make up some excuse, turn on the gaslights, accuse me, like Wolf had, of being off my meds.

So instead I crept over to the end of aisle three and pulled out my phone, in order to record my boyfriend's conversation with the woman whom I believed was his other girlfriend. Which seemed like the only reasonable course of action given my compromised position.

From this position—namely, kneeling on the scuffed linoleum, straw from my huaraches scratching the back of my thighs as I crouched, I couldn't see these two shameless adulterers. But I could hear them. Each word made my chest ache.

"What about this one?" the woman said, her voice melodic.

"I don't think that's big enough," Ben replied.

"But your mother has so much stuff!"

Oh, I thought, so he'll talk to *her* about his mother, he'll talk to *Simone* about his mother, but he won't talk to me? He'll let *this* floozy help take care of his mother, and not me? I'd rather have caught Ben mid-coitus than in the midst of shopping for home goods with another woman. At least that could be chalked up to raw animal impulse. But this? This implied real intimacy, the banal intimacy of daily life, which is the majority of intimacy and, in truth, the one I'd never had.

Over the past few weeks I'd realized that's what I wanted the most: that banal intimacy with Ben. I would have done anything to cultivate it, banged notes over and over on that out-of-tune piano until Mozart finally came out of my fingertips. *Come, take a walk with me,* I wanted to be able to say to him, say until the day I died. *Even if we just talk about television and the weather, with you I will be happy.*

I hated myself all of a sudden, for allowing my hopes to float so high.

"Why don't we start with these," Ben was saying. "We can always come back. Didn't you want to get one of those pill organizers for her, too?"

In retrospect, I can see how this might have served as a useful context clue. But I was so far afield I wasn't thinking too much about context, including my surroundings. Which is why I missed the sound of Ben's and his lady's footsteps, and why by the time they rounded the corner into my aisle I had only a split second to spring to my feet and sprint toward the exit.

I only got halfway down the aisle when I heard Ben say, "Casey? Is that you?"

I whirled around.

"Ben? Ben! Oh my God, I didn't see you there! Hi! Wow, what a coincidence!" I was shifting my weight and swinging my arms around like a rubber-boned lunatic. "I'm here with Lindsey, ha ha. This is 'our place'! Your place too, looks like. Me, oh, well I just got some new closetry!"

"What were you doing just now?" he said. His face had that focused, penetrating expression.

"You know?" I said. "Ha, I can't even remember!"

I came back here looking for"—my eyes scanned the aisle—"bathroom drawer organizers, but then I realized, I don't need them! Plus Lindsey already checked out; she's waiting outside. Anyway, I should let you go. I'm Casey, by the way," I said to the woman, waggling my fingers. "Casey Pendergast. Friend of Ben's. Nice to meet you."

"I'm . . . Maria," the woman said.

Ben had kept that same funny expression on his face. "She's my mom's new in-home aide. We're moving her to the downstairs bedroom so she doesn't have to worry about the stairs."

"Your mom's new in-home care person!" I said. "The downstairs bedroom!"

The cube that I had cubed was morphing, the white-hot clarity in my brain dissolving back into a muddle. The only sense I could make of this snarl in my brain was: me make mistake. And also: he know me make mistake.

I had to get out of there. I started inching backward. "Oh, wow, that's great! I'm so glad you guys found each other. Not found-found, ha ha. Anyway, like I said, Lindsey's waiting for me outside, so I better"—I stuck my thumb toward the exit—"be on my merry way. But, wow—*so* great to meet you, Maria, and so great to see you, Ben, and see you guys together. Not together-together, but—okay I'll talk to you later, yeah?" I was shuffling away with increasing speed. "Cool, cool. Bye!"

I turned and ran.

Outside, I found Lindsey sitting forlornly on the curb. She looked like a kid whose mom had forgotten to pick her up after swim practice. I plopped down beside her and rested my head for a second on her shoulder. Her corn-silk hair brushed against my temple.

"Everything okay?" she said.

I sighed and shook my head.

She put a thin arm around my shoulder. "Me neither."

"I keep messing up," I said. On the *up,* my voice broke in half.

"We all do," she said, and kissed the top of my head. The gesture reminded me of my mother. Not because Louise had made such gestures, but because I had always wished she would.

After a minute, I pulled my head back. I looked at her; she looked back at me.

"I hurt people," I said. "All the time. I don't want to hurt people anymore."

Now it was Lindsey's turn to sigh. "I dunno. I think hurting people is inevitable."

"Why?" I rubbed my forehead with the back of my hand.

She shook her head, shrugged slightly. "'Cause we're afraid," she said simply. "And most of us don't know how to be anything else."

I dug through my ear. It was filled with wax. There was stubble on my legs and my stomach was pushing against the button of my shorts and I wondered if all women felt as disgusting inside their skin as I sometimes did. I looked down at the pavement.

"I ruined things with Ben."

"You did? What? Where? How?"

"He was in The Container Store. I thought he was with another woman."

"He was?!"

"No. I just thought he was. It was his mom's *aide*."

Lindsey shifted her weight. "I was going to say, he didn't seem like the type—"

I laughed despairingly. "Oh, he's not. But apparently I still needed to spy on him? He caught me hiding in the air fresheners."

Lindsey winced. "Oh, Casey."

"I don't know what to do," I said, burying my face in my hands. "I really don't."

"You can apologize. Go back in there. Maybe he'll understand."

I peered through the cracks in my fingers and looked across the parking lot. "Or *maybe*," I said, "we could just go to Applebee's."

Lindsey smiled gently. "If you want to make jokes, that's fine," she said. "But you never have to, not with me."

"Yeah, but," I said through my fingers. "How else can I make you love me?"

Lindsey didn't make me go talk to Ben again.

I think she realized I didn't have it in me. So instead we stood and walked with our arms around each other's shoulders to an oasis that served neon drinks and boneless wings and chicken quesadillas: not alleviating the other's sorrow, oh no, we could never do that, but keeping watch over it, keeping it company.

I didn't hear from Ben until that night. When he finally did call, he told me a story. He had spent, he said, four years with a woman in his early twenties, a woman who'd been with a few really terrible men. Ben did everything to help her feel safe—he called her every night, only had sex at her initiation, apologized and beat himself up every time he did or said something that she called a "trigger"—right up until the day she told him she was having an affair with her boss.

"I can't go through something like that again," he said. "I'm always trying to understand where you're coming from better—but the bullying? The spying? I can't get behind it."

"Okay," I said faintly. I was sitting on my bed, knees hugged to my chest. My windows were open, and I could hear the cacophony of summer birds in the maple. I leaned one cheek on my knee and looked outside. It was the kind of twilight past the beautiful, wistful blues and purples, the time when darkness was inevitable and the day surely done.

"Why did you *do* that today? Right after we—" he started to say more, but his voice was rising, and he stopped himself.

"I know," I said. "I'm a really messed up person."

"I think you're an incredibly special person," he said. His voice caught a little. "I'm just sad things didn't work out."

I startled. "Didn't work out?"

He exhaled audibly. "I need a little time, that's all."

"Please don't go," I said, my voice trembling. "I love you. I can trust you, I'm doing better. It'll just take time."

It was the first time I said it. The *I love you*, I mean. Plain and clear, they were the most honest words I'd said in a long time. In response my breath deepened, I sat up a little straighter, the uncanny feeling I'd been fighting all day dissipated. The whole body changes when you tell the truth; it's just that most of us, as we grow up and forget our bodies, forget this too.

After a silence he said, "I love you too." I could tell he was crying a little because his voice sounded like he'd swallowed a bubble of water. "But I can't do this again."

"Please don't go," I said again. Now I was really crying, for the second time that day.

"I hope everything goes well for you," he said.

"Don't worry about the office—it'll be fine. Most of my work is virtual anyway."

I choked out, "I'm not even thinking about the office."

There was everything and nothing more to say, so we hung up. With my phone still warm in my lap, I put my forehead on my knees and wept.

But it's not enough to cry, is it? For years I'd let crying settle matters. It was a necessary release. I luxuriated in the physical catharsis, felt as clean and refreshed by it as I did after a bath, refusing to allow the tears to reveal the information they contained. Action, for example. Words. A hard examination of what led to them in the first place. Without these steps, crying was sex without love, work without purpose. Fine, important, pleasurable at times. But not enough.

But what was enough? I had never been enough, that much I knew. We are born into this world with a great nameless absence. And it was haunted by this absence, this terrible, yawning lack, that I finally, some hours later, fell asleep.

11

WHAT HAPPENS IN VEGAS

The next day, Monday, I awoke and took inventory. Best friend, gone. Boyfriend, gone. Sabbatical, not happening. I dressed grimly in all black and went into work, resigned to making the best out of the remaining shambles of my existence. I consoled myself with the fact that I still had fifteen percent equity and a ten percent raise, not to mention Lindsey's friendship and my new Elfa closetry. Yes, there were always ways to look on the bright side. Even when your life is in flames, the light can be very pretty. Not!

Celeste called me into her office first thing and gave me the dossier for my final assignment— the tenth asset—before we took Nanü to the VCs. In short, I was to harpoon the white whale of Blue Ocean. A white whale that turned out to be, of all people, Julian North, the one who'd gotten Celeste interested in this Nanü business in the first place. And of all places, she needed me to harpoon him in Vegas, where the annual American Book Fair was taking place.

Celeste explained that the ABF was where publishers and authors acted as hype men for their upcoming books in the hopes that booksellers, jacked up on booze and flattery, would choose those books to be the ones facing out on the shelves. Apparently there were whispers going around the publishing industry, rumors about what Celeste was up to, though all the contracts with Nanü were still confidential and out of the public eye until autumn. Celeste didn't want to start a big publicity push until we'd secured funding and the paperwork to sell PR was final.

Indeed, only Ben's social media activity with Waterman Quartz was live, but even that little partnership was ruffling some feathers. The party line among writers and publishers was that they were completely against the quote-unquote corruption of the literary arts and this quote-unquote disgraceful turn into advertising. But Celeste was well-connected enough that she could burrow beneath the party line, and the unofficial word was that there were plenty more writers ready to cede their quote-unquote artistic integrity if we had the right pitch and dollar amount ready.

Including Julian, who in the years since I saw him speak in college had amassed a number of national awards, as well as publishing one novel that climbed to the top of the bestseller lists. Julian's wife had been diagnosed with a rare and aggressive form of breast cancer. Julian was already two years late on turning in his next novel, a sequel to the bestseller, but apparently, devoted as he was, he was unable to work with his wife so sick.

The treatments weren't going well, either, and they were so expensive that they'd devoured the last of his advance. Word on the street was that he was desperate for cash to keep up with the medical bills. "He may be a literary lion," Celeste said, and sighed. "But even lions have to eat."

Upon hearing this news, instead of feeling uncertainty or moral circumspection, I thought: my God, perhaps my luck is turning already! I guess we want so badly to be okay that even when we're in a pot of hot water and sweating like mad, we're telling ourselves all sorts of encouraging stories, stories like, hmmm, maybe this hot water is good for me, as it will release what Gwyneth Paltrow calls "toxins"; or, oh please, there's no *way* this warm comfy bath could ever become something nefarious and boiling! As Susan always said, my optimism bordered on the deranged, and one of the key symptoms of derangement is selective amnesia.

But look, Vegas was my favorite city in the world, and I was going there to remeet my literary hero, who had already reset my moral compass once, back in college. Maybe, in some limited way, he could do so again. I was getting so wound up and excited to see him that I didn't really listen to Celeste talk about the product that Julian had been pegged to hawk—a new tablet created by a yet-unknown American-made electronics company—and its sexy attributes designed specifically for writers, like voice transcription and front lighting and a stylus in the shape of a quill. I imagined a scenario in which Julian, so impressed with my professionalism and spunk, asked me if I might leave my job at Nanü in order to become his full-time . . . something. Assistant, maybe.

"One more thing," Celeste said as I stood up to leave.

A nervous chill passed through me. I was hoping Ben hadn't contacted her about the end of our romantic liaison out of some weird ethical obligation. I was also hoping Wolf hadn't contacted her out of some need to be a giant dick. "What's up?"

"I was talking to Ben," she said, "at the picnic." She folded her hands on her desk. "He mentioned you were interested in taking acting classes. Said you'd always loved performing and were looking to get involved after a long hiatus."

"He said that?"

She laughed drily. "It was quite . . . touching. It was clear from the conversation that he thinks quite highly of you."

"Well—" I said, clenching my jaw. "I wouldn't say that's always—"

"It got me thinking," she said, and opened her desk drawer. "I wanted to do something for you anyhow, to thank you for the long hours and travel you've put in this summer, a gesture. I've met a number of producers and agents through our dealings with Ellen. If it's all right with you, I'd like to set up a meeting with one or two of them after you get back from Vegas."

"With me?" I said, abashed. "Why would you do that?"

"I know—" Celeste paused to clear her throat. Her words were coming out starched and stiff. "That I don't seem like a particularly—emotional person. But I've grown quite—I suppose— fond of you over the years, and tried my best to cultivate your—talents—and if there is a way for us—ahem"—she coughed slightly—"me—to better use your talents . . . Well—I'm all ears." She sped up and re-professionalized herself once she arrived at the logistics. "I've spoken briefly to an agent who's currently pitching a reality show about twentysomethings working in the city, and she'd like to meet you and see if you're a good fit for the programming. It's also a good way to get Nanü exposure, since they'd probably want to film you in the office."

"Oh my God!" I said, clapping a hand over my mouth in surprise. "I don't—"

I rummaged around the drawers in my brain for something to say, but all I was finding were fortune cookie wrappers and platitudes from yoga teachers. "I don't know what to say," I said, dropping my hand. "Seriously. I'm gobsmacked."

No, an ensemble role on a cable reality show was not exactly what I'd always wanted, but look, at this point, it was probably the closest I could get. I felt my eyes fill with tears, goddamn it, *again*. I was turning into a Lifetime movie. "What I mean is, I'm honored," I said. "Sorry." I dabbed at the corner of my eyes. "I just—I guess I'm also surprised—"

"I'm not as cold and heartless as you all think I am," she said with a faint smile. "You've done a lot for PR this year. You've worked hard, you've wowed everyone you've met, you haven't once complained—"

Well, I thought, not to *you*.

"—and it's about time you were acknowledged."

I wanted to run behind Celeste's desk and hug her. *Mama!* But before I could, she had opened her laptop back up and started typing. "Thank you," I said.

"Don't thank me," she said, putting up a palm in farewell, and I could tell she meant it.

When I was a kid, I had a book of Greek myths that Louise had given to me for my birthday. I remember being constantly appalled by how stupid some of these characters were. "Don't turn around, dummy!" I would shout at Orpheus when he was bringing Eurydice back from the underworld. "She's your mother, you idiot!" I'd yell to Oedipus. But I didn't yell anything to myself that day because fatal flaws are like Magic Eye pictures: you can't see them when you're too close up. It's all just colorful mush.

Thrilled with how the Fates rewarded as capriciously as they punished, I played hooky from work the rest of the afternoon, went home and shut the blinds and, calling it research, rewatched the entire last season of *The Real Housewives* with Ellen Hanks. Boy, is it fun, living in a fantasy. I turned my phone off and got a little day drunk off red wine and ate a lot of popcorn straight from the microwave bag and found myself thinking, God, I am the best and my life is the best and just forget about all that other stuff, Casey! Sure, you had a rough few days, weeks, months. But who cares? Who cares, really? Not you, Casey. Now you've got a pile of money and a reality TV show waiting, you're back and better and you're going to Vegas, a place where there is no past, no future, nothing beyond whatever glorious temptation is right in front of you! You'll be happy now, Casey. You *are* happy. You are. Aren't you?

The American Book Fair was like nothing I'd ever seen before. Or maybe it was like a lot of things I'd seen before, it's just that Vegas made my adrenaline levels much higher and my sense receptors more alert. On the floor of the convention center in Caesars Palace, the best and brightest of the book industry held court. They stood behind skirted tables and alongside huge posters advertising the next greatest best American novel, or memoir, or hard-nosed nonfiction. The crowd at the fair was mixed in the way of gender, and about as mixed in skin color as, say, a gallon drum of vanilla ice cream.

I'd been to advertising conventions before over the years, and though this was a different industry, the interpersonal dynamics were pretty much the same. You could spot the power brokers right away: they tended to wear pointier-toed shoes and more tailored shirts, their skin as bronzed and moisturized as if they'd just stepped off a plane from St. Barts. You could also tell them apart by the circle of admirers that inevitably surrounded them, mostly younger men, who seemed to know more intuitively than women that one way to gain power was just to find it and stand near it and never let it out of your sight. For if you caught these power brokers at the right moment, they would shine some of that power upon you, not altruistically, but with the selfish pleasure of a benefactor. I've always admired the naked ambitions of these sorts of strapping, oxford-shirted, hands-in-the-pockets aw-shucks young men—though I've always wanted to punch them, too.

On the other hand, the women in the convention hall spoke mostly as equals, in small groups, among themselves and with enthusiasm, either unaware of the subtly shifting movements of power or, more likely, already exhausted by it. Not that everyone fell so neatly across these gender lines—but then again, they kind of did.

Then, there were the writers. Oh, the writers! Flown in by their publishing houses, you could spot them right away, too: looking awkward and feral and stoop-shouldered, shuffling around with downward slopes to their mouths, clearly parched for solitude. Yet here they were, forced to be on display, asked to speak to, say, a blowsy gal named Mary Jo who ran an independent bookstore in Boise and was *very* curious about where they got their ideas.

I felt sympathy for the writers. A former poet laureate lurked blackly in one corner of the hall like the Phantom of the Opera; a National Book Award finalist desperately drank cola after diet cola while three old women buzzed around him like gingham flies. Many of them stood by themselves, dazed, in the middle of the room, as the rest of the industry devoted itself to itself.

The exception among these writers was Julian North—my Vegas raison d'être. He was giving the keynote address that evening, and I spotted him in the hall right away, because people seemed to be pulled toward him, as I had been years ago, as if by some horizontal gravity. He looked similar to how I remembered him: not attractive, necessarily, but tall and trim, and with his salt-and-pepper hair, well-cut slacks, and thick square eyeglasses, he was clearly improving with age.

Though my guess was, even before he was famous, he'd always been able to draw people to him. There was an energy that radiated from him that translated into an expressiveness in his face, a receptivity in his gestures, which in turn led people to feel immediately familiar around him. Women and men alike fluttered across his perimeter, touched his sleeve. And Julian, instead of, like many writers, keeping himself at a physical or emotional remove from his admirers, appeared to absorb everything they said and did.

I thought about introducing myself right there on the floor of the convention, but eventually I decided I didn't want to enter the scrum of devotees. Other people's hero worship grossed me out.

Instead I wandered around the hall. I'd chosen my clothes for that day seriously because I wanted Julian to take me seriously, and the only control I had over that, I believed, was through my appearance. I'd picked out a black crepe sheath, black stilettos, and a black crepe blazer I draped over my shoulders, and as I walked I carried my black leather attaché in what I hoped was a very serious manner. Not much in the convention interested me, and I ignored the outposts of consumer goods for sale, book lights and bookmarks and e-readers and leather-bound journals that tied around the middle. Bored and with the bourgeois ennui that strikes at the heart of every midafternoon, I was just about to make like a celebrity couple and split when I heard the nasal honk of a Jersey accent. "Casey? Casey Pendergast? That you?"

Well, well, well. Who should hurtle up behind me in a cloud of perfume, cigarette smoke, and ball-busting vitality but Ellen Hanks? Though we'd emailed some over the summer, I hadn't seen her in person since she'd come to the offices for the first and only time that spring. "Ellen!" I yelped joyfully, turning around and giving her a big hug. "What the hell are you doing here?!"

I was so relieved I wanted to laugh. The Fates were kind! They knew I needed a friend. Vegas wasn't a place for the solo traveler, and neither were most conventions, unless you were a sociopath or, I guess, a billionaire autocrat. Together Ellen and I could bond over being fish out of water with all these publishing types. Or maybe more like walruses out of water, warm-blooded and prone to bellowing.

"I could say the same thing to you!" she pulled back and hit me on the biceps like a softball coach. "Look at you! You look good!" she said to everyone within earshot. "You working out?

Your arms look good. My God, we've got a professional right here!"

"Ha. I wish. You have no idea how happy I am to see you!"

"Oh, I have an idea," Ellen said, and started dragging me by the arm. She looked the same as she had a few months before, tucked into an airtight dress with towering heels, done up with stage hair and makeup. "This thing is a joke. My publisher told me to come here and shill my book, and can you believe it? No one wants to talk about my book! They don't even know who I am! I told one of these broads I was on television, and you know what she said? She says, 'I don't own a television.' Who doesn't own a television? Just because I didn't go to college or write some book nobody's heard of about the . . . who knows . . . war in Iraq. I may've had a ghostwriter, but how many vodka companies have you started, honey?" She linked her arm through mine, though continued to propel me across the room. "What are *you* doing here?"

I told her—she was a friend of Celeste's and a client, I was pretty sure confidentiality didn't matter—I was there to talk with Julian about a sponsorship deal for a new venture PR was running. At the name Ellen rolled her eyes. "That guy. Everyone here's jerking him off every chance they get."

"He's an amazing writer," I said. "Like, pretty

much my favorite writer of all time. Where are we going, by the way?"

"I don't care if he wrote the freaking Bible, it doesn't mean he's not an asshole." Ellen looked like she was about to say something else, but she stopped herself. "We're going to get a drink is where we're going. I just got booked on *Dancing with the Stars* for next season. You're coming with me, I won't take no for an answer—"

Before I could answer her, she turned around, put her arm up, and shouted to what seemed to me no one in particular, "Barry! Barry watch the table, will you? Us girlies are gonna get a drink."

Some distance away a tatted and bepierced man, bald and the size of a tank, gave an affirmative wave.

"That's my fuckboy," Ellen said conspiratorially. "Isn't he great?"

At a bar called Numb, situated right in the center of the gambling floor, Ellen and I ordered supersized frozen cocktails, complete with lids and straws, so you could take them with you while you gambled or swam in one of the numerous pools. Mine was called a Numb Cappuccino!

Ellen gave me a mile-a-minute update on everything that was going on with her—arguments with her publisher, arguments with her producers, arguments with her assistant, haggle, hustle, money, money—which was long enough to get half a vat of alcoholic slushie in my bloodstream. After that, I proceeded to spill the beans on what happened with Wolf and Susan, what happened with Ben, what happened, or might happen, with the casting agent Celeste knew and the reality show I might be getting. "Are you kidding me right now?!" Ellen said about the latter, smacking me on the arm. "That's incredible. I *told* Celeste you were a star. See? Should I make some calls? I know everyone in that town. I could twist some arms for the two of you."

"You don't have to do that," I said, blushing, or flushing from the alcohol.

Ellen looked incredulous. "Oh please. You think you're gonna get anywhere with that attitude? Listen to me. You've got to know what you want"—she smacked one fist in her other palm—"and grab it"—*smack*—"and not"—*smack*—"let"—*smack*—"go. You say you want your man back? Well then, Casey, you gotta *do* something about it! Though be careful, don't do what I did, I've got two restraining orders against me.

"And that bastard," she said, changing subjects abruptly while sucking down something called a Purple Haze. "That Wolf guy. First of all, who names their kid Wolf? He sounds typical. Typical bastard. Reminds me of the time my ex-husband tried to take me to the cleaners after I started making money, saying I owed him back alimony. Doesn't matter, I made his life hell for the six months we were in court." She drank more Purple Haze. "And I loved every minute of it."

"I want to make Wolf's life hell." I was getting mad all over again. "More than anything I want to make things right for Susan. I could prove that she wrote these poems, but she doesn't want me anywhere near her, and anyhow Wolf isn't even remotely afraid of me. He's swinging his dick all over the Internet. The other day he *literally* tweeted 'I'm king of the world' and it wasn't even a cultural reference!"

I took a sip of Numb Cappuccino! I heard the empty *kkkk* sucking sound of the straw that meant I was getting to the bottom. "He feels invincible, and I *hate* it."

Ellen scoffed. "Jerk-off." She pointed at my empty slushie. "You want another one?"

Nothing brings women together more than shared fury over men. Well, that and sharing failed attempts at weight loss. We explored our fury for a long time, let me tell you, until it gradually transitioned to a vast exchange of compliments and "I love you"s and two additional swimming-pool-sized cocktails. We hugged until we lost balance and nearly fell off our bar stools. Other patrons wandered toward and away from the bar, Hawaiian-shirted, eyes glazed from booze and poker chips and oxygen, unfazed by two loud and excitable women validating the shit out of each other. We were there for around two hours, maybe; the thing about Vegas is that it eliminates time. With no windows, day bleeds into night bleeds into a permanent and hazy golden hour where everything is allowed, nothing is forbidden, and indulgence is the highest form of living.

"So what are you going to do about this Wolf guy anyway?" Ellen said finally, circling back to our earlier conversation after our peak drunkenness had faded to a pleasant buzz.

I threw up my hands. "I *literally* have no idea. But now I'm mad, and I want to get even. You have to help me think of something better than just flying to New York and ripping him a new one."

"Okay. Well—wait." Ellen cocked her head. "What're the odds Wolf's in Vegas *right now?* You said he's a writer, didn't you?"

"I dunno," I said. "Oh! But you know how we could figure it out?"

I pulled out my phone and opened the Twitter app.

Sure enough, Wolf had tweeted that he was in #vegas for #ABF. *laughing for no reason cum party w me,* he'd written. "UGH," I said, and threw the phone down on the bar.

"He's here, isn't he?!" Ellen said with glee.

She leaned over to look at the screen, putting her elbows on the bar. She snapped her fingers. "Bartender, can I get a napkin and a pen? Oh, this is good. This is really good. The timing is perfect, we just gotta figure out the details. Let me think—

"Okay," she tapped on the napkin and pushed it toward me after she'd scribbled a few things down. "You're gonna love this. Here's what we're gonna do."

Ellen's diabolical scheme was perfect and made-for-television and precisely this: she'd have her lawyers—or, more likely, one of their summer interns—send Wolf one of the firm's standard cease-and-desist letters. The letter would have to be true, of course, but as Ellen put it, "there is such a thing as true*ish*." The point of the letter was not to *really* sue Wolf, but to scare him into *believing* we could and would, which would compel him, finally, to excise Susan's work from his manuscript. In order to really scare him, we had to be, shall we say, playful with the language about the proof we had and the possible repercussions of his plagiarism.

Sending a letter like that would have been more than enough to assuage my guilty conscience. But because this was Ellen, and Ellen didn't do anything halfway, she declared we had to raise the stakes even higher. "I don't want this asshole messing with you ever again," she said. "What he did to you in New York?" She wagged a finger. "That shit don't fly with Ellen Hanks."

The latter was one of Ellen's most popular taglines from her TV show.

So the second part of the plan was to have Barry, Ellen's bodybuilding fuckboy, deliver the letter to Wolf in person. Ellen said, "Barry'll do what he needs to do to make sure the message gets through, if you know what I mean." She said this completely deadpan, thumping her fist into her open palm, and though I had an urge to guffaw, I held it back. Sometimes you just had to succumb to the outsized reality of a reality TV star.

The lesson I took from the experience was this: whoever said revenge wasn't sweet hadn't plotted revenge while getting brain freeze from a Numb Cappuccino! with a minor celebrity. Revenge wasn't just sweet; it was an opiate. The fog I'd been living with ever since Ben broke up with me—no, since Susan broke up with me— no, since I'd gotten home from Mort and my mother in Milwaukee—no, since I signed on with Nanü four months back—started to clear, and I came upon the glorious sense of purpose I'd been searching for. I felt sunny as a solstice, happy as a ham. Wolf's end, God willing, would be my beginning.

"Why are you doing this?" I said, after Ellen had gotten her lawyer on the phone and texted

Barry. "I mean, don't get me wrong. I don't think I've ever been more grateful for another human being. But—why?"

Ellen sighed and crossed her legs, which was difficult, given the tightness of her dress. "The real reason?" She shrugged. "I like you. If I like you, I like you, it's not that complicated. Where I come from, we look out for our own. And some of these people out there?" She twirled her index finger. "They're awful. They're fucking nuts. Mean, too. And when it comes to people, you're smart, Casey, but don't take this the wrong way, you're real dumb, too."

"What do you mean?" But Ellen's attention had moved away to the casino floor. She was watching something, or someone, but in the blur of lights and sounds and people and desperation masquerading as a good time, it was hard to tell what.

"You know what I need?" she said finally. "I need a manicure. What time is it?"

I checked my phone. "Shit!" It was seven-thirty in the evening. Julian's keynote was at eight.

Ellen said, "Vegas's a time warp, what can I say. Last time I was here I ended up sitting on the floor of the Wynn at five in the morning, my dress up to my waist, and some guy named Stefano feeding me hamburgers. No idea how I got there."

"I've gotta go!" I stood up, pulled my wallet

305

out of my purse to throw down my company card, but Ellen waved her hand away. "Please. This one's on me."

"Okay. Thank you. I mean it. For everything. Oh, and Ellen?" She turned around, and I threw my arms around her. She smelled overpoweringly of perfume and hair products. "I love you."

"You nut job," she said into my hair. "I love you, too."

By the time I got back to the convention center hall, it was nearly empty. The few remaining people were putting white sheets over their book tables and turning off LCD monitors. Even though the ABF folks had done their best to make their event seem hip and glamorous during the day, as the space closed for the night—the cleaning staff was already dragging in vacuums and wheeling in carts—it made me sad to look at what was left once all the shiny, important people were gone. For a convention celebrating what always seemed to me like a necessary human endeavor—using language to make sense of our lives—the room looked awfully small. Outside the hall the rest of Vegas went blithely by, engaged in less demanding pastimes.

It felt wrong, I guess, to see that these books and their guardians meant so little to the rest of Caesars. But of course, people hadn't come to Caesars to read. They'd come to gamble and drink and pretend to be someone else for a while, someone richer and cleverer and unburdened by the past, someone who took risks and said what they meant and wasn't so stinking afraid all the time. In short, people came here to forget their burdens, to immerse themselves in a reality unfamiliar to them and exciting in its unfamiliarity, to remove some steam in this temporary game of make-believe.

But what they didn't know, or maybe they did but had forgotten, was that books did that too. When I was a kid, and I found myself lonely, or afraid, or fed up with my parents or teachers or friends at school, I read. Because books, the good ones, the ones you hold on to and come back to, they never disappoint. They're the best kind of escape because, instead of leading you away from yourself, they end up circling you back to yourself, nice and easy, helping you see things not just as they are, but as you are too.

And though you'd think this circling would be the last thing you'd want, seeing as escapism was what you were after in the first place, it ends up being the best part. Because the people who made those books, they put themselves on the line to do so. They spent a long time working; they gave you the best of what lay inside them, though this may have hurt them too. And you can feel that in the good books; you might even call that feeling love. A feeling so much better than distraction, than pleasure, than obliteration, but boy, so much harder to do.

Yes, I wish I could have said this to those people snapping selfies with Cleopatra, or walking into pillars buried in their phones, or eating or drinking or smoking like crazy just trying to get to—what? where?—that infinity beyond loneliness and fear. But who was I to talk? I, Casey. Settling scores by threats and bodybuilders named Barry whilst press-ganging into the advertising industry.

The keynote was in another hall on the other side of this floor. I went to the bathroom first and splashed water on my face. The drinking, Ellen's kindness, thinking about how much I loved books, it'd all made me a little sentimental and red-eyed. I looked hard at my reflection in the mirror and tried, for a moment, to make peace with what I saw. Not just with how I looked, but what was inside.

Still frowning with the effort, I got a text from Ellen. *Barry says your guys taken care of ;)*

Yes!!!!!!! I wrote back immediately, adding a biceps emoji. Ah well, I'd give peace a chance later.

I snuck into the back of the packed hall to listen to Julian's keynote. It had just started when I arrived, and the audience was hushed, rapt; you could hear a pen drop. I plopped into one of the few open chairs in the back and made, I *guess,* what could have been construed as excessive noise: unwrapping a piece of gum, shrugging off my blazer, trying to turn off my phone but accidentally making it ring, cracking open a can of sparkling water I'd stolen from the convention. When a few guys in front of me turned and frowned, I shot them a look and pumped my shoulders back like *Come at me, bro.* What did they think this was, church?

But actually, that's exactly what they thought it was. Art is as fine a substitute for religion as, say, CrossFit or political ideology, and the secular humanists who packed the hall looked to Julian for direction just like Catholics look to the pope and hippies to tarot. As a prophet, Julian was riveting. The subject of the speech he gave wasn't particularly original—asking the publishing industry how to remain relevant in the media-saturated digital age was by then well-worn territory—but as any good orator knows: it's not *what* you say, it's *how.* As I listened, transported, it became clear that Julian was a master not only at writing, but at delivering his writing in a way that felt, well, *mighty.* His cadence was full of pregnant pauses and alternately hushed and soaring tones, and with his words he opened up the possibilities of the human condition, asked us to expand the capacities of the heart. To an inherently sentimental audience like this one, Julian's connecting of a smaller, more prosaic truth (people need to read more or this industry will become extinct) with a larger and loftier one (we must help people face who they are without flinching) felt like gospel. How could I not love him for giving me this feeling?

I was not alone. Julian was mobbed with admirers and hangers-on after his Q&A, and I figured the only way to get to him was through a war of attrition. Leaning against a fake Roman column, I drank the black coffee ABF had provided for the occasion and shoveled a piece of sheet cake in my mouth, having forgotten once again, or maybe having been too nervous, to eat much that day. The room was full and throbbing with inspiration, and I tried to capture some of it while I thought about how I might convince Julian to get on board.

Beyond the obvious problems of his sick wife's medical bills, Julian didn't appear to be someone motivated by money—a sure sign he'd grown up with a fair amount of it. So I couldn't just appeal to his wallet. No, Julian's entrée into Nanü had to be ideological, something about the revolution starting from within. Promoting a tablet that had custom-made features for writers was a way to combat the war between literature and digital culture he had spoken about in his address. There was no need to fear technology; we had only to make sure we were using it in a way that furthered our empathic capacities. Yes, I thought, high from the sugar, as I grabbed another piece of cake. I was sure that was the right approach.

Time went by indeterminately. I drank more coffee and ate more cake until my hands shook. I was nervous about talking to Julian, infinitely more nervous than I'd been with the other writers. Eventually the crowd thinned; I held my space against the Roman column, until, at what seemed at the time to be my great fortune, a figure appeared at my side.

"You must be Casey Pendergast," Julian North said.

I jumped a mile. "Who, me?!"

He laughed. "Who else?"

"How do you know my name?"

"Celeste Winter told me to be on the lookout for a tall blonde with legs like a gazelle. You seemed to fit the bill. Julian North." He stuck out a hand. We shook.

Something small pinged inside me when he said the thing about a gazelle, but I brushed it off. Just look at what happened with Ben. I was always overreacting. "We've met once before," I blurted out. "You came to my college and spoke a long time ago. You signed my book—it was because of you that I became an English major."

"No kidding." Julian waved goodbye to someone behind me. "I'll take the compliment, don't get me wrong, but my guess is you would've become an English major anyway."

"Why do you say that?"

He smiled knowingly. "My work's made me useless in most ways, but understanding human nature isn't one of them."

"Well—" I said. And I did not know what to say after that.

I figured we would meet up the next day to have a proper chat, seeing as he probably needed to get back to his wife. But it was Julian who suggested that we get something to eat, explained he hadn't had a chance to get dinner before the talk and was rightfully starved. "Me too!" I explained. I thought but did not say, *We have so much in common!*

As we walked out of the room, he put a gentlemanly hand on my back. This seemed normal. Everything Julian did seemed normal, or even better than normal. Magical. Reporters who had written about Julian before always remarked on the force field he had around him. The only reality was what he alone created. Julian was a master at getting people to talk about their personal lives while saying nothing about his own.

Perhaps this explains why I have no clear recollection of moving to the sushi bar at Caesars and ordering a tableful of nigiri and rolls, as well as sake that arrived in an elegant ceramic pitcher. The next thing I remember is pouring my heart out to him about Susan. "She's the reason I came to see you in the first place," I said, dabbing my eyes with a starched napkin. "She's been my best friend for ten years, and now she won't even pick up the phone when I call. I can't believe I was so stupid, trusting this poet guy"—I didn't want to name Wolf directly—"to help get her published. I don't even think I *did* trust him; I just wanted to get back at him by using him like he'd used me."

Julian appeared completely immersed in what I said. "I understand," he said, looking into my eyes.

"You do?"

He nodded without breaking his gaze. I can't even tell you how good that felt. I felt, I suppose, above all else, honored. A man like Julian North, respecting me.

"Sorry to burden you like that," I said, abruptly looking away, because something pinged in me again, he was paying a little *too* much attention, it was making me uncomfortable. But no, actually, I corrected myself, that was my fault. I just wasn't good at accepting heartfelt gestures.

He shook his head and picked up a neatly cut rectangle of tuna. After he swallowed he said, in his mighty way, "It's not a burden. It's life. Everything you're saying, everything you've done, in my own way I've said and done too. Here, between the two of us, we get to be who we are."

"I can't even tell you how relieved it makes me

to hear you say that," I said. More tears popped out from the corners of my eyes. "I'm touched, truly. It's been just—devastating—"

Wait, why was I talking about Susan? How did we get here? Didn't I have a job to do? Julian poured us both another large thimbleful of sake. I tried to course-correct. "Anyway, sorry, I don't know how we got so off—how are you? How's your wife? I was really sorry when Celeste told me the news."

Julian put his chopsticks down and picked up his sake. "She's all right."

"I am sorry," I said. "I really am.

"Umm," I said after another pause. Julian could use silence to his advantage better than anyone I'd ever met. "Should we talk about business?"

He put his glass down and his elbows on the table, interlacing his fingers and placing his chin upon their tips. "Yes. Why not."

So I told him about the tablet and how I thought it might be a useful meeting of the minds between literature and technology, but because I could not keep anything back from that magnet inside of him, I also told him about my moral dilemma with Tracy Mallard and Mort Stillman. "If you're going to come on board with us," I said, and then, correctingly, "with *Nanü,* you should do so with your eyes wide open. That's where I'm at right now. I don't want to manipulate you into doing anything you're not a hundred percent okay with—not that I think I could. It's just you seem like such a good person, and you're doing such good work, and I figure the only way to do business with a good person is to try to be a good person back."

Julian looked at me intently. His eyes were strange, mostly blue, but with a splash of brown in one of them. "I admire you," he said.

"Oh." I blushed at the compliment. He had expressed neither interest nor disinterest in my proposal thus far, so I went on to say that I thought he could be an ambassador of literature in the digital age. "You're the agent of change!" I said. "That's you, everybody listens to you. You're, like, an American hero!"

He laughed a little. "Once one of my readers wrote to me. She was in a hospice in South Florida, stage four liver cancer. She knew she was going to die soon, she said, so she was writing letters to all her heroes, to let them know how much they'd meant to her.

"She could have left it at that, and I could have, too. But I didn't. I told my wife to cancel everything, and I got on the next plane to Florida. By the following morning I was sitting next to her in the hospice. She didn't want me to see her—the room smelled of decay, her body was failing—and she cried when I walked in the door. But I didn't leave. Her family was dead,

315

her husband had left her years before. So I stayed with her till the end."

My eyes filled with more tears. I didn't know why he was telling me this story, but I felt, again, so honored that he considered me a worthy addressee.

"Would you mind waiting here for a second while I go check on my wife?" he said. "I won't be long, and I can tell we're not done talking."

"Oh God, of course," I rushed to say. "Of course. I'll be right here."

Julian paused. "Unless you wanted to come with me? As I said, it'll only be a minute."

"Oh!" I said. This was a strange request. Wasn't it? In Julian's reality it was hard to say. But then again, I was drunk, so what the hell did I know? "Well . . . yeah, I guess," I said fumbling around for my purse. "I don't see why not."

The next thing I remember is standing in front of his door while he tried a couple times, unsuccessfully, to stick his key card in the slot, before the red light finally turned green and the door swung open.

"I'll be right here," I said, motioning to the hallway.

"Don't be silly," Julian said welcomingly. "Come on in."

"But your—" I coughed. "Your wife's sleeping, isn't she?"

Julian saw my expression, laughed. "Oh no. Jill

316

isn't here. I just want to call and check on her."

"Ohhhhhh!" I said. I looked around at my invisible peanut gallery in the hallway. "Right. Okay. Yeah, that makes sense. I mean, of course she's not here, since—"

Trailing off, I followed him.

In hindsight I know how woefully obvious this all seems. It always does, doesn't it? But the brain has a special mechanism that allows us to see only the parts of a person we wish to believe are there. Just look at my mother, spending her life with a man who lied to her half the time. Denial is part of being; dissonance isn't processed very well by our delicate little hippocampi. What I mean is, I started my conversation with Julian that night believing he was an amazing person, and it was an amazing person that I followed into this hotel room.

Julian's room was a suite, complete with a high-wattage view of the Strip. "Can I get you a drink?" he said, disappearing around the corner into what I assumed was a kitchen.

"I'm okay, thanks." I took a seat on an over-stuffed couch, which was part of a whole living area separate from a platformed area, atop which was a king-sized bed. I gave a little whistle. "Nice place you got here!"

"Isn't it? ABF put me up."

I crossed my legs and put my hands on my knees, trying to seem businesslike. Even though, sure, a few beats had felt funny, I was really enjoying our conversation. It was the first time a Nanü writer was speaking to me as a peer, an adult, and not just a kid or hired gun. I wondered how open Julian was to mentorship. I'd never had a male mentor before, only Celeste, but Julian seemed like a person I could learn a lot from about, well, being a person, and right now I needed someone like that in my life.

When he reappeared, he'd taken off his jacket and tie. But everyone needed to kick back after a long day. Hell, five minutes didn't pass from the time I usually got home to when I'd pulled on my sweatpants.

No, it was only when he sat right next to me on the couch, when there were at least four other pieces of furniture to sit upon, that I got another ping. My belly, all of a sudden, began to hurt. A tremor, too, in my brain: on the right side, a quiver, like something was bending that I could not keep straight.

"So tell me more about this tablet," he said.

I smiled, partly with relief. This was about work, after all! I turned to face him. But before I could, he had put a hand on my thigh and was leaning forward, brushing his lips to my neck.

I jerked back. "Oh—ah—what? Sorry—"

"It's okay," he murmured, and leaned forward to kiss me again.

"No!" The sound of shock. "I mean—what are you doing?"

"What do you mean, what am I doing?" he said into my ear, pushing my hands off my knees, pushing my legs apart, and beginning to push his fist between my thighs. In my nerves I felt equal parts arousal and revulsion. He kissed my neck more, and I sighed, not because I wanted to but from the involuntariness of bodily pleasure. Until the thing that had bent in my brain straightened with a snap, and the instinct that has kept humans surviving and women upright kicked in so hard that I jumped to my feet.

"What are you *doing?*" I said again, crossing my arms over my body protectively. "You have a *wife!*"

Julian didn't say anything, only sat there, the bulge in his trousers prominent. "Sit down," he said, as calmly as if we were discussing the weather. He patted the spot where I'd been. I suddenly realized how much older he was. My father's age, were he alive. "Come sit with me."

"No!"

"But you liked it, didn't you?" he said calmly. "You liked the way I felt between your legs?"

"No!" My face was hot, my fists clenched, my ankles crossed.

"I know you liked it," he said, and held up his fingers. "I felt you liking it."

"What the *fuck,* dude," I said. "That's it, I'm leaving." I turned on my heel and headed for the door. I was no longer thinking about work, my future, about venture capitalists, about equity, about books, about television. I was not thinking of Wolf or Susan or Ben or Lindsey or Celeste, Barry or Ellen or Vegas. I had one thought on my mind: I need to get out of here as fast as I can. I need—to *run.*

But before I could Julian was already on his feet, pushing me toward the door and then against it. He turned me roughly around and pulled my dress up around my waist, pinning me there with his body weight and one hand, unzipping his pants and fumbling with my underwear with the other.

"Get off of me!" I screamed, or I might have whimpered, maybe I didn't even say it, I can't remember. I thought, just for a second, about allowing what was about to happen, to happen. So that it might be over with, so that he might be gentle, so that I could close my eyes and remove the part of myself that mattered to another part of the room so that he could do what he wanted and I could be gone.

But I couldn't. I couldn't do that. Whatever hell was right in front of me, leaving my body would bring me no closer to home. The only way out was in, or was it through? The only way was impossible; the only way was necessary. So I gathered up all that impossibility and necessity into the center of myself, where a small girl was also weeping. And with a big inhale and every muscle in my body, with the herculean strength that allows mothers to lift cars off their pinned children, I slammed my body backward into Julian's.

He was weaker than I thought. He stumbled backward, lost his balance, and fell onto the floor. As soon I was above him I started kicking him, over and over, in my stilettos. Then I stomped on his groin. He howled, curled into the fetal position. "You're a monster!" I said. I was probably crying. "A monster!" Probably I said some other stuff too. I kicked him one last time, then I ran to the door.

But I couldn't open the door at first, because he'd bolted the door (he'd bolted the door?). I unbolted it and burst out into the hallway, slamming the door behind me. I was drenched in sweat. My hands were shaking and the only thought I had, only it wasn't a thought, it was an instinct, was that I needed to hit something. No, I needed to hit him. I was trembling so badly I wasn't sure I could keep my balance, but I took off running down the hall. Eventually I had to stop and take off my stilettos. Then, stilettos in hand, I kept running.

I was all the way to the elevators when I realized I'd left my purse in Julian's hotel room.

"Fuck!" I said, and slammed a palm into the closed metal doors. My dress was hanging off one shoulder, my feet blistered from the heels. I limped back to Julian's room with all the power I could muster, my adrenaline still spiked like crazy. The adrenaline decided the safest way for me to get my purse back was to make it a public affair.

"HEY ASSHOLE!" I said, pounding on the door. "I NEED MY PURSE!" God willing one of the neighbors would wake up and come out into the hall to serve as witness.

There was no peep from Julian. I kept at it. "HELLLLLOOOO!" I bellowed. "I KNOW YOU'RE IN THERE! GIVE ME MY PURSE!" What I wanted to say was: give me my purse so I can call the police and file a sexual assault report, but I figured that wouldn't get me very far. "LET ME IN! IT'S THE LEAST YOU CAN DO!"

Finally I heard a deadbolt turn. Julian stood there, still in his trousers and shirt, my purse dangling in his hand. "Hi there," he said, still eerily calm. "Here you go."

I looked at him, mouth agape, until I realized what he was up to.

"You should get some sleep," he said. And it was the way he said this—the absolute lack of culpability it implied, the sense that he hadn't done anything wrong—that caused the wild animal that lived in me to push the door open a little wider, and then push Julian back into his room with all my might. "I should get some sleep?!" this wild animal screamed. "Sleep?! You think I can sleep now?! After this?!"

Julian said nothing, just continued to look at me unflappably. I snatched my purse out of his hand, turned, and started running back toward the elevator. I was still shaking all over, for what else can a body do when trying to make sense of the utterly nonsensical.

I was so overtaken by my wild animal fury that I almost didn't see Wolf Prana in the doorway of his own hotel room. He had his phone out, facing me. He also had a black eye and a puffy lip.

He looked at me and smirked.

"What are you looking at?!" I said, or maybe screamed, I can't remember. Then I faked like I was coming after him. I shouted profanity. He flinched, as I knew he would, but kept his phone up the whole time.

When I got back to my room I took the longest shower of my life. I curled up in a ball beneath the rain spigot and wept. When I got out, I popped a Klonopin, and went to bed praying I would wake up and realize that none of this had ever happened. Through the drawn blinds I saw that it was nearly dawn.

12

. . . Doesn't Stay in Vegas

I still remember many of the stories in the book
of Greek myths my mother gave me. Zeus
turning Io into a cow, Daphne's dad turning her
into a tree, Philomela's tongue getting lopped off
by the king who lured her into the woods. But the
one I remember most is the one about Cassandra.
As the story goes, the god Apollo fell in love
with Cassandra; he wanted to bed her; she said
no. Instead of killing her, or turning her into an
animal, Apollo did something even worse. He
said: fine, leave, do as you like. Run away or
hide or rue the day you met me. But no matter
how far you run or how deep you hide or how
loud you scream, it's too late, your life is over:
I've cursed you. Wait and see. When you speak
the truth it will be heard as a lie, when you state
facts they will be laughed off as heresy. Say what
you will about the world, say what you will about
me, but you're done for, you're doomed, no one
will ever believe you. And you will go mad from
this. Wait and see.

I've spent a lot of time thinking about the last
few hours and minutes of my, if not innocence

exactly, then my obliviousness. When I woke up at noon, the first thing I did was reach for my phone, a reflex, and turn it off of airplane mode, which I'd done before bed so I could avoid being awakened by early morning emails chirping in my inbox. My home screen started flooding with messages, streaming them so fast my phone couldn't keep up. They whirred in quick succession, direct messages from Twitter and notifications to @caseyprepublic, an account I rarely used but kept around because it seemed like a professsional necessity, about five hundred Facebook notifications and the same number of emails, a text from Lindsey saying *HON WHAT'S GOING ON?,* a text from Annie that said *Are you ok?!?!?!* Even Jack had texted: *Call Lindsey were worried!*

Most alarmingly, there was a voicemail from my mother (which I ignored) and a text from Celeste: *Call me. Right away.*

It started to dawn on me, slowly at first, and then all at once, like what happened to the Red Sea after Moses was done with its parting and it came crashing down, that my life as I knew it was over. I didn't know why, exactly. I hadn't looked at the Internet yet. But there was a psychic supernovic flash of knowing. In the near dark distance, something was waiting for me. Something's wide jaws were opening.

My body started doing the strangest things.

I watched these strange things from a distance, with curious detachment. I saw myself jump out of bed, start walking around the room, drop my phone, pick it up again, drop it again, kick it, pick it back up. I saw myself go into the bathroom and come back out right away because I didn't remember why I'd gone in there in the first place. I walked around some more, dropped my phone again, tried to unlock the home screen but my hands were shaking too much, dropped to my knees. It was odd watching myself behave in this way; I was no more familiar to myself than a character in a movie. I saw myself clutch at my throat and tap my chest with my hands and look up toward the ceiling like a drowning person breaching the surface for a second. On some level I knew that was me, but I was neither in, nor of, my body. No. I was far away.

Humans, I would later learn, are the only mammals to have panic attacks. Something faulty in the wiring, or maybe faulty in the way we've set up our civilization, that we come to think we are dying when we are not really dying. Though the truth is that we are dying every moment, every day; becoming too conscious of this fact is the commonest source of our undoing.

Anyway, there I was, in a real bad way, unable to get my act together and certain that my act was about to collapse upon me, when my phone began to ring. Celeste's personal ring, which she had personally chosen. Grieg's "In the Hall of the Mountain King." Years of working for her had conditioned in me a response that nothing could stop, not even death or the threat of it. So I sat up, tried to slow my breath, finally got one deep breath in with a shudder, exhaled, and in the voice, as best I could, of a normal, collected, functional working woman, I answered the phone.

"Hi Celeste, sorry I missed your text." I didn't even bother trying to explain myself. "What's up?"

"What's up?" she said, her voice as tightly coiled as I'd ever heard it, coiled like a snake about to strike. "What's—*up?*"

Then she hung up.

I pulled the phone away from my ear and looked at it, dumbfounded. A text from Celeste rolled in. Just a link.

At nine o'clock that morning, the morning after Julian North assaulted me, prime time for news-dropping and feed-scrolling and the attendees at ABF sitting down at their laptops with a fresh cup of coffee, Wolf Prana tweeted to his thirty thousand followers the video he had taken the previous night of Julian and me facing off in his hotel doorway with the caption, *NORTH'S WHORE FREAKS HOTEL FLOOR #abf #juliannorth #northstar #betterthanfiction #whathappensinvegas #bitchesbecray #northgate.*

There was sound on the video, but I couldn't bear to listen. Julian was in his shirt and trousers in the doorway, looking normal and pleasant. I was standing in my bare feet in the hallway, dress askew, yelling at him furiously until all at once I shoved him back, yelled something again, and then tore off down the hallway and toward the camera like a crazed demon. You could just make out the word "MOTHERFUCKER!" on my lips before the video cut off. This was retweeted fifty times, and was eventually picked up by one of those popular sites dedicated to aggregating noteworthy stuff from the annals of the Internet on an hourly basis, and proceeded to go viral. One million views by noon and counting.

The next tweet from Wolf, at 9:02 a.m., was a *ps Julian's wife dyin of cancer #northgate,* to which he added an emoji of a dead smiley face and a smiley face covered in a surgical mask.

From a public relations perspective, I had to hand it to Wolf. Every PR girl, every journalist, every conspiracy theorist—hell, every advertiser worth her salt, knows that it's not what happens that's important, but the story you make from it. With a few well-timed words, Wolf had managed to turn a situation into a story, a disaster into a joke, a trauma into a meme. I'd seen it happen a million times before to women on the Internet: slut-shaming, fat-shaming, fashion-shaming, naked-photo-shaming, sex-tape-leaking, and the like. But even though such shaming, trolling, dragging, whatever you want to call it, was common, I could only care about it the way I cared about orphans in Romania: which is to say, distantly. It was something that happened to other women, other people, and, though unfortunate, had nothing to do with me.

I just . . . started laughing.

Or I guess it wasn't really a laugh. It was just a breathy sound escaping from my mouth, a half step away from hyperventilation, abetted by violent shaking.

I don't know how long I stayed like that, but I think it was a while.

Eventually, with the same twisted-up sick feeling that made me rubberneck at car crashes on the highway, I tapped the notifications tab on Twitter and started skimming through the comments from members of the hive mind brave enough to tag me.

@wolfprana @caseyprepublic who is this whore hope she rots in hell #northgate

@caseyprepublic DIE BITCH better you than his wife #northgate

@wolfprana @caseyprepublic lost all respect for #juliannorth after this #northgate

@wolfprana i don't think #juliannorth would cheat this woman is clearly crazy!!!

And so on. The general consensus, guided by Wolf, was that I was Julian's scorned mistress.

Wolf had also tweeted a link to the People's Republic website, where my smiling head shot suggested that I enjoyed "reading, reality shows, and having fun wherever I am!"

You can imagine the field day people had with this. Dumb bitch, idiot, witch, slut, whore, crazy, sleaze, psycho, homewrecker, too skinny, too fat, nice tits, shitty rack, sinner, backstabber, demon, she-demon, devil, she-devil, jezebel, monster. Not to mention the death threats and suggestions that I put my head in an oven or drown or hang myself or take a gun and shoot myself—this one still makes me cringe—in the you-know-what. A whole subnation of citizens, who previously knew nothing about me, now wished more than anything that I would die. It's hard to orient to something that disorienting, wrap your head around that unwrappableness. If I could have felt anything I might have cried again, but the part of me that was capable of human emotion had silently excused herself.

It's hardly surprising, but the percentage of people who were outraged by Julian's alleged philandering, while not unsubstantial, was far smaller than the percentage of people outraged by me. I chalk that up to the fact that people thought—just as I once had—that Julian North was an amazing person. A genius. A public intellectual and American treasure. It didn't seem fathomable that he might have a mistress. Julian

North wouldn't *do* that sort of thing, they said. It didn't make sense. He loved his wife. They'd been together for twenty years; look how devoted he'd been. Even if he had had an affair with me, I must have tricked him into it. Seduced him. Some women were like that, they said. You had to be careful around them. Born manipulators.

It all moved so fast. Pictures were circulated of Julian and his wife smiling together at various events. Someone dug up their wedding photos. Someone made a GIF of my screaming. After a few hours, when the initial outrage subsided, I became a punch line for jokes. Someone mashed up Wolf's video with Patsy Cline's version of "Crazy." Someone else superimposed my face onto a Disney cartoon villain. That one got a lot of traffic.

Feminist Twitter, bless them, rose to my defense. There were a couple think pieces on Internet bullying and how living in a patriarchy pits women against each other. But the problem with feminist Twitter and feminist websites is that no one reads them but feminists themselves. The gavel of public opinion had made its ruling, siding with precedent. Julian's reputation would be briefly called into question, then returned to what it had been before. And my reputation was done for.

For a split second, just a split, weaselly, terrifying second, a voice inside my head suggested I take a commenter's advice and end it now, make it easier on everyone, make it easier on myself. Go to the edge and jump, the voice hissed. Better than them pushing you.

But no. No. I shook my head vigorously. I might be done for, but I would not be a tragedy. I fumbled with the phone, called Susan. She didn't pick up. I called Lindsey, but it went straight to voicemail. I got to my feet, which felt like blocks of lead, stretched my arms above my head, and with a high-pitched grunt threw my phone with all my might. It landed against the wall with a heavy clunk that sounded so satisfying I threw it again. I put on running shoes and a sports bra and ninety-dollar yoga pants, and I stuck my key in my bra and headed straight for the hotel gym.

I remember thinking as my feet pounded the conveyor belt on the treadmill: I need to get this out of me. What *this* was, I didn't have a word for, just the feeling of poison rushing through my blood. Unfortunately, the cortisol-fueled exertion made me miss the one stupid person in the hotel who happened to spot me through the gym's windows and snap a photo. *@caseyprepublic basic bitch working out w no remorse for ruining #juliannorth's family*

But I didn't know any of this at the time. I had put my phone away and was letting the reptile part of my brain form a plan. I knew the scandal could go one of two ways: one, it could blow over by the end of the day if a replacement scandal was found; or two, I was dead in the water. I gritted my teeth and ran faster and told myself I would not die in the water, all the while looking at the TV screens with their scrolling headlines of violence in other countries, and heavily made-up women laughing along with the audience in semicircles.

And in order not to die in the water, I was going to have to release my own version of events. I'd call Susan again and ask for the evidence of Wolf's plagiarism. I'd write an open letter explaining why Wolf had released that video—he had it in for me—and how he purposely skewed the context of the video in order to get revenge for a legal and physical roughing up I'd ordered. (Or maybe I'd leave that part out.) Then I'd explain, detail by detail, how Julian had basically lured me back to his hotel room, acted like an old lecher, assaulted me, and denied it, just as countless old lechers had done before. A textbook case. Crystal clear. Straight out of central casting.

There, on the treadmill, this seemed like a reasonable enough plan. I had truth on my side. The truth would set me free.

When I stepped off the treadmill, seven miles had gone by in a quick blur. When I got back to the room, I ran for my phone. I called and left a voicemail for Susan this time in what I'm sure was a manic pitch, asking her to send screenshots of the date stamps from her poetry manuscript. Then I opened my laptop and drafted the open letter. I wanted something in hand, something to read from, when I called Celeste back. Celeste hated mess, and I was going to have to clean up every inch of this one before I talked to her again.

"Before you say anything—" I said as soon as she picked up the phone. I had arranged myself in the desk chair of the hotel room, opened the blinds that had previously shielded me from the blinding sun and synthetic view, and put my power blazer over my sweaty sports bra so that I might convince myself that I was a woman with agency and authority.

"You have literally one minute," Celeste said.

I spoke as fast as I could while still speaking precisely. I left nothing out. I told her I shouldn't have mixed my business and personal affairs, shouldn't have given Wolf Susan's poems, or at the very least should have told her about it. I told her, too, about seeing Ellen, about Ellen's and my drunk scheming, about what we'd had the lawyers and Barry do.

All this took about thirty seconds. For the next thirty seconds I told her what happened with Julian. Except I couldn't get it all out, that part, the clear narrative I'd written down got all muddled and strange, and by the last five seconds I was speaking only haltingly and using words like *he was, um, putting his hands*—and *it was like*—and *I dunno it felt*—and *I remember running*. Sweat was pouring from my armpits and inner thighs by the time I'd finished. I did not cry, because it was the animal in me saying these things, and animals do not cry. When I finished, I put my forehead on the freezing metal desk. I wanted to stay like that forever. My head weighed so much I could barely pick it up.

But I did. Because I had to.

"You done?" Celeste said. I nodded, though she couldn't see me. I looked out upon this shiny artificial city I was in, a city in the desert, a mirage made of glass.

"I'm sorry that happened to you," she said.

"It's okay," I said, though it was not.

"The thing is," she said after a pause. "It happens all the time. It's happened to me too, more than once. Men in the entertainment industry, probably any industry, when they get a little power, they'll use as much as they can get away with. Ask anybody. They see it all the time."

"They—do? Then why doesn't—"

"I'm not trying to make you feel that what happened to you isn't, you know, terrible." She sucked in a breath. "I'm just saying you have to see the bigger picture. I know you don't want to hear this right now, but you need to move on, or you'll become one of those people who"—she

336

paused—"see themselves as victims. And that doesn't play well over time."

"Okay," I said, nodding and nodding. "That makes sense." I didn't know deep down if it did, but there was relief in being given instructions.

"All I'm saying is, do what you need to do to get past this, as soon as you can. That's what I did. This sort of—you can't let it hold you back. I mean what happened with you and Julian."

"Okay," I said again. "Okay." In that silent space inside me that *knew* things, the room where my old antenna used to live, I felt crushed; Celeste's words were making less and less sense. She was telling me, more or less, that what happened was par for the course, a fact of life. What I wanted to tell her but couldn't bear to was: I can't stand that this is a fact of life. As she told me matter-of-factly how the world worked I saw the single most important difference between Celeste and me, and the reason why our relationship was doomed from the beginning. Working for People's Republic, while exhilarating at times, had been a big mistake. I couldn't live with the world as it was, like Celeste. I wanted the world to become what it could be.

"Of course, what happened online goes beyond all that," Celeste said. "Julian's already issued a statement, very well-crafted, obviously, saying—hold on, let me find it." I heard her keyboard clacking. "Here we go. 'Ms. Pendergast, as I understand, is a bright young woman with an active imagination. I believe that she believes that she and I were involved in some kind of relationship, but I can assure you that I did not have an affair with this woman, nor did we engage in any sexual activities. Ms. Pendergast and I met only once, on the evening in question, in the sushi bar of Caesars Palace, at which time Ms. Pendergast attempted to coerce me into a sponsorship deal with her advertising firm, which I refused. After several drinks, Ms. Pendergast became increasingly flirtatious and asked repeatedly that I let her come to my room. I refused, yet she must have followed me there after our meeting.

" 'Of course I did not betray my wife. I love my wife. I have walked beside her for twenty years, and through all stages of her illness. I wish the best for Ms. Pendergast and hope that she is able to get the support she needs in order to treat what appears to be a major mental illness. I imagine she is struggling tremendously right now, and, in light of this, I would ask you to suspend judgment. Indeed, instead of punishing her for an illness she has no control over, offer her your compassion. Mental illness affects over a quarter of Americans every year; I myself suffer from depression. I hope this unfortunate incident allows all of us to be more forthcoming about the struggles we face and how we might better cope.

" 'To Mr. Prana, who posted this video and is widely known as an agent provocateur: please consider the disastrous effects your provocations have caused the next time you use your considerable means for destructive ends. To all of you, thank you in advance for your good wishes, your respect for our privacy, and your continued support of the arts.' "

I exhaled a big *whuff* when Celeste was finished. "Jesus Christ, this guy's a criminal liar!"

"That's not the point," Celeste said sharply. "Wolf should have never taken that video, but you gave him good reason to. What Julian did is inexcusable, but I have yet to hear you take responsibility for the considerable role you played in jerryrigging these particular circumstances. There's a million different things you could have done to avoid this along the way, you know. You could have called me the minute Wolf came on to you in Brooklyn. You could have told me you were talking to him about Susan's poems. You could have come to me the minute it came out that he plagiarized, hell, you could have called me last night after you left Julian's hotel room—" Celeste's voice was rising. "But you didn't, did you. You kept it all from me and plotted and manipulated, and in some way I imagine you liked doing that, didn't you, keeping your secrets, keeping your little sphere of influence—"

"I did *not!*" I burst out.

She made a sound that was some mixture of laughter and fury. "Not to mention antagonizing a *very* important new client *with another client* behind my back. Getting Ellen involved? Come on, Casey. Can you take responsibility for *that,* at least? Wolf emailed me this morning with a photo of the bruises on his face and is threatening to sue Nanü for negligence."

"I'm *sorry!*" Though I was not sorry. Or rather, I was only sorry for myself.

"And to top it all off the most important asset we could have won just shit on us in a nationally released statement. What am I supposed to do with this, Casey? What the fuck am I supposed to do?"

"How the fuck should I know!" I said. I pushed my chair back and stood. "Are you saying it's *my* fault—"

"That's exactly what I'm saying!" Celeste interrupted. "I stuck my neck out for you hundreds of times. I trusted you, and you betrayed my trust. You've failed me, and you've failed yourself. Disappointment doesn't even begin to express—"

"I said I'm sorry!" I exploded. I was stalking around the messy hotel room like a penned-in big cat. "What else do you want me to say?"

"Nothing. I want you to say nothing. I want you to listen. I want you to hear me. I've never been more—" Celeste paused. "You know what? All I'll say is, what a *waste*. What a waste of time and work and potential. As of immediately, you're terminated. I'll have Simone pack up your belongings and ship them to your house."

I stopped pacing. "You're firing me?"

"Did you hear what I just said?"

"Well, you know *what?*" I said. "You can't fire me! I already decided to *quit!*"

"Oh Casey," Celeste said. To call her tone patronizing wouldn't begin to convey it. "There's no need for that."

"Oh yes there—" but before I could finish, she hung up.

"UGH!" For the third time that day, I chucked my phone across the room. I hit a bedside lamp and knocked it over. This time it broke. And then when I went to check out later, I found Celeste had already canceled my company AmEx. I would have to pay.

I purposely kept my head down as I wheeled my suitcase out of my hotel room. The people walking past, gambling and laughing and filling their mouths with colorful food and drink—were they looking at me? Were they talking about me? Had they been on the Internet? Had they seen the video? Did they know who I was? Did they think I was a monster? Was I a monster? How much of monstrousness was innate, and how much was

341

born out of circumstance? How many people believing you were a monster did it take for you to believe it yourself?

The latter was a matter of arithmetic.

The answer, I believe, is not many.

Even if they did not know, I told myself, they knew. They knew just by looking at me that I was not right. I had looked to them my whole life, these strangers, to tell me who I was. I had tried my best to look good, feel good, act good, be good, to please, to shine, but never too brightly. If I had a self that felt like mine and not just an amalgamation of rhetorical tricks and gestures, sure, I might not have needed these strangers' benedictions so badly, but tell me, where the hell in this world was I supposed to learn that? Why would anyone want anyone to be themselves when what they can get instead is a reflection of their own image? For when I tried, those few times, to be what you might call a self—to *act,* to be *subject,* rather than object—I ended up feeling crazy. I ended up feeling bad.

Yes, I was crazy. Yes, I was very bad. Someone and something—or was it everyone, and everything?—had taken a thin paring knife to my body and removed a layer of skin. Then another layer, and another, and another, until all the layers were gone. No need to protect myself anymore. There was nothing to protect in the first place. Come now, I said through my side-eyes to these strangers. I know what you want. Take my body. Push me to the ground and kick my stomach. Chase me through the woods with stones. Turn my ass toward you and push into me while my head bangs against the fountain. I have nothing left, if there was anything in the first place. Do, take, what you wish.

I found myself waiting on the floor of the Caesars lobby, leaning up against this fountain, in the middle of which was a classical marble sculpture. My suitcase was pressed up to my knees. I wanted to see what would happen if I did nothing. Nothing at all. I would wait passively for something to happen to me. Then I would respond, or not respond. I would be very quiet for the rest of my life. That was what they wanted, wasn't it?

Sometimes I think I might have stayed leaning against that fountain forever. I would have let my body disintegrate further and rot, until I was just a skeleton. And they would keep me around at Caesars because people come to Vegas not just for the gambling but for the profane attractions. Sideshows and peep shows and sex shows and freaks. *Look here,* the concierge would say to a group of visitors. *Here are the remains of a girl who went mad, and look, she died of her madness. Isn't that interesting?* And the visitors would take pictures of my skull and nod because, yes, yes, they'd heard that story, or they'd heard a story just like it. It was just like girls to do that sort of thing.

But I did not stay to rot against that fountain because my phone rang. It was Susan. Susan had a specialty ring. She chose it. It was a Yoko Ono song.

I could not bring myself to pick up at first. Shame, see, is a powerful silencer.

But what I could do, however, is pick myself up off the floor and walk unsteadily to the concierge desk with my suitcase. And when the concierge asked, "Taxi?" I could nod yes. I don't believe anymore in gods and angels, but if I did, I would elevate this man among them. He wasn't special-looking, but he had a kind mouth, and eyes that had only respect and courtesy when they met mine. "Of course," he said. "Would you like some water while you wait?"

I nodded again, and he pulled a miniature water bottle from beneath his desk. I know he was just doing his job, but it didn't feel like that at the time; it felt like a life vest.

When I got to the airport, I looked at the arrivals and departures on the screens in front of the ticketing counters, and for a moment I considered getting on the next flight to anywhere. I had nowhere to go, nowhere to be. I had nobody, was nobody. I was alone.

The feeling of standing at an airport with nothing between you and disappearance is so extreme that it's easy to mistake the extremity for ecstasy. Possibilities on the departures screens: Shanghai, Sydney, Frankfurt. So many places where no one knew my name, whereto I might abscond with my shame. It was a deeply unsettling kind of giddiness, which is why it took me a second to come down enough to hear the noise coming from my pocket.

It was Susan again. My phone was ringing.

"Hello?" I said when I answered it. My voice was pitched high and strange.

"Where are you?" Susan said.

"I'm—" I looked up at the departure screens, all these plans, all these people coming and going. "I'm at the airport."

"The Vegas airport?"

"Yes."

"Are you on your way home?"

"N-n-not yet."

"Will you be soon?"

I looked up at the screens again.

"Yes," I said finally.

"Good. Will you call me when you land?"

What was this water all over my face?

"Yes."

"Are you hanging in there?"

"Y-y-y—" I started to shake.

"Oh Casey," Susan said in her most Susany of voices, and that's about when I lost it.

13

THE HOUSE OF DEARTH

I took a cab to Susan's apartment after I landed. She opened the door in sweatpants and an old basketball T-shirt two sizes too big for her. Her hair was piled on one side of her head. I hadn't seen her since the day she kicked me out of the apartment.

"Hi," she said.

"Hi," I said, and started weeping again.

She led me to one of her garage-sale armchairs and made me put my bags down and made me a cup of tea and let me curl up into the chair and hide my face in my chest. As she waited for the kettle to whistle, she filled the heavy silence with some news: Mary London had called her a few days ago. She'd read the story of Susan's that I'd given her and used the contact info in the header to tell her personally not only how good it was, but to inquire on behalf of Mary's own agent about representation. Susan had stammered she didn't yet have an agent, and Mary asked if she'd like to speak with hers, and Susan'd gathered her courage and stammered yes, in fact she was working on a novel she would love to have her read. Mary had said,

347

"Good, send her the first fifty pages," and gave her the agent's email address. Susan said she and the agent were due to talk the following Friday. As she poured the tea and put some pretzels in a bowl, I noticed how buoyant her voice was, how she was standing a little taller, walking with her shoulders back. I didn't think I'd seen Susan undepressed in—God—years, maybe. The sight of her so happy and hopeful was almost enough to make me happy and hopeful. Almost.

"I'm so happy for you," I said. I struggled to lift myself up in the chair despite the crushing weight pressing down upon my body. "I'm also—" I teared up again. "I'm so sorry I did that—without asking—and with Wolf—I know it's so—"

"It's okay," Susan said in a quiet voice. She sat down at the foot of my chair, cross-legged, and tapped her knees. I looked at her. She tapped one of my calves and, when I did nothing, pulled my legs down to her lap and started rubbing my feet. The feeling of her warm hands on my skin unlocked some deeper layer of shock. I stopped crying. My whole body began to shake. She rubbed my feet in silence for I don't know how long, and it was only when the trembling began to slow that Susan let up massaging with her fingers and, instead, squeezed my feet tightly with her hands. There was animal comfort in that pressure. My breath slowed and evened. I inhaled, exhaled.

"Thank you," I finally said. I rolled my shoulders, stretched my neck.

"Thank you," she said, looking up at me.

"I'm so sorry."

"I'm sorry, too."

"You have nothing to be sorry for," I said.

"Yeah I do." After a moment she said, "I haven't been a good friend to you in a long time. I pushed you away. Every time—"

"You had every right to," I said. "I don't even know—I don't even know who I was. Got stuck in a house of mirrors and couldn't see my way out of it." I added, "Not anymore, though. Even if I wanted to—"

"—I put up a wall—" she was saying, shaking her head, but at the last part she looked up. "Wait, what do you mean?"

I told her moment by moment what had happened with Julian, told her how Celeste had fired me, told her what I'd done about Wolf with Ellen: the lawyers, the hit by Barry. Despite ourselves, despite how bad it all was, despite this enormous amount of pain leaching out of me like mercury, we somehow ended up laughing. "Oh my God, Casey," Susan said, wiping her eyes. "What in God's name were you thinking? Getting a Real Housewife to—"

"It was her idea!" I said, putting up my hands.

"I had nothing to do with it! Okay, okay," I immediately conceded. "I had *some*thing to do with it."

"I can't believe it." Susan's voice was appalled, but there was a teensy bit of pride beneath it, like: *Wow, look at this ridiculous thing my friend did on my behalf.*

"Listen, the guy is a rank motherfucker who *stole* your poems. I would've done a lot worse, let me tell you. Still would."

"Well then, maybe *we* should do something," Susan said forcefully, clambering to her feet. She redid the knot in her hair, stuck a bobby pin in the back to catch the strays, and put her hands on her sweatpantsed hips. "The thing that really pisses me off, too, is I bet Celeste would've fired you even if there was nothing between you and Wolf. Fucking Celeste goes whichever way the wind is blowing." Her lip curled a little. "She's doing literally *nothing* to defend you against a *sexual predator,* not to mention—well, you know what? Whatever." Susan exhaled with a puff and ruffled her flyaways. "Fuck her."

I thought about telling Susan that Celeste's motivations were slightly more complicated than that, that the better you knew somebody, the harder it was to claim things about them, to distill them down to one attribute, but Susan was getting energized by her ire, and in turn was energizing me. We worked together all through

350

the night to revise the open letter that I'd written in my hotel room in Vegas. We interspersed the text with the screenshots from Susan's computer with copies of all the poems I'd given to Wolf, complete with the date stamps from when they'd been written and completed. With hopes high, we posted the open letter at nine the next morning on all my social media accounts, emailed a number of feminist blog editors, and direct-messaged a number of Susan's writer friends asking them to repost it. They did immediately. For a half hour, we felt that wonderful gritty joy that speaking one's mind brings.

But then, nothing happened. Absolutely no one cared. It had taken mere moments for the tornado to destroy my life, but that was how news cycles worked. No one's interested in what happens in the days after a tornado sweeps through a town; we're fascinated by the tornado itself. No one likes looking at destruction unless there's a whole lot of other people looking. I don't know what this says about human nature; all I know was that my private wreckage, once revealed publicly, was not as interesting to people as the disaster that caused it.

Sure, yeah, there were a few *Casey Speaks* reblogs, a swell in support from sexual assault prevention organizations, a call from one site to boycott Julian's books, but none of it gained much traction. As for Wolf, the people in the literary world who believed he was an asshole continued to believe he was an asshole, and the people who didn't, didn't. Susan said the best way for her to get revenge was to write a better book. And, once she had enough power from said book, she would, she said, "eviscerate him." But we would see. In the aftermath of our efforts to hold these men responsible, we realized we didn't possess the power to do that. We were just a couple of nobodies, a couple of ladies. Men were innocent until proven guilty. Women were crazy until they were believed.

After the initial swell of hope brought about by reconciling with Susan, I tried to keep my spirits up, but they fell. They fell until I seemed to not even have spirits anymore. I still bought groceries and drove my car and washed my hair and performed essential human functions; there was no Hollywood-style sadness montage where I curled up in my pajamas all day. But I had lost something, and not just my job or my boyfriend or my reputation. Grief, it knocks you flat, and never in the way you expect. I would be signing my name on checks or forms and would notice that even my own name seemed to have nothing to do with me. Casey Pendergast—who was that? The words were meaningless. I mean I did not recognize them, I did not recognize myself, because there was no self. I had neither strength nor will, no I-ness left, to put myself back together again.

After I left Susan's house, I ghostwalked around the city for days, no longer myself but trapped in myself, haunted by my own body, its insistence on remembering what I would've rather ignored. During these drizzly, specter-filled walks, I figured out pretty quickly that I wasn't going to be able to stay in my condo while unemployed—I wasn't what you'd call a penny-pincher, my savings were nonexistent—so I did what I had to do and in short order found a renter, a twenty-two-year-old who'd graduated from college that spring. Her name was Savannah, and she had very nice hair and was very certain about her future success in the field of human resources. I upcharged the rent well past my mortgage so I'd have a little something extra to live on; Savannah either didn't notice or didn't mind.

I also started selling all my beautiful things. I said goodbye to decorative plates, artsy lamps, a two-hundred-dollar juicer. I said hello to pursed-lipped women at consignment shops who hung my best dresses up on a rack and decided how much they were going to pay me for them, which was never enough. I couldn't afford movers, so I packed up what I couldn't sell—the pilled sweaters, the misshapen cottons, the underwear—and gave away what I hated, which was pretty much everything, since it reminded me of a self that I was no more. The self that wore these things and blended these juices was a self that, if not untouched by suffering, did her damnedest to keep it at arm's length through willful blitheness. Such compartmentalizing was no longer possible, and even if it had been, I wanted nothing to do with it anymore.

And at the beginning of October, about a month after I'd gotten home from Vegas, I arrived with two cardboard boxes and an overstuffed suitcase at the door of Lindsey's condo.

"Hello, roomie!" Lindsey said, greeting me in a Japanese-print caftan. "I'm so glad you're here!" She handed me a cup of ginger tea and gave me a giant hug. She'd offered to let me stay with her, rent-free, until I got back on my feet. "We'll call it the Red Tent!" she'd said, referring to a novel where women in biblical times got their periods together.

"You really don't have to do that," I'd said, or groaned. The conversation where she'd invited me to cohabitate had happened on the phone. I'd been lying on the floor of my near-empty living room watching the ceiling fan circulate. *Whatthefuck,* it asked, *whatthefuckwhatthefuck,* on every go-around. I was at the stage where I felt I did not deserve anything, where what happened with Julian was my fault, where the best course of action seemed to be to isolate myself like a wounded animal until I'd either licked myself clean or died of infection. I berated myself incessantly. If only I hadn't taken the job at People's Republic. If only I hadn't agreed to help start up Nanü. If only I had taken that sabbatical. If only I weren't so greedy. If only I hadn't taken those poems from Susan. If only I hadn't bullied Wolf. If only I hadn't gotten drunk on Numb Cappuccinos! If only I hadn't spied on Ben. If only I didn't have to seek retribution for every stupid thing. If only I hadn't been so naïve about Julian. If only I had more self-awareness. If only I had more courage. If only I didn't try so fucking hard to please. If only, from the minute I figured them out, I had set out to follow my dreams. If only, God, if only, if only. A different mother, a different father, a different boss, a different me. You could take all the if-onlys back to the day you were born, if you wanted. Spend enough time with yourself, you might find yourself pretty disappointing.

Which is why none of us should spend too much time alone, isolated without interruption. People need people, and not just virtually. And why I was so lucky the day Lindsey heard my refusal of her invitation and dismissed it so wholeheartedly.

Lindsey's apartment smelled like a Yankee Candle and looked like a Barbie Dreamhouse. It was tidy and we both bent over backward to keep it that way, to put each other at ease. In the weeks to come, I would cook and make her smoothies; she would clean compulsively. Once I'd come home late from a walk and found her using a bleach toothbrush on the tiled kitchen backsplash while a meditation podcast played through her Bluetooth speakers. "I am the change I wish to see," she was repeating, scrubbing in her pink rubber gloves. "I am the change I wish to see."

I, on the other hand, was not the change I wished to see. I was a very sad and ashamed unemployed lady. Halfheartedly I filled out job applications, knowing that I wouldn't get anything, since any employer googling *Casey Pendergast* received a *very* unflattering portrait of yours truly. Even though the Internet was preoccupied with me for a week at most, a week is a jackpot when it comes to data collection. In three months I didn't receive a single call for an interview after applying for God knows how many jobs. Jobs not only in advertising, but anywhere and anything. But no one wanted me.

I would have perhaps plunged deeper into my depression, were it not for Dudley, dear Dudley, Susan's boss, stepping in. Since his portrait studio was right next to Wendys's Books, he'd gotten to know the three Wendys who owned it over the years. Completely independently of Susan asking—he'd just heard her talking with me on the phone one day—he asked if they'd be willing to take me on for the holiday season. They were. After the holidays, there were no guarantees, but still. I showed up on the first day with a découpaged mug for each of the three Wendys and tears in my eyes after stopping into the portrait studio to thank Dudley. "Heavens to Betsy Jean, no need to thank me," he chortled, patting me on the back in a grandfatherly way. "Simply a matter of common decency."

Dudley knew what'd happened on Twitter—Susan'd had to explain it to him—and though he never mentioned anything to me, I could feel him trying all the time, in little ways, to remind me that there was indeed such a thing as common decency. That, even though fifty percent of the world or greater may be real shitty, the other fifty percent are made of people who try hard to do right by other people, people whose hearts are big enough to care about the whole world, not just the people they know in it. They were easy to forget, this other fifty, because they didn't talk as much as the other half, aren't as showy. But they are there, they always are, always have been. Mercy. Look around, train your gaze; you'll see them everywhere eventually. They're beautiful, I'm telling you. Beautiful as a painting.

"Can I help you with something?!" I asked. It was the three-month anniversary of my assault and humiliation, and at Wendys's I was trying very hard to master the power of positive thinking.

"I'm looking for a book called, ah, *The Incendiaries?*" the woman on the other side of the customer service desk said, pulling out a piece of paper to make sure she'd gotten the title right.

"Oh!" I smiled very wide. "Yes, of course!"

The Incendiaries was Julian North's new novel, out just in time for the holidays, and published to rave reviews.

"It's for my book club," the woman said apologetically. She had short gray hair and wore fingerless gloves that appeared to be self-knitted. I'd noticed during my so-far brief tenure in retail that a lot of women felt really apologetic about asking for anything, even if their asking just meant I had to do what was in my job description. "Have you read it?"

"You know!" I said. I tried to end everything I said with an exclamation point. "I haven't read that one yet! But everyone who has seems to really"—I gritted my teeth—"love him!"

I led her to the bestsellers table in the front of the store. In the middle of the table, tucked into one of those metal holders, was a big poster of Tracy Mallard standing contemplatively next to a pond. There was a newspaper, a magazine, a notebook, and a pen on a rock next to her, along with a box of Nature's Harvest granola bars. *The poetry of silence,* said the tag. Beneath it was a short paragraph from Tracy herself:

> There's nothing I love more than a walk in the woods to connect myself back to the earth. Our world might be fraught, but our minds don't have to be. That's why I always carry Nature's Harvest with me. They feed my body and mind and, best of all, they're natural. Just like you and me.™

The Nature's Harvest logo was placed discreetly at the bottom of the ad. Nanü, by the end of that year, was up and thriving. Lindsey, Annie, and Jack had been brought on by Celeste with an attractive and standard start-up package that included stock options and equity. Jack was doing art direction—this poster had his name all over it—and Annie, along with a couple new hires, was doing my job now. Lindsey had taken over what Celeste was calling "asset maintenance"— hand-holding the writers to ensure their corporate projects went smoothly—though she was hoping, as soon as she could, loyal as she was, to get out from under Celeste's gilded thumb.

Most of the other people at PR had not been as lucky. Celeste had sold PR, as expected, to Omnipublic. There were three rounds of huge layoffs, with no explanation from the bosses except that they were looking to cut costs. My and Lindsey's guess was that Celeste got a better price by forgoing PR's independence, and money had mattered more than ever once it was clear she had to get Nanü off the ground herself. (After the Vegas disaster and Julian's public disavowal, the venture capitalists had gotten cold feet.) In a company-wide email that Lindsey had shown me only after I threatened to spill orange juice all over her newly cleaned kitchen floor if she didn't, Celeste wrote that although she was "looking forward to new beginnings," she was also "deeply sorrowful" that the era of People's Republic was coming to an end. She also wrote that she never would have sold PR were it not for the riotously bad press a "troubled former employee" had caused the agency, thereby pinning all the bad blood from the layoffs on me.

If I had any sympathy left for Celeste, any understanding of how she, as my boss, might have felt betrayed by my less-than-honest and under-the-radar plots, it disappeared when I saw that email. People reveal themselves in writing more than anywhere else; they show on the page what in life they keep private. I saw who she was in that email, for the first time, in her entirety. And to be honest, it appalled me.

"Oh," the woman at Wendys's said, taking the hardcover brick with a look of apprehension. "This is longer than I thought it'd be."

"Yes," I said. "I believe his books do run long!"

What I did not say: because he's a megalomaniac!

"My book club's the day after tomorrow," the woman said. "I don't know how I'll get it done."

"Well," I said. I put a hand on my hip and looked toward the ceiling, like I was considering what I was about to tell her for the first time. "I *have* heard it's kind of slow going. You know what you could do, though? I mean, it's a little rascally but—"

"What?" She was smiling. I really loved it when older people got mischievous.

"You *could,*" I said, "since you only have a couple days, just read the reviews on Amazon. Get the gist of the thing without having to"— I waved my hand—"you know, deal with the overwrought, blowhardy, self-important verbiage—"

The woman put her hand over her mouth and laughed. "Don't tell anyone, but I *have* always thought he was a little too big for his britches—"

I clapped my hands. "See?!"

Encouraging customers not to buy Julian's pretentious block of a novel was one of the high points of my days as a seasonal employee at Wendys's. The other high point, of course, was reading. I devoured books on my lunch breaks, used my employee discount to purchase a novel a week, and disappeared into them during my days off. I hadn't read with such voracity since college—I hadn't had time. I'd put in such long hours at PR, plus the culture of advertising had turned my interests away from self-reflection and toward consumer spending—yet it didn't take me long to pick back up the habit. To enter a world of make-believe painstakingly created by another person, to be told a well-crafted story at the exact moment where my life had no narrative: this was joy. A joy that relied not on money or status or reputation, but a joy created between me and a stranger who thought and felt as I did. For minutes, hours, even days at a time, this stranger offered respite from what seemed to me, when I looked out upon the earth, an endless desert of loneliness. Picking up reading again, too, allowed Susan and me to connect in a way we hadn't for months. This made up for the lowlights of being a seasonal employee at Wendys's: long hours and low pay and cranky customers, to name a few. But even with these lowlights, I often returned home with a lighter heart than I'd had when I arrived at the store, having spent the day surrounded by books, and people who loved them.

Including my new friend Chris, a fellow seasonal employee at Wendys's and another one of those people whose presence in my life was a great gift and therefore a challenge to my more or less constant despair over the fact that the world was a shithole. Chris identified as non-binary trans, used the pronoun "they," and, along with being the most millennial of all the millennials I knew, was also the funniest person I'd ever met, despite the fact that one of their favorite sources of humor was making fun of how white I was (Chris was black). We originally bonded over slam poetry. Chris was way famous around town, in that milieu anyway; was friends with Gina, Susan's friend; and had made it to the national championships the year before. When I told them I'd "done some slam" in college, they laughed so hard I thought I might need to pull down the defibrillator in the break room, where we were sitting at the Formica table. "GIRL," they'd said, still laughing, shaking their head. "You? What the hell were you writing about, losing your *Canada Goose* jacket at a frat party? Or, no, let me guess—your *eating disorder?*"

"Um, *no,*" I'd said, though of course that was exactly what I'd written about.

It was at the same Formica table in the break room that I was reading the newspaper on my phone at the end of my shift, waiting for the bus since I was trying to save on gas money, when Chris burst in, septum pierced, jean-jacketed, saying, "Oh my GOD did you hear the news?" Chris was like a sunbeam when they entered the room—bright light everywhere.

I looked up. I had just been reading about a drone strike. "What news?"

"Ellen Hanks is coming to our store!"

I dropped my phone with a clatter on the table. "She is?! Wait, you know who Ellen Hanks is?"

"I'm like obsessed with *Real Housewives*. If she turns up I'm literally going TO DIE. I love her! She's like my favorite person on Instagram. Do you know she just wrote a memoir?" Chris paused slightly for a huge intake of breath. "Why didn't you think I knew who Ellen Hanks was? Because—"

"No," I said, before they could even finish, "because isn't *Real Housewives* a little bougey for you and your, like, radical anarchy?"

"Real Housewives is anarchy," Chris said, throwing their body down in a plastic chair across from mine and grabbing a clementine from a tangled mesh bag the Wendys had given their employees for Christmas. "Where else do you get to see skinny white girls punching each other on TV?"

"Good point," I said. What I didn't say was that I knew Ellen, that one might even say I knew her well, if you counted conspiring to commit assault and battery together. No one at Wendys's knew about my former life, unless they googled me, but I'd deleted all my social media accounts and shied away from hanging out with any coworkers besides Chris. I felt safe around Chris, unlike with most new people. Which I think is always true with people whom you can look straight in the eye and see at once that they, too, have traveled out to the edge of things; perhaps even, or more likely, way farther out than you.

Anyway, Ellen and I hadn't talked much since I'd been fired. I don't think she put it together that the guy who'd posted the video of me was the same guy who her fuckboy Barry had beat up, and I didn't want to subject her to my inferno. Ben had actually called, too, sometime in that first week, but I didn't call him back, either. Or my mother. I couldn't bear it. I wanted only to take refuge in books and Lindsey and Susan and my new friend Chris, whose laughter in the break room was like a lit match to my extinguished heart-fire.

Minds and hearts are fragile things, you know. I lost both of mine for a little while. Only the special people, the special books—the ones that remind you that, though, yes, you died before, you can still come alive again—help you find them.

As for those other people, the less-special ones—well, I had figured I'd just hide from them till the end of time.

But then again—Ellen, coming to the store. It would be worth not-hiding for just one of her huge and overperfumed hugs.

"Why are you smiling like that?" Chris said. "You look crazy."

"Nothing? I'm just—" I smiled wider, then put

my hands to my cheeks. "I think I might actually be happy."

Chris looked at me like there was a pile of screws falling out of my ears. "Uh yeah, you *should* be happy," they said, jazzing their hands only half-ironically. "It's the HOLLIIIDDAAAYYYSS!"

On my bus ride home, we passed through a pedestrian shopping district. I stared through the dark into department store windows trimmed with fake snow and fake evergreens and fake bodies draped with down and wool and cashmere. I passed an Encore with full-bodied mannequins dressed in full-coverage lingerie, accompanied by two large posters. The first one said BE MERRY! And the other one was a tag that I just knew Mary London had written, even though it was unattributed: KEEP YOUR FRIENDS AND YOUR BREASTS CLOSE THIS SEASON. No one at Encore was clever enough to come up with something like that without Mary at the helm.

I trundled off the bus along with a whole bunch of other people, people who looked different from me, people I hadn't had to be around when I'd driven around in my car all the time, insulated by layers of metal and glass. I had begun to find it comforting, this anonymous, liminal community, sitting shoulder-to-shoulder with other bodies. Some days it was the only touch I received. My phone buzzed with a text from Susan. *What are you up to tonight, muffin?*

Gettin busy, I'd written back, *with my lover, Mr. TV*

You want to make it a threesome?

I smiled. *Foursome. I'll text Lindsey.*

During a commercial break, after a particularly exciting sequence in *The Bachelorette* where the heroine got to take a hot air balloon ride with one of her honeys, Lindsey muted the TV. "We need to catch up," she said earnestly. "Susan, I want to hear about what's happening with your book! I keep forgetting to ask you about it."

The three of us were drinking wine and eating cheese and crackers on Lindsey's matching sofa and loveseat, which were beige suede and had had no stains right up to the night I'd laid out like a corpse and fallen asleep watching *Pride and Prejudice* with a bag of peanut butter M&M'S. Lindsey had out a bevy of pillows and blankets for us; her living room was like a marshmallow world. In answer to Lindsey's question Susan smiled, a small smile, like she'd been keeping some pleasure a secret for a long time and was slowly getting used to revealing it in public.

"I knew it!" I said when I saw that smile. "You're not forgetting, she's just shy. But I think it's going well," I told Lindsey.

"I can tell," Lindsey said, smiling back. She

brushed a hair back from her face and her bangles clicked. "I finished *The House of Mirth*, by the way. Did you?"

"I did!" I said. Susan had given me her copy the last time she came over, said she thought it "might be useful." Lindsey, inspired, had bought her own copy on her Kindle immediately. "First meeting of the Red Tent Book Club!" she'd said, maybe a little too excitedly for Susan, who, with her terror of organized anything, saw the distance between social clubs and neo-Nazism as perilously small.

I said, "Um, Susan, I'm not sure how long it's been since you read it but—you know she *dies* in the end, right?"

The "she" I was referring to was Lily Bart, the heroine of *The House of Mirth* who gets kicked out of her tony New York City social milieu after false accusations of an affair and dies penniless in a boarding house. The parallels, if you wanted to see them, were there.

"I know," Susan said, leaning forward, elbows on her knees. "But she dies honestly—"

"She's still *dead!*" I said, just as Lindsey was saying, "But she died finally admitting she loved Lawrence! And Lawrence loved her too!"

"—and her death is the final nail in the coffin," Susan said, using her index finger, as she always did, when she knew she was making a good point, "for Wharton to show the cowardice of upper class morality and the bullshit falsity of bourgeois—"

"If only he would have gotten there in time," Lindsey said wistfully.

I was surprised to feel that I was smiling again, for what must have been a record twice in one day. How strange, this smile. How incongruous. Because I didn't really know how to be a person anymore, didn't really know much of anything.

And yet.

Sometimes I was just . . . fine.

Sometimes I even felt a boundless love in my heart.

Sometimes.

As I continued to pat my cheeks in wonderment, Susan and Lindsey entered into a very gentle argument—the only kind of argument Lindsey, as a self-described "highly sensitive person" could handle—about whether or not *The House of Mirth* was a love story. Susan maintained it was a social satire; Lindsey kept saying, "But the chemistry!" I listened for a while, continuing to smile at my friends, at how sweet they both were.

"That reminds me," Lindsey said after a while, seemingly out of nowhere. She turned to me. "Have you talked to Ben?"

"What? Oh—no." I shrugged casually. Very casually. "He called, like, right after all that . . ." I waved a hand. "But I didn't call him back."

"And why not?" Susan said pointedly.

"It's nice that he called," Lindsey offered.

"Did he leave a message?" said Susan.

"No," I said. "Which is why I didn't call back."

"You should call him back," Susan said. "She's not going to call him back," she said to Lindsey.

"She might!" Lindsey said.

"You guys, I can hear you!" I pointed to my chest. "I am literally right here!"

"She's afraid," Susan said to Lindsey, as if I hadn't said anything. "Which is understandable. But she's going to have to stop being afraid sometime. Don't you think?"

14

A (Green) Room of One's Own

The day of Ellen's reading I was scheduled to close the store, but I asked a fellow seasonal employee to trade my closing shift for her opener on the condition that I hard-clean the bathrooms at the end of mine, so that she'd only have to spot clean at the end of hers. A not-insubstantial concession, seeing as our restrooms were unpotpourried and open to the public.

Let me tell you, it's a special feeling, scrubbing toilets used merely as approximations a mere forty-five minutes before meeting up with a minor celebrity friend with whom you've previously drunk Numb Cappuccinos! By the time I was done, I had toilet scum on my knees and sweat under my arms, and I hadn't thought to bring a change of clothes.

While I cleaned, Chris, along with several other employees, had been charged with setting up the event area for Ellen's reading. We were expecting a full house. There was a table stacked high with copies of Ellen's memoir, *All Real*. The title was, of course, the same tagline that we'd come up with for her personal brand campaign, and the cover-sized close-up of her face was the same photograph Lindsey had spent countless hours photoshopping. Seeing my team's work in this completed, public form brought on a surge of pride that existed simultaneously alongside a more familiar sense of loss.

The book had been included in a "Holiday Gift Ideas!" segment on our CBS affiliate's early morning show and written up in the local paper. By six-thirty there were already thirty people milling around for the seven p.m. proceedings, the literary equivalent of a sold-out stadium. Someone had brought a case of Ellen's fitness water, Ellian!, and samples of her nitrate-free beef sticks, Hankfurters!, for the event, and I grabbed one of each on my way to confab with Chris, who was wearing a headset and directing the other employees with the high-octane duress of a stage manager at the Emmys.

"AV?" Chris was barking into the foam micro-phone strapped across their cheek as I approached. "AV, do you copy? . . . yeah, ALEX, I'm talking to you. Who else would I be talking to? We're gonna need to cut down on the reverb up here, do you copy?"

"Hello, commander," I said, giving them a hug. "Can I help with anything? Also, do I smell like toilet-bowl cleaner?"

"What? Oh God, yes, you do," Chris said, pulling away. "And no, it's too late. This is a disaster. The show starts in twenty minutes and our star is LITERALLY nowhere to be found."

I didn't bother pointing out that we were not at a show, we were at a reading at a local bookstore, because Chris was enjoying the hell out of playing their role as a distressed general, and I felt it only right that I indulge them. "That is LITERALLY crazy," I said.

"RIGHT?! If she's not here in five I'm LITERALLY calling the police." Chris pushed the foam mic closer to their mouth. "What'd you say, Alex? . . . You what? . . . Are you KIDDING ME right now?!"

"Listen." I put a hand on Chris's arm. "I know this might not be the best, you know, *timing*"— at that Chris began preparing to look affronted— "but I thought you should know before she gets here that I kinda know Ellen. Well, not kinda. I mean, I do know her. From the old days. Before the fire."

That's how Chris and I had decided to refer to my humiliation: the fire. We'd gone out for drinks one night, and I'd told them briefly about Julian and Wolf and Celeste and Las Vegas. It was still hard to talk about; I winced the whole time, but I'd gotten out the most important details. "I *knew* you looked familiar!" Chris had said, unfazed and with a big smile after I'd finished, smacking me on the arm. "I was like, didn't I see that girl on Giphy?"

I continued. "Don't worry, she'll be here, she's

never missed an appearance in her life. I think you guys are gonna hit it off great, but if you see us talking just—be cool, all right? Don't like tackle her from behind or anything. Ellen's fear-aggressive."

Chris put their hands on their hips and looked at me exasperatedly. "What is wrong with you?! You waited until RIGHT NOW to tell me you know Ellen Hanks?"

I threw up my hands. "I didn't know when to bring it up!"

"What?" Chris spoke into their headpiece. "Okay, DON'T MOVE. I'm coming." To me: "Maybe one of the million times I was telling you what I'd read on *Us Weekly* dot com, for one thing!"

"I know, I know, I'm sorry!" I felt stupid and unnecessarily secretive. Now that I was free from the subterfuge of Nanü and PR, I especially hated keeping secrets. "I have issues!"

Chris and I had bonded that night at that bar over our shared issues. At one point they'd said, "You know, if I were an animal? I'd probably be one of those rescue dogs that'll never trust a man no matter how long he's lived with his happy suburban family," and I'd laughed until I cried.

"Don't apologize, just make her come out for drinks with us!" Chris called back to me as they hustled to fix whatever mess Alex had made.

I took a seat in the second row, on the far side,

so I could catch Ellen's eye without appearing too desperate. I was afraid of that a lot those days, appearing desperate. Or, really, appearing anything. Over the months I'd started wearing hats and clothes that had less shape. I made little eye contact; I had not wanted to be seen by anybody. Not just because I was still paranoid that people would recognize my face. I just didn't want eyes on me. My skin, my face. I could not bear eyes on me yet. I was afraid of what they might find if they looked. The seats were slowly filling in around me with various sizes and shapes of humans, and it wouldn't have been impossible for me to lean behind, in front, or to the side to say *hello, how are you, how's your day going*— the sort of thing I'd always done with strangers, my whole life, curious creature that I was.

But I didn't. I had lost that part of myself. It had died. Likely people had forgotten about me, if they'd ever thought of me at all beyond five seconds of my face on a screen or my name as a punch line. But I hadn't forgotten. I still haven't forgotten.

That's why I've had to put this all down.

Every morning when I woke up, for a brief moment, I thought to myself: perhaps *this* is the day when I stop feeling ashamed. But then I would swing my legs over to the side of the bed and the shame would return, a dense cloud inside my skull. Occasionally, over the course of the day, the fog would clear, for a second or two—when I was reading, or if I encountered beauty out in the world—and I would catch a glimpse of this enormous landscape of freedom. I would think, this is what your whole life can feel like, each moment, if you can just accept everything that has ever—but then as soon as I began to finish this thought the fog would start to roll back in.

I'd become accustomed to the fog over the past three months; I'd forgotten that a world existed beyond the fog, that there were thousands of miles of different altitudes and climes. So I curled into myself while I waited for Ellen to appear. Because I was afraid of the Internet, I didn't take out my phone. I just sat there, small and quiet. I'd lost weight in the past months, but not in a fun way. There were lines on my face and an expression behind my eyes that I did not like. I avoided mirrors as much as I could.

Oh well. It was, I counseled myself, fine to be alone. Because, I counseled myself, alone is what we always are. Even, I counseled myself, when we pretend otherwise.

"Move your jacket, will you?" a familiar voice said.

I looked up. Susan was standing at the end of the row, her puffy coat gathered in her arms. Her long hair was brushed, her eyes clear. She looked playful and happy.

I did a double take. "What're you doing here?"

"What do you mean, what am I doing here?" she handed me my coat and purse before sitting down next to me. She placed a still-cold-from-the-outdoors hand on my back. "Do you really think I'd let you come face-to-face with your former life by yourself?"

"Oh—for crying out loud!" I reached over and gave her a hug. We laid our heads on each other's shoulders. I hadn't asked her to come because I'd been embarrassed. Because it's so embarrassing to ask for help. Because it's so embarrassing to be helpless. This despite the fact that when we see our friends helpless, we feel such a great rush of tenderness.

But Susan, she knew to help me anyway. I didn't even have to ask.

"Thank you."

She lifted her head and reached for her purse. "Gum?" she said, taking out a foil-wrapped stick.

"Sure." I plucked one from the minty envelope.

"I quit smoking," she said, breaking the sugar-dusty green stick in half before popping it in her mouth. "As of yesterday. Which is good, but it means I've chewed like ten packs of gum between now and then. I'm going to end up one of those cadavers with a ten pound wad in her stomach."

"Whatever! Still counts as progress." I chewed. "Speaking of progress, as of yesterday, *I* decided to quit feeling sorry for myself and have entered, like, a deep period of misanthropy instead."

She laughed. "That is progress!"

Then I laughed. "I hate," I said, laughing, "everybody." This made her laugh some more, and then I laughed some more, and I could feel some of the poison in me exit into the atmosphere, high up in the sky where it couldn't hurt anyone.

"Ahhhhhhh," Susan said, stretching her arms out wide. "Life. *La vie.*"

"It'll kill you, I'll tell you what."

She put her head back on my shoulder, and I rested mine on hers. We sat like that for a while. Time stopped being linear and became a series of moments that stacked on top of each other like translucent building blocks. I was snuggling into my mother's chest, my best friend from kindergarten was hugging me so hard I could barely breathe, I was at the movies, folded into the first boy I'd ever fallen in love with, I was standing over a riverside cliff with Susan looking at a sunset when we were nineteen, I was alone in the pinewoods behind my parents' house naming trees (you *are* a birch, you *are* a maple) and finding solace in their company. It was the very opposite feeling of what had happened in the aftermath of Celeste and Wolf and Julian, when I'd fallen into a sinkhole, which bottomed out into other sinkholes, comprised of every bad memory I'd had and some I hadn't even known existed: memories of punishment and correction, moments of neglect and abandonment.

But for a second there, in the bookstore, when time spanned vertically instead of horizontally, and love was at the center of the line, I forgot all about that.

It's so simple, I know, but perhaps all it takes to mend, in the end, is people who love you. Who find you when you are lost, who come out with a flashlight when you've gone too far into the woods. They call out your name, you hear it, you are reminded of yourself. They remind you. They remember you. They remember you.

And so you return the call. You put yourself back together again. Because, my God, you love them too.

"What are you going to say to her?" Susan said.

"You know, I haven't gotten that far? I was hoping to just lay down at her feet and start weeping."

"I like it. Very efficient."

"And elegant!" I said. "My modus operandi these days. Hence why you might have found that I am smelling of women's toilets."

She sniffed me. "You smell fine."

"You sure?"

Before Susan could respond, Ellen came blasting up to the podium out of nowhere with a cloud of white fur trailing behind her. The shape and texture of her jacket was not unlike that of the abominable snowman from the Claymation adaptation of a popular Christmas story Lindsey and I had just watched on network television while waiting for our Korean skincare face masks to dry.

"Hello, hello, hello, hello, hello." Ellen was shrugging off her jacket and panting into the microphone. The microphone was squealing. Her hair, as usual, was a perfectly coiffed brunette helmet, her body fatless as a chicken breast, her fingers covered with jeweled rings and her skin an evenly sprayed bronze. To her right I saw Chris motioning furiously to their AV team, a.k.a. Alex, who was standing next to a single amplifier. Chris drew a finger across their neck.

"Hi, hi, sorry I'm late, everybody. I'm Ellen Hanks, but I guess you know that already." The audience laughed appreciatively. We were primed to appreciate Ellen, prepared to adore everything she said. Hell, she could have spoken through a dirty sock puppet and we would've been thrilled. "It's been a god-awful day, my Uber driver got lost, and I have no idea where my assistant is right now. I lost her at the mall. But look—you're all working women. You know how it is."

We laughed appreciatively again. I looked around. It was true, the audience was made up entirely of women, mainly age thirty-five to sixty, though a few skewed younger like Susan and me. I saw Ellen's eyes scan the audience, looking for a familiar face. It was her adopted hometown, after all. When her eyes met mine, I gave her a shy little wave. Immediately her face lit up. And then mine lit up, because being excited to see someone, and seeing they're excited to see you, is the best possible outcome of the human impulse to mirror, not to mention one of the best feelings in the world.

"To be honest, I don't even know what to say to you ladies tonight," Ellen said after a beat, throwing both elbows on the podium and leaning forward. "You've probably all read the book already. Even if you haven't, you probably know everything there is to know about my life. My life's an open book, right? I've been traveling around talking about this book for, what, a month now. And one thing I've learned from this experience, or whatever, is that, my God, you ladies have a lot of stories. Story after story! I sit at that table back there"—she motioned to the table piled high with her books—"after readings, signing books and chatting with you girls, and it's unbelievable, you come up to me and tell me things that freaking blow my mind! I'm thinking to myself as they talk, Jesus Christ, why am I famous? You're the one who should be famous! This one woman in Seattle, to get out of her shitty marriage, she started working secretly as a seamstress and taking small amounts of money out of the joint checking account so she could leave her asshole husband and have some money in the bank already. And another woman? This was in Boston, she got fucking—excuse my language—raped walking home one night after bar close and you know what she did? She started her own business! An all-girls taxi service! Talk about making lemonade, am I right?

"Anyway, the reason I bring this up—it's gonna sound a little crazy, but let's be honest, you know I always sound a little crazy—is I got this idea after Boston that I want these readings to be more like conversations. Seems stupid to stand up here and read something you guys have already read and tell you stuff you already know. I'm tired of talking. I've been talking my whole life. I've been talking for a month straight. You talk. At this point you've got a lot more to say than I do."

She stepped back from the podium and gestured toward us.

"Come on then!"

Those of us in the audience, who were prepared only to passively receive entertainment that evening, stirred uncomfortably. We were not sure how to proceed, how to initiate, how to, oh, what do you call it: create something for ourselves out of negative space instead of waiting for someone to give us instructions.

Chris, for their part, was looking like they might shit their pants. This had not been written into the Emmy broadcast!

"Come on!" Ellen said. She flapped her arms like a hype man. "Up, up!"

When no one came forward right away, she leaned into the microphone. "Casey Pendergast," she said in a singsong voice. "I'm lookin' right at you."

I waved. *Hi!* my hand said. *Stop that right now, thanks!*

"Yes!" Susan whispered, poking me in the ribs. "Go up there!"

"Come on uuuuuuuup heeeeeeeeeere," Ellen sang. "You guys, Casey's a dear friend of mine who's freaking hilarious, a freaking star. I've known her for a while now and she's a total nut job, a real great girl. She got into some trouble a while back but—well, I'll let Casey fill you in on that. Anyway, Casey, we need you up here! Girls, can we get some applause for Casey?"

I crossed my arms over my chest and stuck my hands in my armpits. I looked at Ellen and smiled. *STOP!* my smile said. *I am trying to erase myself from the public record, please and thank you!*

"Come on!" Susan whispered. "This is perfect!"

"I can't!" I whispered back.

"Yes, you can!"

"I don't want to!"

"Yes, you do! When have you ever said no to a microphone?!"

"I'm not ready!"

"You're never going to be ready! You just have to do it!"

I looked at her as she said this, the bright hopefulness in her face. "I'll be here the whole time!" she said. This coming from Susan, of all people, who had buried herself away in books and papers for so long and was finally, finally, inching her way back out into real life with the help of Mary London and Gina and her agent and maybe, just maybe, in spite of all the fuckups, with a little help from me. Maybe this is all friends really need to do for each other. Find refuge in each other, yes, but also nudge each other forward; because love is both risk and refuge.

"Casey!" Ellen yelled. She waggled her fingers at me. "We're waaaaiiiting!"

I looked at her. I looked at Susan.

"Casey," Susan said. "You have to go."

"Ugggggghhhhhhh," I said. After a pause: "FINE."

I was met with a warm smattering of applause when I got to the podium. A sea of fifty pale, wintry faces stared back at me. "Ah," I said. "Hello." The microphone shrieked, as they tend to do in these more vulnerable moments.

"My name is Casey Pendergast," I said slowly.

"Some of you, um, may have heard of me. As Ellen hinted, I got into some trouble a few months back and my name was briefly sort of all over the Internet."

I didn't know what else to say. It was clear that my name registered, among about a fifth of the audience; there was at least a shred of recognition. These were bookish people, after all. I saw furrowed brows and cocked heads from some of them, as if they were trying to place me. Crossed arms from others, as if they'd already heard what'd happened and made up their minds. A few pulled out their phones, I imagined, to do a Google search.

I felt a wave of dread, watching this, but it was coupled with the sense that what was happening was already happening. It was too late to run, to hide. I had to speak, to act. In ancient Rome, the word *fata* denoted words spoken by the gods, but by the Dark Ages, *fate* started to mean something a little more nuanced: something like "the spirit that guides you." What this spirit is—divine or ordinary, neurochemical or fantastic—well, who am I to say. But what cannot be argued is the presence, across space and time, of a plain old human impulse to *do* something about what plagues us. To be our own remedy, as well as our own worst enemy. I have felt this impulse toward remedy before and I felt it then. Which is why I plunged ahead.

"Anyway, that incident from a few months back has got me thinking. I've had a lot of time to think lately, haha, after losing my job and apartment and, ah, identity and whatnot. I've been spending a lot of time alone, away from my computer, and I have to tell you, it was hard at first. I was kind of addicted to social media. Who isn't? But I got used to the silence eventually, and honestly, I prefer it. Not all the time, of course, but it sure is better than falling into pits of self-loathing on Facebook and Instagram.

"Now that I've got a little distance, I can see that all that—What do moms call it?—*screen time* doesn't do great things for my brain. You can't squeeze a life into two dimensions. Or you can, but it comes at a cost. For me, that cost has been a gradual whittling down. Not just of my waist, because of course we women always are trying to do that, but of my, you know, *personness*.

"I just thought, well, maybe if I can make myself and my life the right size, and document myself and my life in the way I'm supposed to, some of these more—how can I put it—*longstanding* personal problems might get whittled down, too. Like my longing for purpose beyond self-interest. My desire for meaning too, I guess. Plus grief, and rage, although grief and rage are basically the same thing. I really thought I could fix these immutable problems by focusing on aesthetics. Which I know sounds deranged, but isn't this what visual culture teaches us? What advertising teaches us? That so long as things around us are beautiful, nothing will hurt?

"But things do hurt. I don't know about you, but people have *messed me up*. Worse, I've messed *myself* up. And I've messed *other* people up, because *I* was messed up. It's a vicious cycle. And when I finally realized I'd been sabotaging myself, putting rotting eggs in rotting baskets, it was too late. I didn't know how to stop. Luckily, or unluckily, who knows anymore, I didn't have to. Someone—some man—stopped me."

Hmm. This was a strange beginning, and not the direction I thought I was going to go. The audience looked a little bewildered. Except for Susan, who gave me a thumbs-up.

But what I was figuring out, whether I liked it or not, was that the best-laid plans ended up in disaster just as often as the unlaid ones. Life, generally speaking, was a disaster, and ended the same way for everybody. Might as well, my mouth was informing me, speak from the heart. A heart that was not just broken apart but spreading out, expanding, covering so much more territory than it used to.

Yeah, yeah, I'd heard other people refer to adversity—a word I loathed for its scrubbed-clean quality—as a gift. Illness, loss, suffering. I would never *personally* refer to my eager participation in a morally bankrupt business venture, my increasingly shitty behavior therein, a sexual assault, and a Twitter shaming campaign as gifts. But that's just me. If you *were* to ask me, I would say gifts are good friends and funny jokes and oral sex, not the crude and pitiless end of life as I knew it.

And yet. As time went on, I would begin to think of all this stuff that'd happened as my rock. My rock of ages, an element of my life that was heavy and unmovable. No matter how hard I tried to shove it away, or chip at it, it was going to live with me, in me, as permanent as my clownishness and the color of my eyes. Which meant that if I was going to live, if I was going to become who I was, I was going to have to, if not love this rock, at least make a bargain with it.

I was going to have to say, hello, rock. I see you. I know all your edges. I understand the cost of your presence. I understand the rights you give me too. The cost, thanks a lot, buddy, is very expensive, and, because the body remembers, I'll be remitting payment for the rest of my life.

But at the same time, I see that the rights you entitle me to are many. Thanks to you, I know what it means to suffer. Thanks to you, I know my suffering is not that special, because everybody suffers, and believing I am somehow entitled to a suffering-free life is not only very silly but a recipe for despair. I feel that now when I meet people, every single day: that life is hard and everyone's doing their best and most of us know that our best still isn't good enough for at least one person we've let down, or one element we've forgotten, and somehow we have to keep going, we have to live with that. It's all the same, we're all the same, don't you see? Our struggles are so similar. I try to no longer ignore this sameness, even though I still do sometimes, because I'm human. Thanks to you, I've never felt more alone. But I've never felt less alone, either.

Because if there's one thing that you've given me, rock, that could maybe be called a "gift," it's that there's a kind of love in the world that is fundamentally impersonal and therefore ever-present. And so when things fall apart, as they always will, that love will always be around. Because it's not the kind of love you see in movies and television, it's not romance and fireworks. It's just a feeling of not being separate. From anything. Not being separate from pain, not joy, nor birds or refugees or mass shooters or trees. It's a feeling that I am the world, and the world is me. And I will not close off that world, rock. For that love is what keeps me living.

Anyway.

I continued. "It's funny, isn't it? How size in men is bragged about—big dicks, big guts, big egos, big personalities—and rewarded in all sorts of creepy ways. How size in women is discouraged conversely. I've spent my whole life watching men dominate women and watching women be dominated. Show me a powerful man and I'll show you a string of silenced women in his wake. Politicians. Business moguls. Hollywood stars. Writers. It's always been bad for these women—but it's even worse with the Internet. Do you know how many death threats I got after the incident I was involved in went viral? And I'm nobody—this pales compared to what real public figures go through. People were telling me to *kill* myself. Our public square has become a public whipping post. For a while I thought I would die of shame."

The room was silent. I heard only breath and the swish of fabric adjusting on seats. My brain was silent too, that synaptic hush that occurs when the mind settles and syncs up with the body.

"But Ellen is shameless, and I mean that in the best way. Nothing about her is small, save for her tiny, tiny body, which we'll set aside for—well, whatever, girl wants to work out two hours a day to keep herself tight, that's her prerogative. But think about her *personality*. It's huge! She's not afraid of anyone, any man, and she doesn't want you to be, either. You know her story: South Jersey, tough family, bad marriage, a thousand failed enterprises. But the story you don't always

390

hear—and what I'm so glad is in the book—is how ferocious her past has made her, how loud she is when she cares about something, and how loyal she is to her friends.

"So this trouble I ran into a while back? Here's some context: a dude stole some work from my best friend and passed it off as his own. When I confronted this dude about it, he claimed he hadn't done anything. What's worse, he called me crazy. Which made me feel crazy! But Ellen made me feel the opposite of crazy. She listened to me. She believed me. What's more, she helped me out.

"Did her help actually work out for the best? Well, no. It ended in catastrophe, the aftermath of which ended up going viral. But catastrophe or not, there aren't that many people in the world who a hundred percent have my back, and Ellen's one of them. She's loyal as hell, and in her own bizarre way, she really wants to make the world a better place.

"So if Ellen writes a book? Of course I'm going to read the book. But not just because she's my friend. Because she's honest. The only thing dishonest about *All Real* is the airbrushing on the cover—sorry to blow your cover, Ellen—"

Ellen honked a laugh, uncrossed her legs, and shouted a conciliatory "it's true" to the audience.

"—And aren't we all, at this moment, starved

for honesty? I guess what I'm trying to say is . . ." I said. At some point I had taken the ratty foam mic off its stand and was pacing around the front of the reading area like an evangelist at a rinky-dink revival. "I think that if we stop shouting for a second and *listen* to each other like Ellen is suggesting, if we speak and write about what really matters, and do it with honesty, we can make a better world than the one that's currently provided. A world where we're not inflicting pain and violence. A world beyond vanity and money and self-documentation. A world where we don't have to shrink ourselves down to a little two-dimensional box. A world, like Ellen was saying, made of stories. Shared stories. Stories that matter. A world where we speak *and* receive a common language.

"They are women's greatest currency, you know. Stories. They keep a lot of us alive. But we've stopped sharing them. Instead we parrot what other people say and cut each other off at the knees and sometimes cut out speech entirely in favor of a duck-face selfie, and I don't know about you, but I'm *tired* of that.

"Yes, I'm furious, and what's more, I've *finally* recovered my speech. And I have things I need to *tell* you. You have things to tell *me*. Dare we disturb the universe by raising our voices? Can we? Will we? We can, we will, and what's more—we must."

When I put the microphone back into the podium slot I saw that my hands were trembling. Not because I was frightened, as before. But because I had told the truth, and the truth had released something. The truth had set me free.

Sure, not everyone needs to tell the truth in front of a live audience to feel that kind of liberation. But I, Casey Pendergast, am not most people. For a long time I thought that was the worst thing about me—the whole not-being-most-people thing—but it turns out it's the best thing about me. Turns out it's the best thing about everybody.

The audience burst into whoops and applause. Ellen gave me a giant hug, which gave me a mouthful of white rabbit fur. "That was amazing," she said over my shoulder. "Fucking brilliant. Tell me, does my breath smell bad? I'm worried I ate too much garlic."

I smelled it. "No, it smells fine. Do I smell like toilets?"

"What?" she sniffed. "No, I don't think so. Oh, wait—" she dashed up to the microphone. "Casey Pendergast, am I right, ladies? Give her another round of applause."

They did. I stood there, hands clasped bashfully in front of my chest.

"You guys can line up in the back there for the signing. There're free bottles of Ellian! and samples of Hankfurters!, and if we're out someone'll run out and get some more. Thank you all for coming. Be sure to say hi to Casey here also, and if you're not following me on Twitter, Instagram, and Facebook, you better freaking start! Goodnight, everybody!" And with that, she stepped away from the mic.

"Hey," she said a second later in her typical ADD way, rummaging through her purse and shrugging off her jacket. She found what she was looking for, a tiny vial of roll-on perfume, and exposed her wrists. "What are you doing at five-thirty tomorrow morning?"

"Um," I said. "Sleeping?"

She capped the perfume, then, as an after-thought, handed it to me. "You wanna meet me at the Channel 27 studios?"

I took off the cap. It smelled like Ellen. "Why?"

"Whaddaya mean, why? Do you want to or not?"

"Um—" I paused. There were many reasons not to go. Sleep, for one. Two, I had been too fragile as of late to do anything spontaneous. Number three, I had also been keeping my life carefully contained, wherein I could wear leggings as pants and remain certain that I would never again harm anybody, that no one would ever again harm me.

"Sure," I heard myself say.

Curiosity killed the Casey! But look, maybe it saved her, too.

"Attagirl," Ellen said.

"Attagirl!" Susan said, appearing beside me. She gave me a big hug. "I don't know where that came from, but wow."

"Really?"

"YES."

"Thank you."

"You're welcome."

"No, I mean for—"

"I know what you mean."

"Okay," I said. I looked at Susan, but I got shy all of a sudden and hid my chin in my shoulder. "I love you. Oh, Ellen, this is Susan, by the way. My best friend? The one I told you about."

"I love you too," Susan was saying, right as Ellen burst in. "I love both of you!" she said, blowing out of our vicinity toward the back of the store for her signing. "Jesus Christ, you whack-a-doodles. You do my heart good."

15

A Lady's Guide to Literature

W e're on in five," our PA, Tony, said, dabbing my face with pancake foundation. I was already blown out and wardrobed and arrayed splendidly in a Danish modern chair that half faced the chair beside it, the other half facing our three-camera setup and live studio audience. My little local daytime talk show that could, *A Lady's Guide to Literature*, had reached its hundredth episode, and we had a very special show planned.

About a year had gone by since Ellen had dragged me at five-thirty in the morning to the Channel 27 studios and demanded they take a look at the YouTube video someone had uploaded of my, I'll admit, unfocused but *very* impassioned speech at Wendys's the night before. "You see this kid?" she said to the producers. Ellen had already regrammed/tweeted/Facebooked the clip, and it had received a surprising number of views. Not as many, of course, as the video of my going apeshit on Julian North, but enough for Ellen to be convinced that there was an audience for my kind of kooky but heartfelt public performance. "She's a star, I've known it from the minute I met her. Haven't I, Casey? You guys are idiots if you don't find a way to use her on your network."

We had arrived there, ostensibly, for Ellen to record a holiday fitness segment for the morning news show, one of those "don't get fat at Christmas with tips x, y, z!" bits. So you can imagine the producers were surprised to find themselves in a pitch meeting when they only had about thirty minutes to get her makeup on and mic affixed and go over the segment with the morning hosts. But that was the thing about Ellen. You didn't really have much of a say about what was happening when she was around. It was good to have friends like that, friends who saw the world not only as their oyster, but themselves as its pearl. They encourage you, these people; what I mean is, they *give you courage.* And so these producer guys, who ordinarily might have dismissed a gal like me outright for not only having *zero* experience in television, but also a *terrible* online reputation, eventually found themselves nodding in agreement with Ellen.

It hadn't hurt, of course, that the old judge who'd presided over the network's ten-to-ten-thirty-a.m. time slot with his cantankerous but ultimately good-hearted courtroom show had been killed in an unfortunate Segway accident over Thanksgiving. And that also, even at his show's peak, the judge had grabbed only about three percent of the market share. But the truth of life is that sometimes what it takes to get somewhere is talent and hard work, and sometimes all it takes is being in the right place with the right people at the right time. Sometimes this works for us, sometimes against us. In this case, after a string of bad luck that had felt more like a ball and chain around my neck, I finally caught a break.

"What kind of show are we talking about here?" one of the producers, his name was Gary, said. He had a New Zealand accent and spoke to Ellen as if I wasn't there.

Ellen looked at me. "Well . . ." I said. I was hesitant at first; I pulled at the ends of my sleeves. "So you know how Oprah had a book club, right?"

Ellen stomped on my foot beneath the round table. *Get after it!* the pain in my foot said. I raised my voice. "And it was, like, really successful?"

Gary and the other two nodded.

"But then—" my voice was quavering. I steadied it. "Oprah went off the air, and along with it, the televised book club did too. And so far no one's come forward to replace it. Right?"

Gary and the other two nodded again.

"So in business terms"—emboldened by their not-immediate dismissal, I sat up straighter, continued with my shoulders back—"you could say that no one has replaced this particular element of Oprah's market share. There are plenty of women trying to replace Oprah, of course, in syndication, but none of them have been able to replicate what she did in terms of reading and readership. In business terms"—I cleared my throat in what I hoped seemed to be a businesslike way—"we would call this a blue ocean. An uncontested market space, if you've never heard the term. In this case, the uncontested market space has not only financial incentives, both for the network as well as the publishing industry, but also cultural incentives for women who are at home during the day, maybe working, maybe with small kids, who want more options beyond home repair or cooking shows or celebrity news.

"I'm not saying I want to or can be the next Oprah—no one can ever replace Oprah, may God rest her soul. No, I know she's still alive," I hurried to correct Gary, who'd raised a paternal finger. "What I am saying, however, is that I'd like to replace Oprah's Book Club. Just think: an interactive book club with a live studio audience, where people at home can also participate through social media. We'll bring in authors—I already know a ton—and we'll have segments, too, where women, regular women, can write and tell their own stories. Nothing like this has ever been done before, and if we don't do it, someone else will. And anyway, I promise you that this need will make the network way more money than that judge, God *actually* rest his soul, has been making you, if you want to get all bottom-line about it.

"So," I said, finally taking a breath. "What do you think?"

I'd had another strange feeling when I finished. Another one of those fated moments. Guided by the spirit things. I had not consciously thought about any of what I'd said before. Everything I'd said was brand new to me. And yet, there it was, fully formed. Waiting for me to be ready to say it.

The producers had nodded in approval.

"You've got yourself a deal!" Ellen had said, and stuck out a hand to Gary.

"Are you her manager?" another one of them had said.

Ellen had looked offended. "No, I'm not her manager," she'd snapped. "I'm Ellen Hanks, do I look like I'm someone's manager? I'm her friend! You should get one sometime."

Not to think ill of people—oh, but who am I kidding, I think ill of people all the time—but I think one of the reasons Gary and the producers had originally agreed to the show was because they thought it was going to be a train wreck. People like watching train wrecks. The original sizzle reel for the show called me "disgraced Internet phenomenon Casey Pendergast." I think they were hoping people would tune in out of schadenfreude.

And the thing is, *A Lady's Guide to Literature* was a train wreck, at least at the beginning. Audiences didn't know what to make of a book club that met Monday through Thursday. How were they supposed to talk about *one* book for an entire week? Without getting distracted and digressing into conversations about men and children and TV shows? On top of that, were women really that interested in hearing real-life stories from other ordinary women like them? Were authors really that interesting to talk to? Were enough people even reading books to assemble a critical mass? There were a lot of questions we didn't have the answer to.

Yes, people were put off by the newness of the format, and initial Nielsen returns were low. The network started breathing down our necks right away, but one of the things that Ellen, who was the executive producer, kept pressing upon them was that they had to be patient. "She'll grow on 'em," Ellen had told them. "She grows on everybody. Just wait and see."

And I had. Slowly and steadily. Ellen co-hosted with me every Thursday as much as her schedule allowed. I'd also brought on Susan's friend Gina for a poetry segment called *Slamz A Lot*, Chris for a segment called *YQY*, focusing on "literature from the margins," and Susan for a weekly segment called *A Room of Your Own*, comprised of advice and prompts for aspiring writers. By the time Susan's debut novel, *I Don't F* With You*, was ready to burst onto the literary stage, she had enough of a social media platform that her big fancy New York publishing house agreed to send her on a nationwide tour. Her first stop was our hundredth episode. The plan was for her to blog about her tour for the show's website, which hopefully would be good publicity for both of us.

So it was true what Ellen said about all boats rising, what went around, came back around. But it happened, I'd found, so much more slowly than I'd hoped. I wanted change to happen all at once; I wanted the arc of justice to hurry up and finish its rainbow right in my lap. But that's not how it works. Real change, lasting change, takes a long time.

But like the melting glaciers gradually raising the sea levels, the show and my friends were slowly moving up in the world. Lindsey had quit Nanü, sold her equity, started massage school, and had spent the summer training with a shamanic healer somewhere in Alaska. She was hoping to establish an LLC for herself in "healing and ceremonial leadership." I employed her from time to time for the crew during stressful stretches, and she also came on the show once a month for a roundup of the newest self-help books.

All the old pain she'd been carrying behind her eyes had been left up somewhere in the Arctic Circle, and she seemed peaceful. She lived a life that suited her more than advertising ever could, a life of quiet skin care treatments, yoga, and monasticism. If I did not always understand what the hell she was talking about, I always knew her heart was in the right place.

And speaking of hearts and their right places, Louise had started writing me letters after I got back from Vegas, though I'd never returned her call. The first one quoted a line from a storybook that she had read to me, over and over, when I was a little girl. *I'll love you forever/I'll like you for always/as long as I'm living/my baby you'll be*. Under her name there was a postscript. *I am here for you in whatever way you need me.* Though the lines from the story only seemed to underscore the fundamental problem—I was not a baby, for one, nor was I *hers*—it was clear that my mother was sincerely sending me love from the height of her capacities, and though those heights were, well, a good fifty feet lower than what I thought I needed, I would no longer ignore her; I would not keep her out of my heart. So I wrote her back, and she wrote me back, and that was how we had stayed in touch for months now, a letter a week from both of us, both signing them *with love*. She had floated a suggestion in her last letter that she come visit me, but I had not responded to it yet; the odds of my saying yes were around fifty-fifty, about the same odds that the visit would be a catastrophe.

As for my other mother, Celeste had called me up after *Lady's Guide* had started getting good press, ostensibly to congratulate me, but more likely to make sure that whatever influence I was acquiring would never be used to go after hers. We had a very civil ten-minute conversation, and I haven't spoken to her since. I had less and less time for people with a lot of self-interest, comparatively little empathy, and zero interest in mucking with the proportions. I wished her no harm, though, especially when I imagined her keeping very, very far away from me. Say, on Pluto. Yes, when I imagined Celeste on Pluto, I had so much kindness in my heart; I felt so much inner peace.

When it came to Wolf or Julian, well, my heart had a more complicated position. As the viewership and influence of *Lady's Guide* continued to grow, I thought of them more and more. Not because I was "grateful for adversity" or felt I owed them anything, but because I could see myself in them, truly. I was as human as they were, the part of me they had wounded I would and could not remove, and the part of me that could wound other people, I would and could not remove either. And I became more aware of power and abuses of power, became more watchful of my own actions as I gained a little power, became more determined to use my influence wisely, ethically, and never at the expense of others.

Which is maybe a better place, a more thoughtful place, to end up than the land of forgiveness, a place that might just be too saccharine for me. Susan says forgiveness is just a philosophical construction anyway, a con put in place by those in power against those who have no power, so that the responsibility of coming to terms with bad shit keeps falling to the latter.

So I believe instead in *forgiverness,* which for me means waiting for these assholes who fucked with me to take some responsibility for their actions. And I, in order to make this practice copacetic, will have to in turn approach those with whom *I* grievously fucked, bowing my head and admitting that *I,* too, must take responsibility, and no, I don't want their forgiveness; I'm just coming around to own up to what I did. If they forgive me, great. But that's not the point. The point is that it's not just useful but necessary to hold oneself to account, to say, "I am at fault, I have done you wrong," while looking into the eyes of the person who was wronged—and what's more, to mean it.

Which is why, after the show gained some

momentum, I called up Simone. She didn't answer, but I left a long voicemail apologizing for whaling on her so hard during sumo wrestling and, in general, treating her as my mortal enemy. She didn't call back, ostensibly too busy rolling around in piles of Nanü money. Undeterred by this initial failure, I also called the writers I'd recruited to Nanü and told them how sorry I was for roping them into the business and asked what I could do to make their lives easier, how I could set things right. The ones whom I got ahold of—Izzy, Betty, Geoffrey, Tracy, and of course, Mary—somewhat surprisingly said no. They didn't mind the work, they said, and with the exception of Tracy, who remained sweetly oblivious to earthly matters, they clearly enjoyed the jump in pay. To assuage my conscience more than theirs, which appeared, collectively, to be unconcerned, I not only had them all as guests on the show, I also worked with the three Wendys, with whom I had a fruitful partnership, to ensure at least these authors' books were always facing outward on the shelves.

Indeed, over the summer, the Wendys had allowed me a table, right by the checkout, with a sign that read A LADY'S GUIDE: SIZZLING PICKS! All the Nanü writers got a place there, too, including Johnny Hard, who'd disappeared off the face of the planet after getting paid for his White Castle commercial treatment, and whom I thought about frequently and with a great deal of regret. And Mort, who had died that spring (after a courageous battle with Parkinson's) at the age of eighty-eight, got his own table. Mort and I had emailed back and forth a few times—he'd been so encouraging when the show had initially floundered, told me it was a success even if I only had a single viewer, because the point was not to be successful but rather to make something of "real moral value"—and I cried when I read the news of his passing. *Lady's Guide* was planning on going on the road that spring, when the new wings of the Milwaukee Jewish museum were scheduled to open. I hoped to dedicate the entire week to Mort's books and his legacy.

Blessedly, kind of, both Julian and Wolf received their public comeuppance eventually. During Susan's book tour, she nabbed a spot on National Public Radio, and during the course of the interview was asked about periods of difficulty she'd had as an artist prior to her success. She brought up Wolf's plagiarism, how much it had wounded her, how much she'd felt erased and negated from her own language; she was canny enough to call him out right when there was some momentum behind her, enough momentum for the accusation to be taken seriously. After that, a number of commenters came forward and said that lines from their poems or blogs had been stolen by Wolf, too. Bits and pieces, so there was always plausible deniability, but the small accusations together added up to something real. He became, quickly, the subject of his own Internet shaming campaign, at the end of which his career as a writer was dead in the water. For a minute.

Then he moved to Hollywood.

With Julian, justice took a lot longer, the results were even more gray, and it took a lot more people. Fifty of us in total. Women. We found out about each other one at a time. I talked about Julian's assault once on my show, just a little, not using his name, it was still really difficult for me to find any words, let alone speak his, and anyway I didn't want the show to be *about* me, per se, just *starring* me. There's a difference. Afterward, a woman who'd watched the episode emailed us. Turned out she'd been groped by Julian after an event he'd done the last time he was in town for a reading.

Thank you for saying something, she'd written. *I tried to convince myself it hadn't happened, or at least that I was overreacting, that it'd been consensual or something. But it didn't work, and I've been a wreck. Keeping it a secret—I haven't even told my husband—it's made me sick. I've just felt stuck, you know? Just knowing I'm not alone makes me feel better.*

Naturally, I responded right away. This exchange started a whole chain of correspondence, and other women—by the way, this took *forever*—linked to us one at a time via message boards and discreet social media posts and word of mouth, until we'd amassed enough testimonies that a lawyer, recommended by Ellen, thought we could bring it to a criminal trial. Keep in mind this process would take five years. Keep in mind that although fifty counts of sexual assault were brought against him, he was found guilty of only three. Keep in mind the judge brought his sentence, which could have been decades, down to a two-year parole, in consideration of the length of time these charges had taken to be brought to court and the relative ill health of the defendant, whose wife had finally lost her courageous battle with cancer. Julian's personal reputation took a serious hit at the time, but his reputation as a writer didn't. Just a few months before his trial, he was nominated for the Man Booker Prize.

Julian was too good of a storyteller for us to change his own story. But life is long and likely he will die before me, and history will not be kind to him, not if I have anything to say about it. And I have a lot to say about it. So do others. And every day there are more of us, and every day we fear less.

That day—the hundredth episode of *A Lady's Guide to Literature*—Susan, as I said, was scheduled to appear, but there was also a mystery guest: a guest that not even I knew about, someone who would take the stage for a surprise. Audiences got a real kick out of my outsized reactions; the producers were always throwing stuff like that my way. At Thanksgiving, they'd had me read a children's book to a live turkey.

"One minute!" Tony said, stepping away from me with one final pouf of foundation to my face. The way the set was designed was very informal, like a girlfriend's living room, deep-cushioned and brightly decorated, complete with *very* large bowls of popcorn and *very* filled glasses of wine for my guests and me, as well as for the studio-audience members, many of whom would be invited on set during the shooting. The thing that made *Lady's Guide* different from other shows—and Ellen and I were dead set on this—was its interactive quality. The show was live, and on the wall behind me were three large monitors that automatically updated the show's Facebook, Twitter, and Instagram accounts so that viewers could participate. They were also invited to take selfies with the books we discussed and tag them with #Ladysread, and about once a month we chose one of these women to be a guest on the show, or, if they lived far away, to Skype in. One of these women had even gotten a book deal, after spending her segment talking about her childhood spent in the wings of Cirque du Soleil, where both her parents had been performers. It was this sort of incremental individual-and-collective forward movement that made my heart sing.

I smoothed my pencil skirt over my legs—I was a talk show host; I had to dress the part—and crossed my legs to their most flattering angle. We had a full crowd, all ages, mostly women. I waved to them as the lights shifted and set. "WHAT IS UP?" I called out to them.

"WHOOOOOOOO!" they said.

"I'm so happy to see you! Thank you so much for coming!"

They kept whooing and clapping. Yes, it was someone's job to get them to do that before I came onstage, but I swear, the show had a real festive quality to it, and not only because of the drinking. Probably this had something to do with the fact that I was genuinely thrilled to be there. Something to do with the fact that, for the first time, I was more or less all right with being me. And, for the first time, really participating in the world I lived in, as it was, as it could be, wholeheartedly. Which came first, this participation or the all-rightness, I can't be sure, but I'm fairly certain they exist symbiotically.

"Thirty seconds!" someone said. I looked down at my index cards of notes about Susan's book, plus things I just wanted to talk to her about. We were both so busy it was hard for us to find time for each other those days. When I saw her backstage, we'd both squealed so loudly and hugged so hard that the PAs had to pull us apart, worried about our microphones and makeup.

"In five, four, three . . ." Tony counted down the rest with his fingers until I saw the red lights appear on the cameras.

"Hi!" I heard myself say, as I'd said ninety-nine times before. "I'm Casey Pendergast! And welcome to . . ." I waited for the synthesized drumroll. "A Lady's Guide to Literature!"

My god. So loud was the thump of my heart when I saw Ben Dickinson step out from the wings that I thought it would jump right out of my chest and bounce toward him like a basketball. Susan, of course, knew exactly who the mystery guest was—she'd talked to the producers and set the whole thing up herself, though Lindsey might've had a hand in it, too. They'd been bugging me for ages now to return his call, but I hadn't. Couldn't have borne it then. Still couldn't bear it. In fact, I still couldn't bear dating, period.

Sure, occasionally I'd force myself to message someone back on a dating app and go out for a dreadful hour-and-a-half date at a passable bar, but it all seemed like such a waste of time. Which I think was less about the inherent wastefulness of such time and more about the fact that I wasn't ready. What an impossible task, intimacy, even more so as we get older. Two people with all this baggage, all these wounds to accidentally stick thumbs in, plus biological and gender differences—I believed every step I took toward someone took place on a minefield. Everywhere I looked I saw danger. It seemed easier, safer, to throw myself into work and friendships and my two-hundred-dollar vibrator.

So I did.

The audience had been informed by Susan, who was onstage with me at the time, that Ben and I were old friends, so it was not entirely beyond the realm of anyone's imagination that I would react as I did to seeing him: standing up, knees wobbling, palms asweat. We hugged in front of everybody. He smelled just as I remembered, but he looked a little older: there were more gray strands in his beard, more lines around his eyes. He was wearing the same midnight-blue velvet blazer he'd worn the first day I'd met him. "Pendergast!" he said, holding me back at arm's length. "It's so good to see you!" He kept his hands on my shoulders a little longer than necessary.

"It is?" My face erupted into flame. "I mean, ah, it is! Good to see you too, I mean!"

"Whooooooo!" the audience said.

The chemistry. The audience could tell. No matter how far we'd been from each other, physically and emotionally, no matter the hurt and the harm, the chemistry had not gone away.

Ben was on the show, ostensibly, to discuss his new book, a collection of mostly previously published essays that included a new, and very moving, piece about his mother's Alzheimer's. I had been sent an advance copy—by his publisher, I thought, who sent the show books all the time—and read the whole thing despite the ache in my chest every time I cracked the spine. However, we didn't stay on the subject for too long. After Susan discreetly gave up her chair and disappeared offstage, the two of us, Ben and I, immediately fell back into the easy rapport that had linked us in the first place, and linked us still.

"So you! The show!" he said, picking up a handful of popcorn and tossing the kernels into his mouth. Chewing, he continued. "I'm so happy for you. Seems like a dream come true."

"It's pretty dreamy," I said. "Well, first it was a nightmare, but then things turned around." I found that I was sliding farther and farther down in my chair. The stage lights were making me very warm. "Which is life, I guess."

"That's a good life," Ben said. He was looking at me in his lasery way. "A pretty great life, in fact."

"It is," I said. Small tears pricked my eyes. "I'm lucky."

"Me, too." His eyes didn't leave mine.

The tears threatened to brim and spill. I blinked them back. "Why does it take us so long to figure out we're lucky?"

The audience was quiet. Or maybe it was that I could not hear anything except the quiet thrum in Ben's rib cage, the place where his tender heart lay.

"Because we're not supposed to feel lucky. We're supposed to want more."

I brought my ring finger to the corner of my eyes, and dabbed. "What if I feel lucky, *and* I want more?"

Ben smiled, just a little, that boyish smile I'd fallen in love with. "Welcome back, Casey," he said.

After the cameras stopped rolling, during the meet and greet I did with guests after every episode, during which they were invited onstage to hang out and take pictures and ask me whatever they wanted, a number of them requested that Ben become a show regular.

"Oh," I brushed it off as politely as I could. "I don't know about that."

"But you two are so wonderful together!" They would say, holding my forearm with their manicured, motherly hands.

"Oh, well!" A banal but essential truth along with do unto others, brush and floss, and sleep eight hours: we don't really hear things until we're ready to hear them.

There was a party scheduled for that evening at one of those karaoke bars you can rent the entirety of. My request. Loving the spotlight, and all that. But I'd promised the crew that I wasn't going to sing. It was *their* night; I wanted them to have their own turn under the lights; I wanted them to get drunk and silly and eat catered sushi and feel that expansiveness I felt when I got onstage, which I was lucky enough now to do almost every day. Ellen, who was insanely busy filming a new season of *Real Housewives*, had also sworn she'd cut out early from some shoot she had at a nearby wine bar and stop by, so long as she could rap her favorite song by Bone Thugs-n-Harmony. She was also providing a case of her signature-branded vodka, and free shapewear for everybody.

Me, to commemorate the hundredth episode, I'd taken a lesson in editing from a crew member and had subsequently made a very heartfelt photo montage and film for the crew. It was called *Memories*, and its soundtrack was a compilation of all the best high school graduation songs. I'd put it on fifty flash drives that I'd had specially made for every crew member. They were purple, and on the side they said, *Love Casey,* which was both a valediction and command.

Anyway, I saw Ben talking to Susan after the

meet and greet. Whaddaya know: it turned out that she'd invited him to the after party. Which was funny, because I'd planned on *not* inviting him to the after party. Susan seemed very pleased about this. Ben looked about as circumspect as I imagined I did.

"We're going to have such a good time!" Susan laughed, and pushed me a little closer toward him.

Six hours, two drinks, and metric ton of California rolls later, I found myself at a table alone with Ben while a cameraman named Lars stood under a disco ball and sang his heart out to Bruce Springsteen. Susan, I thought, glancing over, was absolutely going to hook up with Lars that night. He was her type, a bearded Viking giant with a heart of gold and giant hands. She was watching him intently and clapping with appreciation at no particular point in the song. The lights were dimmed, with swirling neon colors bouncing off darkened walls. Ben and I were talking, talking, talking, talking. We'd always been able to talk. And have fun, and have sex, and laugh together.

But the rest of it, Jesus, was so goddamn *difficult*.

"You seeing anyone right now?" Ben said eventually, and, I thought, a little too casually, picking up his beer bottle and swilling the contents.

I shook my head and said, also too casually, "I've been busy. You?"

"Nah." He took a sip. "Busy, too."

"Mmmhmm."

"I've never minded being alone."

"Me neither."

"Though it does get lonely," he said.

"People make you lonely, too," I said, and put a strawful of club soda in my mouth. It was not that I'd quit drinking, but for some reason I didn't want to get drunk around him. It felt—the strange word that came to mind was *disrespectful*. "By the way, how's your mom doing?"

"Not all people," he said at the same time. Then he looked right at me. "Not great. Sometimes I think it'd be a whole lot easier if I just stuck her in one of those memory care facilities, but—I just can't. She's my mom, I'm stuck with her.

"And sometimes you want to be stuck with people," he said after a pause, his gaze never leaving mine. "You know?"

Oh, what was I going to say to that? I'll tell you what I could have said. I could have said, yes, I do know. Some people make you feel the opposite of lonely; they make you feel not only that you aren't as awful as you secretly fear you are, but in fact that you are more wonderful, more astonishing, more full of riches and wisdom and beauty than you ever would have thought possible. These people, so few and far between, you belong to them. You belong with them. You wrap your longing around them, they wrap theirs around you. They become your longing. And you become their longing too.

And with this belonging, this belonging, this yoking, paradoxically, comes freedom. I could have said: I have always felt I belonged with you. I could have said: and the stronger that feeling becomes the more my fear intensifies. I could have said: because I've been wounded, and I've wounded. I could have said: because I've already ruined things with you once and I'm terrified of doing it again.

But I didn't want to say that. Because what he had asked me for, all that time ago, was a clean slate. And even if I could never give that to him fully, I could at least try to not scribble all over the slate before we started writing something together. Not just my story. The story of us, together.

So what I said instead was, "I know."

And then I reached across the table and took his hand.

It was as warm as I remembered it.

ACKNOWLEDGMENTS

To my teachers—Charles Baxter, Nicole Grunzke, Jan Jirak, Kate O'Reilly, Julie Schumacher—for being, as Steinbeck said, artists of people.

To my agent, Michelle Brower, for changing my life.

To my editor, Anna Pitoniak, for the reassuring hand at my back, which nudged me further and wider than I ever thought I could go.

To my sister-writers—Lara Avery, Kate Galle, Elizabeth Greenwood, Jackie Olsen, Carrie Schuettpelz, Emma Törzs—for mopping my brow while I gave birth to this thing and for being such geniuses in your own right. Special thanks to Molly Weingart for your singular, tenacious loyalty. Special thanks, too, to Carrie Lorig, for allowing me to lift a line from your poem, "The Pulp v. The Throne" *(there is everyone at the lessening of your wounds),* which I didn't believe at first but has proven itself over and over.

To my supporters, cheerleaders, and patrons— Rick Baker, for your generosity of spirit and the peace of Flatrock; Luke Finsaas, for your instrumental brainstorming in the early stages;

Nancy Angelo and Nancy McCauley, for the refuge of 18 Plu; Jack Franson, for lots of stuff but especially what you said that night at Marinitas; Studio 2 Café and The Loft Literary Center, for letting me pace around your property like a crazy person; and, of course, the Kimmel Harding Nelson Center for the Arts, the Minnesota State Arts Board, The MacDowell Colony, the Ucross Foundation, and the University of Minnesota MFA Program, for the time and space to both goof around and go to the places that scared me.

To everyone at Random House—Gina Centrello, Avideh Bashirrad, Theresa Zoro, Christine Mykityshyn, Leigh Marchant, Andrea DeWerd—for your formidable intelligence and foresight, and for believing in this book. It is an honor to be in the room with you.

To my friends—Elizabeth Abbott, Isaac Butler, Ginny Green, Katie Hensel, Helene McCallum, Emily Meisler, Neil Pearson, Alexis Platt, Jordan Poast, Jenn Schaal, Ginny Sievers, Andrea Uptmor, Mandy Warren, Hannah Wydeven, Matt Zinsli—for loving me even when I disappear for months at a time, and even clapping like I'm some American hero when I come back around, dazed and blinking. You are the flowers in the garden of my life, or whatever that quote is.

To my students, current and former, for helping me see the world anew, and bringing me joy.

To my family, without whom I am not.

And last, but certainly not least, to Ben, my boon, the real one. You came later but you made all the difference.

About the Author

Sally Franson grew up in Madison, Wisconsin, and was educated at Barnard College and the University of Minnesota. Her work has appeared in *The Guardian*, *The Best American Travel Writing*, and on NPR, among other places. She lives in Minneapolis.

sallyfranson.com
Facebook.com/sally.franson
Twitter: @sallyjf
Instagram: @sallyjf

Center Point Large Print
600 Brooks Road / PO Box 1
Thorndike, ME 04986-0001 USA

(207) 568-3717

US & Canada:
1 800 929-9108
www.centerpointlargeprint.com